The Long Way Home

Kevin Bannister

The Long Way Home by Kevin Bannister

This is a work of historical fiction. While based upon historical events, any similarity to any person, circumstance or event is purely coincidental and related to the efforts of the author to portray the characters in historically accurate representations.

Cover design by Christine Horner
Interior design by Jacqueline Cook

ISBN: 978-1-61179-361-1 (Paperback)
ISBN: 978-1-61179-362-8 (e-book)

10 9 8 7 6 5 4 3 2 1

BISAC Subject Headings:
FIC014000 FICTION / Historical
FIC002000 FICTION / Action & Adventure
FIC049040 FICTION / African American / Historical

Address all correspondence to:
Fireship Press, LLC
P.O. Box 68412
Tucson, AZ 85737
fireshipinfo@gmail.com

Or visit our website at:
www.fireshippress.com

"*The Long Way Home* is an inspirational and harrowing historical drama. Though the men pass through many different settings on their quest for a free life, *The Long Way Home* is very much a character driven story at heart. I'd definitely recommend it to all historical fiction fans."

—K.C. Finn, author of the *Caecilius Rex* saga, *The Secret Star* and *The Book of Shade* and the bestselling and award-winning novel *The Mind's Eye*.

"An epic work. I was mesmerized by the intensity and power of this work that brings to light heroes I hadn't know about. Bannister's writing is lyrical and elegant, at times I would feel compelled to stop and re-read an especially memorable passage. I loved this book. *The Long Way Home* is most highly recommended."

—Jack Magnus, Readers Favorite

"It takes more than a good imagination to write a spellbinding historical novel but *The Long Way Home* is a success on many, many levels; a tale that will speak to the hearts of readers with eloquence. Bannister has successfully combined historical facts with glowing imagination to deliver a masterpiece that will be well received by lovers of historical fiction. The characters are extraordinarily compelling, strung with the kind of courage one would find only in persons fighting between death and freedom."

—Romvald Dzemo, author of *Courage To Embrace Yourself* and *You Can't Be A Failure*.

"*The Long Way Home* by Kevin Bannister takes us back to the eighteenth century when blacks were fleeing colonial America as slaves or freemen and later settled in Nova Scotia. The main protagonists, Thomas Peters and Murphy Steele, are historical figures who lived during this time. Fast paced and poignant...this novel is a tribute to these two forgotten heroes."

—Maria Beltran, playwright, author, past chairwoman of Women In Literary Arts Inc.

To my wife and best friend Lorraine

Acknowledgements

Many thanks to my editor, Lorraine Delp, for being meticulous, skillful, and judicious, and for sticking with it. Special thanks also to Mary Lou and Jacquie at Fireship Press for their advice and support.

A big thank-you to my reviewers who were so kind and generous. My website, www.longwayhomebook.ca, was designed and built by my daughter, Rebekah Bannister, and for that I am very grateful.

Most important, my heartfelt thanks to Lorraine Bannister, who supported me and helped with my research, then edited, proof-read, formatted and helped with the final editing. Without her help *The Long Way Home* could never have been completed.

The Long Way Home

Kevin Bannister

FIRESHIP
PRESS

One

When we ran, they tracked us down, dragged us back, and whipped us.

I had never thought of running. I was young, not old enough to do a man's work but old enough to know when to keep quiet and when to sneak a mouthful when nobody was looking. I was in the kitchen, cleaning the floor and minding the cook, and when she asked me to chop wood, that's what I did.

When you're chopping wood with a fine, sharp ax, the blade goes right through the wood, no matter how thick, so you can chop a cord before dinner without even breaking a sweat. But when you're chopping with a rusty ax, your blade gets stuck at every blow and you have to pick up the wood over your head with your stuck blade and then strike it down hard on a rock to make the ax bite through. That gets tiresome even if you're like me and you look at the wood to pick out the wavy grain and see just where you should strike to make the ax slide through.

It so happened that I was lifting one mighty big stump over my head with my blade stuck halfway down when Thomas appeared around the outside corner of the building.

"What are you doing?"

"Well what does it look like?"

"It looks like either you forgot how to cut wood or you're trying out some new kind of chopping. Either way it looks like you're going to break that ax or maybe cut your own head off."

"I guess you've never cut wood with a rusty blade."

I didn't really know Thomas very well. All I knew was that he was a little older than me, old enough to work in the shop with the field machines. I had heard talk that he was born a prince, but he sure didn't look like one now, standing by me with his dirty clothes on and sweat running down his forehead and dripping off his nose. Thomas had come to this place a while ago. I had heard him talk before and that man could talk.

Everyone would listen to him just because he made you think about things. I guess he must have been royalty because people wanted to listen to him even though he had no wife, no family, nothing behind him at all.

"If that blade is so damn bad, why don't you get a stone and work on it?"

"I think I'll just wait for you to get one for me, seeing you're so smart about this cutting business."

"All right then, I'll do that."

Before I could bring that stump back down on the rock, the blade still embedded in it, he'd opened the door to the kitchen, stepped inside, and asked the cook for a stone and a little oil to work the ax up. I heard that part because the kitchen door was still open, but I didn't hear the rest because the door swung shut.

I swung down hard on the ax, hitting the block of wood against the striking rock. Still it didn't cleave through and the blade of the ax stuck fast again, halfway through the wood. I put one foot beside the blade and pulled back hard but it stayed stuck, squeezed between the two sides of the cut. As I raised the ax above my head again, with the stump wrapped tightly 'round it, the kitchen door whipped open. Thomas jumped down the stairs to the ground and ran a few steps into the yard. The door swung shut but only for an instant as the cook, Jean, came out and stood at the top of the stairs.

Who knows why we decide on the spur of the moment to do one

thing and not another? Would we change our decisions if we knew the trouble that would follow? We don't decide how our lives are going to be shaped through one big decision, but instead through a whole series of little choices. There is rarely a big crossroads that we stand before to shape our lives. It seems to me that we mostly just go with what moves us at the time, not thinking about the future when we make a choice.

When Thomas came out of the kitchen on the run, I knew what had happened. I knew it even before I saw that he had a loaf of bread in his hand. The cook, standing at the top of the stairs with her hand on her hips, said nothing. I let the ax blade and the stump fall to the ground, still holding on to the handle.

"Let's go," Thomas said.

"Go where?"

"Let's get out of here."

I could have done several things—grabbed him, kept cutting with that dull blade, ran away, even just yelled. But I didn't do any of that—the plain fact is that none of that even crossed my mind. I went over to Thomas and we both walked into the bush at the end of the yard. Jean turned without a word and went back into the kitchen.

"Should we run?"

"She won't tell on us."

"Where do we go?"

"Through the bush and then we'll see."

We walked on an old animal path through the scrub willows and tall grass and the trail got wider, but softer too. I kept thinking I heard dogs barking back from where we'd come, but when I stopped to listen all I could hear was the wind through the trees. Thomas never slowed and never said a word. He just kept walking at a strong, steady pace, the loaf of bread in his hand. Finally, with the trail so soft that my feet sank a little with every step, he halted.

"Why are we stopping here?"

"I have never been farther than this. If you want to go back, now's the time."

"Nothing to go back for."

"Your momma will be missing you pretty soon."

"I have no family here."

"They'll beat us if they catch us."

"Best make sure they don't catch us, then. You got a plan or are we just sort of walking and hoping?"

He smiled at me.

"When we get through this swamp we can camp for the night. If we keep off the roads and keep walking on the trails, we should be all right to the coast. I've been there for supplies. I think we can crew on a fishing boat and get up north."

"I never saw myself as a fisherman."

"I guess you never saw yourself as a runaway neither until I came along. If I were you, I'd try thinking of myself as a free man and then maybe you'll be happy being just about anything but somebody's slave."

Thomas was older than me but not much bigger. The truth is that I've never been too sure just how old I am. I barely remember being taken from my folks and my raising was left to anyone who happened to be handy. Until the last year, I'd been working for the teacher, cleaning the schoolhouse and tidying up the yard. She was the one who taught me to read and write. She taught me a few other things, too, like where I lived now, and where in the world my ancestors had come from, and where there weren't any slaves because it wasn't allowed. She taught me after the white kids had finished their lessons and there was no one about.

Then they took me from the schoolhouse and gave me to the cook for kitchen duties and that was the end of the teaching. By then I knew how to read and I'd taken books from the master's house when I was doing meal clean-up so I could read when I was alone. I kept the books in a hole under a tree in the woods that we'd just walked through. When I was let out of the kitchen and before the light faded, I would walk to the tree and read until the night closed in. I had *Macbeth* and *King Lear* and a worn-out book of rhymes, but my favorite was the Bible. My favorite story in that book was about Joseph, son of Jacob, and I dreamed sometimes of being the slave who became the ruler of a new country. As we walked through the swamp, I was thinking about the books and I was thinking of what it would be like to be a fisherman. My toes were making small dents in the soft ground and there was brackish water all around in little pools, but our trail seemed to wind between the stagnant ponds and we never got wet.

"Are you hungry?" Thomas asked.

"No, I'm wondering if you were really a prince like people say, and if you know the story of Joseph."

"Yeah, I know that story, but I don't see what it's got to do with us walking through this stinking swamp. As to being a prince, I'll tell you about that when we get out of here. I'm getting peckish myself but I think we should get out before dark so we're not wandering in this bog with no light."

The moon had appeared and it was still light enough to see when the ground got harder and began to go up. After a little while, we climbed out of the swamp and into a small meadow between thick groups of trees. Thomas motioned over to the edge of the forest where the path continued after crossing the clearing.

"Let's make our bed there and have a bite."

"Do you know where we are?"

"I know well enough. They'll be missing us by now but they'll have trouble clambering through that bog on horses. Likely they'll have to go round by road, even if they do figure out which direction we went. We're fine here for the night, I think."

He handed me a chunk of the loaf.

"What's your name?"

"Murphy."

"Do you have a last name?"

"Steele, Murphy Steele."

"Murphy, I'm Thomas Peters. I wasn't born Thomas Peters, and if you want to hear my story, I'll tell you while we go looking for the creek that makes that bog so we can have some fresh water."

As we walked at the edge of the clearing, eating the loaf and looking for clear water, Thomas told me the story of his beginnings.

"In my country, my name is Adekola Akande. It means 'one who is full of determination' and it was given to me when I was born because the birthing was so long. I was the first-born child in one of the ruling families of my country. My family ruled the area beside the Ogun River under the big rock, and we had many horses and much good land that went into the forest around our farms. My father's house had fifty rooms and each room had leopard skins and fine carvings. We lived well.

"My father, Taiwo, ruled with his twin brother, Kehinde, over our land and in the tribal council for the entire region. He was a good ruler and the people respected him. My father believed in earning the respect of the people by leading them justly. Our leaders stay in power only as long as the people let them—this was something that my father understood very well. He employed a teacher for me and I was taught, starting when I could barely walk, the ways of a leader.

"My teacher was from Arabia—he had been taken from the Ijebu when we raided them, just before I was born. He was a slave there but my father offered him his freedom if he agreed to remain with us and teach his newborn son. My father respected the Arab because he spoke five languages and understood war, history, geography, and politics.

"His name was Haafizah. He had been an Arab trader before being captured and enslaved by the Ijebu. Haafizah had travelled many miles and picked up the customs and languages of many countries. He taught me how to speak Arabic, English, and Spanish. More importantly, he taught me how to watch people closely to see what they are thinking, how to make alliances for my own benefit, how to speak with passion and directness, how to persuade people to follow me, and how to be a just leader.

"In our land we were often at war, sometimes with our neighbors and, always, with the white traders who came to steal our people. The whites took many people, either through trade with our enemies who had taken them in battles or by capturing them on our own land in raids, and we would not see them again. We did not know what became of them until my teacher said that they had been taken over the ocean and enslaved.

"We fought the white traders when they came and when there were too many to fight we took refuge in the rocks and mud walls of the city. We hunted the leopards and alligators. I was engaged to be married and life was fine.

"One day while I was hunting in the bush with two companions, white men appeared from the surrounding trees and took me and my friends captive. They bound our hands and marched us through the bush, out of our land and to the coast. On the way I talked with a Dahomey guide who was working for the white men. He told me that I had been betrayed by my uncle and sold into slavery.

"When my people do not wish to be led by an old ruler, they find a parrot's nest and send it to the chief. The nest must have several of the blue eggs of the parrot in it. When the chief receives the nest, he knows that his reign is over and he takes to his bed and refuses to eat. Then one night, when he is sleeping, the village women creep into his room and strangle him, and a new ruler is proclaimed.

"My father received a parrot's nest shortly before my hunt but, still being a strong, powerful man, and suspecting treachery, he did not accept that this was the will of the people. He refused to give up his power and did not retreat to his room and continued to rule our land. The Dahomey guide told me that my uncle had sent the nest to my father, planning to destroy his brother then seize complete power for himself. When that plan failed, he turned to our old enemies, the Ijebu, and schemed with them to kidnap me and sell me into slavery. My uncle thought that, through this deception, my father would be easily persuaded to give up power. The white traders would be blamed.

"Our enemies were happy to oblige, thinking that with my nation divided, they would be able to press their conflict with us. They arranged with the traders to steal me while I was on the hunt. The whites marched us to the coast. On the beach, we were led in front of the captains of the ships that took us across the ocean. These men squeezed our arms and legs, licked our cheeks, and inspected our teeth before agreeing on a price with the traders who had captured us.

"My two hunting companions had also been taken to the ship. The three of us, and many more, were placed on wooden, slatted shelves below the deck. We lay on the slats with our heads lined up in the middle of the ship and our hands chained to a single cable that ran down both sides of an aisle.

"After one day, the stench and filth were overwhelming. After a week, we had almost become accustomed to it until we came back below decks after eating. Then the odor and despair cloaked us like a dark, heavy mist and we fell to retching and choking on our miserable racks.

"We were on the ocean for sixty-two days. There were 201 of us that started the voyage. Many were ancient enemies with feuds and conflicts that crossed tribal lines. But, in our misery, we were brothers, united in our suffering and, also, in our hatred. The man lying on your one side and the man lying on your other side were your family and your caretakers and your children. They looked to you and you looked to them.

"We were allowed on the deck twice a day. In the morning, we were fed a shell of mashed yam and rice and in the afternoon we were fed a shell of mashed beet and rice. In the evening we were given one shell of water from a bucket that a crew member brought to where we lay. We were allowed on the deck in groups of twenty. At the start of the voyage, it took several hours to feed us all. By the beginning of the third week, we began to die, so the feeding period became shorter and shorter as the days went by. When the man beside you died, you had to drag him up on deck before your meal time and throw him overboard.

"Several, including one of my hunting companions, Bosede, refused to eat. They were whipped. If they still refused, they were thrown overboard. Others prayed and moaned all day and, as a result, declined rapidly.

"I did not do either.

"Haafizah had taught me that my first duty always was to survive so that I would be strong and able when others weakened. I knew that I would need my strength when we reached our destination. I was determined to be strong enough to return home and repay my enemies. I did not reveal to the crew that I could speak English so that I was able to listen as they discussed their plans. When I received my mash, I reached deep in the tub in order to scoop up whatever liquid and bugs were at the bottom along with as much food as I could fit in the shell. I told my hunting friend to eat so that he might live but he refused and was thrown overboard. My other companion despaired and got stomach sick after forty days and died two days later. I told the others on the ship to eat as much as they could, to use their anger as a weapon, to contemplate revenge instead of prayer, and to think about the future when we would fall upon our enemies, both on the ship and at home.

"After fifty days, many had died. But for the next twelve days, only ten died. The rest had become hardened. I knew from the chatter from the crew members that we would be making landfall soon. I told my people that when we reached our destination we would likely not be kept together but would be sent many different places. I asked them to remember me, remember where they had come from, remember our trip, and to remember that we had become a community of many tribes that would be dedicated to freedom for ourselves.

"I told them to remember what it was to be free and to hold that memory as a torch through the dark paths that we would be walking as slaves in the new land. I asked them to be like the leopard which always remembers his freedom and can never be tamed, no matter how long he is caged or whipped or given fine meat to eat. I told them to be leopards that pace and plot and wait for that single chance to kill their careless captors with one unexpected leap.

"The ship was anchored at a new coastline and small boats were lowered to take us to shore. I was chained with nine others and we were rowed to a busy dock where several white men bid to purchase us. These men repeated the indignities of the men on our home coast, poking, prodding, licking us, and prying our mouths wide to check our teeth. The man who paid the money to take me away was the man who owns the farm where we work. He tied my hands together with thick rope and led me behind his horse. When we got to his farm, he sent me to work in the field but the foreman sent me to the shop when he saw that I could figure out how to repair the equipment.

"There's our spring."

Thomas pointed at a small water flow, bubbling out of the ground beneath a large oak tree. We both took long drinks and sat on the tops of the roots where they protruded above the earth. The dark had spread and even with the moon's glow it was now difficult to see where we had come from.

"So with all that do you plan to kill the master?"

"At first I did want to kill him, and his wife and children too, but I came to see that killing him was not the answer for me because they'd kill me then and there would be no one to lead our people home."

"I don't have a home anywhere but here."

"Well, now you're back to being content to be somebody's slave. Your home isn't there, where you will be whipped for wanting to live your own life. Your home is anywhere you can live a free life, and that isn't in this country."

I had no clear thoughts about what Thomas had told me. My only memory was of this land, my only life was as a slave, even though the teacher had told me about countries where everyone was free. I could not think about how to become a free man myself. But I did intend to think about what Thomas had said and, as I lay back with my head against the tree root and floated off to sleep, thoughts of lying on the wretched shelves of the transport ship flared through my mind.

When I woke the next day, a whiskery old horse nose was six inches above me. A white face peered along the side of the animal.

"Well look at this, this fellow's about ready to join the day."

"I figured he was just about done with his beauty sleep when we rode up. C'mon get to your feet."

The short man jumped down from his horse and tied my hands together, then knotted the end of the rope around his saddle. The other man had already tied Thomas to his horse.

"You two have got a little bit of running ahead of you now. I imagine you'll get right sick of looking at that horse's butt by the time we get you back to Richardson's," he said.

The man laughed and swung into the saddle. His stumpy-legged partner said something under his breath and they both laughed again. Thomas sidled up to me, careful not to attract the attention of the two men.

"You take note of the features of those two maggots. One day we'll be the ones doing the laughing. We've got a long road ahead of us. You think on this: they're not going to kill us, they've got too much money in us. So we need to endure."

I looked over at Thomas and nodded. He moved back behind the horse.

The road back to the farm was terrible. We ran as far as we could, then we were dragged. The horses never slowed. The pebbly surface of the road tore the skin off our legs and feet and the undersides of our arms. Even our faces were bruised by rocks. Hatred was born in me on that long, rough road back to the farm.

When we reached the farm, they untied the ropes and left us in a heap on the ground. We were both conscious but unable to speak, unable even to sit up. The master, Richardson, paid the two trackers and their horses slowly sauntered out of the farmyard. He turned to us.

"Tomorrow will be the day of reckoning for you two. Tonight you can rest and get cleaned up and maybe eat if anyone will feed you. Tomorrow you will face your punishment."

Most of the workers were afraid to help us, but Jean shamed four men into carrying us into the kitchen and she gave us water with honey and bowls of potato soup.

"You boys are in for it now. What were you thinking? Now you're going to get whipped as sure as day, and for what?"

Thomas had a black bruise on his forehead and his lip was bleeding, but he did manage a small smile.

"We might have got away."

"Yeah and I might have been a princess with a stable full of horses. But instead I'm a cook with enough to eat every day and a roof over my head at night. You boys are fixing to be half dead in my kitchen and more than that after they get through with you tomorrow."

Thomas turned on his side and groaned.

"The easy way to tame someone is not by whipping the hell out of them. That way grows hate and trouble for the future. The best way to make someone a slave is to make them feel grateful for being alive by giving them just enough to keep living. That way they feel they owe something to those who keep them slaves," he said.

"Well my kitchen may not be on the path to freedom but the truth is that both you and I are in it right now and you're about to get the whipping of your life tomorrow and I'm not. So I guess I don't see how you're any closer to being free than I am. Maybe further away since I'm going to be able to get around tomorrow and you're not."

Jean turned and went over to her bed in the corner of the kitchen and lay down. Thomas and I lay on the mat on the floor, shivering as the night drew close. It seemed to me that the night lasted a long, long time. Of course I was scared of what the morning was going to bring, but I also wanted to get it over with. After surviving the brutal way home, I knew that a whipping would not do me in.

The fact of the matter is that the whipping was bad but the straw was worse. That's what I remember the most—the straw bales that we were stretched on. Richardson's foreman took me by my hands and pulled me over two small straw bales, then put two more straw bales under my legs. My hands were each tied to a post in the barn and my feet to the front wheels of a hay wagon. Thomas was stretched out at my feet. We were whipped at the same time, two foremen standing on top of us and just dying to get at us with cutting braids made from twisted leather shanks. Each time the leather whip came down, the man with the whip hand would jump in the air and drive the thin, cutting piece of leather with the strength of his full weight behind it. Every time he did that, the hard ends of the straw nailed into my chest and my poor, raw legs. The foreman had gathered all the people from the farm—fifteen of them—to the barn to watch us get whipped and the women cried and the men sighed at the sight.

After thirty-five strokes, when the whip had become one constant wheel of pain rolling down my back, and my spit had turned into a solid lump in my throat, the foreman called an end to it.

"Look at these miserable buggers. Look and see what happens if you run. You can't get away; there's nowhere to run. You will be dragged back here and whipped. If you have a family, they will be whipped too. So think on that."

They untied us and left us on the floor of the barn. Everybody went back to work except Jean and a worker who fixed the tools with Thomas. The cook helped me to the kitchen and Thomas went with the mechanic back to the machine shed. He was bleeding, front and back, and slumped onto his friend's shoulder.

I just looked at him and stumbled away with the cook. Every morning and every night for two weeks, she smeared white grease from the stove onto my legs and chest and back and, every day while I lay unable to work, she brought me food and my strength returned as my wounds healed.

"You won't run again, will you?"

"Nope, I think one dragging and whipping is enough for me."

"I've seen this before. Sometimes boys just have to try something and see what happens. When it doesn't work, well, then they are fine and everything goes back to normal. Best thing for you is to settle down and forget all these fancy notions."

But here's the thing. People on that farm treated me differently after the beating. All of them treated me differently, not just my people but the whites too. I wasn't just a poor boy anymore. People looked at me with respect. The whites had fear in their eyes; I saw them glance my way and then move their gaze quickly away, afraid to look too closely.

My hatred, a creature born when the rope was woven around my hands at the back of the horse, had been nurtured, shaped, and educated during the long drag home and the bloody beating. It was now a terrible monster living in me and feasting on every wayward glance from the foreman, every order from Richardson, every taunt from the white children. It was the creature looking out of my eyes that scared the whites.

A month after the beating I was mostly healed and back working in the kitchen. I was at work cutting wood in the yard again when Thomas appeared at the corner of the kitchen.

"Good to see you got that ax sharpened up. Or maybe you just finally learned how to cut wood? Either way it seems you aren't going to cut your head off anymore."

"No. I thought I'd leave it to you to get me into trouble."

"Don't you think we should be moving out of here?"

"There is no 'we' here. There's you and your crazy ideas. Then there's me, working here, eating every day, sleeping every night, and keeping out of trouble."

Thomas looked at me.

"You must think I'm an idiot or something. Any fool with half a brain can see that if you don't get out of here, you're going to bury that ax in Richardson's head. Fact is, you look as crazy as a rabid fox and I'm just about scared to even have you with me."

I had been thinking about how I could get back at the sorry excuses who had dragged me back and at the foreman who had whipped me. Truth is, I hadn't thought of much else. I'd been sneaking out at night to read my Bible by the edge of the woods and it struck me that my idea of getting back at evil folk was pretty much the same as what was written there.

"I know what you want," he said. "I want it too, which is likely a good thing because, when the time comes, I don't think I want to get in your way, but you are never going to get the chance by cowering here like a whipped dog."

So it was that we ran again. This time I took the ax with me.

Two

We walked along the same path through the forest, past the trees where I had hid my books, and then through the bog.

Thomas was silent, but kept glancing at me. Finally, as we drew near to the place where we had slept during our first run, he laughed.

"Why did you bring that ax? Do you intend on chopping down a few old trees?"

"I intend on not getting dragged again behind some old nag. I intend on using this ax to help me with that if they catch us."

"If you hit somebody with that," Thomas said, "they'll kill you, sure as you're standing. The thing is this, you need to focus yourself and you need to pick your spots so as to not waste your anger until you can really use it. Fact is, I need you to stick around."

I looked at Thomas out of the corner of my eye.

"What does all that blather mean? You talk a mean streak but I don't get a lot of it. That story you told about the parrot's nest still bugs the hell out of me. So what if you were an old king? Why the hell would you wait in your room for the women to strangle you? That story doesn't make any more sense than you do. And now you're saying we should just roll over and wait. For what?"

We walked past our old dirt beds and on to a road that ran behind the forest. Thomas began walking quickly down the road and I hurried to keep up.

"If we keep heading this way, we'll get to the water and then we can crew up on a ship. But we'll have to get off this road and into the trees in a hurry if we hear horses coming up behind."

We walked along the road for several minutes before he spoke again.

"Listen to this.

"In my country there was a man, the unluckiest man you could ever know. He was out with his young brother on a big leopard hunt that went deep into the forest. He spotted the leopard high in a tree and called for his brother to help him kill it. But before he could throw his spear, the leopard jumped and knocked him to the ground. His brother yelled and the leopard left the unlucky man, jumped on his brother, and killed him before leaping back into the forest.

"The man was crazy in his grief and anger. His anger was all the harder to bear because he blamed himself for his brother's death. Guilt, a cruel master, seized him. As soon as he could, he went back into the forest to hunt the leopard by himself.

"But hunting alone is very hard, especially when you're hunting for an animal as smart and clever as a leopard, which will lie in wait, invisible and calculating. The man was gone a long time and did not even see the leopard. When he returned to his home, he discovered that a war party of our enemy had killed his other brother while he was gone.

"Now the unlucky man was beyond grief. He blamed himself again. His mindless and thoughtless hunt of the leopard had left his family weakened and his other brother had been killed. He swore vengeance on his enemies and went, alone, to track them.

"He came upon the enemy after several days, but when he ran heedlessly into their camp, they scattered like feathers on the wind and he was unable to find even one of them to kill. He had to return to his home without being satisfied.

"This time, when he came home he discovered that his wife had slept with his neighbor and both had fled into the forest to escape his wrath. His vows of revenge and insults echoed through the village and he quickly followed their tracks, thoughts of vengeance on the enemy warriors and leopard put aside.

16

"He followed the tracks for many miles but eventually lost them in a swamp where he wandered for hours before finally finding his way out and returning home. He greeted his only son upon his return, not knowing that he had brought a swamp fever back with him. His son sickened with the stomach pain and died soon after.

"Now the unlucky man did not know whom to seek vengeance on. He thought that he had been forsaken. With no hope, no faith, and no reason to live, the unlucky man became feeble and died."

I looked at Thomas.

"What kind of sad story is that? Are you saying it was the man's fault that all those bad things happened? How can you blame him for being unlucky?"

"Well, if he had thought a bit before blindly casting about like a wounded buffalo, he may have actually had his revenge. All I'm saying is that if he'd waited to put a group of hunters together, it would have included his other brother. They might have killed the leopard and none of the rest would have happened. If you really want revenge, if you really want to get back at those who dragged you and whipped you, you'd better think a little bit before you start striking out. Otherwise you won't get your revenge and they'll kill you before you get anything done. But if you wait and think and act in a reasoned way, you might gain your freedom and others might, too."

I didn't say anything for several minutes. We walked past an old white man who was shuffling along and carrying a basket of eggs, but he didn't even glance at us. We went past two farmyards where the dogs barked, but we didn't hear anyone coming after us.

"How exactly will I know when the time is right?"

"You'll know it when it comes, if you think it through, but our revenge won't be without purpose and it won't just be to strike back at the master. When we strike there will be many of us and we'll be striking to be free men forever, and no more looking over our shoulders to see who's coming."

"So if we get caught again, I'm just supposed to stand still."

"You're not supposed to do anything. You do what you want but, as sure as day follows night, if you use that ax on any white man, that will be the last thing you do. That means you won't have any real revenge and the bastards will have won. What I'm hoping is that we will not get caught this time. We can do more good as free men. I don't like the idea of being whipped any more than you do, but if we do get caught I want you to hold on to your anger and remember there will be another chance for us."

As the shadows grew long, we stopped at the edge of the woods. I ran back to the old man whom we had passed and offered him the ax in exchange for his eggs and water flask. He was happy to make the trade. We were happy too, and at least had something for supper. We made our bed and a cold, hard bed it was. It was a full moon and the road was still visible from our resting place.

Despite the cold ground, I slept well. We were on the road again just after dawn but we hadn't gone more than a mile before four horsemen burst from the trees and trapped us. I'll never know if they were just lucky to find us or if the old man gave us up. We stood there like dumb oxen waiting for our yokes.

The way back was hard but not as bad as the first time. Maybe Richardson had told the hunters not to drag us since he didn't get work from us while we healed, or maybe they were just not inclined to drag a man for mile after mile, but I doubt that. You have to be a mean bastard with no thought of anyone but yourself to be a bounty hunter.

We ran for miles and when we couldn't run, we walked and the horses slowed to walk with us. It was dark when we got back to the farmyard and we were chained by our wrists to the barn posts and left for the night. Finally left alone, I turned to Thomas.

"What will they do to us this time?"

"Well you can count on a whipping, that's for sure. What else, I don't know."

"I'll tell you this. You got me to give up that ax, but I am never going to sit there like some damn pigeon again. I don't care what the hell happens to me, I'm not about to let them take me again without a fight."

Thomas looked at me and laughed.

"You're already thinking about the next time and we aren't even finished with this time yet. You would surely fit in well with that unlucky man from my home that I was telling you about. Still, you have the fire and it is better to have the fire than not, even if that flame ends up consuming us both."

"I get the story of the unlucky man, but I still don't get the story of the parrot's nest. Why would anyone just consent to give up power and be strangled in his bed?"

Thomas laughed again and shifted his wrist chains so that he was looking directly at me around the edge of the post.

"It seems to me that you should understand that very well, seeing as how you are quite willing to accept your own death if you can take a few with you. The question you're asking me you could just as easily ask yourself and the answer is the same. If you care about something or somebody more than you care about your own life, then logic and reason have no power over you. You want revenge more than you want to hold on to your life. To the leaders of my homeland, the history of justice and tradition and popular support is more important than their own lives. The people are their lives. When they lose the support of the people, they believe that their own lives are over. The women just carry out the request."

I kind of understood what Murphy was saying, but his story was coming from the point of view of a ruler and my experiences were of a common man, a slave. I understood that everyone in his community had a part to play but my own freedom was all that mattered to me.

A sickly yellow moon shone over the yard. No one, not even Jean, came to us during that hard night and we were thirsty, cold, and scared. The chains bit at my wrists and I could not sleep, dreading the morning and hoping for the trouble to come sooner so that it could be over sooner.

I could not have predicted the horror that was to come.

In the morning, Richardson appeared with his foreman. He asked one of the men to build a cooking fire and two others to stretch us over the straw bales. We were whipped in the same fashion as the first time, the ends of the straw sticking to my stomach and the whip leaving my back in agony. By the time we had received thirty lashes each, all the people of the farm had gathered at the barn. Richardson turned to them.

"These two are troublemakers. No one can run from here. I own you. All of you."

Richardson took a long metal poker from the fire. It was straight for three feet, then shaped into the letter *R* at the end. The *R* was orange hot, the ends of the letter glistening like liquid with the heat. The farmer told one of the foremen to sit on my shoulders with his knees, pinning my arms to the ground. The other foreman kneeled, gripped my head, and turned my face so that my left cheek was turned up.

Richardson took the poker and pressed the *R* into my exposed cheek. The dry acrid smell of the smoke from my branded cheek made the watching workers squint and cover their mouths. I know this because my face, turned in the heavy hands of the foreman, was fixed on the watching crowd. I had vowed not to scream, no matter the punishment, but as the pain from the burn seized me, my voice was unleashed. I could not cry but a series of small mumbles and moans came from my mouth and I saw Jean, standing at the front of the crowd, bury her face in her apron, her shoulders hunched and shaking.

Finally the iron was removed, the hands lifted from my head, and Richardson and his foremen moved on to Thomas. I heard no words or sounds from my friend when the sour smoke again curled up. The iron, cooled slightly by my branding, was left on Thomas longer and the smoke filled the barn. All I heard was a sharp intake of breath and then nothing.

Richardson said nothing more and walked from the barn with his foremen. Jean and several men dragged us into the kitchen. Neither of us said anything. We were barely able to breathe. Jean got lard from the stove and smeared it on our cheeks and our backs. She was sobbing quietly and murmuring a prayer under her breath. I could not speak for a day and a night, which was more than long enough to add a measure of hate to my already large stockpile.

Three

Richardson's latest torture suited his purpose well. The brands on our cheeks, while a constant worry for infection and a source of agony that crawled up our heads and down our necks, did not keep us from working for very long. Our backs, thick with scars from the first whipping, were not greatly damaged by the second. Thomas was back at work in three days and I returned to my labor in four.

Jean tended me like a nurse.

"When you run again, you tell me and I'll put something out for you."

"I don't think I'll be running again."

"That's just what you said last time."

The farm foremen contrived to keep Thomas and me apart and it was rare that I saw him. When I did, the foreman kept a close eye on us and we did not speak. I was mainly given jobs that did not bring me into contact with any of the other workers on the farm. I was taken from working in the kitchen, and put to special work that left me by myself. For several months I was left alone with an ax to clear a small grove of trees, my ankle banded with iron and attached with a heavy chain to a large log that I could pull to move from tree to tree, but could not travel with for any distance.

The new work suited my disposition.

I hated the foremen for their arrogance, despised Richardson for his cruelty, and was ashamed of my fellows for their passivity. I was more than happy to work alone all day and my thoughts of vengeance and escape simmered like broth in a pot. Everyone on the farm avoided me. Some were worried about being associated with me and some were afraid of what they saw in me. The foremen treated me like a captured bear, keeping me in chains and hauling me from one job to another. I never said a word to them.

Everyone avoided me except Jean.

* * *

The months of solitary work passed into years. As the years drifted by, I grew solid and strong, bitter and remote. My ankle band, applied every morning when I went into the fields or forest, wore a thick ring of red scar tissue around my leg so that when the band was removed it appeared that one leg was thicker than the other. My muscles were strong from dragging the cursed log and swinging the ax day after day.

I still slept in a corner of the kitchen, as I had since I was a boy. I seldom talked to Jean anymore, preferring to keep my black thoughts to myself. Eventually I lapsed into a sullen silence, even as Jean continued to speak to me. I could see that she was worried. One evening she came to me after the light had faded from the open door.

"Murphy, you need to leave this place."

"And go where?"

"Murphy, you need to find a place where you can rest. You need to run away or you'll die here. You're an outcast, feared and hated by everyone. Worse, you hate yourself."

"If I run I'll get caught and whipped or worse."

"And if you stay here your heart will turn into rock. I told you to endure but I no longer think that's right for you. The price is too steep."

I turned over to sleep and Jean went to her bed.

The foreman came to fetch me as dawn broke. We went to a small boggy field where I had been digging a drainage ditch. The ditch wended its way from the bog to a creek. Richardson likely planned on planting the field next year after the water drained. I had been digging it for two months. The foreman led me to my companion log and snapped on the ankle band and the lock. He gave me a small loaf with cheese and a flask of water and left without a word.

That morning crept by in its usual way, the sun blazing in the sky. I dug slowly in the heavy, water-soaked soil and finally stopped for lunch, pulling my log to a dry spot where I could sit. After eating, I fell asleep in the warmth, lying beside the log. I was shaken awake. Thomas was standing beside me, a wide grin on his face.

"Well what sort of work is that? Good thing it was me that found you and not the boss."

I shook my head to clear the last remnants of sleep.

"If you've come around just to plague me again you might as well go back where you came from. I'm not interested in anything you have to sell."

"That's a mighty hard attitude coming from someone with their leg tied to some big log, and lying alone in a swamp. You may have noticed that I don't have a tree attached to my leg, and I sure as blazes have a sunnier outlook."

"What do you want?"

"I want to take that band off your leg and I want to get you out of here."

Thomas had two burlap bags with him. The bigger one jangled as he emptied it on the ground. Several tools fell out—a hammer, a file, several pieces of wire of varying thicknesses, a couple of chisels, two screwdrivers, and two implements with narrow shanks and hooks on the end.

"Let's have a look at that thing."

"You can't be here. This is going to end up poorly, like it always does with you. Someone's going to miss those tools or maybe miss you and the first place they'll look is out here."

"Well that's where you're wrong. My foreman is gone all day and they all trust me so much now that they just leave me on my own, and I'm responsible for these tools so I doubt anyone's going to see they're missing. If we get this band off soon we can get out of here and have a big head start."

I thought back to Jean's words. I thought of myself, lying like a staked animal on the grass and I thought of the whippings and I felt the hard scar of the *R* on my cheek. Mostly I thought about how good it was when Thomas and I were walking down the road when we ran the second time.

"All right."

Thomas grabbed my foot and looked at the iron band.

"I don't know if I can work it off or not. I think we should try to jimmy that lock open."

He took the two pieces of wire and the hooked tools and put them in the keyhole of the lock. It was a simple padlock that was locked with a key that the foreman kept. After a couple of minutes of moving the pieces around in the keyhole to no effect, Thomas dropped the tools and grabbed the screwdriver but he could not lever the lock open. He picked up the hammer and chisel.

"This is it then. This is going to hurt some, I imagine, so brace yourself."

Thomas took the chisel and applied the end to the lock where one post entered and swung with the hammer. My ankle was jerked hard but the lock did not open. Before his next swing I grabbed my leg with both hands so it would not move. He took another, harder swing and, although the lock refused to open, a slash appeared on the post where it entered the lock. Five more swings with the band biting into my ankle each time and the padlock hung limply by one post, the other post severed. Thomas removed the lock and I swung the band back on its hinge.

"Wasn't too much to that lock."

"Easy for you to say when it was my leg getting hit. Where're we going now?"

"Back our old way. They won't miss either of us 'til night and then they won't be able to look for us in the dark, so if we make the road by nightfall and keep walking we should be all right."

Thomas left the bag of tools on the ground but hoisted the other bag on his shoulder. We took off through the bog and soon we hit upon our old trail. Down through the wet dips we walked and up through the same old dry rises. At dusk we passed our leafy beds of a few years back and then got onto the road. We walked slowly but steadily along the scruffy road, the trees on each side looming large in the gathering darkness and keeping us on edge. Several times we thought we heard hoof-beats and scuttled into the woods, but no horses appeared.

After a couple of hours, Thomas stopped and sat on a log at the edge of the woods. He reached into the burlap bag and pulled out two loaves of bread and a sealed jug of water.

"Where did you get all that?"

"Jean came to see me a couple of days back on some phony errand. She said I better get you out of here quickly or you're going to get yourself in big trouble."

I didn't say anything but sat there looking at the ground. Thomas stared at me for a minute and then smiled.

"Yeah, I can see that she was right. So I figured it was time to get going. First chance I got when they left me by myself, I took the tools and went to the kitchen where Jean gave me some food. Then I went on to you. Jean has a special fondness for you, despite your bad attitude and nasty thoughts."

"That's rich coming from you. You're the cause of all my misery. If it weren't for you, I'd be at the farm with no marks on my back, no brand on my cheek, and no welt on my leg. I wouldn't have been walking around with a big damn log attached to me and I wouldn't be having everybody hating me."

"I don't think you'd be the friendly, loveable simpleton no matter what, but the plain fact is that you know the way back. If you want to be someone's slave, suit yourself."

"Let me see that bag."

Jean had given him loaves, water, cheese, and a roasted chicken in the bag. I took a chicken leg and began to eat. We ate like free people that night and when we were stuffed we lay back for a while in the grass.

"What have you been doing for the last couple of years?"

"Working in the shop. Thinking about things. Trying to get along. Planning. Wondering what in hell you were doing."

"You must have been getting on better than me if they were all right with leaving you alone."

"Well, Murphy, I was the perfect little slave. While you were scaring the hell out of the foremen with your hostile looks, I was getting along and making everyone happy. I heard about your trials and it made me angry, but we've got bigger things ahead so I just kept my mouth shut and got along. These people are pretty dumb. If it doesn't hit them on the head they don't see it."

"Don't see how you could get along like that."

"I was hoping we would get another chance and we did."

Thomas lay back in the grass, his head and shoulders resting against a large tree. The moon shone through the leaves and the road was a silver slash stretching into the distance. The owls were calling softly to each other and I was nearly asleep when he jumped to his feet.

"C'mon, let's go before we fall asleep here. I'll tell you a story while we walk."

Thomas picked up the bag and walked down to the pale road.

"I want to tell you a story about the most dangerous animal in my country. This animal is not the biggest animal, not the cruelest, not the strongest, but it is the smartest and the most patient. It is the one animal that knows that there is a future.

"When my father was young he decided to make pets of the two most dangerous animals he could find. So he set a leopard trap and he set a buffalo trap. The leopard trap was set so that when the cat walked between two trees, two hunters hidden in the trees yanked on ropes and caught the animal in woven vines that made a net on the ground beneath the trees. The trap was located on a game trail—even so, it took several days for the leopard to appear and all that while the hunters waited in their trees, their food and water by their sides. When the leopard was finally captured it was taken to my father's yard and put in a strong pen where there was food.

"Catching the buffalo was even more difficult. The hunters did not know how to capture a buffalo alive, but they finally settled on the idea of wounding the animal so that it could not run or attack, and then driving it home. They managed to separate out a young bull and one of the hunters speared the buffalo in its leg so that it was hobbled, and drove it slowly home and into a different pen.

"My father was very pleased with the beasts and had a special feast for the hunters who captured them. He began the process of taming the leopard by personally feeding meat to it through the walls of the pen every day. As he fed it, he talked softly and slowly. At first the cat watched him carefully but hung back. Then it began to eat after he had left. Finally, the leopard came up as he dropped the meat into the pen, and eventually, it would eat the meat as he held it from outside. After a couple of months the leopard would eat the meat right out of my father's hand. Every time it came up to my father, his guards with spears at their sides, he would feed the cat a bit of meat and talk softly to it.

"He tried the same approach with the buffalo, feeding it sweet grass and seeds. At first the animal refused to eat at all. Then it would eat only when my father had walked away. Every time he came near the fence, the buffalo, now healed, would put its head down and charge. After a few months, my father had made no progress at all with the buffalo. At the mere sound of a voice, especially my father's, the animal would toss its heavy horns, swing its head from side to side and paw at the earth. A dog that had the misfortune of straying into the pen was gored by the monster. It was fatal to go inside the pen and dangerous even to go close. After the buffalo killed another dog, my father realized it was too dangerous to keep the beast and had it killed.

"One time, as the leopard was being fed, my father took a braided leash and dropped it over the cat's head. It was not long before the leopard allowed itself to be led around inside the pen and then be taken outside. The animal sat quietly beside my father and he fed it the finest pieces of meat. My father was very pleased with the leopard and decided, on his birthday, to take the leash off. As soon as he did, the leopard sprang up and bounded into the forest before either my father or the guards could act. By the time they got to the edge of the trees, the animal was long gone.

"I ask you, which animal was the most clever and the most dangerous? Do you think it was the untamed buffalo, destroying everything that ventured into his pen? Or the leopard, apparently tamed by tender meat but looking to escape and be free and able to kill at the first chance?"

I looked over at Thomas. His head was outlined in the moonlight and I could see his eyes sparkling like dew-drops. He was smiling and I knew damn well how he wanted me to answer. Knowing that, I answered the way he wanted me to anyway, seeing as how he had cut the band from my leg and set me out on this adventure.

"The buffalo's the most dangerous," I said. "He'd kill anyone who got in the pen out of sheer madness whereas the leopard just wanted to be free."

"You're wrong. The buffalo, which was as terrible an animal as you'd want to run into, was slaughtered by my father after he got tired of trying to tame him. Our family had a huge feast of buffalo meat.

"On the other hand, the leopard, which had seemed as tame as a dog for months while it waited for its chance to escape, killed a lone hunter two days after it ran into the woods. We knew it was our leopard because it didn't eat any of the hunter, just killed him and left him there for us to find. It killed another man two weeks later, and a third a month after that. We never caught a glimpse of it."

The lonely road was an ugly break between the trees. I thought of what it would be like to be hunting alone in a fantastic world where spotted death lay in wait. And I thought of the terror of having crushing jaws fixed on the back of my neck, lying face down in the dirt; no escape, no forgiveness, and no mercy.

"I see your point. I'm the buffalo, mindless and blind and cruel, and you're the leopard, smart and thoughtful and patient. You know what I'd really like?"

"What?"

"Sometime, in your stories, I want to be the smart guy. I want to be the hunter who's smart enough to get a group of his friends together to get his revenge. I want to be the leopard and I want you to be the dumb old buffalo."

Thomas looked at me and he smiled. Then he began to chuckle and then to laugh. I couldn't help smiling myself and soon we were both laughing so hard that we had to sit at the edge of the road.

"Yeah, you got it. I'll be the dumb old buffalo next time. Sometimes when I talk with you I get the feeling that maybe I'm the slow one already. There's a lot to be said for patience, biding your time and waiting for a chance but, you know, you're right too. There's also something to be said for being so damn solitary that people fear you and there's a lot right about acting swiftly, strongly, and in a direct way. There's no right path, that's the only sure thing, and when we get together, I realize that. You surely do keep me from thinking I've got a corner on the truth."

We both laughed again and I shook my head like a wet dog. After a moment we began walking down the road. It was easy to see our way and the road was quiet. Thomas walked on quickly. The sun was beginning to rise before he spoke again.

"Can you imagine owning slaves?"

"I imagine many things, most of them to do with the men who tortured us, but no, I can't feature owning someone. Can you?"

"Don't have to imagine it. My family had slaves that we'd captured. We never branded them but we did whip them if they tried to escape. Or for a whole range of other things we didn't like. It's my shame that I did this without thought and without regard. Worst of all, with no regret at the time. These things and more from a past that I cannot change haunt me. As surely as the shadows swallow the light of day, my past cruelties devour my life. I think, over and over, about each one."

He stopped.

I was stunned, not so much that Thomas had been an owner of slaves but, more, that he was plagued by his past ownership. He was the strong one, the one with the plan and the one who always figured things out. This was the first sign I saw that Thomas ever doubted himself. We walked in silence. The day dawned and still we walked down that hard road to the coast and freedom. Thomas had nothing more to say and I could not fill the terrible quiet. I considered my twisted life and uncertain future, my mind wandering from one grim thought to another. I thought of my unknown parents and I thought of the teacher who had taught me to read and write, taught me to see the world, and encouraged me to think.

It was this memory, finally, that led me to thoughts of my book tree and my Bible. I knew what it was that Thomas needed. I grabbed him by the arm.

"You need to make peace with yourself and with God. Atonement. Remember the story about the parrot's nest? You told me the rulers in your country are defined by the way they rule, that their lives are dedicated to their people. When they are unable to live for their people, they accept that their lives are finished. You have great things ahead of you. You have to find out what these things are, and then you'll know how to atone for your past cruelties, and then God will remove your demons."

He looked at me sideways. We walked on in silence.

The sun, now high in the sky, spread a gold sheen on the road and it stretched, a path to the future, for miles and miles.

Four

We were captured as the day turned to dusk. It happened just as we were thinking that this time we had actually escaped. One minute we were walking; the next, we crested a sharp hill and saw with terror a team of bays and a wagon stretched across the road. A man with a gun was leaning against the back of the wagon. We heard hoof-beats from behind and a boy on a horse appeared, gun in hand.

"That's it then. C'mon here and lay yourselves down in this wagon. Cover up with the canvas. All the way up, over your heads. If you peek out, I'll blow your feet off."

We lay under the canvas and the wagon pulled off with a start. After just a few minutes we stopped, the canvas was pulled back, and the teamster motioned with his head for us to jump off. He no longer had his gun but we were covered by the boy, still on horseback and watching us closely. We were in a small farmyard, the barn on one side and a worn house on the other.

"In the barn, both of you."

The twilight grew into deep night. We were tied fast, our backs to a large pole in the middle of the barn, and our wrists knotted together behind us. For a while, I strained against the ropes but the knots held. There was nothing to say.

The dark had drained from the barn and light had started to creep in when the man appeared at the door. He cocked his head to one side, spit out of the corner of his mouth, and began to speak.

"Here's the thing. Richardson is as mean as a stuck hog. He's the most ornery man in the county. If I turn you back to him, he'll give me a bounty of ten pounds each, which is a bit of money. Now I know you've run before, it's plain on your face and I know damn well that he'll string you up if he lays hands on you this time."

He paused and looked at us.

"But there's a fellow I know in Wilmington who will give me forty pounds each for you in a straight sale. Now that's a powerful amount of money that I surely could use. If I get caught smuggling you, I'll be a thief and maybe shot for my trouble. It's a long trip with danger all the way. It's a tough choice and I'm going to put it to you two. You can take your chances with me and Wilmington. Or you can maybe hang with Richardson."

I twisted my head around so I could look directly at the man.

"You'll drag us all the way?"

"Nope, I want you there whole and looking fine. You'll be in the back of the wagon, covered with the canvas. There's no profit in me beating you up and you won't be tied, neither. If you want to run, then run. I'll put out the word and Richardson's men will have you with nooses around your necks before you can jump."

The man came over and untied the ropes binding us to the pole. He went and sat on a step leading to the barn loft.

"What's it to be?"

I looked over at Thomas, who was rubbing his raw wrists.

"Thomas, what do you say? I think we maybe should take our chances on Wilmington."

"Well, we can't go back."

We stood, twisting our necks where they had cramped. The man led us to the wagon and the boy came out of the house and gave us water flasks, bread, and cheese. We leaned against the wagon's gate as the farmer pointed his finger at us.

"Boys, if you want to talk now you go right ahead but listen up to me, when we get going you have to stay silent. If I say hush, you lie quiet and still as you can 'til I say so. If you need something, you just say 'Jackson' real quiet and I'll stop the wagon."

Jackson and his boy went into the barn and came back out with large sacks of oats that they put in the back of the wagon. There were a couple of pieces of post, some thick rope, and a few old halters in the far corner. Jackson told the boy to look after things while he was gone and then looked at us.

"You can lie against these sacks and they'll make your ride a little easier."

He went back into the house for a few minutes and came back with two small burlap bags with supplies that he placed beside him on the seat. We crawled into the back and pulled the canvas over our heads and, a moment later, he clicked at the horses and we pulled out.

The next week settled into a routine. During the day we lay still, trying to be comfortable on our oat-sack pillows. At night, Jackson pulled into a farm, putting the horses in the barn and being careful to leave the wagon behind a building and out of sight of the house so Thomas and I could stand and stretch. In the morning he brought water, bread, cheese, and sometimes chicken and apples. We ate half in the morning and saved the rest for night.

The track to Wilmington was divided by rivers, the road swallowed by the water at one bank only to be carved anew on the far shore. The small rivers were easily forded, the horses pulling the wagon along riverbeds worn hard by previous travelers, but finally we came to a large river where Jackson stopped and waited for twilight.

As the sun set, he told us to get out of the wagon.

"Just walk behind the wagon here in the water and give it a push if we get stuck. The water's not deep, it won't be over your knees."

The path across the river bottom was hard-packed but narrow. The horses, stepping surely through the water, easily pulled the lightened wagon. Thomas and I trudged along behind with the current making our steps difficult and slow. Just past halfway, the wagon settled into a dip and the horses strained to pull it out.

"Now, give the wagon a push so we can get out of here."

We pushed. The wagon lurched and settled forward. The horses pulled sharply and the wagon jerked across to the far bank. Thomas and I clambered out of the water and sat on a log by the river's edge.

"We'll stay here for the night and leave at first light."

In the morning we settled back into the wagon and Jackson pulled out. We hadn't gone more than a couple of hours before he told us to lie still. I heard the sound of hoof-beats from behind and soon a horse snorted from the side of the wagon where Thomas lay like a stone statue. The sound of voices filtered through the canvas.

"Hey there. Beautiful day, isn't it?"

"Good enough, I guess."

"Where you headed?"

"Just down the road a piece."

The horse moved to my side of the wagon.

"I'm looking for a couple of runaways. You'll know them for sure. They've got a mark on their faces. Now you haven't seen anything like that have you?"

"Nope, haven't seen a soul. I'll keep a lookout though."

The bounty hunter shifted the horse to the front of the wagon.

"What's in the back of the wagon?"

"Sacks of oats. My old dog."

"You say your dog? Mind if I have a look?"

"Can if you like, but here's the thing. My dog is lying back there and he's sick, kind of drooling and twitching. We're going down to the doc's to see if he can give him some medicine. Since he took to being sick he's been even more ornery than usual and he never was a friendly type. He won't hardly even listen to me but feel free to have a look if you want. Just watch when you peel that canvas back that he doesn't jump out at you."

There was a long pause. I held my breath and looked at Thomas out of the corner of my eye. Finally we heard the bounty hunter let out a long breath and we heard the horse turn away from the wagon.

"Well that's all right. There's a reward out so if you see those runaways, tie them to a tree and you'll make yourself some money. Have a good day, neighbor, and I hope your dog gets better."

The horse trotted away and the wagon slowly pulled forward. I waited for a long while and then turned over and looked at Thomas.

"You recognize that voice?"

"Oh yeah, one of the riders who dragged us all the way back to Richardson's."

"One day I'm going to kill that bastard."

Later that night, after Jackson had left the wagon behind a barn and stabled the horses, I sat on the edge of the wagon and talked with Thomas.

"I could reach over and strangle him in his seat. We could take the wagon ourselves."

"Two things can happen if you do that. Neither of them are any good."

"What?"

"First is he'll hear us get up and shoot us. Second is that if you kill him then for sure whoever grabs us will shoot us."

"Could be we'll have a wagon that will take us to the coast."

"Nobody's going to let a couple of branded runaways drive a wagon anywhere on this road. The first person to see us will take our heads off."

I was silent. Thomas looked over at me.

"I know a bit about Wilmington."

"How's that?"

"Jean told me. Before Richardson took her she lived in North Carolina and as far as she knows her kids are still there."

"I didn't even know she was married, let alone had any kids."

"Yep, that comes from never looking beyond your own nose. Turns out she had a husband there and a family. Her husband got whipped for talking back, got sick through his cuts, and died. Jean got sold south to Richardson. Her son and daughter were old enough to work on their own so they were kept in Wilmington."

"How come she got sold out?"

"Bastard couldn't get enough work out of her. Guess she was grieving her husband."

"What did she say about Wilmington?"

"I didn't ask her much, not knowing we'd be headed that way. She did say some things were a little different there, that her family lived in their own shack, and that some of her friends even worked out and got paid for it."

"You believe that?"

"Nope."

The next three weeks were a stretch of tedium. We crawled along the road at a steady, slow pace and splashed through the streams. I found a knot-hole in a plank on the floor of the wagon and watched the earth and water flow by. This was my only amusement. Nobody talked during the day, we met few travelers, and the nights were fixed to the same old routine. Thomas kept me awake some nights by tossing and moaning in his sleep.

One evening, we came to another large river and Jackson told us to get out again and walk behind the wagon. The water was up halfway between my knee and my thigh and the horses were having a tough time of it. Everything was fine until just before we reached the far shore. The front wheels of the wagon settled into a rut on the river floor and would not move. Jackson jumped off his seat. Moving in front of the team, he grabbed their harnesses and pulled, yelling at us to push hard.

Suddenly the team lurched. The horses had finally found footing on the bottom and stumbled up the bank, and Jackson fell on his back to one side and into the water. Before he could scramble to his knees, I was on him. I sat on his chest, my knees pushing into his armpits and my hands around his throat. His face was beneath the water, his eyes round moons, the breath leaking out of his nose and mouth in small, dribbling bubbles.

Jackson's hands waved at my arms but he had no traction, his feet slipping beneath him. Behind me I heard yelling, then felt pawing at my back. I could feel Jackson slipping away, his legs losing their small strength. His eyes looked at me and I looked directly back, calm as the night and sure as death.

There was a sudden whoosh of air behind me and the world disappeared.

When I woke, I had a blinding headache and I was lying on the bank beside the horses. Jackson was sitting beside me and Thomas was leaning against a tree, the gun in his hands. I looked at my friend, I looked at the gun, and I looked at Jackson.

"You hit me on the god-damn head."

"You were fixing to kill him."

"Yeah."

"We'd decided not to."

"You decided not to; I decided to. I can't believe you hit me on the head with a damn piece of wood to save this old man who's going to sell us."

"Not to save him, to save us."

"Yeah, if you say so."

Jackson looked up at me, the marks from my fingers still flushed on his neck, his eyes watery and hollow and his skin the color of dust.

"Can't believe you'd kill me after me treating you so well."

"So well, you say, when you're just going to sell us to another Richardson. I don't see you as having such a warm heart. You look more like a slave trader than a saint to me."

"You know what, I'm just a dirt-scrabble farmer. Nothing to my name but these horses. I'm just trying to get by."

"On our backs."

"I've half a mind to turn you over no matter the lost money."

"Try it and I'll finish the job before the words have left your mouth. Thomas, give me the damn gun and I'll finish him here."

Thomas stood looking at me, his face strained. The gun rested in the crook of his arm.

"I'm keeping the gun. I'll tell you both what's going to happen now. First off, we're going to crawl back into that wagon and, Jackson, you're going to get back on the seat. When you get to a farm, you go and do your usual stuff. Thomas and I will stay quiet in the back. Tomorrow we'll carry on."

"What about the gun?"

"I'll hold it for safekeeping."

37

The team walked on and came to a farmyard. Jackson stabled the horses and went into the house. The wagon was left behind a grain bin. I was still brooding about the river and being hit on the head by my friend.

"Should have let me kill him."

"Except you have no plan after that. Now we're just about done."

"I don't see that. We've got the gun, we can go where we want."

"No, we can't."

"I still can't fathom that you hit me on the head. What the hell got into you?"

"What got into me? Well what the hell got into you? I'm still thinking how we're going to get out of this mess. Jackson would as soon shoot you as look at you now. Why couldn't you just wait until Wilmington and we could make some plans?"

"I'm sick of your plans. Sooner you realize that nothing's going to change unless we make it change, the better off we're both going to be. Another thing, if you don't start acting instead of plotting and scheming, we're going to be old before we're free. This is our chance, right here and now."

"Chance to do what? We don't know where we are. We don't know a soul except the man you tried to kill. We aren't just simple runaways now with what you did. They could hang us now and no one would speak up."

"I never featured you as a coward."

Thomas turned slowly where he was sitting on the edge of the wagon.

"Don't ever say that to me again."

"You'd best be acting like you had a spine then. Another thing. I see you tossing around every night in your sleep. I expect you're having nasty dreams. I think you'd best consider what I said to you before. You need to do something to atone for owning slaves yourself."

"Yeah, well that may be but I don't see myself doing much to help anyone when I can't even figure out how to get us out of this spot."

"How about this? We've got a chance to make a run right here and now."

"The truth is that I think I've got to help more people than just myself. As of right now I can't help anyone."

I kicked at a rock that lay beside the wagon wheel.

"Remember when I asked you a long time back if you knew the story of Joseph?"

"Yeah."

"I like that story. He was sold into slavery but won the favor of the king and came back as a ruler. You remember why?"

"No."

"He had dreams that told the future and he could tell other people's futures by their dreams. I think I can maybe do that too sometimes."

"So now you're a seer as well as a killer."

"I've not killed anyone and I'm not claiming to be a seer. But I've had the same dream, over and over, since we ran the first time. We're both in it and there's a lot more like us. They're following us, but it's mostly you that's leading and we're running over a bridge. There's guns and cannons all around but all I have is a big knife like a sword in my hand. There's screaming and yelling and the noise is terrific. I've had this dream more times than I can count."

"What happens?"

"When we get to the bottom of the bridge there's three men getting ready to shoot us and their faces are as white as the full moon. I stab two of them before they can raise their weapons. I don't know what happens to the last one."

"For God's sake, does everything in your mind revolve around violence and meanness?"

"Yeah, pretty much like everything else in the world."

Thomas put the gun inside the wagon.

"I need to get some sleep and figure out how to make things right for us. Are you planning to run tonight?"

"Nope, I'll stick with you through this thing. That's clear in my dream, we're there together."

Five

If Thomas actually made plans to get us out of our jam, he never did reveal them to me. That night we slept quietly in the back of the wagon, the gun resting between us. Jackson crept out in the night and took his gun back, and in the morning greeted us with bread in one hand and the gun in the other.

"We've got a little ways to go yet. Might as well get at it. I'm going to tell you this and then nothing else. I'm ready to move on and finish this thing. If we have any more trouble, I'll turn you both over to the bounty man and that'll be it."

We crawled into our usual places and the wagon moved out.

The rest of the trip to Wilmington was without excitement. On we rolled, over hard-packed road, shallow streams and, once more, a fast-flowing river. This was crossed with the usual pushing and cursing until we arrived on the far bank, wet but whole.

I chafed at our inactivity and spoke little to Thomas. He watched me carefully, a wary look in his eyes. I felt that we had lost our chance for freedom and lay sullen and withdrawn as the miles passed under our planked floor.

One morning before setting out, Jackson brought us some chicken legs and cake. He told us that we would be in Wilmington that afternoon. Later, as the sun began to warm the canvas, I heard him ask directions to William Campbell's house and, with the shadows growing longer, he finally pulled the wagon to a halt and told us to get out.

Campbell's house was a large, white, two-story building. Jackson told us to wait by the wagon as he walked up the stairs to the front door and spoke a moment to an unseen person who answered his knock and disappeared inside. A few minutes later he appeared with another man. That man looked us up and down.

"They're big enough, anyways."

"And strong and clever. Young enough to do anything you want them to and old enough to know how to do it. They'll be prime hands at anything you set them to."

"Branded though. Could be a handful and there will be men looking for them, sure enough."

"Those are old scars—these boys didn't cause me any trouble at all. Besides, out here you see everyone coming miles before they get here. You're getting them cheap, you know that."

The two men walked back into the house and, shortly, Jackson re-appeared.

"It's all done. This here is your new place. If you can manage to get along, you'll be fine."

He took his seat in the wagon and drove away. Campbell appeared at the doorway and came down the steps. He carefully looked us over, up and down, and then came over to me and stared at my face.

"What work did you do?"

"Cutting trees, clearing pasture."

"You start cutting tomorrow—Sam will show you where to go. What about you?"

"Worked fixing machines."

"The mill then. Go with Sam tonight and I'll get someone to show you where it is tomorrow."

He turned away to go back in the house but hesitated on the wide, white staircase.

"What are your names?"

"Murphy."

"Thomas."

"I can see you've been runaways before. If you run I'll get the hunters and dogs after you. If you cause any trouble, you'll be whipped. If you behave, you'll get your meals and a place to sleep with a roof on it."

Campbell turned and went back into the house. A short man with a gimpy leg came out and told us to follow him.

"Where are you boys from?"

"South, Louisiana way."

"Who's to the forest?"

"Me."

"Good, you look like you could carry a couple of trees under your arms."

"Sam."

"Yeah, that's me. I'll give you a bit of advice. Stay quiet, don't run, don't cause trouble, and we'll all get along fine. They don't treat us too bad here, and nobody but nobody wants that to change."

Sam looked hard at me and then over to Thomas.

"Moses will take you to the mill tomorrow."

We walked across the yard to a small cabin in a leafy grove.

"This is where we sleep. The men with families are over in those cabins and the single women are behind the kitchen. If you're caught over there after dark you'll be whipped. You'll take all your meals where you work. Don't ever go near the house unless you're asked and don't cause problems with the other workers. You get the top bunks."

Sam had the bunk beneath me, and Moses, who worked in the mill, was in the other lower bunk. The next morning, Sam and I headed for the woods while Moses and Thomas went to the mill.

Sam and I were the only workers in the forest. Our job was to cut down and limb the large pine trees that jostled with the poplar and birch for footing. It was dangerous and tiring but I grew to love the work. Every morning, Sam and I picked up the food sacks left on the steps of the cabin and headed to the small pasture where the team of working grays was staked. Sam harnessed the pair to a flat-bed wagon with stout wheels and we set off for the woods. He selected the trees to be cut and set me to cutting them while he finished limbing the trunks from the previous day. When I was finished cutting I helped him with the trimming.

I was given oil and a stone to keep my ax sharp and clean. It bit through the wood with a satisfying liquid sound. Sam rarely spoke, which suited me and made us good working partners. Every evening we used the team to load the logs on the wagon, hitch the pair up again, and drive to the mill. At the yard, we chained the log ends to a sturdy post and pulled away. The logs slid off the back of the wagon with a thundering crash.

The mill was located close to the bunkhouse and we usually gave Thomas and Moses a ride back. Thomas was content with his work in the mill but it was clear to me that he was thinking about another opportunity to gain our freedom. We did not yet trust our bunkhouse companions and we were rarely able to speak alone. His night-time tossing and turning and moaning continued and several times woke us all up.

* * *

Our daily routine was as established and regular as the movement of the sun. The days slipped into months and the months to years. One sunny day in 1774, Sam drove the team into the mill yard while I sat on a log on the back of the wagon. When we arrived at the yard, there was the sound of angry voices. We jumped off the wagon and peered through the dirty windows of the mill office. We could easily hear the conversation inside. Inside, we saw Campbell, red-faced and sweating, jabbing his finger in the chest of a smaller man.

"I want you off my property. Now."

"I have no intention of leaving until you give me your accounting records."

"You have no right to my books."

"By the authority of His Majesty, I declare that you must turn over your records to me. We believe that you have not submitted your proper taxes for several years. If you have not paid your full taxes you will be fined and jailed."

"I'll not be giving any more money to tyrants. Go back to the hole you came from and don't bother coming back."

"The books or the police. What's it to be?"

Campbell made no reply to this but moved closer to the smaller man and put his hands around the man's neck. Instead of squeezing, he half-dragged and half-carried the man to the door and out to the yard. The tax collector's feet dangled inches above the ground, the toes of his boots dragging in the dust. He tried to yell but a series of small gasps were all that came from his mouth.

As the two stumbled out of the door, a number of men on horses arrived in the yard, a horse and wagon following behind. Three of the men jumped from their horses and grabbed the unfortunate fellow. The other two horsemen went to the back of the wagon and re-appeared with a heavy iron pot, a burlap bag, and six pillows.

Sam and I pressed against the wall of the mill. The men took no notice of us. Thomas and Moses appeared in the doorway, staying in the shadow of the opening.

Campbell, his hands still firmly around the neck of the tax collector, yelled at the men to bind the man's hands behind him, and the man with the wagon took a length of rope from beneath his seat and tied the man's hands firmly together. Another went to the pile of firewood stacked against the wall of the mill and rapidly built a fire in the middle of the yard.

Two men were required to lift the heavy pot onto the fire. After a little while, the pot began smoking. A heavy, acrid black cloud reduced the sun to a pale circle with little light and no warmth. The tax collector stood in the center of the yard, unmoving and silent. Campbell turned to the man with the wagon.

"Took your damn sweet time."

"We knew he was coming for you but we weren't sure when. We only just heard about it."

"How many other places has he been at?"

"You're the ninth but I hear there are more to come."

"Not if we take care of this here. I'm sick of sending money across the ocean. We've more than paid for our freedom from tyrants and bullies."

The tax collector moved towards Campbell, his lips dry and his eyes swollen and round.

"You're looking at treason if you assault an officer of His Majesty's government. Whatever you do will be paid back in full."

But, Campbell, still red-faced, was unmoved by the tax collector's words.

"Could be you should think about saving your own skin. There are no officials around and no soldiers to protect you, and I don't see your pathetic king anywhere here. Don't expect the police neither. Fact is, all you've got here is the Sons of Liberty and you maybe should be nice to us so we don't string you up when we're done."

Campbell went over to the pot of tar. The wagon man brought a thick piece of wood and the two men carefully hooked the handle of the pot and lifted it from the fire. They placed it gingerly on the ground. Through the smoke I could see the tar inside the pot, huge bubbles cresting on the oily black surface. Campbell took a large brush from the burlap bag. He went over to the pot and dipped the brush into the tar. It came out thick and glistening, the greasy mixture smoking on the hairs of the brush and dripping shiny black teardrops in the dust.

The tax collector's eyes went glassy with fear as Campbell approached him. He tried to back up, but one of the Sons of Liberty tripped him and he fell to the ground. Another townsman sat on his legs.

"This is to remember us by. I reckon you won't be stealing any of our money anymore, and tell your thieving king to expect more of the same if he sends anyone else here. This is our land and we intend to live as free men. If I were you, I'd close my eyes tight."

Campbell took the brush and made a single stroke across the side of the collector's face and down his neck. The tar stuck to the poor man's face, his skin already red along the edges of the black covering. Now he screamed, a single high note resonating through the yard and bouncing off the walls of the mill. Two more Sons of Liberty grabbed brushes from the sack and began tarring the tax collector. One tore off the man's shirt.

By the time the tar was cooling and thickening, the man was covered from head to waist. He lay on the ground, no longer screaming, but moaning with a low animal sound. Thomas looked over at me, his face pale and hollow. His eyes warned me to stay still.

The man could not get up. He struggled to stand, but his pain and fear left him lying on the ground. The dust attached to the tar, turning the color from absolute black to a mottled gray. His eyes looked wildly about as if looking for safety and his mouth opened as if he was going to speak. But he could not find words to say and finally he raised himself to a sitting position, his head down and his shoulders hunched.

Campbell grabbed two of the pillows and, tearing them open with a short knife, spilled the contents over the man. The feathers floated down like big flakes of snow, at first speckling the tar lightly and then covering more and more. Soon the man was covered with small white feathers. Now looking like a strange bird brought down to earth by an evil hand, the man lay still as the Sons of Liberty emptied the remaining pillows.

Eventually, the men lifted the tax collector into the back of the wagon. Campbell spoke briefly to the driver.

"Leave him on the big dock. The Brits will find him soon enough there. I'll get my coat and be there in a minute."

The wagon and horsemen clattered out of the yard and Thomas and Moses melted back into the mill as Campbell went for his coat. Campbell then mounted his horse and left the mill yard as Sam and I emptied our cart of logs. Moses and Thomas joined us for the short ride to the cabin.

That night we lay on our bunks as the darkness crept in. Moses was on his back, kicking softly at the wooden slats beneath the straw tick of the upper bunk. His arms were folded on his chest, his feet tapping out a regular rhythm.

"I've never seen anything like that. Never thought there'd be anything so purely evil."

Thomas poked his head around the edge of the bed.

"There's plenty of evil in the world, enough to go around, for sure, but I never did see anything like that neither and I hope I never do again. Worse though, there's nothing to be done. It's always like that. You can see the evil but you can't do anything about it. Quit kicking my bed will you."

"They say the British will give us our freedom."

"Moses, how long have you been here?"

"Long back as I can think."

"Has anybody ever given you anything?"

"Well I've heard talk there's going to be war. The Brits say they'll give us property and make us free if we fight for them."

"Might just be that the property isn't theirs to give. They're just as likely to own slaves—" Thomas looked at me before he finished his thought "—as anyone else. Fact is, anyone will be a master given half a chance."

Sam rarely said anything, but tonight he swung his legs over the side of his bunk and sat on the edge.

"I'll tell you boys something. There's going to be a war coming sure as I'm sitting here and I'll tell you why. It's because these Sons of Liberty and others like them want to have their own laws, pay taxes to their own states, run their own shows. I've heard Campbell work himself up into a righteous rage about it. They don't want the British telling them what to do anymore. They don't want to be slaves but they don't care that we're the real slaves. They don't even think about us. There's a war coming sure as hell but it won't help us."

We all sat up. It was the most that Sam had talked at one time and he wasn't finished.

"I'll tell you something else. It's not true to say everyone will be someone's master if they're given a chance. It's sign of a poor character to want to own someone. There's plenty of folk in this town who don't own slaves and there's lots more north, I reckon. There are places on this earth that don't have slaves at all. So don't you go telling me that everyone would own slaves if they could. Sounds to me like you're trying to sell something that you need to own yourself."

Thomas stopped swinging his legs and looked square at me as he spoke.

"I never seen a place without slaves but that doesn't mean that such a place doesn't exist and it doesn't mean that such a place couldn't be made. I've been thinking for a little while now that maybe it could. So maybe I am wrong about that but I am pretty sure a war is not going to help us."

Before he could finish his thought, Moses jumped in again.

"If there's a war coming I want to be on the side that's against Campbell and his friends. Hell, I don't care about property, I'll do it for the fun of it. I've had a bellyful of men like him and if I could get my chance for a little payback, I wouldn't object."

Thomas laughed.

"You must be Murphy's long-lost brother. I've always thought we should pick a fight we have a chance of winning. This might be it but it might not be, too. If not, it'll be the worse for us. But you and Murphy, well I guess you'll just flail away at anything without a whole lot of thinking ahead of time."

I jumped down.

"Better to fight than to lie on your bunk every night thinking of what might have been, or what could be, or what should have been if you'd only had the backbone to do something. You can stay here daydreaming if you want, but if a war comes and we get to fight these men who own us, and who put this brand on my face and these marks on my back, you can bet I'm there. Moses, you just let me know the time and place."

Sam looked up at me.

"Murphy, the plain fact is you have the strength of two of us. Maybe three of me. I think I'm too old and sore to fight any wars but I'll do anything I can to help the two of you if it comes to it. You can count on me for that."

I turned my back on Thomas and walked to the open door and sat on the step. Moses joined me. We sat together through the gathering gloom, watching the moon and the shadows and thinking thoughts of conquest and war.

Six

By tarring the tax collector, the Sons of Liberty had created a malaise in Wilmington that enveloped the town. All the residents were nervous, anticipating retribution from the British and scared of the slaves rising up to take advantage of the rumored British offer to secure their freedom and give them property.

I didn't have to hear what they were saying to know they were scared. All I had to do was look at them to see their faces cast down, their eyes glancing off to the side. Fear of a local rebellion made the town council pass laws forbidding slaves from meeting together in groups. While we did not know if there was any truth to the British offer, it was debated, over and over, in our cabin at night and in every other bunkhouse in town.

The fate of the tax collector was also debated. I didn't know how anyone could survive the attack that I'd witnessed. On the other hand, I wasn't sure if I would have thought that anyone could survive being tied behind a horse, dragged for many miles over a rocky road, and then whipped. The British had few friends in town. It was rumored that the mayor and local police were, if not active members of the Sons of Liberty, at least sympathetic to their cause. But it was also true that the judges and government authorities were British and were intent on enforcing British law and customs. They were viewed with increasing hostility.

We heard that the governor had gone into a rage when told of the tar and feathering and sworn that the outlaws would be punished. However, the Sons of Liberty had melted back into the general population and would have remained invisible but for their inability to keep quiet about their misdeeds.

I was told this story by Sam and, knowing his prudent nature, believed it to be true in every detail. His brother worked in the stables attached to the Elijah Tavern.

It seemed that the wagon driver who took part in the tarring had been well into his cups at the tavern a few weeks after the assault, and took to boasting about the cruel deed to all around. The patrons included two British soldiers who were off-duty and in plain clothes. All the customers, including the wagon driver, were aware that the two men were soldiers, so everyone else was careful in talk and action.

The drunk wagon driver must have been convinced that he was beyond the reach of the British. In any event, he talked loudly and persistently of his role in the tarring. One of the soldiers slipped out of the tavern, his friend staying behind to keep an eye on the foolish teamster. The soldier took a horse from the stable and left at top speed. Shortly thereafter, well before the fool had finished his boasting, the governor appeared in the yard along with a contingent of British soldiers.

The boastful driver was arrested on the spot and taken to the British barracks where he was held, awaiting a decision from the judiciary. This was not long in coming. Two days after the arrest, a notice was put on trees and posts in the town. It proclaimed that the man, one William Johnston, had been convicted of treason and was to be punished by being hanged, drawn, and quartered.

Sam, in his usual dry manner, told me that death by being hanged, drawn, and quartered was the common British punishment for treason and, in point of fact, had been administered on previous occasions. It involved the poor unfortunate being hanged for just a few moments, then cut down and seated on the ground, his hands tied behind his back. Half-dead from being strung up, the victim's stomach was then slit, his intestines pulled out and either boiled in a steaming pot or burned over an open fire. It was only with the final step of the punishment, when his head and limbs were hacked off, that the horror ended.

The British rulers, masters at exquisite and diabolical tortures, particularly favored this public display because the victim would generally live for a prolonged period of time while his innards were boiled or burned.

Johnston was to be executed in the yard of the tavern where he was discovered. This was meant, Sam said, as a warning by the governor to the townsfolk against subversive behavior. The results were almost directly opposite to what was intended. After the mandatory parade through town with Johnston, the unfortunate driver was led, dazed and bleeding, through a silent row of his friends up the steps to the hastily-constructed gallows.

The governor had recruited a member of the local police to be the hangman. This executioner did his job well, in fact, a little too well, because when the body dangling beneath the platform was cut down, it was discovered that Johnston had cheated the governor and his officials by dying before he could be gutted alive.

Sam told me that his brother told him that this was a huge relief to the crowd gathered in the tavern yard but put the hard-headed governor into yet another rage. He blamed the hangman, who claimed lack of experience as his defense. Then he blamed his officials for not hiring a competent executioner. Finally he blamed the crowd for being disobedient and rebellious.

Feeling a need to do something, the governor ordered the tavern torched. British soldiers burned the Elijah and the attached stables to the ground and it was fortunate that surrounding buildings, and, perhaps all of Wilmington, didn't burn along with the tavern. Of course, the effect of these actions on the local populace was to harden anti-royalist feeling and hatred of the British. The Sons of Liberty gained followers.

All of this, the normally quiet Sam told me while we were limbing trees. I had one question.

"What about Campbell and the others?"

"What about them?"

"Well do you think they'll be arrested? I mean, they were there with Johnston and he must have told the British who they were."

"He likely did tell them but I doubt they'll be arresting Campbell, he's got too much money and too much pull with the governor. Johnston was a simple teamster, no holdings at all, no money and not too bright, perfect to be hanged. Now everybody can go back to doing what they were doing before. Justice has been served."

Sam smiled like a big old cat that's swallowed a mouse.

"But I'll tell you another thing. This war business is just starting up. We've got a war coming as sure as you're standing there and when it comes it's going to change things for everybody for good. You want to be sure you pick the right side. The right side means the side that will give us freedom and let us start over. You and Moses best think hard on that before you go running off because once you make up your mind, there won't be any going back. Make sure you pick the side that will let you be free, that's all that matters."

I had been thinking about it. The British offer to give us freedom and property sounded good. The best part of the whole deal to me was the chance to get back at the men who kept me a slave. The British were not to be trusted any more than Campbell and his friends but if the offer was real, it was a chance to feed my need for revenge and gain my freedom at the same time.

Thoughts of running away filled my head. Moses and I made excited plans every night, only to re-think them in the morning light. Sam listened to us but rarely spoke. Thomas would generally leave our shack and go off into the night when we started to talk, coming back when we were drowsy. One night, as evening settled in, he pulled me to one side and asked if he could talk with me for a few minutes. We wandered down to the pasture and leaned against the rail fence.

"I've been meaning to talk with you for a while. The simple truth is that I'm moving out of the cabin."

"What do you mean moving out?"

"I'm moving out and moving into my own place."

"How'd you manage that?"

He smiled awkwardly.

"I'm moving into the family side."

"You?"

"Yeah."

"How did that happen?"

Thomas just looked at me for a moment.

"The why of it is I've got this girl. She works in the kitchen. You likely know her. Her name is Sally."

I looked at my friend. He was as serious as could be.

"Well I'll be. Sure I know her, she leaves our food sacks."

"Yeah. She came out to the mill a few times with lunch. I got to talking with her and she started coming out more and more and here we are."

I was quiet. I wasn't sure if it was harder to think about the cabin without Thomas or to picture him with a family.

"You know they won't let you marry."

"We don't care. She's due in a couple of months and we're as good as married now. Truth is, she's a fine woman and I'm pleased about the whole thing."

"Well of course I'm happy for you. Surprised, I guess, but happy. Congratulations."

"Thanks. There's something else too. I've met Jean's daughter."

"Where?"

"In town. She came into the mill last week. She works for the family that runs the hardware store and has her bed above the store. Her name's Mary. She knows all about us and especially you."

"What do you mean?"

"I guess Jean must have heard that you were out here. You know how things are, word just gets around somehow. Mary asked me about you. She said Jean was worried. If I were you I might want to get to know her. She sure seems like a good-hearted woman and she cuts a fine figure."

"I don't need to get to know a woman."

"I figured you might say that, you being so sociable and all. Suit yourself."

"Did she say where her brother was at? Didn't you say Jean had a son, too?"

Thomas's face darkened and he looked across the pasture.

"Mary doesn't know where he is. He was sold to a man who was going to sell him to a plantation owner on those islands down south. That was the last she ever saw or heard of him. She's worried because her brother is like you and generally acts before he thinks."

"As opposed to just dreaming, like you. You being in the family way and all I guess you've no longer got any hope for freedom or anything else. Just going to be stuck a slave forever right?"

Thomas laughed.

"Well I figure she'll let me out every now and then. My kids won't be slaves, that's for sure. So I guess I'll be doing something to make sure that's true but I want to wait a little and see how things are shaping up in this war that's coming. We've got different ways, you and I. We do now and we always have, but that's not to say I don't want it as bad as you. Maybe for different reasons but I feel it just as strong."

I started to speak but Thomas wasn't finished.

"I'm going to move out tomorrow but we're friends and more forever. I know you'll be leaving soon with Moses but that's not my way right now so I'm telling you to be careful even though I know you won't be. Our thoughts aren't the same today but I need you with me down the road because no one can beat us when we work together."

"Don't you worry about me. I'll have a place for you on my farm. You can visit when this is over."

Thomas turned and we walked back to the cabin. I followed him, silent and thoughtful. When I got to the bunkhouse, Moses was sitting on the step. He motioned at me to sit and we talked for a long time about our escape.

Seven

Moses and I talked and talked.

The plain truth was that we did not know where to go, how to escape, or even what to expect from the British if we did get away. The elusive chance of freedom for runaways remained just a rumor. There was no real offer, no place where we knew to go, and no war to fight.

Wilmington remained on a knife's edge, the people wary and hesitant. A strange feverish energy possessed the slaves as they swung from the news of promised freedom to the despair of daily life. I began to lose hope that anything would change.

The days, weeks, and months slipped away. I saw Thomas most nights when we gave him and Moses a ride from the mill. Sometimes I visited with him and his family, which now included his daughter, Clairy. Thomas was troubled by the local tensions. We had heard reports of small slave uprisings which had been quickly put down by the local authorities, often with cruel results. We rarely discussed these events, each already knowing the other's opinion about violence in the interest of freedom.

Finally, when I was almost at the point of resignation, Sam brought news that changed everything. His brother had been put to work at a different livery by the unfortunate owner of the Elijah

Tavern. There were many travelers through this stable and Sam's brother heard stories from far and wide, but this particular news was extraordinary. Sam talked to Moses and me as we lay on our ticks.

"You boys aren't going to believe this one. My brother told me that he's heard that the British have said that any slave who makes it to Britain is a free man. Seems there was a trial about a slave who was brought to Britain and was going to be sold to a sugar plantation owner in the Caribbean. Somerset was the slave's name. Anyways, Somerset was nobody's fool and when he found out he was bound for Jamaica, he got some local help and took the whole thing to court. The British judge decided that, since slavery does not exist in Britain, Somerset must be set free. He can't be bought or sold."

Sam sat on the edge of his bunk, shaking his gray head with wonder, but I wasn't sure what this meant for us.

"Well, all that sounds good for those in Britain, but it doesn't help us in the colonies, does it?"

"That's the best part. First of all, there's a couple of slaves up north who got wind of this Somerset business and they've gone and got themselves a lawyer."

Sam stopped and looked at me. I'd jumped off the top bunk and was pacing around the small cabin. Now I was the one shaking my head. Sam looked at me and grinned.

"Yeah, I said they got a town lawyer, believe it or not. They got themselves a lawyer and they've taken the whole thing to court. They say that since Britain has made slaves free on British property, all the slaves in the colonies are free too."

"Are they going to win?"

"Not likely. My brother says there's no way they'll let them win. They don't think British laws apply over here."

"Then why should we care about all this?"

"Well that business up north is a shot for us anyways, win or lose, but the best part of this whole thing for you boys is something else entirely. It's sitting right there in the harbor."

"What do you mean, sitting there? I wish you would get to the point."

But Sam was a master of drawing the conversation out and rationing his information.

"It's not my fault you're thick as a brick. Use your head. What's in the harbor as clear as the big nose on Moses' face?"

I had no idea what he was talking about but I did think he was about as difficult as a one-eyed mule. Moses, however, got the drift of things right off.

"British ships. Warships."

"Now, you see, Moses here has got a head on his shoulders even if you don't or maybe he just looks around now and then, sort of to get the lay of the land. What does he see but British ships in the harbor."

"Yeah, yeah but I still don't know how that's going to help us get out of here."

Sam leaned back on his bunk and linked his fingers together under the back of his head.

"British warships are British property right? They're owned by the British government. Now, the law over there has said that all slaves on British property are free men. The ships are British property. With those ships sitting there in the harbor, it means if you can get to the ships you'll be free. You might have to fight in this war that's coming on the side of the British but you'll fight as free men."

I could see it clearly now. This was the chance we'd been waiting for. If Moses and I could get to one of the British ships that were always coming and going off Wilmington, we'd be free.

"How do we get on one of those ships?"

"Now that's going to be the hard part. We need to work on that a little bit but don't you worry. If you two can hold yourselves together for a few days, I think maybe my brother and I will work something out. You just keep doing things in the usual way; don't breathe a word of this to anyone and I'll do some thinking and working out how this is going to happen."

With that, he stretched out on his bunk and went to sleep.

The days, slow before, seemed to crawl by now and Sam would not speak to either Moses or me about his plans. Three days passed before he talked with us again, just as the three of us were getting ready for sleep.

"Two nights is the time. There's a British warship in the harbor called the *Otter*. Two nights from now it will be pitch black, no moon at all. So that's when you go. Get yourself ready with whatever you need. We'll take the wagon to the wheelwright in Wilmington to get one of the wheels fixed. You will be in the back under a canvas. Thomas and I will leave the wagon in the wheelwright's yard, down near the docks, to be fixed the next day. That night you boys will creep out and pick up a rowboat that will be left tied to a dock piling. You can row out to the *Otter*."

Sam was as serious as his words. He stretched his neck to look at me.

"Now listen carefully. My brother says the patrols in town are doubled since the news about the court case came from Britain. Any slip at all—and I mean anything—will get us all in trouble. There's already been four hanged and there'll be more before this is all over. If they catch you, you're dead. No second chance. No trial. You will just be strung up. So you have to be careful, and you can't tell a soul."

"What about Thomas?"

"He already knows. He's the one who came up with the bones of the plan. Figure you can row out to the boat?"

"Yeah, between the two of us."

"All right, now we sleep."

Two days later, I was as skittish as a scalded cat. It was all I could bring myself to do to help load our few logs on the back of the wagon. We set off to the mill. Sam parked the wagon behind the back of the mill and we used the team to take the logs off. Thomas and Moses appeared and, as quick as thought, we jumped in the back of the wagon and pulled the canvas over our heads. I talked to Thomas through the sheet.

"Kind of reminds me of something from the past back here. No wonder you had the idea for it."

"Yeah. That best be the last thing you say. Remember, stay there until it is truly dark, so dark you can't see across the wheelwright's yard, and don't move at all. There might be people about."

The wagon lurched ahead and Moses and I lay still for a long time. Eventually we heard Thomas and Sam unhitching the horses from the wagon and slowly walking away. There were a few voices but the evening was coming on and most folk were going home to dinner. The dark slowly crept in and we lay, not moving and not talking, waiting for the blackness of true night.

Finally, when I judged the darkness to be complete, I lifted one edge of the canvas and peeked out. There was nobody around and the far edge of the yard was not visible. Moses and I jumped out and ran to the nearby fence. Keeping close to fences when we could, we made the short run to the dock and then waded into the water. We went below the dock, between the pilings, and slowly made our way along.

About halfway to the end of the dock we came across the rowboat floating quietly between the pilings. The water was up to our waists and we were about to pull up into the boat when we heard voices at the land end of the dock. Quickly Moses and I ducked down into the water so that our faces were the only parts above the waterline. We grabbed onto the hull of the rowboat to keep our balance, our faces pressed tightly against the wooden sides. The voices came closer.

"I'm mighty tired of doing this every night. For what? I wish to hell we'd get going with fighting if we're going to. I mean, we've been doing nothing for so long it seems like that's just about all we're meant to do."

"They're making plans, I'm telling you. We'll find out about it soon enough. Besides, this isn't so bad. I mean, it's a nice night, it's quiet, and I got myself a bottle here that I might even share with you if you can stop complaining for a minute or two."

"Twist my arm."

The two men laughed and walked over our heads on the spaced planks. They went to the far end of the dock, at the water's edge, and sat with their legs hanging over. We could faintly see their feet dangling just above the surface of the water.

Moses whispered quietly to me.

"I hope they leave before it gets light. Otherwise we're finished."

"Don't worry, they'll be gone long before that. They don't want to be found down here drinking. We just got to keep quiet and wait it out."

But waiting was hard. We still had a ways to row, the water was cold, and it was difficult to keep our balance while the rowboat bobbed up and down with the waves. We could hear the men talking and laughing but we couldn't make out their words. Finally one of them tossed the bottle out into the water and we heard them getting to their feet. They walked back over our heads, laughing and spitting, and finally their voices faded and the dock stopped trembling with their footsteps.

We scrambled quickly into the rowboat. There was a set of oars lying inside and I fitted them into the locks and began rowing under the dock. When I came to the end I did not look back but continued to row, hard and steady, into open water.

The trip to the *Otter* was strange but uneventful. Rowing through the blackness seemed beyond the confines of the earth, as if we had entered a different universe where time didn't exist. Finally, after an unknown interval, we drew near the lights of the ship and hailed the night watch. A voice from the ship came back down to us.

"Who hails us?"

"Moses and Murphy, two runaway slaves looking for sanctuary."

"Wait a moment. I'll throw a couple of lines."

Two ropes came hurtling out of the night, landing in the water just beyond our little boat. Moses grabbed them both and gave one to me. We wrapped the ropes around us and began climbing up the side of the big ship. Before we got halfway up the side of the *Otter*, someone yelled at us to hold on and the ropes were pulled hard and steady so we landed in a heap on the deck. Four men were looking down at us and laughing.

"Well what have we got here? Two black fish caught in a black night. Someone go and get Joe and tell him we've got a couple of his countrymen out for a midnight swim."

One of the men left the group and came back with a black man who was grumbling and yawning.

"This better be good, boys. If you're going to be waking me up out of my sleep we better be sinking or fighting. This doesn't look like either. What are your names?"

"Murphy and Moses."

"Runaways. My name's Joe Harris. Here's what we're going to do. These boys are going to take you to get dry clothes and some food, if you want it. Then you're going to sleep for a while and I'm going to try to get back to sleep. In the morning, the captain and I will have a talk and I'll let you know what his plan is. Sound all right?"

"Yeah," I said, "but I sure hope you can use us."

We turned to go with one of the men to get dry clothes. Joe, still yawning, said one more thing to us before he disappeared into the bowels of the ship.

"Fellas, I know what you've been through and I know how hard it is to get out here. I was a runaway too and I got the whip marks on my back to prove it. One thing: if you want to fight with us in this here war that's coming as sure as you're standing here, then you've got nothing more to worry about. If you're just looking for a free ride this is not the place for you."

With those last words he stepped below deck. Moses and I were led into a small room with bunk beds. There were clothes in the cupboard. We weren't hungry but we surely were cold and tired and sleep was a blessing to us both.

I lay on the bottom bunk, half asleep but too excited to close my eyes.

"Moses?"

"Yeah."

"We made it. Moses, we're free. We're going to be like every other free man now. No more someone buying or selling us. No more someone owning us. That'll never happen again. That Joe, he was a slave too and look at him now. He's a free man and he's a leader. That can be us too, Moses."

But my friend was asleep, snoring softly like a peaceful child in the arms of his mother.

Eight

The *Otter* lay in the harbor for several days.

Talk among the sailors on the frigate was that we should shell Wilmington, hang the Sons of Liberty, and put an end to the local unrest through military action. Their officers, however, counseled patience and planning, which reminded me of my past discussions with Thomas. I missed my old friend already. I wished he was on the *Otter* so we could celebrate freedom together.

Joe Harris was the pilot of the ship. He had previously been the property of a Norfolk merchant who mixed smuggling with business. Joe knew every tidal flat, every inlet, and every hidden shoal along the coast. He was Matthew Squire's right hand.

Squire, a captain who had originally said that runaways were not welcome on his ship, had changed his mind when Harris crawled into a tender from the *Otter* that had put into land for supplies. The former slave had a considerable knowledge of local sailing conditions, an intelligence which was used to great advantage by the captain.

Since that chance encounter, the *Otter* had ranged along the coast with impunity. Rebel businesses were raided, shipping blockaded, and British troops transported. The importance of Harris to the British was not lost on the Sons of Liberty. When they captured another British tender sent to shore for supplies near Hampton, the rebels refused to give up either the boat, its equipment, or the supplies until the British surrendered Harris to them. Squire replied by blockading the town.

All of this was told to Moses and me by Joe as he waited for our sailing orders. There were ten other runaways on the *Otter* and more were training at a base in Virginia.

When we finally sailed, it was a huge relief to me and seemed the final confirmation that I was not bound to any man or any place.

It was a short voyage to Norfolk. We went to shore with the British soldiers in seven small boats, weaving between wrecks that the rebels had sunk through the harbor to deter landing.

Squire spoke to us before we left the *Otter*.

"You have been charged with guarding the ammunition on shore against the rascals who would steal it and use it for their own treasonous purpose. You may also be ordered to seize weapons that the traitors have already stolen. Some of you are regulars and some are runaways, but you are all acting for His Majesty, for Britain, and for the honor of the *Otter*, and I expect all of you to demonstrate respect, courage, and loyalty."

The regular soldiers responded with three cheers.

The runaways looked on, uncertain but hopeful. Moses looked at me and raised his eyebrows.

"All that cheering is fine but we've got nothing to fight with. It's hard to fight without any weapons. Hope they give us something on shore that's going to be of some use to us."

"All I need is a big stick."

"Well we haven't even got that, now."

On shore, Moses got his wish. The British provided us with their long musket, Brown Bess. The runaways from the *Otter*, along with forty-one other former slaves and the regular redcoats, drilled every day.

It amazed me how fast the redcoats could load and shoot Brown Bess.

Open the cartridge box. Grab a cartridge. Bite off the end. Pour some powder into the pan of the lock. Close the pan. Drop the rest of the cartridge into the barrel. Remove the rammer and ram it home. Return the rammer and make ready to shoot by cocking the lock. Aim at the enemy.

Four times a minute for four minutes. After four minutes, even the best marksman had to stop for fear of fouling his piece.

Several of the runaways were also adept at firing Brown Bess, having learned how to use a firearm when they were slaves. This surprised me. None of the slaves I'd previously met had been taught about guns, but the runaways at Norfolk had come from all over, and had different experiences.

I was even more surprised by Moses, who had a natural talent for the musket. It was all I could do to remember the loading sequence, but my friend, steady and thoughtful, was able to out-shoot all but the best redcoats after a week's practice. One day, after we'd been drilling all morning, we lined up to shoot at a target fifty yards away. Moses hit the target three times before I'd even finished loading. I looked over at him getting ready to shoot again.

"Moses, you are a born marksman."

"What?"

"You were born to this. How do you do it?"

"I just think it through at night when I'm lying waiting for sleep. I think the routine over and over in my mind and then the next day it works well. I really want it to work."

"More than me I guess."

Our sergeant, a runaway named Titus, walked past.

"Steele, you ever going to fire that thing? Or are you figuring on talking the enemy to death?"

"I'll tell you what, sir."

"What?"

"You let me stay close to my friend Moses, here, and let him fire away. If you give me a big club or something, I reckon I'll do my damage with that."

"You planning on just walking up to them and knocking them on the head, are you? Steele, that doesn't sound like a good plan to me."

I did want some kind of head knocker. By the end of the second week I could load and fire Brown Bess once a minute when I was thinking very hard and nothing went wrong. Hitting anything was another matter. Moses took to calling my musket 'Brown Miss.' I was starting to wonder if I'd be any good at all when it came to a battle.

The redcoat captain addressed the group of runaways at the end of the second week.

"Next week we will be going into battle under Lord Dunmore. You're about as ready as can be. You men will fight as one unit, called the Royal Ethiopian Regiment. You'll wear these uniforms. When we get to the fight, you'll follow what your sergeant says and remember what you're fighting for."

The uniforms were red with white stitching across the breast that stated 'Liberty to Slaves.' I wondered what the Sons of Liberty would think when they saw the Regiment lining up across from them, and I smiled.

* * *

The road to war was short.

On Monday, we marched ten miles to Kemp's Landing, where the rebels had a large camp. We marched in regimental form, with the redcoats about seventy strong in a center block and the Ethiopian Regiment, along with a few local loyalists, flanking the British. As we approached the Virginians, gunfire erupted from the surrounding woods. It was largely directed at the British, who continued their steady march along the road.

Titus directed our regiment to go wide, through the bog that bordered the woods. We moved quickly to the edge of the thicket and established our line behind the rebels, who were clearly visible only fifty yards away. Moses quickly brought his gun to sight. He looked over at me, still loading my musket.

"See that fellow over there by the dead tree?"

"Yep."

"Watch."

His Brown Bess fired and the unfortunate Virginian fell straight back against the tree, as if resting. His buckskin shirt had a black hole in it, now seeping red. We could easily see this from where we stood in the thicket. The rebels were confused by being fired on from our side as well as from the British on the road. They began to retreat deeper into the trees and most of our shots were now bouncing off of trunks and branches.

I had managed to get off one shot, to no effect, and was struggling to load again. When I looked up, I could see the enemy moving deeper into the woods. It was clear that even our best marksmen would have no further luck.

Moses was still firing into the retreating Virginians, who were not firing back. I jumped up and ran into the woods as the firing from the Regiment died away.

In just a few seconds, I was next to the Virginian that Moses had shot. Another rebel was behind the tree trying to load his musket, his eyes wide and frightened and his fingers clumsy. I thrust my musket, bayonet fixed, at his stomach, but my arm was impaired by his wounded friend who was still slumped against the front of the tree. Though barely alive, he had enough strength to nudge the blade. The bayonet went wide of the Virginian's stomach and ripped through the loose buckskin on his arm. It ended stuck in the tree, pinning the man's arm. He dropped his weapon.

The terrified man turned to me, his white face a mixture of fear, despair, and hope. I knew how he felt. I'd felt the same way, being dragged by a horse all the way back to Richardson's. I'd felt that way before the whip came down and before the smoking brand was applied to my face.

I picked up his weapon and, holding the long barrel like a spear, thrust the butt into the man's face. Once. Twice. Three times, and blood erupted in a huge gush from his destroyed mouth and ran in small streams from his ears. He said nothing, his hands fluttering, one still pinned to the tree by my musket. I turned to the wounded soldier and was about to smash him with his friend's weapon when I felt a hand on my arm. It was Titus.

66

"He's dead, Steele. They're both dead. Son, you have a mean old bear in you and maybe something uglier still. I do believe you were right, you need a different weapon than a gun. Come see me when we get back to camp."

The road back to camp was a lot easier than the march to Kemp's Landing. Our spirits were high and the road disappeared beneath our feet. At our base near Norfolk, everyone was already buzzing with the news of our victory. That night we celebrated, redcoats and runaways alike, the camp alive with laughter as we joked around the fires.

The following day, just before noon, I went to see my sergeant. Titus was leaning against a tree next to his tent.

"Steele, I want to give you something. It was given to me by Lord Dunmore but I've got a feeling that it's more use to you than me. It might be that you never do learn to fire that Bess properly. It seems like you might like fighting a little closer in."

Titus pulled a short sword from beneath his tunic and gave it to me.

"This weapon is called a Roman sword. See, it's short and fine for close-in work. Steele, I don't know if you know about the Romans but they were fighting a couple of thousand years ago. They invented this sword because it's the best when your enemy is right on you and you on him. You can move it quickly, you can thrust it deep, and it's thick so you can parry anything. I have the thought that you'll be doing more close-in work than me. One other thing, Steele. Kemp's Landing was easy but the next one likely won't be the same. You best wait for orders before you go trying to win the war all by yourself."

The soldiers were emboldened by the battle at Kemp's Landing. No redcoats or Ethiopian Regiment members had been lost, we had killed several rebels and captured many more. Two days after Sergeant Titus and I talked, we paraded the captured Virginians through the streets of Norfolk. To my surprise, a large number of the townsfolk lined our route and cheered our troops.

The rarely-seen Lord Dunmore led the parade through Norfolk

and posted a declaration on the posts and walls around the courthouse. It said that all slaves who were able and willing to bear arms should join the British military and would be granted freedom. When I read it, I was excited and hoped that the news would reach Thomas. Surely this would be encouragement for him to join the British troops and claim his freedom.

News of the proclamation did travel quickly. The Royal Ethiopian Regiment had numbered around fifty soldiers for the Kemp's Landing battle but now there were three hundred volunteers and more came every day. Local men arrived to swell the ranks of the loyalists. For the Regiment, the increased number of runaways meant a more definite chain of command even though we had never been officially sworn into the British army. Titus, formerly our sergeant, was now our colonel. The British would not officially make any runaway an officer but, unofficially, Colonel Tye, as we now called him, was in charge of the entire Regiment.

Moses, as steady as his aim, was made a sergeant. He had the original members of the Regiment under his command. Our new orders were not long in coming. The new sergeant spoke to us one day in the early afternoon.

"The rebels are marching. They mean to get us out of Norfolk, but to get here they have to pass over the river at Great Bridge. We'll get there today so we can stop them when they try to cross over. Pack the tents and be ready to march early tonight."

We marched the short way to Great Bridge during the evening and arrived there in the early morning hours. The British had constructed a small fort at our end of the bridge. Across the water of the Elizabeth River we could see the camp of the Virginians, which seemed to stretch on for a long way along the river flats.

The land along the river was swampy and stank of decay. The upcoming battle, on uncertain ground and against a numerous and waiting enemy, would be fearsome.

With these thoughts floating through my mind, I fell asleep, a roof of stars over my head.

Nine

Great Bridge was a poor crossing built over a dreary river.

The redcoats, loyalists, and former slaves occupied a small fort on the Norfolk side of the crossing. From there, our forces lobbed cannonballs at the Virginians who were camped a little way back of the bridge on the other side of the river. The balls, hissing through the air like so many snakes, hit nothing but the boggy water of the river or the swamp on the far bank. The rebels returned fire when the whim struck them, again to no effect. Surrounding both armies was a vast marsh, bordered by sink-holes and stunted bushes.

The British had fired the buildings that had previously stood on our side of the river, and the blackened ash that remained continued to smoke. The landscape was as desolate as any I had ever seen. It didn't help my mood to see that the Virginians clearly had many more troops than we could hope to muster and were firmly entrenched behind dirt embankments.

Moses was also not in a favorable mood.

"Murphy, this whole thing doesn't seem right to me. How are we going to get over that bridge? The damn planks are out, and besides, it's too narrow and if we do get over we have to run down that little road all the way to where they're dug in down there."

The words were hardly out of his mouth when Colonel Tye came along and told Moses to get some men together and hammer planks across the bridge. Starting at the end of the bridge near the British fort, this seemed like an easy task. Sporadic shot from the Virginians could not reach us there.

However, while the British had removed the planks so that the rebels could not easily cross the bridge, the Virginians had greased the cross rails so that the redcoats could not sneak up on them. It was a measure of the progress of the war that both parties worried about the other while taking no offensive action of their own. The biggest problem we faced when we began hammering the planks on to the cross rails was actually staying on the bridge without slipping off. The first man who clambered onto the bridge promptly lost his grip on the greased rail and fell through to the water below. He clambered onto our bank amidst much laughter from our army.

After that we took our time and moved carefully, wiping the rail ahead as well as we could with our shirts. Moses slipped as he led us up one greasy rail, but I grabbed him with one hand as he went over the side.

"Watch your step or you'll be swimming in a minute."

"Not with you around, I think. This is a miserable job in a bad place. I just don't see how we can do any good here."

It took us all day to nail the planks. The rebels were camped well beyond the far end of the bridge so that we were able to complete the construction without being hit by any enemy fire. When we got back to our tents, Colonel Tye came by our campfire. He told us we would attack the rebels at first light the next day.

"You boys should get as much sleep as you can. I doubt there'll be much time tomorrow for napping. You'll be going in with the first wave of redcoats. Moses, you come with me."

Moses was gone a long time and when he came back, his face was drawn. He pulled me over to one side, away from the campfire where the rest of the unit was eating in silence.

"We're to be right behind the redcoats, over the bridge and on the attack. The other units will be behind us or down the river to draw the rebels away. We're to hold fire until the redcoats shoot, then we'll fire while they reload."

"Sounds like a plan."

"Yeah, but how are we supposed to hit them? They're going to be hiding and we're going to be wide open. Once we get on that road there'll be nowhere to hide. We'll be sitting ducks and we still won't be able to reach them with any sort of accuracy."

"I don't figure on hiding. After the first shots you can count on me being gone. I'll be on them before they know what hit them."

"I don't know, Murphy, I have a bad feeling about this. I think we're going to have to be really lucky."

Moses was silent for a couple of minutes.

"You ever think on what's going on back at Campbell's?"

"Well, I try not to."

"Yeah."

He took a drink from his flask.

"You know, I liked working in the mill. It suited me fine."

"Yeah and how'd you like being someone's slave?"

"I know all that. I'm just saying I didn't plan on having to be in somebody's war. I just wanted to have my own life and mind my own business."

"You knew what was going to happen when we snuck aboard the *Otter*."

"It's different for you. You like all this fighting. I just want to live my life and get along."

I picked up my short sword and felt its edge. Since Colonel Tye had given it to me, I had worked on the sword every day, polishing and sharpening and getting the feel of its weight.

"Moses, I know what you want but I'm going to tell you the same thing I told Thomas. If you want something, you have to fight for it. Nobody is going to give it to you. We're fighting for a good thing here and that's the right to be free men. There's nobody at the mill going to give that to you."

"And what if you lose your arm here? What if you get your leg shot off? Or maybe you get killed? It's not worth it then, is it?"

"Yeah, it's worth it to me. All of that and more could have

happened at Campbell's and I stood no chance of having a life there. I don't know what's going to happen tomorrow but I know that whatever happens, it'll happen to me as a free man, fighting for something that I think is right. It's not my way to bide my time and hope that better things are around the corner. I just got to make things happen myself."

Moses got up from the ground. He held out his hand and pulled me to my feet.

"Murphy, you have a heart as big as the sky. I was feeling a little blue but you've got me remembering why we're here. I'm glad we'll be fighting together tomorrow."

"Me too, since I still can't hit the side of a barn and you can shoot a fly off the roof. And I'll tell you something else. A long while ago, when Thomas and I were running away from that son of a bitch down south, I had a dream that Thomas would be leading an army of slaves across a bridge. I was beside him. But now I see that it was you I was dreaming about way back then. Not Thomas. It's you who will be leading us across that bridge tomorrow and I'll be happy to be beside you."

It was barely dawn the next day when we formed up behind the redcoats. There were forty-six healthy and strong soldiers in our unit, all of them veterans of Kemp's Landing. The rest of the Regiment formed behind us as we crossed the bridge.

The Virginians did not seem to hear us coming and we easily marched over the bridge on our new planks and down the road toward their embankments. The trail from the bridge was narrow, with swampy ground and dark pools of stinking water on each side. The redcoats, marching six abreast ahead of us, filled the road with row after row of quiet men. There was silence—no gunfire, no voices, no cannon. Walking with Moses at the front edge of our unit, I could clearly see the front of the column, many rows ahead of us.

As the first row of the redcoats got close to the rebel embankment, now visible though the mist of the swamp, gunfire erupted from the Virginians. The rebel soldiers could still not be seen but the enemy gunfire took down the first three rows of the British, including their captain, who fell with a wound in his leg. The soldiers behind their fallen comrades fired their muskets at the top of the embankment and then tried to move back towards us to reload, but the road was narrow and several bumped into their friends as these fellows tried to fire, causing the second volley of shots from the British to go largely astray.

In any event, there was nothing to shoot at, no enemy to be seen, and no charge possible. The hidden shooting was relentless while the British staggered and stumbled on the narrow road, some falling into the swamp, others wounded and dying on the road itself, their torn bodies and moans adding to the confusion.

As the number of soldiers in front of us dwindled and the air clouded with smoke, Moses turned to me.

"What in God's name are we going to shoot at? There's no target anywhere."

"Moses, we've got to get around the earthworks or we're all going to fall on this miserable road."

I stepped out into the swamp, thinking I could walk along the side of the road and avoid the congestion, but the ground gave way beneath my feet and I was quickly up to my ankles in sucking mud. Moses, stumbling over the bloody bodies draped across the narrow trail, led the Regiment forward past the British soldiers who were frantically reloading. There were still no enemy soldiers visible on the embankment, although we could see their guns poking through the dirt. Moses turned to his troops.

"Aim for their guns boys."

The Ethiopians aimed quickly and fired. It was tough to see if any damage was done and the enemy fire continued. As we fell back to enable the redcoats to fire again, the British captain, bleeding from the leg, stood up as if uninjured and raised his hat in the air with a flourish.

The redcoats, bayonets fixed and filled with renewed vigor, gave a huge cheer and surged forward. The enemy fire paused for a minute, as if the Virginians were stunned by the wave of red now advancing on the run towards their position. It was barely fifty yards to the enemy line and the British soldiers were quickly at the base of the embankment. The Regiment, Moses and I in the lead, ran quickly behind the redcoats.

At the foot of the earthworks, the British paused for a moment as their captain, limping but still waving his hat, began climbing up the dirt. At once there was a loud cheer from behind the works and the Virginians, clad in their golden buckskins, rose up and fired two huge volleys down on us. The British captain, now shot through the arm, staggered back and was hit by two more shots through the chest. As he fell back into the arms of his soldiers, another ball hit him in the head. More musket fire rained down on us. There was nowhere to hide. A few brave souls tried to scale the earthen wall but were cut down before getting to the top. Several of the soldiers in our unit had been hit and lay in the dirt, wailing like children. Moses looked at me and gestured above the din to go back to the bridge. I nodded. We turned and, with the rest of our unit, began picking our way back. The trouble was that the men behind us, who made up most of the Ethiopian Regiment, did not know of the disaster at the front of the column. They continued to surge forward even as we desperately staggered back into them. The redcoats were frantic to get out of the withering fire and threw their own friends off the road and into the swamp in their mindless drive to safety.

Finally, the entire unit turned towards the bridge and began running back. Moses and I, at the very back of the column, helped one poor fellow who had taken a ball in his thigh. He hung between us, his arms around our shoulders, as the fire from the Virginians dwindled. When we reached the point where the road ended and the bridge began, we heard a cry from behind and turned to see the Virginians mounting a counter-attack.

Moses and I dragged our companion up onto the bridge and hauled him across to the British side, then turned with the redcoats and re-crossed the bridge to face the oncoming rebels. But, as we did, Moses uttered a short cry and pitched head first off the bridge and into the river. I peered over the edge but could not see my friend in the murky water. Frantically calling his name, I finally saw him lying on the muddy bank, his legs dangling in the water.

I scrambled down the bank. The Virginians had stopped their advance a short distance away from the bridge as the British fired on them.

"Moses. Moses."

My friend, lying on his stomach with his head turned to one side, looked at me but did not speak. I turned him over on his back. On his chest, clear across the neat 'Liberty to Slaves' stitching, was a large wound. Blood oozed from the edge of the wound and seeped down the front of his trousers. Moses did not speak but looked directly in my face, the glow fading from his eyes, his breath coming in short gasps. Finally his light dwindled and died and my friend's fingers clenched on my arm.

I sat there in the blood and mud and decay. I thought of Moses and his simple, solid hopes, now drained in this terrible wasteland. I thought of my own hardships, all leading to this useless end, and I howled, not like a man but like a beaten dog. Scrambling back up the riverbank, I ran directly at the rebels, who were now advancing slowly towards the bridge. My sword was in my hand and my eyes were wide open. I didn't see individual soldiers and had no regard for their muskets or swords.

The first shot hit me after ten paces. It pricked my arm, just above the elbow, but there was little pain. Five more strides and another musket ball struck me, this one in my leg. It flung my leg backwards but was not enough to slow me down. By then I was on the first of the Virginians, a small front line of five men. I could see their faces, pale, drawn, and scared of the terror that had risen on them from below the bridge. Then I was on the first of them, my short sword slashing and cutting off his arm as if it was a pale sapling. His neighbor fell with a quick cut across his eyes. The third man turned and ran as I directed my attention to him. And then I felt something slam into my head, above my right ear, and I fell into a deep well, black and still.

Ten

The world was a place of searing light, of hard knocks and murmuring voices. It smelled of blood and horse sweat.

I was lying on the bed of a narrow wagon, the sun shining like a torch in my eyes. My arm and leg hurt but my head was the worst. Someone had wrapped a thick bandage around my forehead and beneath it my skull throbbed with each beat of my heart. I slowly raised my head and looked around. The waterfront was close by and we were approaching the docks. On either side of the wagon walked soldiers—members of the Regiment as well as redcoats.

Behind us stretched other wagons filled with injured soldiers and supplies. I tapped the driver of the wagon on the shoulder.

"What's going on?"

"Loading up. We're getting out of here."

"Where we going?"

"We're going up to New York but I'm not sure where you're going. First on a hospital ship, I guess, and then wherever they tell you to go. Colonel Tye wants to see you, if you can stand."

The wagon stopped and I eased off the back.

"Where do I go?"

"He's likely down there by the boats."

I limped down to the dock and spotted Colonel Tye directing

the loading of the Regiment into small tenders. The boats were transporting soldiers out to the British ships in the harbor.

"Colonel Tye."

"Murphy Steele. Good to see you up and around. They said at the hospital that you might finally wake up today and here you are."

"How long have I been out?"

"Well we carried you back to Norfolk five days ago. The doc said you're lucky to be alive."

"I've been out for five days?"

"Yep, and the plain fact is that you'd be dead and buried by now if we hadn't hauled you off that bridge. I never have seen anything like that. You were maybe planning on killing all the rebels yourself?"

"They didn't take the bridge?"

"Funny thing is they kind of lost heart after your little charge. They went back to their camp and left us to get clear of the bridge. Yeah. I've got something of yours here."

Colonel Tye reached into the bag lying near his feet and gave me my sword.

"What now?"

"For us, we go on to New York and fight again. For you, there's the hospital ship until you're right. I'd tell you to just leave after that, but I know you wouldn't go. So I guess you should come back to see me and I'll figure out what to do with you."

"I'm good now."

"No you're not. You look like hell; you can hardly hold your head still for the pain of it and you can't put much weight on that bad leg. The war will be here waiting for you. The doc says you might have to sleep a lot for a while. The ball creased your head and you're going to have headaches for some time. You're just damn lucky you don't have a hole in the middle of your skull."

I felt the sword in my hand. It was strong and solid. I thought about Moses lying on the bank of the river and the fire began to surge through my blood again.

"Did you get Moses?"

"We got all the ones that were close to the bridge. They're

all buried by the river there. I'm sorry about Moses. It was a bad business from the start. If I started telling you all the regrets I have about the whole affair, we'd be talking here for the next year."

He looked at me, then beyond to the wagons drawing up to the dock, filled with wounded soldiers.

"The truth is, sometimes we just have to take the hand we've been dealt and do the best we can with it. My hand was that crap bridge and that skinny road. So we did what we could and took our licking but it won't be the last battle and next time maybe we won't get a bad deal. You get yourself fixed up and then we'll have a little talk."

Colonel Tye turned from me and walked back towards the wagons still coming down to the dock. A British sailor came over.

"Boyo," he said, grabbing my kit bag, "you come with me." He led me to a tender and helped me down. I sat at the front and the rest of the boat filled with wounded soldiers, most sitting silently. Two were lying on stretchers.

The tender quickly took us to a ship in the harbor—the *Ranger*—already half full of wounded soldiers. During the next day the ship became more and more crowded. I found a small space at the stern where I could sit. A nurse, harried and anxious, came by once and asked how I felt, but mostly I slept.

The wounds in my leg and arm, barely a week old, were already healing. Neither ball had hit bone and both wounds had been treated in Norfolk. I would have scars to show from the battle but no lasting effect. The slash on my head was another matter. The ball had grazed my skull above my ear and the cut itself had mostly healed but I was plagued by severe headaches and slept both day and night.

The *Ranger* did not move from the harbor.

We lay at anchor, stinking, hot, and miserable. More and more runaways joined our sorry ship. These runaways were eager for accounts of the battles at Kemp's Landing and Great Bridge but sometimes I feigned sleep, not wanting to talk to anyone. The crew built wooden sleeping shelves on the deck and added more bunks below decks. Still there was not enough room for everyone to lie down at once. The nurse came by once every couple of days to change my dressings but the surgeon never talked to me. There were many men on the *Ranger* who were desperately wounded and more each day became sick, either with the pox or a fever. Every morning, the dead, weighed down with cannonballs, were slipped into the sea.

I felt like I was sleepwalking through a hellish place where the only escape was to sink beneath the waves. We had no blankets to keep warm at night, little to eat, and no idea of our future. The worst of it all was that between my injury, the loss of Moses, and the misery aboard, I no longer cared what happened to me.

I was hunkered down in my spot, nodding in a daze, when yet another tender pulled up to the *Ranger*. I heard the boat bumping against the side and the excited voices of a new load of runaways climbing up the rope ladder. I was so disinterested that I didn't bother looking up.

"Why is it that most every time I find you, you're sleeping?"

Standing over me with a grin as wide as his face was Thomas, a jar of clear water in one hand and a canvas bag in the other. It was the first time in a long time that I felt a smile crease my face.

"It's about time you got here. I was getting tired of waiting."

"I can see that. First thing you need to do is drink this water. Second thing you need to do is eat this chicken."

Thomas pulled two chicken legs out of the bag.

"How'd you know I was here?"

"Tell you what. You drink and eat and I'll talk. There's more chicken where that came from."

The sight and smell of the chicken made me hungry. The water was beautiful.

"A fellow on shore told me you were out here. I'd been asking for a while. Many of them know who you are but it took a while before I could find someone who knew what ship you were on. Some say you're a crazy man, others say you're a hero. Of course that's no surprise to me, at least the first part."

"Yeah."

"Anyways, I got a lift on that tender and here you are. Must say, you might have picked brighter surroundings."

"Thomas, it all went wrong at Great Bridge. Moses is dead and lots more. I couldn't do anything about it."

His face darkened.

"I know. I know it all. The fellow who sent me to this rat-trap, Colonel Tye, told me. He said something else too. He said you couldn't do anything about Moses, and that it was just a mess from start to finish."

"How'd you get to Norfolk?"

"Came in style, in a wagon behind your two old workhorses. Campbell up and left a month ago along with most of Wilmington. The masters figured it was about time to skip town, so there we were, slaves without owners. Sam and I loaded the wagon with all sorts of stuff, hitched up the team and started heading north. We heard about the battles and we figured we might find you here somewhere."

"What about Sally and Clairy?"

"They're waiting for us by the wagon."

"Nobody stopped you from coming?"

"Too late for that. All those who might have stopped us are either running to join the rebel army or just plain running away. Nobody's worried about looking for runaways right now. Campbell is long gone, who knows where."

There was a noise by the side of the *Ranger*. Thomas looked at me.

"That tender's fixing to be going back to shore. You want help standing up?"

"No. I don't know why I didn't think of leaving this hell-hole before. I was a fool for just sitting here."

"I imagine it's kind of hard to think when you're all shot up and you got nothing to eat or drink."

Thomas helped me to my feet and I limped over to the ladder that led down to the tender. I clambered down and the small boat struck out for land. All the wounded had long since been moved and the redcoats had also been taken to ships waiting in the harbor, but the dock remained crowded with runaways from places all around

Norfolk, hoping to leave the town before it was left to the rebels.

Thomas led me through the crowd to the alley where the wagon was parked. Sitting in the driver's seat was Sam. Before I could say anything, he jumped from the seat and put his arms around me.

"Oh boy, I never did think I'd see you again."

"Sam. I'm sorry about Moses."

"That's not your fault, son."

"Thanks for coming for me."

"Of course we came looking for you. Now why don't you go lie down in the back of the wagon and we'll get out of here."

I went to the back of the wagon. Sally and Clairy were sitting along one side and another woman was sitting on the other side. They helped me up and I lay on a blanket between several bags. Thomas sat next to Sam on the driver's seat. As the wagon pulled out of the alley, I drifted off to sleep, my head resting on a bag of grain.

It was night when I woke and the stars were blazing above my head. My friends were sitting around a small fire. I had three blankets on top of me and still I was cold.

I could hear Sally talking.

"Thomas, you've got to get us to a place where we can let him rest and get better. We can't just drag him around the country. He needs some decent food and water and he needs a proper bed."

"I know, I know, Sally. I'm worried about the sickness. Half of the runaways on that ship had the pox or swamp fever."

I drifted back to sleep, shivering beneath my blankets. It was daylight when I woke. Thomas and Sam were standing at the bottom of the wagon looking at me. We were in a small farmyard next to an old house that I didn't recognize.

"Do you need us to carry you in? Or can you walk it?"

"Where are we?"

"Why we're home, Murphy. Or, at least, we're somewhere that's going to be home for a while and a nice place it is too. Old but tidy and warm, I think. The owners have gone off to fight the British or something and left it to us."

I stumbled off the wagon. Sam and Thomas each took an arm

and half-carried me into the house. They sat me on a bed in the front room and took my shoes off. I was so hot and tired; I lay back on the bed and went back to sleep without another word.

* * *

"Murphy."

"Murphy."

I could hear the voice but I wasn't sure if I was dreaming. Climbing out of sleep was like scaling a slippery tree—halfway up I wanted to slip back down. I wanted to stay where it was warm and dark and safe, but the voice kept on calling and finally I made it to the top and woke up.

"Yeah."

"Murphy, you're back with us. How do you feel?"

"Let me think for a minute."

I felt pretty good. My head didn't ache at all and I wasn't hot or cold. Truth was, I felt comfortable, lying back on a thick bed with a pillow beneath my head and a good-looking woman putting a cold cloth on my forehead.

"I feel fine. I'm kind of hungry but I feel pretty darn good."

"I'll go get some soup."

The woman stood up and left the room. Thomas poked his head in the door and, seeing I was awake, came in and sat on the edge of the bed.

"We were wondering for a while if you were going to stay in this sorrowful world."

"How long have I been lying here?"

"You've been in this room for six days but there were a couple of days we couldn't keep you in bed, you were stomping around the room and ranting. We had to put a chair against the door to keep you in."

"I'm as hungry as a horse. Have I been eating anything?"

"That good woman that was just here has been feeding you soup every time your eyes were open. She's hardly ever left the room. Don't you remember any of it?"

82

"You know, I don't recall a thing. Last I remember you were helping me into this house. I do recall lying on the bed but that's it. I must have had the fever."

"Yeah, and it's a good thing you didn't get any sicker or you wouldn't be talking to me. Still, it was a near thing, Murphy. I think you got off that ship just in time."

My nurse walked back into the room. She smiled at me as I started to pull off the blankets.

"Nope. You'll be staying in that bed for a while. Besides which you got no clothes on and you don't want to be scaring Clairy. You eat this soup and rest. In a few days I'll think about letting you out of bed."

While she fed me the soup, the woman told me that my fever had taken a long time to break. I'd slept with just a single thin blanket on top of me as my body raged with a sickly heat and I'd often raved in a strange voice with words that no one could understand. My temperature had finally started to decline the previous day.

During the next few days, I began to eat more and sleep less. There was plenty to eat and drink and I began to feel strong. Thomas came and stood by the side of the bed.

"Are you about ready to get up yet?"

"Yeah, if she lets me. She keeps a pretty firm hand on things in here."

"She saved your skin. You'd still be sick or likely dead if it wasn't for her."

"Who is she?"

"For god's sake Murphy. Haven't you asked her name?"

"I was getting to it."

My nurse walked in the room and looked at us as if we were sharing a secret that she should know. Thomas took her by the arm and led her over to me.

"Murphy Steele, I'd like to introduce you to the woman who saved your life, Mary Brown. Mary Brown, I'd like to introduce you to the man who, for some reason that escapes me right now, both you and your mother seem to have taken a shine to, Murphy Steele."

Mary came over and sat on the edge of the bed.

"But Thomas, I already know Murphy. Why I took his clothes off just the other day when he was so fevered."

Thomas, with a wide grin on his face, walked out of the room.

Mary reached into the chest at the foot of the bed and took out my clean clothes. She was smiling too.

Eleven

We left the farmhouse the next day. My plan was to head north and end up in New York, where I could find Colonel Tye and the rest of the Ethiopian Regiment. Thomas remained undecided on his course in the war.

"I'm not sure about joining the British. I don't trust them. It could be that the best idea for me is to wait and see how this war turns out."

"If the rebels win, you'll stay a slave."

"Yeah, and if the British win, do you really think they'll give us our freedom? If they don't then we're back to being slaves and maybe hanged for choosing the wrong side. I've got a family to think about."

Sam and Thomas sat in the front of the wagon and I leaned in the bed against the back of the seat. Mary, Sally, and Clairy sat along the edges. The wagon was stuffed with bags of food and supplies.

"Thomas, people look up to you. You have a way of speaking and thinking that people respect. You can be a leader in this; someone other slaves will follow. I'm not talking just about the actual fighting, but in places where you can change men's minds and point people to better lives. When this war is over we'll need people like you, but you could start now by leading as a soldier."

"I know it."

We frequently saw other travelers, but they paid little attention to us. Many houses were abandoned, the owners off to fight in the war or perhaps to find a home away from the fighting. As each day wore on, we tried to find an empty house where we could spend the night. When we were unable to locate an abandoned house, we spent the night just off the road and slept under the stars. In the midst of war, it was an oddly pleasant, restful time.

A few days after the start of our journey, Mary came and sat down. The others were boiling stew over a small fire just off the side of the road. I was a little way back of the fire, leaning against a rotting log.

"Murphy, are you feeling all right?"

"Yeah. I haven't felt better in a long while. I feel like a free man, free to go where I please and when I please. Nobody's looking over my shoulder or telling me what to do."

Mary looked over at me.

"Do you know what happened after you and Moses left Campbell's?"

"No, I didn't hear."

"They blamed Sam. They said it was his fault you ran away."

"How did they figure that? They didn't know how we got away."

"No, they didn't know. They guessed a little of it, I think, but what it came down to was they wanted to blame someone. So they blamed Sam. He was responsible for the wagon and he was the only one left from the three of you."

"It wasn't his fault."

"Murphy, you ought to know by now that things don't work that way. They could blame him, so they did."

"What happened then?"

"They were going to whip him. Thirty times they said, then slit his ears so everyone would know what he did. They were going to do it in front of the mill so the town would see. They told everyone, but that day, when Sam was dragged out and tied to the post in front of the mill, Thomas left his work and came to the door."

"Thomas did that."

"Yes, he had to, don't you see. It would have killed Sam. There's more, Murphy. All the slaves in the town had been brought together at the mill to watch Sam get whipped. The masters got us all there to watch as a warning to us. So when Thomas came out of the mill, there were three hundred slaves in the yard and twenty masters. He walked into the crowd and climbed up on this big stack of lumber and started yelling at Campbell."

"What did he say?"

"Well, the thing is, they'd tied Sam to the pole but they weren't quite ready to whip him. So Thomas yelled that it wasn't Sam's fault that you and Moses had run. Thomas said it was Campbell who was to blame. He said Campbell was worse than the British king and that the slaves just wanted to be free. Just like the rebels. He told Campbell he was a sorrow to God, that it was a sin to own another man. He said Sam should be let go. Then he told the crowd they should never settle for being slaves. He told them that the fight for freedom for themselves and their families was a noble fight. He said you and Moses were heroes. He said lots more."

"What did Campbell do?"

"He couldn't do anything. The whole crowd got more and more riled up. They started yelling at Campbell to set Sam free and they surged forward towards the post. Campbell was in a rage as Thomas spoke but he couldn't get to him to stop him and neither could the other owners. Thomas kept right on speaking and the crowd got more and more excited. He said he'd thought up the plan to get you and Moses out of there and he said he was proud to help you and would do it again. Campbell was so mad it looked like his face might catch fire, but he couldn't do anything. By now he was also getting scared, real scared. So he backed up into the mill with a couple of his friends and barricaded the door. The rest of the owners disappeared into the town."

"What about Sam?"

"He was still tied to the post. The slaves at the front of the crowd let him go. Then they lifted Thomas up on their shoulders and they paraded him around the town. All of them were yelling and shaking their fists in the air. There was no one to stop them. Half the town had already left, thinking that the British were coming."

I looked over at Mary. Her face was glowing and her eyes sparkled with the light from the fire and her memory of that fantastic day.

"You know Thomas. He's not about to back down. So Sam, Thomas, Sally, and Clairy stayed in your old bunkhouse that night. The next morning, Campbell came calling. He had five other members of the Sons of Liberty with him. They battered down the door of the bunkhouse and they grabbed Thomas and Sam. They stood them up on the wagon, tied their hands, and threw nooses over a nearby tree limb. They didn't say a word, but Sally is nobody's fool. She sent Clairy around the back of the bunkhouse off to town. Clairy told the first slave she saw what was going on. That fellow rounded up forty friends before you could take a breath. They went as fast as they could to Campbell's. Meanwhile Sally was wailing and carrying on and jumping up on the wagon and doing just about anything else she could think of to waste time. When she was finally carried off the wagon and held by the side of the tree, why, old Maude came out of the kitchen and she started crying and climbing up and grabbing Sam's legs. They finally took her down, and Campbell and his gang were getting really angry by now.

"So they moved the wagon to the tree and were just about to put the nooses over Sam and Thomas and tie them off when around the corner of the cabin came one of the men from the field. First thing he did was whistle, low and short, and the horses with the wagon moved towards him so that they were no longer under the tree. Well, Campbell went crazy and he yelled at one of his friends to get the wagon back. But the horses would not back up, not while the field-man, Joseph, kept whispering things to them. So another fellow had to grab Joseph and take him inside the bunkhouse and finally they brought the horses around and put the wagon back under the tree.

"By this time, the slaves that Clairy met were coming into the yard. Campbell tried to bluff his way out. He told them that they were all going to hang if they didn't go home, but none of them listened. They got closer and closer in a circle around him and the wagon. Some of them had clubs and some had pitchforks. Campbell had a gun but he knew if he used it they'd kill him. All this time Thomas and Sam hadn't said a word. Finally, Thomas spoke up. He told Campbell to cut Sam and him loose and leave Wilmington.

"Campbell was mad but he was also very, very scared, so he cut the rope on their wrists without a word. Then he made his way through the crowd back to his house. The next day he and his family were gone."

Mary turned to me.

"Murphy, we need leaders. I don't know how this war is going to turn out. I know you think everything will be fine, that we'll all be free after the war, and I know the British have made promises, but what I'm saying to you is to stick with Thomas. He listens to you. We, all of us, need you two to be together. The men at the dock, the soldiers, they all know you. You're a hero. They say you're fearless, and when Thomas speaks he grabs our hearts. Together you two can do amazing things. My mother knew this a long time ago. Now I know it's true. Our time is coming, but only if you work together."

Sam came over from the fire.

"If you two are through with your chat, maybe you'd like to come and have some food. It smells ready to me."

The stew was good. That night, I lay on my back and watched the moon flicker through the trees. The future was as uncertain as ever but now I saw for the first time how we could shape it ourselves. It was a future for all the slaves, for everyone who wanted to be free. I was starting to see how Thomas and I could make that future come true.

When we were just a few miles outside New York, we camped by the side of the road. We were drinking our tea before bed when a traveler came into the light around our fire. He had a large pack on his back.

"Do you have room around your fire for another body?"

I looked at him closely but, before I could say anything, Thomas spoke up.

"Depends. Who are you and where are you going?"

"Matthew's my name. Matthew Stone. And I'm going down to the fighting in Virginia."

"What do you plan on doing down there?"

"Why, I'm going to fight those damn British scoundrels."

I didn't change my expression, but my right hand went to the sword attached to my belt. I started to take the thick knife out of its scabbard. Thomas looked over at me, his eyes hard, but before I could take the sword all the way out, Mary put her hand on my wrist. I stopped. She looked closely at the visitor.

"Are you a runaway?"

"No. Ferguson went to fight the British and he told all of us to do the same before he left. He told us we were free to fight and when we got rid of the British we'd be free men."

"You can sit. Have some tea."

Stone took his pack off and sat down opposite me.

"Thanks. It's a long walk. You folks going the same way?"

"No, we're heading for New York."

"Why, you're almost there, but I wouldn't go into New York. The British are all over and you can't hardly move."

I could barely sit still. If it wasn't Mary tightening her grip, it was Thomas fixing me with his glare. But if they didn't want me to move I could still speak.

"Why do you think your owner will let you go after the war?"

"He said he would."

"He owned you before. Hard for me to see how his mind's going to be different after the war. You know the British have outlawed slavery."

"I heard that, but it was a British ship that stole me from my home. Why trust them now? My thought is that I'm better off throwing in my lot with Ferguson. He treated us all right before all this trouble. If we can get rid of the British, maybe we can make our own country here."

I got up to look for more wood for the fire. Thomas followed as I moved out of the circle and went back into the woods.

"Would you have killed that man?"

"Yes, in a second."

"As he sat at our fire, drinking our tea?"

"Yes."

"He had no ill will toward us. You'd kill him though he didn't raise a hand to us?"

"Yes."

Thomas was silent for a minute. He stopped scuffing at the dirt and turned to me.

"Well that's the difference between us I guess. I couldn't kill a man without a thought."

"Just because I don't have your thoughts doesn't mean I don't have thoughts."

"All right then."

"Here's what I'm thinking. That fellow is going to join up with our enemies. When he does, maybe he'll kill me in the next battle. Maybe you or Sam. Maybe it will be in a year or two and he kills Sally, or Clairy, or Mary. Or maybe he kills somebody we don't know who could keep on living if I'd killed that fellow at our fire."

"He's a slave like us. He just made a different decision."

"He's a slave all right but he's not like me at all. His decision keeps him a slave. I'm a free man, and against everything he's fighting for. His decision might cost a free man his life. You shouldn't be so quick to make allowances for someone who will look to kill you or your family. There are no compromises in war, only kill or being killed."

Thomas went and sat in the dark against a big rock.

"There's still time. You could go back and kill him."

"Yeah, I could. In fact, I was thinking about doing just that."

"When we get to New York, you going to join up with that Colonel Tye again?"

"Yeah. Have you decided what you're going to do?"

"Well I'm a free man now. I'm not sure why I should do any fighting."

"You won't be a free man until you fight for your freedom."

91

"What about the fighting I did for you? I've already been nearly strung up for your freedom."

"I heard about that. You figure that's the end of it, you get to walk away now?"

"What do you mean?"

"You think you can whip up the crowd so that they all want to follow you and then just go away. Tell them it was all a big mistake. Just run away."

"Nobody in New York knows what happened in Wilmington."

"Not yet, but they will."

"Maybe. Maybe not."

"The people knowing in New York has nothing to do with it. You're never going to be able to sleep as long as you turn your back on yourself. You still have to make amends for owning slaves yourself. Only way you can do that is by helping all those slaves out there, not just yourself. I know you can do it and so do you. Question is if you have the guts for it."

"You're a son of a bitch. I ought to smack you for the way you talk to me."

"Yeah but you won't. You know I'm right. If you want, you can come with me to Colonel Tye, or you can keep on in your own world and work hard at not thinking about those dying out there so that you can be a free man. Me, I'm going back to the fire to maybe put my little knife under our visitor's ribs."

But when I got back to the fire, the visitor was gone. I questioned Mary.

"He drank his tea and left. Said he wanted to put a few miles on in the cool of the night."

"Huh."

"When you left the fire, he asked who you were. I told him and he didn't stay long after that."

"What the hell?"

"Murphy, all the slaves know your name. You're the runaway who charged the whole rebel line without a gun. You're the one who led the fight at Great Bridge. Those fighting with the rebels are scared and hate you and those fighting with the redcoats want to fight beside you. They all know you."

We drove into New York the next day. A British soldier directed us to a collection of tents. We found one that was empty and moved in for the night. I was anxious to find Colonel Tye, and Mary, Sally, and Clairy were going to look for work in the kitchen that supplied the soldiers. Sam said he'd take the women to the kitchen tomorrow and would find work himself in the British stables.

Mary and I talked outside the tent.

"Mary, I know I'm not the prettiest face and I know I can be a trial to you and to everyone else. I know I can be rough and hard and quick to anger. I'm not about to ask you to wait for me. I don't know how long this war's going to be."

"Wait for what?"

"Well I just kind of hoped that, you and I, we'd be together after all. That's what I mean. I mean I'm going off and for who knows how long. So I can't ask you to wait for me to come back so we can be together. But I'd like you to wait if you would."

Mary looked at me sideways.

"It's a good thing you fight better than you talk. I'll make it easy for you, seeing that your brain's not connected to your mouth. I've been waiting for a while and I figure I can wait a while longer, but don't go and get yourself killed. Maybe let someone else lead the charge once in a while. Thomas might take a turn or two."

"I don't think he's coming with me."

"Of course he is. You think he's going to let you go and get shot at again without him being there? He's already disgusted with himself for letting you go without him the first time."

Thomas was the first up the next day. He jostled me on the shoulder as I lay, half-awake, by the canvas door.

"C'mon, let's go. I said my good-byes last night and I don't want to say them again."

I grabbed my bag and we set off for the camp of the Royal Ethiopian Regiment.

Twelve

The Regiment sprawled like a wounded, stinking beast, its gray canvas hide dirty and wrinkled. We could smell the decay and hear the moaning of the sick before we reached the base camp. The filthy hospital tents stretched along the outer ring of the main encampment. Just beyond the tents lay carts piled with bodies waiting for burial in the morning, bluebottle flies already swarming around the noxious liquid accumulating beneath each wagon. Inside this loathsome circle lay Canvas Town, home of the Regiment and, at its very center, Colonel Tye sat behind a small desk in his own tent.

"Murphy Steele."

"Colonel Tye."

"I was afraid I'd sent you to your death on those sick ships, but now I see you've come here to die with us. Are you feeling better?"

"I'm healed and healthy."

"Who's your friend?"

"Thomas Peters."

"Peters. From Wilmington, I think."

"Yes."

Colonel Tye, thin and drawn, stood up from behind the desk and looked closely at Thomas.

"Did I meet you in Norfolk? Are you the fellow who led the riot in Wilmington?"

"Yes, I asked you where Murphy was when you were at the dock in Norfolk. As to Wilmington, it wasn't a riot. We were trying to prevent a murder, more like."

"I see."

The Regimental leader went back behind his desk. He took out a notebook from a drawer and came to an open page. When he looked up again he glanced at Thomas and smiled.

"What a surprise to see Steele is a friend to a man who started a riot. The two of you have got the runaways talking. Peters, do you plan on joining up with me and Steele here?"

"Yes."

"All right. Do you know how to fire a musket?"

"No."

"Well, that can be taught. God knows we've got the time for it. Here's the situation, boys. There are about seven hundred members of the Regiment in Canvas Town now. Fewer and fewer every day. Each day there are more runaways coming here, looking to join up, but for every fellow who joins us there's four who get sick and die from the pox or swamp fever or some other disease. We've lost more to the pox than we ever lost in any battle. We've had more than three thousand runaways come to us, but most of them have died, either on those god-forsaken ships or here in this dreary place. And here we sit, getting sick and tired and bored."

He looked hard at us.

"You know what happens when men sit around, bored and hungry and sick for wanting to fight? They start thinking of their homes, maybe their wives, and they get angry quickly, even with their friends. Pretty soon they don't want to listen to orders and then they think they should wander off home. Follow me."

Colonel Tye stood up, strode past us, and left the tent.

"I want you to get a tent and set it up right near me. You'll report directly to me and you'll have the ranks of sergeants in the Regiment. Don't go near the hospital tents unless you have to. The supply and mess tents are just over there. Tell them I sent you. Steele, you teach Peters what little you know about shooting a musket. I'll see you both again in a week."

He turned, but just before he went back in his tent, Colonel Tye looked back at me.

"Steele, it's good to see you still have that sword. It may come in useful yet. I'll bet you boys haven't even officially signed up. Go find Waddle, the British officer in charge of this mess, and get him to swear you in."

Waddle was easy to locate—he was puking his guts out behind his tent. When we came up on him, he weakly gestured with his hand at the next white tent and said to see Captain Martin.

Sitting outside on a big wooden chair, as calm as a toad in the sun, was the Captain. He looked at us between the smoke rings from his pipe and gestured us into his tent without a word. Inside, he picked up two Bibles and swore us both in together. Thomas and I repeated Captain Martin's words as he spoke them, each of us with a hand on a Bible. I still remember the words to the oath. I swore that I entered freely and voluntarily into His Majesty's Service and enlisted myself without the least compulsion or persuasion into the Negro Company commanded by Captain Martin. I would demean myself in an orderly and faithful manner and would cheerfully obey all such directions as I would receive from my said Captain or the Officers under his Command.

As I repeated his words, I couldn't help but think of the battles, the running from slavery, and the sickness. To me, the words I spoke were the final step on my personal road to being free and complete, and I have often thought of that insignificant oath, spoken long after my allegiance had been proven many times, as the culmination of my fight for freedom. There would be many more battles and trials ahead but, from that point forward, I knew that the world now saw me as a free man, able to swear a binding oath and respected by the British as a man with the power to direct his own life.

Afterwards we shook hands all around and Captain Martin went back to blowing smoke rings in his chair. I shook Thomas's hand too and, when I did, I looked into his watery eyes and knew that he had felt the same way about the oath.

* * *

It was many months before anyone in the Regiment went to war.

We drilled, ate, and slept. We argued, dreamed about warring, dreamed of life after the war. Many got the pox and died, and many more got swamp fever, or ship fever, or yellow fever, or typhus, or pneumonia. Some of these died but most got better and returned from the dreaded hospital tents—thin and quiet. We heard stories of the redcoats fighting the rebels in standing battles, some involving large armies, but we were never called to fight.

In the fall of 1777, Colonel Tye ordered Thomas and me to take thirty men and start building a prison in New York. Thousands of rebels had been captured in two large clashes—the Battle of Long Island and the Battle of Fort Washington. These men were being held in prison ships in the harbor, a situation that resulted in starvation and filth, and one that the British wished to resolve so that the ships could be sent back into action. We were sent to rebuild a former warehouse—named the Sugar House—into a prison, a job that took us all winter and well into the next summer. As we finished one section of the brick building, the prisoners were moved into the cells. With them came their British guards.

While our construction unit continued to live in tents near the Sugar House during that harsh winter, we were provisioned with warm coats and enough food to keep from starving. Every Sunday we were given leave to attend church, so we met Mary, Sally, and Clairy on the steps of St. Paul's. They were living, warm and dry, in barracks in New York. Mary worked in the British kitchen and Sally and Clairy were in the laundry. Each Sunday, Mary brought food she had saved during the week and we had a special lunch, outside if the weather was fine, or in the church basement during the cold months.

The days passed quickly while we worked on the Sugar House and it would have been easy to forget we were at war if not for the moaning of the prisoners beneath our feet as we built new cells on

97

the second story of the huge warehouse. One cold day early in the fall, I stood in the prison yard looking up at the third floor window. We were putting bars on the upper windows and were nearly finished with our work at the Sugar House. As I looked up, a white face appeared at a barred window on the first floor.

"Hey."

"Hey what?"

"Could you get us some food? We're starving here."

"Ask the guards."

"We're not allowed to speak to them. C'mon we're dying in here. We've eaten our boots. We got no blankets or coats or anything. You know what we get to eat—a bowl of broth and two chunks of bread and peas. You can help us."

"No, I can't."

"We've got nothing to eat and half of us in here are sick with the pox. Can't you get us some meat? Will you let us just die here?"

I walked back inside and went up to the second floor. We were nearly finished building the second and third floor cells. Thomas grabbed his lunch bag and we headed back to our tent.

"There was a fellow in the window."

"What window?"

"The window on the ground floor. The one that looks into the cell."

"Yeah."

"He said they're starving and sick and cold in there."

"Well they're prisoners."

"Yeah but they're starving to death. They've eaten their shoes and belts."

"Well, what do you think, Murphy? Our fellows are starving and sick back at the main camp and they're not our enemies, they're runaways like us."

"Yeah, I know. But I hate to sit back and watch someone starve to death."

"Be thankful that you're not a guard. They've got to watch it all the time."

"Those guards are animals. They're part of the problem."

But Thomas was right. There was no way to get food to the prisoners and no reason to do it, anyway, when so many members of the Regiment were starving and sick and cold. My concern was inconsistent and without reason but still it nagged like a sore tooth. Thomas had little use for my complaints.

"The guards may be bad but they're British at least. What in hell is the matter with you? You wanted to kill some poor boy who stopped by our camp a while back just because he was a rebel. Now you want to save these prisoners who have likely killed some redcoats. I don't know, Murphy. You're hard to figure."

"The thing is, I know how he feels."

"Who?"

"The prisoner who talked to me. I know what it's like to be hungry and hopeless and desperate. Yeah, I would have killed that boy who stopped at our fire. But I can't abide torturing someone. It doesn't feel right. I'm kind of surprised you think it's all right."

"Murphy, I don't think it's all right. What I think is that it's suffering and that's what war is all about. Haven't you noticed that there's lots of misery, enough for us all? And here's what else I think. I think that we need to pay attention to staying alive here. That means keeping out of the way, doing our job, eating when we can, and trying to stay healthy."

"Yeah."

"Another thing. You've got someone waiting for you and I've got a family. We can get out of this war with our freedom and make lives for ourselves. Real lives where we can raise children who will be free. This isn't our war; the redcoats aren't our saviors. They're using us to fight their battles. That's fine if we get our freedom out of it, but who cares who wins the war as long as we can be free. I don't care about any of these soldiers on either side, or their generals, or their big words. I just want to survive."

"You don't care about fighting."

"Yeah, I care. I hope we don't have to fight. I like it just fine building this prison. I hope we have a few more to build and then

99

the war ends. I don't want either one of us to get killed in someone else's war. You've told me a hundred times, Murphy, that this is our chance, and now I believe it too. Our chance for freedom, that's our goal. Not a slave country. Not an old king. Not some land that's not ours anyway. Freedom. That's our war, to be free men and have free wives and free children on our own land, making our own way. All of this other stuff is just our work to get there."

"What if the British lose?"

"I hope they don't because it will make things easier for us if they win. I figure there's a chance they'll live up to what they say and grant us land. If they lose, I think we should strike out for their colony north of here. In any event, we'll have to see which way things are going as the war winds down. Meanwhile we have to keep our heads down and remember what our goal is and stay out of trouble."

"All right, Thomas. All right. Let's just go."

We walked back to our small camp and began packing up our tents to return to Canvas Town. The wind, colder by the day, was picking up as the night drew near. I could feel the chill creeping into my toes, up my legs, and along my spine where the scars from my whippings so long ago had never faded.

Thirteen

Thomas was right about one thing. There was more than enough misery to go around. When we got back to the main encampment of the Ethiopian Regiment, the hospital tents were still there, the wagons of death were still stinking beside them, and a huge ditch had been dug to hold the dead. The only change was that the number of tents for the Regiment soldiers had shrunk. Colonel Tye was still in his tent in the middle of the encampment.

"Good to have you boys back."

"Where are the tents? Where is everyone?"

"Well this is it, fellows. This is all that's left. Everyone else is dead, sick, or gone. We've got about a hundred left, I figure. If we stay here long enough there won't be enough to do any damage to anybody."

Colonel Tye was a man working on devouring himself. His command had shrunk to one hundred from close to a thousand while rotting in its own inactivity. Every death had diminished our leader until now he was little better than a wraith. Our small unit struck our tents close to the colonel's. Each day we got our tiny measure of food and sat idly, waiting for orders that never came. It was a particularly hard winter, the snow packed up outside the tents, the cold wind ripping through the walls. One day, Thomas stood up after our breakfast of hard bread.

"I'm going to see Colonel Tye."

"All right."

We walked into the colonel's tent without announcement. Our leader was at his desk, sipping tea and reading a bound notebook. Thomas put both hands on the colonel's desk.

"Do you think our cooks know how to cook meat?"

"I expect they do."

"Well why don't we ever get any meat to eat?"

"You got to have meat to cook it."

"All right. Here's what I think. I think I should get our unit together and go get a few cows for this camp. I figure there's likely a few to be taken on some of the farms around here."

"We have no orders to go raiding."

"Yeah. Here's the thing. I know you can't order it, but Murphy and I can do it and I just want to make sure the cooks will handle it if we bring a cow in here."

Colonel Tye leaned back in his chair and locked both hands behind his head.

"All I can tell you is that everyone in this camp has to eat meat or none of us will. You should likely leave your uniforms with the laundry to get cleaned for the next few days."

Raiding for cattle was easy. It was a simple matter to round up a herd as they nibbled at the grass poking through the snow or munched on hay. We never saw the owners of the cows. The war had produced many raiding parties of runaway slaves, dispossessed loyalists, or angry rebels. We were just another group of armed men in the countryside and the farmers had learned to keep their doors shut and curtains drawn if they didn't want trouble. Some of the marauders were as inclined to violence as to stealing food and there were few cattlemen who valued their herds above their lives.

We drove the cows back to the pens beside the stables and, for the rest of the winter and spring, meat was not in short supply for the Regiment. The war swirled around us in the spring with rumors of battles while we still sat in our miserable tents. There were now less than eighty Regiment members, with twenty-six left in our unit.

Colonel Tye came to us one day in May with the sun high in the sky.

"We're moving out tomorrow. Get everybody in the Regiment ready to go by dawn."

"Where are we going?"

"To catch up with the British. There's going to be a big battle and we're invited."

The road to the main force of the redcoats was clogged with soldiers, runaway slaves, and fleeing loyalists. The British, leaving the Philadelphia area and heading to Sandy Hook where ships waited to take them to New York, were stretched in a column many miles long. Colonel Tye had been a slave on a farm in the area and knew every back road and quick detour, but it still took a long time to get to redcoat headquarters. We arrived very early in the morning, just as the rebels were moving into position to attack the British column. For the Regiment members, the Battle of Monmouth was a strange affair. We stood on a nearby hill and watched the two huge armies face each other. The heat was oppressive and we could not help but feel sorry for the redcoats with their bearskin and leather caps. Several British soldiers collapsed in the lines with heatstroke before the fight began.

Although both armies were in strict order as the battle began, the rebels soon broke ranks and began running back to the main rebel force. The redcoats took off in hot pursuit. However, just when it seemed that the British would win the day, the entire rebel army turned and rushed back into the fray. Fierce fighting resulted in the redcoats retreating back to the road and their original position.

All this we could see from our vantage point, as, like generals, we watched from atop the hill while the thrust of battle took place below. A small group of rebels broke off from the main group and, following a man dressed entirely in blue, began running around the main battle to attempt to get behind the redcoats and encircle the British army. As this group reached the road, Colonel Tye turned to Thomas and myself at the head of the Regiment and told us to bring our troops to battle with this group of rebels.

We ran in quick time down the hill and stopped a short distance from the flank of the rebel group. The rebels paused in their advance and began forming a line to fire at us, but before they were able to take a shot, Thomas yelled to fire and we unleashed a musket volley directly into their ranks. The rebels had numbered about fifty when we came down the hill, and there were now only twenty left standing. The rest were moaning or silent on the ground. With my sword in hand, I ran toward the line where the remaining rebels stood, dazed, their loaded guns in their uncertain hands, but as I got close to the nearest rebel, I tripped over a wounded soldier's leg and sprawled on the dirt. I looked up in time to see a rebel getting ready to stick me with his raised musket, bayonet fixed. The man was so close that I could see the sweat beading on his sun-blasted face and his wide eyes fixed on my Liberty to Slaves stitching. There was no time to move.

As the man hitched his bayonet higher to bring it down in full force on my stomach, I saw a sharp musket flash from very close and the rebel's face exploded. His gun slipped from his fingers and he fell face-first on my chest. I quickly scrambled up, my chest covered in red. Colonel Tye stood beside me. He smiled crookedly.

"Am I to make a career out of saving you?"

"So it would seem."

"I'm just not sure if you're trying to get yourself killed or if you're just plain clumsy," he said. "Well, it looks like this fight is over."

I could see the blue-uniformed leader of the rebel group waving a light blue handkerchief in the air. The remnants of his unit, now only fifteen or so strong, stood in a circle around the man, their guns on the ground. Standing down twenty yards away, the Regiment watched as Colonel Tye, Thomas, and I walked to the small group.

"Sir, the day is yours," said the rebel leader.

"Yes. Leave your weapons on the ground and walk before us back to the regiment."

We marched the captured soldiers back to the hill. The battle was winding down under its own weight with no clear victor as heat and exhaustion defeated both rebels and redcoats. The British packed their wounded on wagons and continued their slow march down the road while the rebels made camp for the night. We loaded up on provisions at the supply tent and Colonel Tye received new orders at headquarters. As we finished loading the wagons, our leader pulled up next to me.

"We're taking them to your old work place."

"The Sugar House."

"Yep."

"That place is a hell-hole."

"So I've heard. They say the prison ships are worse."

The march to the Sugar House was without incident. When we got to the prison, the guards refused to accept our prisoners, saying they were overcrowded. Thomas and I stood beside Colonel Tye as he discussed the problem with the prison warden.

"I told them before, I've got no room here for prisoners. We're stuffed as it is and the prisoners have little to eat. We can't take them."

"My orders are to bring them here and I can tell you you'll have quite a few more to put somewhere when the redcoats get here."

The warden looked hard at the prisoners and harder still at the blue-clad officer at the head of their ragged group.

"You, sir. Do you have money?"

The officer just looked at the warden as if the man had asked him a question that was beyond his understanding; as if, in fact, the entire reality of his being faced with imprisonment in a hideous jail that reeked, even where he stood beyond its walls, was beyond his comprehension.

"Do you have money? Where is your family?"

"My father owns a mill. My brother's a farmer."

"Do you have money?"

"Some. I can get more."

The warden looked at the other prisoners. He looked at me and he looked at Thomas and he looked at Colonel Tye. Finally, he called for his guards.

"Pick ten of the worst prisoners in the worst cell. Hang them."

"For what?"

"For whatever you want. Say for disobedience. Or for what

strikes you. Now listen, just hang those that don't have money. Then put these new ones in their old cells."

One of the guards looked closely at our prisoners.

"We'll be tight for room."

"Yeah, we will, but maybe we can make use of this fellow's money."

Colonel Tye turned away from the warden. Thomas and I formed up the Regiment and we left the prison yard as the first of the ten unfortunate men was dragged out of the Sugar House. We marched back to our camp. Thomas and I talked as we made our way.

"It wasn't much of a fight."

"Just the way I like it."

"Yeah and how'd you like to be one of those poor fellows who got hanged?"

"I don't think I'd like that at all, which is why I don't ever plan on putting myself in a position to get caught or killed."

"Right."

"What do you mean?"

"We're in a war here, in case you hadn't noticed. You can get killed any time."

"With the sort of war we've been in, I like my chances. We mostly sit around."

Colonel Tye drew up to our wagon just as Thomas finished.

"Boys, I don't think we'll be doing that much more. We've got new orders."

"For what?"

"For raiding, for taking prisoners, for warring. I guess they figure we can handle it now since we caught this last lot. I'm forming a new brigade and you two are going to be my sergeants. It'll be called the Black Brigade. Pick the fifty fighters you want out of the Regiment and send the rest over to the redcoats. They'll make them up into another unit. Then come and see me."

Colonel Tye rode off. I looked straight ahead and Thomas glanced in my direction.

"Well, there you go. So much for our nice quiet war."

Fourteen

Colonel Tye took our small Black Brigade to Sandy Hook, where we made our camp. The area was familiar to our leader. He had been the slave of a particularly cruel Monmouth County farmer, a man who had promised Colonel Tye his freedom when he reached manhood but, when the time came, had reneged on his promise. Tye knew every hiding spot and path through the numerous swamps in the area. He also knew the sympathies of a lot of the residents.

Our orders were simple. We were to provision the British army that was camped nearby and we were to seize any rebels we came across. We were to kill any that offered resistance. Most of our raids were simple. We would focus on a farm that a runaway had pointed out or one that a deserter had told us belonged to a rebel sympathizer. We would arrive at the farm just before dark, carrying torches and yelling. It was rare that anyone would even open the front door as we took cows and horses and anything else that we pleased from the barn. Most times we didn't bother with the house.

All through the cold winter, we kept the redcoats and ourselves provisioned. We had lost two men from the brigade. The first had fallen from his horse, been dragged for a short while, and finally hit his head on a rock, while returning from a raid in the pitch darkness. The other man was shot from the window of a farmhouse as we took five cows. Astride his horse, Colonel Tye watched with a face like a mask as our soldier pumped out his blood on the cool, dark earth. He turned to Thomas and me.

"Get everybody out of the house."

"How do we do that?"

"Tell them they have to the count of ten to get out before we burn them out."

Thomas went close to the house but away from the window where the shot had come from. He yelled at the farmer to surrender or be burned. He said he'd count to ten. At the count of nine, the farmer and his young family appeared at the door and walked into the yard. The young man looked up at Colonel Tye on his horse.

"Please, could you spare us the cows? They're all we've got."

But the colonel said nothing to the man. Instead, he told Thomas to set the barn, the storage shed, and the house on fire. I looked at our leader.

"The house, too?"

"You have a problem with my order, Murphy?"

"No, sir. But the house? It's damn cold here tonight and those babes are young."

"I expect a little fire will warm us all up."

Thomas took a torch and lit the house himself. The other soldiers fired the barn, the shed, and even a planked wagon that was loaded with firewood. The whole farmyard became a vast inferno. It enveloped the bordering trees and raced along the tops of the wheat showing above the snow. Colonel Tye ordered the Black Brigade to herd the cows back to our camp and we left the yard. Thomas sat beside me on the wagon. I looked back as we pulled out and the miserable farmer was sitting on the ground as if pole-axed, his crying wife huddled beside him with the children under her skirts.

"Thomas, that doesn't feel right."

"Yup."

"Those people are going to freeze and they've got children too."

"Maybe so."

"Nothing left to eat there."

"Nope."

"We should maybe have taken them prisoners."

"What, and put them in the Sugar House, you think?"

"No, somewhere else."

"Maybe we should keep them in our tent. Murphy, they shot Billy. You saw that. What did you do when they shot Moses?"

"That was different. They were soldiers that shot Moses and he was my friend."

"Billy was Daniel's friend. Didn't you see him trying to stop that poor boy from bleeding his life out on the snow? Don't tell me that stuff about soldiers. This is a war, Murphy; everybody who's against us here is a soldier and our enemy and will kill us if they get a chance. This isn't our land. We are in the country of our enemy and everyone might kill us. They all hate us."

"Yeah, the babies and women too."

"A woman can shoot a gun. You don't know that it wasn't her that shot Billy. If they shoot at us they deserve to die."

Most of our raids in that harsh winter were for supplies, but as spring turned to summer, our fights became more focused and deadly. One night Colonel Tye came to us with a new order.

"Tonight we go to capture Joseph Murray. You know who he is?"

"No."

"He's hanged about twenty loyalist farmers simply because they're not rebels. We've got orders to capture him so he can be executed here in front of everyone. We'll take half the brigade. Pick out twenty men. I'll want both of you, too."

The rebel's house was well-lit when we rode up. We could hear loud voices from inside. Colonel Tye stopped his horse just outside the gate into the yard.

"Bad luck for his friends. It looks to me like he's having a party. Murphy, you and Thomas take five men and go around the back. Cut them off if they try to make a run for it. I'll take the rest and knock on the front door. Remember, we're to capture him, not kill him."

Thomas and I went around to the back. We could see through the back window but the voices were coming from the front of the house.

Suddenly, all went quiet and we could hear Colonel Tye's voice, low and calm. Thomas opened the back door and we went through the kitchen of the house into the front parlor, where Colonel Tye was talking to three men who were all standing. I didn't recognize the man nearest me but I sure did know the other two as they turned to see who we were.

"Thomas. It's the bounty hunters. The very same ones that dragged us when we ran the first time."

But Thomas, his eyes like small blazing coals, had already taken a small skinning knife from his tunic. Before Colonel Tye could utter a warning, my friend grabbed the man nearest to him. This was the small bounty hunter who had made jokes as he bounced us along the road back to Richardson's. Thomas took the man from behind, his thick arm around the man's chin. As he raised the small man backwards off his feet, Thomas took his knife and drew it along the man's throat. Instantly, a spout of blood burst out and the bounty hunter collapsed on the floor, gurgling and clutching his severed throat. As the man slipped to the floor, his friend, the other bounty hunter from so long ago, took a long sword out of his belt and slashed at Thomas, catching him on the arm and backing him into a chair, but the long sword is a poor weapon in a closed space. I drew my short sword and, before the rebel could parry my swing in the narrow room, buried the weapon in his stomach.

The end of the Roman sword struck against his spine but I lifted hard with all my strength, upward and deep, so that his body was raised off the ground. His sword fell with a clang on the floor. With a huge wrench, I pulled the bloody blade out and the man fell next to his friend.

Murray turned to face me, a wicked knife in his hand, but as he moved to stab me, Colonel Tye raised his musket, bayonet fixed, and ran the rebel leader clear through his side, just under his ribs. The tip of the bayonet showed on the other side of his stomach and Murray slipped to his knees, moaning, as the colonel withdrew his musket. Colonel Tye turned to one of the brigade soldiers standing wide-eyed behind him.

"Drag him outside and fire the house. Murphy, can you help Thomas out?"

"Yeah."

"All right."

We went outside. The soldiers had leaned the dying Murray against a post in the yard. The house was beginning to burn. The edge of the sword had caught Thomas just below his shoulder but it was a flesh wound and already the flow of blood was lessening. Colonel Tye came up to us as I tied a bandage around Thomas's arm.

"What was that about?"

"Those two dragged us when we ran away. They dragged us all the way back to the farm and they laughed about it the whole way. Then we were whipped."

"I see. It was their bad luck that you were here today. Murray's bad luck too, I guess."

I helped Thomas up into the wagon. He lay in the bed and I drove the team.

"Well, what the hell, Thomas?"

"What?"

"What the hell happened in there? We were supposed to capture them."

"You were going to let them walk out alive?"

"Yes. No. I'm not sure what I would have done. I never got the chance to think."

"I couldn't let them go."

"You're the one always telling me to ease off and to not be vengeful. To take things easy and keep my head down."

"Yeah."

"Well?"

"Do I look like a saint to you, Murphy? That Bible you're always talking about. How many gods are in that book? Just one, I figure, and he's not here tonight. I'm just trying to do the best I can."

"All right. But the second man could have killed you. He surely was going to have a go at it after you cut his buddy."

"I wasn't worried about him."

111

"Why?"

"I figured he was yours."

"Yeah."

"Those men needed killing, so don't ask me to be sorry. I'll never be sorry for it and I won't waste a minute worrying about it. Fact is, I'm glad we got the chance."

"All right."

"It doesn't change anything. We've still got to get through this war best we can. We got lots of good life ahead of us. What I said before is right."

"Yeah."

Thomas closed his eyes and lay still as the wagon rolled on to Sandy Point. Colonel Tye rode up beside us, sitting high and straight on his horse. He looked at Thomas, sleeping in the back, and he looked hard at me, but he didn't say a thing.

Our leader never did say another word to us about what happened in Joseph Murray's house. We didn't know how he explained it to his commander. Thomas's wound healed quickly, leaving yet another evil-looking slash on his scar-crossed body. The killings at Murray's house did have one unanticipated consequence. The Monmouth rebels were now terrified of the Black Brigade and haunted by the threat of more runaways joining our ranks. Our raids continued through the summer, made easier by the killings, as rebel sympathizers were reluctant to offer resistance to men who would as soon kill them as take them to prison. Colonel Tye's name was used by mothers to scare their children into good behavior and the Black Brigade encountered no resistance as we took cows and horses and any other supplies we needed from rebel farms. Rebel leaders were left at the Sugar House. That dreadful place was now turning over prisoners at such a quick rate through starvation, hanging, or fatal flogging, that it had room for the steady flow of prisoners sent to it by the redcoats.

In early September 1780, with the air crisp and fresh, the Black Brigade was dispatched to Joshua Huddy's house. The building was a solid log home with small windows and an imposing oak door.

Huddy was a well-known rebel leader. He and his wife refused to surrender and opened up on our group with musket fire when we arrived at his home. We took cover behind the wagons and farm implements but it was difficult to get close enough to the building to fire it. Colonel Tye, wounded slightly in the wrist from a musket ball, ordered half the Brigade to fire, at his command, at the front of the building while the rest torched the back of the house. We piled straw and loose lumber onto the small blaze at the rear of the building and the fire began to crawl up the back wall. Huddy and his wife were soon smoked out and surrendered through the front door. Colonel Tye ordered ten soldiers to take the two captives to the prison ships on the coast and we returned to our camp at Sandy Point.

Four days after our raid at Huddy's house, I was sitting on a stump outside our tent, eating a bowl of beef stew. Thomas had been sent with half the Brigade back to the Sugar House to do some repairs on the old building. Colonel Tye walked over from his tent and sat on a log next to my fire.

"Colonel."

"Murphy."

"You want some stew? There's lots here."

"Nope. My neck's so damn sore I can hardly move. My mouth is tight, too."

He was talking through his teeth as if his jaw was frozen in place.

"You should go to the hospital tent and see if the surgeon can do something."

"Yeah, I should, but I hate that place. Most of the men that go there don't come back."

I looked at Colonel Tye. His lips were curled back from his front teeth and when he turned to look at me, he moved his whole body, his neck fixed on the top of his shoulders and seemingly unable to swivel. I put my stew bowl down on the stump.

"I'm going to get a doctor to come here. I'll be back soon."

The surgeon seemed eager to leave his wretched tent. I took him to Colonel Tye, who was still sitting on the log looking thoughtful. The surgeon brought a small canvas bag and, after taking one look, asked our commander if he had any wounds or cuts. Colonel Tye showed him his wrist where the musket ball had nicked him. The small wound had become black and evil-smelling under the dirty bandage. The doctor, holding Colonel Tye's hand in his own, took out a small, thin-bladed knife and a short length of oak. He called me over.

"You'll have to hold him still. Colonel Tye, we have to cut out all that inflammation. Now this is going to hurt. Your man here will hold your arm and you put this wood between your teeth. Bite down. Hard."

Colonel Tye didn't say a word but pried his teeth open with the stick, inserted the wood in his mouth, and clamped his teeth down hard. There were tears in the corners of his eyes. I moved behind the colonel and wrapped my arms completely around him. He had seemed to shrink in the last few days and it was easy for me to encircle both his waist and his upper limbs. His sore wrist dangled from his lower arm. The doctor took his hand and began cutting the rotten flesh from the Colonel's wrist.

It took several minutes for the sharp little knife to draw blood. The skin, almost green with some vile infection, sloughed off easily enough, foul-smelling yellow fluid spilling on the ground. The surgeon then cut into the surrounding pink tissue, deep enough to cause the blood to flow. All this time, Colonel Tye, unmoving, had bitten hard on the oak, his teeth denting and splintering the hard wood. After the surgeon was finished, he heated up a small vial of turpentine in the fire and poured the contents on the open wound. He gave Colonel Tye a flask of opium and several small bandages and advised him to soak the bandages with opium twice a day and apply them to his frozen jaw.

After the surgeon left, Colonel Tye sat by my fire for a long time. He held his injured wrist.

"Murphy, it's been quite a trip."

"Yeah."

"You know what's happening, don't you?"

"Yeah."

"This war will be over sometime but this country isn't going to change, no matter who wins. Not for you or Thomas. Maybe for your children or their children. If the British win, it'll be back to the good old slave days. And if the rebels win it will be back to the good old slave days."

"Yeah, we figured that too."

"You and Thomas have got to get out of the country at the end of the war. No matter what, you go up over the border. Just don't stay here. Go somewhere you can make a life. You're the best soldier I've ever met and a damn good man, too. I'm proud that you fought with me."

"What do you want me to do?"

"I want you to help me up to that hospital tent tomorrow morning. Then I want you to not see me again."

The next day, I helped Colonel Tye up to the hospital tent. The surgeon from the previous day was not surprised to see us. He helped the commander into a small cot by the doorway. I turned to Colonel Tye before I left.

"There's no help for this, I guess?"

"No, Murphy, not this time."

"You're about the finest man I've ever met."

"Murphy, although this country isn't going to change, you can. You'll have choices after the war. This fight is about freedom for you and your children. All those hard times we've had over the past months were the best part of my life. We were fighting for our freedom. Fighting together side by side and trusting each other. That makes up for all the whippings before. I never thought I'd see free runaways fighting together for their freedom in one brigade, and to have been able to lead such fine men... well, it's a life anyone would envy."

I turned my face away but the Colonel wasn't through.

"You grab hold of your freedom, Murphy. You grab tight and don't let go. When your children are born, you tell them about our battles and what it means to be a free man so they know how much their freedom cost and won't let anyone take it away."

Fifteen

We buried Colonel Tye in a separate grave in the cemetery outside the hospital tent. I thought back to when I had met him. Then I remembered Moses and our escape from Campbell's six years past. Lying still and scared in the back of the wooden wagon seemed so long ago and so distant that I sometimes wondered if I had imagined the details.

Our lives were now measured by our time at war. It seemed to me we had been warring, or waiting for war, all our lives. We were continually amazed to be alive when so many had died. Death was a constant companion, waiting to claim us through disease, through an enemy's musket, through a series of coincidences that ended in a mass grave.

The war itself had degenerated from a clash of ideals to a fight between men who did not remember and could not contemplate its original causes. Reason had long since fled and chaos and depravity had taken its place. Bizarre atrocities, not considered by civilized men in normal times, had become not only commonplace and accepted, but praised and advocated. When Thomas and I had seen the taxman tarred and feathered in 1774, I thought that the world could have no darker secrets for me. In that, as in so many things, I was wrong. The evils of the world can never be plumbed. There is always another level of despair and cruelty.

After we buried Colonel Tye, the Black Brigade was left not only without a leader but also without any sense of direction or goal. Most of the former runaways had gone to the redcoats and been formed into a new unit called the Black Pioneers. Our raids ceased and we sat in our tents, waiting for something to spark us out of lethargy. Finally, as fall began to creep towards winter, we were told to join the redcoats under Colonel Banastre Tarleton in South Carolina as he continued his campaign. Thomas turned to me as we stood leaning on the rail of the ship taking us to join up with the redcoats.

"Do you know what they call Tarleton?"

"Bloody Ban."

"You know why?"

"Yeah, because of the Buford Massacre, but I heard he was fired on by a rebel who had surrendered."

Everyone knew the story of the Buford Massacre but nobody had the same details. Bloody Ban Tarleton, infamous among the rebels for giving no quarter and for being utterly ruthless, had led the redcoats in battle against the Virginians under Abraham Buford. After fierce fighting, the rebels waved the white surrender flag and dropped their weapons, but instead of accepting the surrender, the British renewed their attack on the unfortunate rebels using sabers from horseback on the now-defenseless Virginians.

Some said one of the rebels had started the slaughter by grabbing a weapon and firing on Tarleton after already surrendering. Others, however, said the attack was unprovoked and vicious. Since the Buford Massacre, Tarleton had embarked on several raids and had vowed to take no prisoners in further battles. It was a measure of the new level of cruelty in the war that this comment was easily accepted, even praised, by loyalists. The rebels used "Tarleton's Quarter" as a reason for their own new strategy of taking no prisoners.

"Murphy, he killed the wounded on the field. They were protected by a white flag and his men put them to the saber."

"Yeah. And we starved men in prison and burned a family out in the middle of winter. We killed rebels in cold blood. Thomas, let's not go down this road. I can't summon up any more anger over what happens in this war."

We were floating on the ocean of war like the debris of ships. We had no direction or sense of stability. We had no way to measure our own progress in the war. We did not know if we were winning or losing and barely cared if we were doing anything as a small brigade to advance the cause of the British. Each battle moved us like a wave, sometimes sinking us below the surface and always taking us in a new direction, not of our choosing but aimless and evil. The war had made us put aside our old fancies of right and wrong. We had become uncertain of our own standards.

We were joined on our ship by our new commander, Colonel Stephen Blucke, a man uneasy with his command. He was quick to tell us that he had been a free man in the Caribbean before the war. I wasn't sure if he was nervous about leading a group of runaway slaves or unhappy with finding himself lost in this inferno. The colonel had been an advisor with the redcoats before being named to his first command.

The Black Brigade was reduced to thirty-two soldiers and it was unclear to me how we could help the redcoats, who numbered just over one hundred, with much of anything. Our first order in South Carolina was to capture the Swamp Fox—the rebel, Francis Marion—who was conducting a running war against the redcoats and Tarleton. We camped on the estate of General Richard Richardson, a rebel leader who had been killed and buried six weeks before. The name of the estate brought back harsh memories of our old master, but the general had no apparent kinship with the cruel tyrant of our youth.

Marion was rumored to be headquartered near the Richardson house in Ox Swamp, and Colonel Tarleton was determined to track him down. Every day we formed groups and hunted a different part of the swamp, a dangerous place filled with sink-holes, hidden trails, and endless hiding places. Bloody Ban, a vengeful man, was convinced that his archenemy was holed up in the swamp and became angrier and angrier as we were unable to find his hiding spot.

General Richardson's young wife and two small children visited his grave, which was in a quiet corner of the estate, every morning, leaving bouquets of flowers on the side of the mounded earth. One dawn, after we had been looking for the Swamp Fox for almost two weeks, Tarleton called the entire Regiment and the redcoats to the grave. We stood there for almost two hours until the young widow and her family arrived. Tarleton beckoned the widow to his side.

"Ma'am, I'm going to ask you one more time. Do you know where Marion is?"

"No, sir, I'm sure I do not. I can't tell you what I do not know."

Tarleton turned to Colonel Blucke.

"Colonel Blucke, order your men to dig up General Richardson."

"What?"

"Dig up the body. Now."

General Richardson's widow covered her face with her hands. Her children, already crying in the midst of the troops gathered around the grave, wailed louder. Blucke, his face blank, turned to Thomas.

"Order the men to dig up the body."

"No, I can't do that."

"What?"

"It's a bad order and I won't pass it down to other men. Murphy, help me here."

There were two shovels leaning on a tree near the grave. I grabbed them both and passed one to Thomas. It was a simple matter for us to dig through the loosely-packed earth. The morning air was cool and we made good progress. In short order we hit the plain pine coffin and tied ropes around the handles so the troops on top of the grave could haul the box out. Richardson's wife and children were now sitting on the ground near the grave, his unfortunate widow staring out across the garden, with her arms around her children. Tarleton and Blucke were standing near the widow as we scrambled out of the grave. Blucke ordered two brigade members to open the coffin and lift the corpse out of its resting place.

The soldiers glanced at Thomas, then opened the pine box and lifted the dead general out. Richardson had been buried for six weeks in the moist ground. His fine white shirt stuck to his wasted body in several places, merging with his flesh in an ungodly mess. A wave of foul air wafted over the troops. Several of the brigade and more of the redcoats retched when the body was lifted out of its box.

Tarleton, grinning like a demon, took Richardson's widow by the arm and led her over to her husband's body. He asked a redcoat to bring a travel chair and had the remains propped up in the chair. The corpse was utterly limp and liquid so that his body did not sit in the chair, but rather settled into it like a large lump of wet clay. Most unsettling was the dead man's face, his paper lips drawn back from his teeth in a snarling grin, and his eyelids crumbling away from his eyeballs. The general's wife turned her face from the horrific sight and put her hands over her children's eyes. Tarleton told the poor woman to order lunch for the officers.

"An outdoor lunch, I think, will be fine, with bread and chicken. There should be something good to eat in such fine company."

Colonel Blucke stayed with the unhappy diners while the rest of the Black Brigade and the redcoats went back to the tents. Thomas and I walked together at the front of the unit. He looked straight ahead as he talked.

"I don't suppose you've got much to say about that."

"I don't know, Thomas. I just can't begin to think what'll be next."

"You know how, long ago, you said I have to make amends for owning slaves myself?"

"Yeah. The Bible says you have to atone for your sins."

"Does it say when it all ends?"

"What do you mean?"

"I mean how much atonement does God need from a man? I'm sorry enough already for three lifetimes. I'm not sure how much sorrier I can get."

"Well, I don't think it's like that."

"What's it like, then?"

"I think you've got to figure out a way to help other people out.

Your own troubles don't count for much unless they show you how to be a better person. That's what the Bible says suffering is about. It doesn't make any difference how much you think you've suffered or how much regret you feel about what you did. It's what you do about it."

"Your Bible says that all this is just a way of teaching me how to help others?"

"Sort of. Yeah."

"It seems to me that I've been helping the British win this war for quite a while now. How will I know when I've helped out enough to make up for my bad deeds?"

"You'll know because you'll be able to sleep through the night without bad dreams. You'll feel better about yourself and you won't care about asking how much more you have to do."

"All right."

"There's more."

"What?"

"You won't reach that point."

"What do you mean?"

"Well, you can work to forgive yourself for owning slaves or for any other bad thing. You can work for God's forgiveness by doing right things now but you won't ever get there, no matter how hard you try."

"The hell you say."

"Yeah. I think the Bible is telling us that the good part is in the trying. I mean, we can't be perfect so we're always going to feel guilty about something or other, but we can work at lessening that by doing as much good as we can."

"So what then?"

"Here's how I figure it. I see it as your fate to lead us out of this land that isn't ours and to a place where all of us can be free. To a place we can call our own where our children can live without fear. But my fate is different. I have this fire in me to strike out. Most times I can keep it under control, but not all the time. So I think I do God's will by being his sword, by cutting down as many of these evil men as I can."

Thomas looked at me sideways.

"How do you know what's right? You might cut down someone who's doing right because you think he's doing wrong. What makes you the judge?"

"C'mon. You know well enough what's right or wrong. Does anyone think Bloody Ban is reasoned and right? Who thinks it's good to starve a man to death in a cold prison? Or brand someone with a hot iron? What about pouring hot tar on someone? Anyone figure that's right? It's not like there's such a shortage of evil anywhere that it's hard to sort out what's slightly good or maybe a little bad. There's enough in the world to straighten out before we get to the little wrongs. Everywhere we go there are evil men, unchecked and grinning at the dumb and the gullible. I know this for sure—if those of us who aren't evil don't act as violent and unforgiving as those that are bad through and through, why then the evil men will just roll over all of us."

Thomas was silent for a minute.

"We've still got to get through this without getting ourselves killed."

"Yeah, I know, Thomas. That's another trial."

We sat in our tents awaiting orders for most of the day. Toward dusk, a messenger called us to rejoin Colonel Blucke at the graveside of General Richardson.

When the Black Brigade arrived at the rebel leader's open grave, the dead general was still in the chair. His widow had been tied face-first to a tree, her arms wrapped around the trunk. Bloody Ban and Colonel Blucke were standing beside the tree and the redcoats had already gathered in a large circle. The leader of the redcoats had a long whip in his hand, the leather coils lying at his feet. He turned to the tied woman.

"Last chance, Mrs. Richardson. Where's Marion?"

But the dead general's wife did not speak; in fact, she looked like she was deaf and dumb, her cheek resting on the rough surface of the tree. The long whip curled though the air and sliced across the woman's back. She made no sound as the leather carved her skin.

Colonel Tarleton did not stop until Mrs. Richardson's legs sagged and she hung from the tree by her knotted wrists. Then he ordered her cut down and taken to the house. Several redcoats carried the unconscious woman by her shoulders and legs the short distance to the building. The remainder of the British army trailed behind. Colonel Blucke and the Black Brigade walked at the back of the column. Our colonel turned to me.

"Will you go back and bury the general?"

"Yeah. Thomas and I will catch up later."

We went back to the grave and carefully placed General Richardson back in his coffin, then lowered the box to the bottom of the grave with ropes. It was as simple to cover the coffin as it had been to uncover it earlier in the day. As we finished our task in the cool evening, a high shrieking filled the air. A large pillar of smoke was rising from the barn near the house. Thomas and I patted down the grave and hurried to the Black Brigade, which had assembled behind the redcoats in the farmyard. By the time we reached Colonel Blucke, the barn and several outbuildings had been fired and flames reached high from the smoking roofs into the starry sky. The colonel seemed captivated by the spectacle, his eyes fixed on the barn as it creaked and groaned. From inside the building, we could hear the pigs screaming as they were devoured by the flames. I turned to Blucke as the cries split the night.

"Colonel, the pigs are burning alive. Let's let them out."

"Too late for them, and for the cattle and horses, also."

As he spoke, a fearful noise arose from the far end of the structure as the fire reached the cows and horses stabled there. The terrible sound, at first a mix of low grunts and high-pitched whinnying, became intense and steady as the fire reached the far wall and pieces of flaming wood fell from the old roof with crashes and showers of sparks. I could not turn away. I was gripped in the jaws of the war and had become an agent of death and pain everywhere I went, even to farm animals.

"Colonel, why didn't we get the animals out before we fired the barn?"

"Colonel Tarleton wouldn't allow it. He said the animals were owned by rebels, so they had to die like rebels."

I thought that the burning of the barn animals marked the end of the horrors of that night. The troops stood silent and still in the yard amidst the insanity, the dark sky filled with clouds of inky smoke, the air charged with strange sounds. Thomas and I stood with the rest, afraid to act, as the fire curled at the edges of our diminished humanity.

The night, however, held still one more spectacle for our weary eyes. Tarleton, not content with the firing of the barn and farm buildings, ordered his men to burn down the house. Straw was hastily packed against the outside walls of the frame house and the building was set ablaze.

As flames began to crawl up the walls and along the edge of the windows and doors, a loud crying came from inside the house. Thomas grabbed my arm.

"Murphy, he's locked the widow and children in the house."

Before I could say anything, Thomas began running towards the door of the house, which had been tied by its knob with a length of rope to a clasp on the frame. As he neared the steps, Colonel Tarleton charged up on horseback and blocked his path.

"Where do you think you're going?"

"In there. I'll not watch them burn alive."

"You'll do as you're told."

Thomas made a move to go around the horse but Tarleton quickly moved his horse to my friend's side and, drawing his saber, sliced him across the chest. Thomas fell to the ground and lay still, his Liberty to Slaves shirt soaking quickly with blood. I ran to his side, crouched, and lifted his head.

"Thomas."

"Murphy, I'm all right, I've just got to get my wind. Go get the widow."

Bloody Ban had stopped his horse next to my friend and was looking down at both of us, his face blank, saber in hand. I stood up from my crouch quickly. As I rose, I grabbed his ankle and tossed him over the side of the horse. The British colonel's saber flew from his hand on impact. Looking at me with unfocused eyes, Tarleton tried to drag himself to his knees, but, dazed, could not rise. None of the redcoats moved to help him.

Without another thought, I ran to the front door of the house. The fire had spread around the doorway but the door itself had not caught and it was a simple matter to cut the rope with my sword. As I opened the door, a blast of smoke and fire belched out. The heat was fierce. I waited for the fireball to subside before running into the house, bent at the waist and with my hand over my mouth.

The widow was sitting on the floor in the front hall with her two children under her skirts. The children were crying but Mrs. Richardson remained quiet, the back of her dress soaked with blood from the whipping. I picked her up easily and lodged her under my right arm. Then I grabbed the children by the backs of their shirts, one in each hand. The fire had consumed the ceiling and was rapidly growing, but I was just a little way from the front door and made it back and through in a few stumbling steps.

Thomas was sitting slightly away from the house, dabbing at the blood oozing from his chest. Colonel Tarleton was nowhere to be seen. I carried the Richardson family to Thomas and laid them on the ground. The widow and her children gasped and choked and took great gulps of air. The fire in the barn was fading and there were no more sounds from the animals. The only sound in the night was cracking from the burning house as timbers and walls collapsed and sparks and flames shot out.

As I was catching my breath sitting next to Thomas, Colonel Tarleton rode up.

"Both of you will be flogged and then hanged."

I did not have the breath to say anything.

"I think not."

Colonel Blucke had walked up. In the crackling from the inferno, I had not heard him coming to join us.

"I think not, Colonel Tarleton. These men are under my command."

"They disobeyed orders and assaulted a British officer."

"Yes, they did."

"I'll see them at the end of a rope."

"Not this day. I think we've had enough of you this day."

"I'll take this up with General Clinton."

"Yes. Well, when you see General Clinton, give him my regards, will you? I was his advisor for the past three years."

Tarleton grunted and moved his horse back to the redcoats. Colonel Blucke turned to Thomas and me.

"You two need to get out of here. Tonight. General Clinton is my friend and he won't let Tarleton do anything against my wishes, but Tarleton might not have second thoughts about hanging you tonight and then explaining later. He might come back with some redcoats."

"What about the widow?"

"I'll send her and the children off to her neighbors. Tarleton will move on to something else. You go back to the camp in New York. I'll take care of things here and catch up with you later."

Colonel Blucke turned and helped the widow to her feet. She stumbled off with her children into the night, the colonel and the rest of the Black Brigade following behind.

"Thomas, are you all right to walk?"

"Yeah. It hurts when I breathe but I can walk a piece, I think."

The day was over, the night already wrapping around the faltering flames as we walked down the lane from the estate and turned toward New York. The road was friendly and familiar, unusual in the strange land of chaos and destruction where we now lived.

Sixteen

The night was still as we walked away from the Richardson estate. The light of the fire was fading into an orange glow on the horizon. It was a cool and moist darkness, frogs chirping in the ditches and barely-seen great birds rising with a flutter of wings from the roadside bushes. It reminded me of our walk from slavery so long ago.

"If you end up with any more scars, I doubt Sally will even want you back."

"You're not so pretty yourself. I don't think Mary will find those burns on your arms all that cute and not having any hair only makes you look meaner than usual. I didn't think that was possible."

I ran my hand over the top of my head. The fire had scorched off my hair and left small black burn marks on my forearms. I looked over at my friend.

"I sometimes think you tell me things just to keep me quiet and then go about doing just what I was talking about. Didn't you tell me we had to make sure we got through this thing alive? To stay quiet and keep low? It doesn't seem to fit with you running to the house and trying to get yourself killed by Tarleton."

"Hell, Murphy, we couldn't just let her and the children burn in there. I mean, we might as well just join them if that's what we've turned into. Besides, you weren't too slow to get to that door yourself and what about tipping him off the horse?"

I looked over at Thomas. He was smiling and I started to laugh, thinking of Bloody Ban flying over his horse and sprawling on the ground.

"Yeah, you know, I felt like I could pick up the whole horse if I had to."

"That I would like to see."

The more we thought about Tarleton flying over his horse and stumbling on the ground, the more we laughed. It had been a long, long time since we'd laughed.

The road to New York was uneventful. We slept through most of the day and traveled at night. Seeing our regimental uniforms, the loyalists that we met gave us food and water. Glancing at our fearful countenance, the few rebels whose paths we crossed were content to stay out of our way. We set up a tent at our former spot and waited for Colonel Blucke. The Black Brigade and our colonel arrived several days later. Colonel Blucke called us to his tent. He told us the Brigade was being merged into the Black Pioneers and would be used for support work in the future.

"You can keep the Black Brigade uniforms if you want. Tarleton has gone off raiding again."

"Is anything to be done with us?"

"Nothing. He's going to try to forget it. He knows General Clinton won't give him satisfaction. The plain fact is that his own officers don't like what went on at the Richardson place. So long as you keep quiet, things will blow over."

"Do we have orders?"

"Yeah. You're to take ten men and go back to the Sugar House to make some repairs. When you're done with that, I want you to build some barracks on Water Street."

It was the best news we could have hoped for. Now not only were we out of the way of the war's path, we would also be able to see Sally, Clairy, and Mary again. We would be able to go to church, lunch on Mary's food, and walk the streets of New York.

The Sugar House had become, if anything, worse. The prisoners, crowded together in each dingy cell, moaned and begged at the windows in a pathetic way, and the guards, hardened by years of stone ears and blind eyes, had become caricatures of themselves, guarding ghosts of men who were no longer capable of escape. We lived on the top floor as we worked steadily through the cold winter. While we kept warm around our stove and had ample supplies, the prisoners below suffered as the temperatures dropped steadily. It was the coldest winter since our escape from Richardson's. The moans of the dying men below us were constant and miserable, and reminded us of where we were and of the war still raging.

I no longer thought of helping the prisoners. The time between our last work at the Sugar House and our current repairs had warped and twisted me. Any sympathy for the poor prisoners below had been scoured from me by evil men with bad intent. The crucible of unending war had left me empty and bitter.

Then there was Mary.

Mary had changed little while the war swirled around. It amazed and discomfited me that she was still there, faithful and constant, not caring about the wounds or the past battles or the future uncertainty. She never questioned me about the war. She simply accepted that now we could be together again. Sally and Clairy were steadfast with Thomas and we all soon resumed our Sunday lunches, now at Trinity; but things could not be the same as before.

I was restless and uncertain and, one day, after Sunday service, Mary gave me a Bible. She said that Thomas was worried about me and had told her that I used to read it. As the spring finally arrived in New York and gave the freezing men below some relief, I began reading the book as I had many years before. Now it touched me in a way it previously had not. I knew what it was like to wage war, to suffer frustrations and pain, to be challenged at every turn, to be angry at God, and discouraged by man. I felt that the Bible was directed to me personally and I started reading and re-reading sections every night.

At the beginning of the summer, I began to have strange dreams.

Every night I dreamed of a battle where all the slaves rose up against their owners and, throwing off their chains, rampaged through the country. There was a huge army of slaves armed with clubs and pitchforks and long knives. The rebel forces, puny in comparison, shrank before the onslaught. My dream always ended the same horrific way. The slave army, having rolled through the rebel forces, tore through the neighboring towns, butchering every inhabitant and firing every building. Women were slaughtered as they stood, and their children, clutching desperately at their mothers' skirts, were bludgeoned by passing soldiers. No one was spared.

This dream, repeated night after night, left me sweating and dazed in the early-morning light. During the day, I was plagued by the smells and sounds of the tortured prisoners below, and at night I was haunted by the wails and cries of the dying children. I was more affected by the horrors of my dream than by the regular day-time tribulations. I told Thomas of my recurring dream and he looked at me strangely, but Thomas was suffering trials of his own. He had always been a restless sleeper and now, plagued by the terrible memories of the war, he had taken to leaving the barracks at night to roam the streets of New York. From there it was a short step to frequenting the bars in the neighborhood. Many nights, Thomas left the building as I lay sweating in my bunk. In the morning he would come back, shaky and silent. I rarely went with him since I could not drink without becoming drunk and when drunk I was not good company.

I could not tell Mary about my dream.

Her opinion of me mattered more to me than anything and I would not have her thinking I was crazy. So the nights passed, each one filled the same way and each one dreaded more than its predecessor. Thomas was as alone in the wasteland of his mind, as I was in the desolation of my dream.

Late that summer, my descent to madness was complete.

I was walking along the street on my way to see Mary at Trinity Church when a Voice spoke to me. There was no one on the street. The Voice told me to tell General Clinton that he was to advise the rebels that if they did not surrender all their troops to the British at once, God's wrath would fall on them and all the slaves would fight against them. The Voice said that God would be on the side of the slaves. I looked about for a person but there was no one there. My world had become so strange and unreal that I was not surprised by the Voice or its message. I did not feel compelled to tell anyone of my experience since I was unsure if it was part of my waking world or my dream. I continued on to Trinity and Mary and I attended service, although I was sufficiently unsettled that I did not remain for lunch.

But the Voice would not stay away. It spoke to me at different times every day. I now feared the day as much as the night. The message was always the same and it stated that I was to be the messenger. Many simple men in the Bible had been messengers for God and I wondered if I was to be one now. Even Thomas, as alone as he was in his own world, noticed my distraction. One morning, as I was still shaking off the daze of my nightly dream, he turned to me.

"Murphy, what in hell is the matter with you?"

"It's that damn dream."

"More than that, I think."

"Yeah."

"So?"

"I've been hearing this Voice. It keeps commanding me to tell Clinton to tell the rebels to give up or they'll be slaughtered by all the slaves."

Thomas turned to look directly at me.

"Yeah. I know how it sounds. What can I say to you? This Voice talks to me every day. So now I have the same dream every night and the same message every day and it's all crazy."

"No."

"What do you mean?"

"No. Murphy, you're the sanest man I know. The sanest man I've ever met. Do you think, after all the stuff we've seen, all the stuff we've gone through, that we should now just carry on like everyone else? We'd have to be crazy to be normal. I think God has chosen you to be his messenger, just like all those other fellows that I hear about in the Bible."

"What do I do now?"

"Well now, I guess you'd better get yourself off to General Clinton and tell him what he should say to the rebels."

Dressed in the uniform of the Black Brigade, I left for General Clinton's headquarters the next morning.

Located at the very center of the long and narrow barracks hall of the redcoats, the office of General Clinton was easy to find. General Clinton's secretary, an imposing man in a glittering uniform, sitting at a desk outside the general's office, said that there was no way that the general was going to see me, even if my mission was vital. I asked the secretary for a pen and paper and, sitting on the floor in a corner of the hall leading to the general's office, wrote out the message from the Voice. The man looked at me strangely when I brought the page back to him. He asked me to sit in the chair across the desk from him.

"So you can write. Let me look at this."

The secretary read the page quickly, then peered over the top edge with curious eyes.

"Murphy Steele. Black Brigade. Black Pioneers now, I guess."

"Yes."

"I think I might have heard your name. Let me think. Yes. Kemp's Landing. No. Great Bridge, I think."

"Both. Were you there?"

"No. Before my time, I'm afraid. Heard that you charged the whole damn rebel lot by yourself. They got so rattled they ran back to their holes. Should have got a medal for that, I'd say. Others say so, too. But I suppose they never give you people medals, do they?"

"Guess you think I'm crazy with that message."

"No, I do not. Murphy, I've been with General Clinton long enough to see many, many things that are crazy. Crazy through and through. Hmm. The Black Brigade. You were with Colonel Tarleton too, weren't you? Yes. Well, Murphy Steele, you'll have to go further than this Voice to convince me or General Clinton that you're crazy.

Interesting, though. Do you think God talks to you?"

"No. Maybe. I'm not sure."

"Me neither. I mean, I don't know if God talks to men. I used to be very religious. I believed in all sorts of miracles and God talking to men and so on. Then I came to this war. Now I don't believe so much. I mean, if He's talking, nobody's listening. Except you, it seems. Don't really know if that makes you lucky or unlucky."

"I can't sleep anymore."

"Well that just makes you a man, doesn't it? Not any more cursed than the rest of us."

"I guess."

"All right. Here's the thing. General Clinton won't see you, but I give you my word I will give this to him. I also believe that he will give your writing serious thought. I know that General Clinton has heard of you and I can tell you he will not dismiss what you say out of hand, no matter how strange it is. Is that good enough for you?"

"I guess so, as long as he gets it."

"Yes. He will, I promise you, and he will read it."

"Thank you."

"Good-bye, Murphy Steele. I can tell you're a good man. I'm honored to have met you. I hope you find freedom when this is all over."

"Good-bye."

I left the barracks feeling as light as air. The kindness of strangers was something I had forgotten. The secretary's care seemed out of proportion, as if he was now, by a simple action, giving me a great gift. That thought stayed with me and buoyed my walk back to the Sugar House.

Seventeen

I did not expect God's message to end the war. I had no expectations left in that war-weary time. I did not think that the rebels would surrender or that the slaves would rise up in a huge army or even that General Clinton would send the message to General Washington.

I knew that men were wayward and followed their own changing desires. The Bible was full of ignored messages and scorned messengers. I was the messenger and I had delivered the message. It was enough for me simply to complete my task. Others could face the consequences if they did not heed the message.

Telling my message did, however, give me relief. I no longer had the same terrible dream and no longer lived my daylight hours in fear of strange commands from an unseen voice. I received no further instructions.

I had learned that there were still good men left in the world, men who would take me at my word and who would believe my message had importance simply because I said it did. The secretary of General Clinton, a man I had never met before, had lifted me from self-pity. I felt that his small kindness had restored my own humanity and, more importantly, given me hope for the future.

As strength and meaning returned to me, Thomas continued down his dreary road of frustration and despair. My friend rarely remained in the barracks past nightfall. During the day he was sullen and withdrawn, speaking little and working slowly and deliberately. Even when our job changed and we began work on the barracks, he continued to leave at night to go to unknown places.

We continued to visit with Mary and Sally on Sundays when they were able to leave work and we got permission to go to church. Mary and I were sitting on the steps one sunny autumn day after service when she turned to me.

"Murphy, what's the matter with Thomas?"

"How do you mean?"

"Well, he's going downhill. Sally's worried and so am I."

"I don't know. I don't know what to do about it."

"Sally's pregnant and she's worried that she's going to be left alone."

"I think Thomas needs to get some things clear in his head. He blames himself for bad things in the past and takes everyone's pain on himself."

"It doesn't look to me like he's doing a good job of thinking straight. You'd best be looking out for him, Murphy."

I looked over at Mary. It had become quite clear to me that when she had her mind made up, there was no sense in further discussion.

"All right, Mary. I'll keep a closer eye on him."

That night, when Thomas began moving to the door, I went with him. He looked hard at me but said nothing and we walked together from the barracks to the quiet street below. I had expected Thomas to go to a nearby ale house. Instead, we simply walked through the chilly, nearly deserted streets for miles. We walked past shuttered stores and quiet houses, past garish whores and lively pubs, past redcoats with suspicious, hard faces. Finally we stopped at a small park and sat on a bench beneath oak trees. The seat of the bench was covered with large leaves from the bare trees.

"Thomas, what is this all about?"

"The walking you mean?"

"Well, yeah, the walking and the leaving every night. I thought you were out drinking."

"Sometimes I drink but most nights I just walk."

"Sally and Mary are worried about you."

"Murphy, I'm thinking of going up north. I'm thinking of leaving this country and starting out somewhere else."

"Where up north?"

"Up past the war. Somewhere that I can make a life for my family and actually create a future for Sally and Clairy without this never-ending war."

"What about the rest of us?"

"That's what's holding me back. I'm not sure why but I feel responsible for the runaways, like I owe them something I can't pay back if I move up north."

"You do."

"I do what?"

"You do owe them. You owe all of them to be the best you can be and that means leading them to a better life, to freedom, to all those things you used to talk about."

"Murphy, I'm not leading anyone to anything in this place. We're not doing anything but getting old, and meanwhile the war goes on and we're no further ahead. I want things to be better now, not sometime in the future. Some of us aren't going to make it if we have to wait too long."

I looked at my friend. He was leaning forward on the bench, his eyes looking at the ground between his knees.

"Are you talking about yourself when you say some of us won't make it?"

"Murphy, things just go on and nothing gets any better. Time passes but we're still slaves. Now our masters are the redcoats. I never thought it would take this long."

"But Thomas, we're not slaves anymore, we're soldiers. Yeah, we have to follow orders but that's the same with soldiers everywhere. That doesn't make us slaves and every step we take to being free men who own land and have rights is going to help those who come after."

"What do you mean, come after?"

"Well, you know Sally's pregnant don't you? No, it's plain to see you don't. She hasn't told you, which shows what frame of mind you've been in. So now you've got two children, maybe more to come. Every step we take to being free men will make it easier for your children. Have you thought of that?"

"No."

"You can be a selfish, self-centered man. Everyone looks up to you and expects you to lead and you spend a good part of your time complaining and moaning. You're not the first person to have sorrows and regrets."

"Thanks for that."

"You've got a family to look out for and friends too, and there's a whole group of people just like yourself who need you to lead them to better things. You act like you're the first person to wish that things were different than they are. You're thinking like a child."

"I'm the only one who had slaves."

"Maybe. Maybe not. Who the hell knows what anyone did in the past? We've all got our dark corners. We're all just trying to get by and not get swallowed by our own evil creations. If you want to make up for a past mistake, you've got to do right by the people who follow you."

"Yeah, except I'm not doing anything here to help anyone."

"Wait. You will. We'll all have our chance. The war won't go on forever."

"Hard to see why I should listen to someone who sees visions and talks to God."

"He talked to me. All I did was listen."

"Still."

"Yeah, you're much better off talking to whores or drunks. Or sorry fools like yourself who nod their heads every time you start moaning and groaning, hoping you might buy them another beer."

I had more to say but before I could take a breath, Thomas stood up. I thought he was ready to leave but as I rose too, he hit me hard and square on the nose. I sat back on the bench and my nose began bleeding down my chin, dripping on the Liberty to Slaves stitching on my shirt.

"Damn. You've broken my nose."

I went to stand up again and he hit me again, this time on the side of my head. My ear began pounding. I was mostly surprised. Thomas would always be the leader, but I had never pictured him as much of a fighter. He wasn't nearly as big or as rough as me. As he swung with his left hand to hit me again, I ducked and caught him straight under the chin. His teeth clacked together and his eyes rolled back in his head. He fell back on the ground. I sat on the bench and tipped my nose back to stop the bleeding. Thomas lay insensible at my feet.

It took a long time for the bleeding to stop. I sat on the bench, my neck tipped back, looking through the bleak branches of the oak trees to the starry sky. All these years and this is what it had come to, the two of us fighting like thugs. And maybe he was right, maybe the war would go on for a long time and we wouldn't be able to make a real life for ourselves, but I didn't believe it. Since God had given me a message, I'd believed that better things were meant for all of us runaways. Otherwise, there was no sense in the message. I'd come to think that maybe that was the real value of God talking to me—it gave me hope that we really did have a future as free men.

After the bleeding stopped, I picked Thomas up and slung him over my shoulder. It was a dead-black night, still and quiet. I turned out of the park and began walking back to the barracks. I wasn't sure I could carry Thomas all the miles back, but I sure as hell could try.

We'd gone maybe halfway when I walked past a couple of pubs with loud whores and muttering men leaning against the walls. The whores called after me as I shuffled past, Thomas on my shoulder.

"Hey c'mon. What have you got there? Let us see."

They pushed forward and blocked my path. I stood there with my friend still on my shoulder, uncertain where to go. One of the women came around in front of me and began picking at Thomas's boots. I gave her a short kick and she sprawled back into the wall, knocking one of the shadowy men into his companion. That man came up to where I stood.

"You just about knocked me over."

"Sorry."

"Sorry is not good enough."

"Sorry is about all I've got right now and I don't have time to stand around arguing with you."

"Is that so? You're Black Brigade, right?" The man turned to his friends. "Hey, look at this. We've got a couple of the Black Brigade here. Well, one anyways, the other looks half dead."

Two more villainous-looking men joined the man standing in front of me. I looked at the men and, taking Thomas off my shoulder, sat him down like a sack of grain against the wall. The closest man spit on the ground and pointed his finger at me.

"The Black Brigade killed my brother down south. You're all ruthless bastards. You should all have stayed on the plantation. As soon as we win this war that's just where we'll send you, too."

"Sorry, Jack. I'm just trying to get back to my barracks. I've got no quarrel with you."

"You're just full of sorry, aren't you?"

The men rushed me in a group, knocking me to the ground before I could get my balance. We rolled in the dirt like hogs but they were all drunk and had no sense of working together. I jumped to my feet while the others were still scrambling in the dust. The nearest man was on all fours trying to figure out how to stand. I went over to him and kicked into his lowered face as hard as I could with my heavy boots. He grunted once and collapsed onto his stomach. The other two men had stumbled to their feet. The man who had spoken to me brought a long sword out of his belt and waved it over his head like a saber, cursing me in a braying voice. Before he could slash with the weapon, I stepped in right next to him and stuck my Roman sword in his belly, twisting hard. When I stepped back, he sank to his knees. He sat back on his legs, a hollow, surprised look on his face.

The last man hesitated, a small sword like my own in his hand. As I turned to look at him, I noticed movement at the wall of the tavern. A fourth man was standing there, a long musket in his hand that was aimed squarely at my chest. From that distance, short enough that even a bad shot would not miss and long enough that I could not reach him before he shot, the barrel of the gun looked huge, a cannon in the small street outside the tavern. I was frozen, uncertain of my next step. The man was so close that I could see his throat move as he swallowed hard and let go of a short breath, the last thing he would do before he fired.

As the man exhaled, Thomas, slumped against the wall beside him, twisted around and plunged his skinning knife into the man's leg, just above the knee. The fellow screamed, a short sharp sound, and, dropping the musket into the dirt, hobbled back into the doorway of the tavern, his hands scrabbling at the knife sticking straight out of his leg.

The other man, still standing in the road with his sword in his hand, took a hasty look at his friend and took off running. I went over to Thomas, who had raised himself up and was leaning against the wall.

"Can you walk?"

"I think so."

"Let's get out of here."

We started out walking fast, Thomas leaning against me. A short distance from the tavern, we started hearing angry voices from people pursuing us, and Thomas and I began to run. My nose had begun bleeding again and I was breathing like a flopping fish, but soon we were running flat out through the quiet streets. We did not stop running until we were a short distance from the barracks. Then we leaned against a post and listened but there was no sound at all. We walked the rest of the way back to our base. Thomas looked over at me as I dabbed my bloody nose with my shirt.

"Do you think they'll report us?"

"No. Who would they report us to? I don't think the redcoats will listen to a bunch of drunk rebels. There's no worry of that."

"Yeah. That's what I figured too."

We sat for a few minutes on the steps leading up to the barracks. The night had drawn close but there were no sounds. No rebel would venture close to the barracks. Thomas was rubbing the back of his neck.

"That was a hell of a night. How come the back of my head hurts?"

"I hit you on the chin."

"Yeah."

"Well your head snapped back. It happens every time. That's the best way to put someone to sleep."

"Huh. Listen. I'm sorry about hitting you."

"I never would have thought you had it in you."

"How's your nose?"

"Broke."

"Sorry."

"Yeah. Don't do it again. That's it. If you're planning to keep up this night stuff, I'm going to bring a big club along. That was as bad as the war. Too bad you slept through most of it."

"Yeah. Did you have any plans for that guy at the wall? Nice work on the other three, but he was the one with the gun."

"Well, I didn't see him at first, but then you were relaxing right next to him."

"What?"

"I thought that since you were just sitting around watching you might want to, you know, get involved somewhere along the line. I couldn't see you sitting on your hands watching me get shot, even if you did break my nose."

"You know you were right about what you said. Everything you said."

"Yeah, I know."

"I've just been feeling sorry for myself."

Thomas stood up and looked down at me.

"I think we've got important things left to do. You're right, the war won't last forever. When it's over, our people are going to need us."

"Yeah. So maybe we should stop fighting like stray cats in the middle of the night."

"Yeah."

He turned and walked up the steps and I followed him into the barracks, where the night moans and grunts from the sleeping men were a warm welcome.

Eighteen

The reports we heard from the war front were not encouraging. As the winter wore on, we could feel commitment slipping from the redcoats as each missed opportunity and outright defeat piled on previous losses. Most of the soldiers were regulars from Britain and it was difficult to stay focused on victory when your home country was not threatened and you were an ocean away from friends and family. We rarely saw Colonel Blucke or anyone else from headquarters. Our small company was left alone to build new barracks, a job that became more meaningless as the days of a lost war struggled into months.

Still, we were reasonably content.

Everyone took advantage of our situation in New York to attend church, drink at local taverns, and even attend dances and parties. We became torn between wanting the war to end so that we could become free men, and fearing that the end would mean a resumption of our previous lives of slavery and desperation. Although the British had promised us our freedom, it became clear that they would not win this war and that the rebels might have revenge and enslavement on their minds, particularly for runaways who had fought against them.

Thomas had not embarked on further midnight wanderings. Now

he was calm, quiet, and peaceful, as if he had an internal source of wisdom that the rest of us did not. I found his new-found serenity barely tolerable but it was better than following him into unknown dangers at night. Besides, I knew that not only was Thomas not a saint, but he had more than his share of hidden sorrows and past mistakes. My nose had healed with a small lump on the bridge and slanted slightly to one side. Mary said it made me look like a hawk that had flown into a tree and bent its beak.

Mary was my strength.

At times I was frustrated with God for allowing the war to drag on. I worried that the British would leave us to the cruelties of the rebels and I worried that Thomas would not lead us out of our purgatory. Mostly I raged at myself. I had become accustomed to fighting, to settling scores through violence, and now was obliged to wait while others fought to determine an outcome that would shape my future. I had never stopped thinking about taking vengeance on my former masters, and although I had learned that satisfaction from revenge was fleeting, I was still driven to that remedy. My inactivity was a sore that festered and could only be cleansed through action. Worst of all, Mary would not marry me while the war continued.

It was clear she loved me, but it was also clear that Mary wanted to have a normal life, a life that did not mean meeting just once a week at church. I was rough and big and ugly and none of that mattered to Mary. She was faithful and stalwart. Mary was reasoned when I was not. She was as passionate as only a returning lover can be and as beautiful and lively as a summer storm. I was confounded by her love for me and afraid to talk of it in case it proved to be a sweet mist that would melt away if looked at directly. I could not believe my good fortune.

As the summer season wore on, it was impossible for me to think of a life without Mary.

"I wish you'd marry me."

"I will."

"Now, I mean. Why do we have to wait?"

"I've told you all this before. I want to get married in our own church, after the war, when we can have a house and a family, and live like regular folks. Besides, you're a soldier."

"Yeah."

"So you might get killed."

"Well we could all of us get killed at any time, I think."

In the fall of 1782 we began hearing rumors that the war was ending. We heard that the British were negotiating to pull the redcoats out of the colony and we began to get anxious. One day, with a cold wind whipping down the streets of New York, Colonel Blucke arrived at the barracks and called me over to a corner of the room.

"The war is over, at least for us."

"What do you mean?"

"I mean the British are pulling out."

"What's to become of us?"

"I don't know. One of the conditions in the peace agreement that they are arguing about is that all property taken in the war will be returned to the rebels. The slave owners are starting to come to New York to take back their runaways."

"What?"

"Yes, the British aren't sure what to do."

"But we're not property. We were given our freedom."

"So they said."

"I'll not go back as a slave."

"Yeah. Well some of the slaves in New York have already been taken by their owners back to the plantations. They were taken right out of their beds and sent back by ship."

It was terrible news. If the British were going to leave us to the mercy of the rebels, there was no hope of gaining our freedom. The best we could hope for was enslavement, but more likely the peace agreement would mean death for the members of the Black Brigade, who had fought so hard against them.

"What should we do?"

"Wait and see what happens and keep a low profile. You should keep your men close together and guard against anyone taking any soldiers from the unit. I know General Carleton is concerned about the agreement. I think he might change things here. I'll keep you informed."

Colonel Blucke went back to his headquarters. Thomas was obtaining supplies and did not return to the barracks until just before night. He was dismayed when I told him the Colonel's news and thought that we should take our leader's advice. We told the men to stay together when they left the barracks and to not cause any trouble in the town that might lead their former masters to descend upon them.

It was a mild winter to start 1783 and we were cooped up inside the barracks, still building bunks and rooms for no one. The men were worried and the pace of the work slackened from its already slow tempo. There was no word from Colonel Blucke. We felt like we lived in a secret fortress within New York, hidden from the slave hunters and blending into the background of the city.

We had not seen Sam for a very long time, although we heard that he had gone on many sorties with the British, taking care of their horses. The last we heard was a story of him going on board a ship bound for a raid further up the coast. He was to manage the horses and calm them. After that, there was no word of our friend at all. Several times I went to the stables to ask about Sam but there was never any news, either of him or of the ship he was on. Both had vanished.

In the spring, New York began to be evacuated. The white loyalists of the city boarded British ships bound for Nova Scotia or London. We still did not know our fate and our soldiers began talking darkly of fighting their way to the northern border. When Colonel Blucke came to the barracks for a second time, Thomas and I were not sure whether we should be encouraged or dismayed.

"Good news boys. We're to be protected. The British have said that any former slave who joined up with them will be considered free."

Thomas looked sideways at Blucke.

"That's great news from the British, but what do the rebels say?"

"They're not happy, but there's nothing they can do. They don't want to go back to fighting over it."

"Now what?"

"Now you're free. You'll be discharged from the British army. You'll receive a certificate allowing you to be evacuated from New York and you can go to London or to Nova Scotia or to Florida, if you want."

"When is this going to happen?"

"Not until everyone else is out. The Black Pioneers and the redcoats will be the last to go."

"Where are you going?"

"To Nova Scotia, I think. I see a lot of opportunity there for someone like me who has some contacts in the government."

Colonel Blucke's news was a huge relief for all of us. We sat on our bunks in the barracks and talked long into the night about our plans. Thomas and I both counseled caution since we were not out of New York yet and we were still worried about the slave hunters, but the men could think of little but their future freedom in a different country. Most of them wanted to go to Nova Scotia, where it was said there was abundant land and no slavery. Thomas was not so sure. Many of the loyalists had already departed for Nova Scotia and several had taken their slaves with them. It was hard to see how former runaways could live peacefully beside slave owners. It was clear to both of us that going to Florida would likely only mean enslavement again in the future. The alternative was to board a ship for London and it was even more uncertain how a former slave could make a life for himself in that country.

Mary resolved matters for me when I saw her that Sunday.

"I heard news about my mother."

"Jean. What kind of news? From where?"

"A redcoat told me. Who'd have thought that? He saw Jean a year ago when she was nursing him at the hospital across town. She knew I was in New York but she didn't know where I was. Anyway, he didn't know her, of course, but she came up to him and asked if he would keep his eyes open for me since he was heading for the redcoat barracks. He had the goodness to do it. He said she told him she was going to Nova Scotia and she'd try to track us down there."

"Mary."

"It is wonderful news, isn't it? I mean, how did she get away from Richardson's and how did she get on a British ship? But who cares? She's going to Nova Scotia and we'll see her soon and then she can tell us herself."

"Is that where you want to go?"

"Why sure. Of course. Where else would we go? We can get some land there and farm and raise a family, and my mother will be there. It will be perfect. It couldn't be any better. The redcoat said my mother told him that if he couldn't find me, to find you instead. She told him you and Thomas are heroes in the South. She said that all the slaves down South know your names and what you've done and especially where you came from."

"Thomas and I aren't sure about going to Nova Scotia. There's going to be a lot of loyalists with slaves there."

"Murphy, it has to be Nova Scotia."

"Did they give you and Sally freedom to be evacuated yet?"

"No, but they told us if we're married and our husbands got protection from the British to be evacuated, then we could go too. That was fine with Sally, of course, and I said I'm married and used your last name."

"Huh."

"What do you mean, 'Huh'?"

"Well it sounds like it's all right to be married to me to get on a ship but it's not all right to be just plain married for the sake of it."

Mary looked away from me and down at her hands. She was silent for a moment.

"Murphy, I took care of you when you were nearly dead. I've sat alone at night and wondered if someone was shooting you, or stabbing you, or maybe flogging you to death. I've wondered if you would even make it to the end of the war. All that and more I've thought and dreaded. I waited so that we can have a good life and I waited because you're a good man. You're the only man for me.

There, that's it. So don't you start feeling sorry for yourself. I'll marry you the minute our feet touch the ground in Nova Scotia, if you like. But don't start getting all weak and mopey and sorry for yourself. It doesn't suit you."

"Weak and mopey and sorry for myself?"

"That's just what I said."

"All right, but I'm going to hold you to your word in Nova Scotia."

"You do that, Murphy."

Now that the soldiers knew they were to be evacuated, it was hard to control their excitement. We continued to stay in the barracks in New York but we did no further work. We remained in the building most of the day as, despite the British sanction, there were still reports of bounty hunters stealing former slaves from the city. Later in the summer, as we were becoming both bored and anxious, we were moved to a tent encampment near the docks and were posted to help with the loading of the departing ships.

The dock was a busy place, with loyalists boarding ships bound for many different places. The ones going to Nova Scotia intrigued us the most, of course, and we took long looks at the loyalists boarding these. It was hard to watch those crowded vessels leaving for a land we were already beginning to think of as our own while we languished in New York, but it was not until the cold winds of November began to blow that we were told to board the *Joseph*.

Mary, Sally, Clairy, and the baby, John Peters, born late in the spring, met us at the dock. As we boarded the ship, a British officer checked off our names on a long list.

We cast off for Nova Scotia on a stormy day. The *Joseph* creaked and groaned as she turned before the strong wind, taking us to a land of peace, prosperity, and freedom, where we could make our home and begin our lives anew.

Nineteen

The wind that had blown us clear of New York had strengthened to a full gale within a few days. Two sails had blown away and most of the passengers were sick and miserable as the *Joseph* bucked and shivered through the waves. There was no relief in sight. Thick, dark clouds lined the horizon and the wind continued to push us farther and farther from Nova Scotia.

"Why does nothing come easy for us?"

Thomas looked up at me from where he kneeled on the deck of the *Joseph*. The ship gave a violent start. My friend had a wretched look on his face as he clutched at his stomach and gazed wildly around.

I didn't feel sick. The rolling of the ship did not bother my stomach and I ate well while others groaned on deck. I wondered where we were going to be when the storm ended and how seaworthy the ancient *Joseph* really was, particularly when two of the rusting old cannons at the stern broke their chains and went cascading over the side, taking part of the railing and a section of hull with them.

"I don't think it's all that bad. I mean, we're free, the air is fresh, and we've got nobody ordering us around. How bad can that be?"

But my friend was beyond conversation.

Captain Mitchell came up to me later that night as I stood at the railing watching the *Joseph* split the foaming waves and race across the Atlantic. He stood quietly for several minutes looking out over the stormy water.

"Quite a sight, isn't it?"

"Yes, I've never seen the likes of it before. It's really exciting."

"So you're not a sailor then. How is it you're not sick like everyone else? Even half of the crew is sick."

"It's an odd thing. I feel good, hungry actually, if anything."

"You must have a strong stomach."

The master of the *Joseph* leaned on the rail and looked straight down.

"Did you fight in the war?"

"Yeah, for a while we all did, but we sat around in New York for a time."

"Did you ever kill anyone?"

"Yeah."

"I never killed anyone. Not sure I could, really, although I've done some things that were on the shady side of the street."

"You could if you had to."

"Maybe. It feels strange to me to be hired by the redcoats, but they were running out of transport ships and I guess the timing was tight. I'm used to sailing this old girl and staying out of the way of the rebels, the British, and the police. I'm not much for sticking a knife in someone or shooting a musket."

"Me neither."

"What do you mean?"

"Shooting, I mean. I never could aim, and as for a knife, it was a case of sticking or being stuck. Anyone could do that."

"So you say, but there's some that are better than others. I think you're likely one of them."

"Maybe."

"It's Murphy, isn't it? You know what, Murphy?"

"What?"

"This is the part I like the best. Sailing in a really bad storm with who knows what to come, everyone sick but a few crew members.

150

It's better still for me with a hole in the hull and the railing off and the water coming in every time there's a big wave. When the wind is howling, the ocean is roaring, and the *Joseph* is riding along the tops of the waves like a mad horseman, well, that's the best part of life to me."

"You like that the best?"

"Yeah, it's the best of all. When I'm close to death, when I can actually feel my fear in my stomach and my head feels like splitting from the tension, that's the best. It's then that I feel that if I can get through this, I can live forever."

"Huh."

"It's the same for you, isn't it? I can see it in your face. You know that feeling when you're just about to die, but you don't. That's why you like the fighting, isn't it? It's when you know you're really alive."

I didn't say anything and we stood in silence at the rail. The only sounds were the smacking of the rain, the wind howling against the thumping lines, and the bow hissing through the waves.

"So what are you going to do in Nova Scotia?"

"I'm going to get a farm and maybe do some logging."

"How's that going to work?"

"What do you mean?"

"Well, I think it's hard to go from being really alive to being half-dead. Do you think being a farmer is going to be enough for you? The danger grabs you, doesn't it? You can't forget it. When it gets too quiet, you'll get an itch to stir up some trouble just to make sure you're still living. So what are you going to do about it in Nova Scotia? I've taken loads of soldiers to Nova Scotia before. Many of them are the same as you, not fit to live in civilized society."

"I think I'll be all right with the quiet."

"Maybe. I know I don't fit in. Every time I'm in port for a while, I get so I'm just thirsting to get back out here. Everything is too safe and already decided for me there."

"I think a bit of safety might be fine."

"You think that now, but after a while I'm thinking you'll want something that cuts closer to the bone."

"I want to make a life with a family and a home and quiet days."

"All I'm saying is that I think you'll find it hard to be happy sitting in front of a cozy fire in your house. You can try and maybe you can put it away in the back of your mind, but you're never going to be satisfied until you find yourself poking the dragon again. That's the way I am and that's why you and me are standing here watching this storm play with us."

"So does that mean we might be fixing to die out here?"

The captain took a long look at the sky and then out at the shrouded horizon.

"I would say no, not this time. Likely as not we can limp to Bermuda, I think. It all depends on how long this lasts, but I kind of doubt we'll be in Nova Scotia too soon. It's been nice talking to you, Murphy. If you ever get tired of farming, look me up. I could use a hand that doesn't ever get seasick."

Captain Mitchell turned and walked to the stern of the ship to look at the damaged hull. I stayed at the bow, watching the waves and wondering about Nova Scotia.

The storm played itself out the next day. The wind and rain died down and the waves stopped crashing against the hull. We staggered our way towards Bermuda and sailed into the harbor the following day under a clear blue sky. Flatts Village lay at the end of the inlet. It was a strange place with shacks and ramshackle houses clinging to the edge of the water and larger houses hanging off the hills surrounding the inlet. Captain Mitchell went directly ashore to arrange for provisions and workers from the boatyards to fix the hole in the *Joseph*. We stayed on board, lying on the deck in the hot sun.

Thomas, Mary, and Sally were recovering from their sickness. They were still gaunt and drawn, hollowed by the storm, while the children were already bored and restless. When Captain Mitchell returned from shore in the small rowboat, I asked him if I could take Clairy and little John into the village to look around. He was happy to let me use the boat.

There was not much to the village. There were a couple of ale-houses and shops but most of Flatts Village was made up of ordinary cabins, many small fishing huts, and several large plantation-style houses on the hills up from the water. The dock itself was surrounded by shanties and ship-building and repair yards. We wandered through the streets looking at the houses and poking our heads into the shops. Later, we walked up the winding road that curled up the hill. I put John on my shoulders and Clairy, now a young woman, walked along beside me. Near the top of the hill, looking out over the harbor, were a small church and a cemetery. The slaves of the town were buried on one side of the cemetery, where the land began to slope away. The masters were on the high side, on the far side of the church. I found this out when we began looking at the headstones and saw the names of the dead and their inscriptions. I had never seen that before. At Richardson's, the slaves held a service every Sunday in the barn while the master's family and foremen went to the brick church in town. We had our own graveyard at the farm, in the small field behind the schoolhouse, but only slaves were buried there. It was strange in Bermuda to see separate burial areas in the same churchyard. On the way back down the road and through the town, I looked more closely at the people and they stared back at us.

When we returned to the waterfront, we sat on the edge of the dock for a little while, looking back down the inlet to where the *Joseph* nestled in the calm waters of the harbor. The yards on either side of the dock were busy as the workers spent the winter months making repairs on the many vessels lined along the shore. It was a short row back to the *Joseph* and Thomas, looking brighter than I'd seen him for several days, helped us aboard.

Captain Mitchell hired workers to repair the *Joseph* but they would not be available for several weeks. Meanwhile, he met with British officers on shore and secured provisions. Thomas and I sometimes helped him ferry the food and supplies back to the ship, but most of the time we simply waited for the ship to be made whole again. We were all free to use the rowboat to go into town, but as there was not much to see in Flatts Village, most of our time was spent on board the ship. One day I did take the rowboat and

Mary and I went into the village. We thought we might work a little at a small farm up from the waterfront and buy some fresh fish on the dock.

As we walked up the hill, we passed a small staked pen near a large house. In this enclosure were four people, three men and a woman, sitting on the ground. Between them was a large bowl of fish scraps and yams and a jar of water. I stopped and talked to the man leaning against the side of the pen nearest the road.

"What are you doing in there?"

"Just waiting."

"For what?"

"Tomorrow. Tomorrow we get sold off."

"What do you mean?"

"You're new here, aren't you? The master died last week so now we're to be sold off at auction tomorrow."

"Are they afraid you'd run off?"

"Yep, and that's because I've already run twice. Look at my ears."

The man had stood up as we talked. I leaned my head through a large gap in the vertical stakes and looked at his face. He moved his head from side to side and I could see that his ears had been slit from the lobe all the way to the top so that each ear was sliced in half.

"See. One ear for each time I ran."

"There's not too many places to run to here, I would think, it being an island and all."

"Well you might be wrong there. There's lots of runaways in the caves by the sea. If you can get there, you got a chance of getting away. The masters don't like to go there because they know they might not come back. From there, maybe a person might sneak on a privateer or a pirate ship."

"How come the British don't put a stop to this?"

"Those lobster-backs aren't any use for anything. They come and they go but things just go on here like they always have."

Mary came over and asked me to walk on with her but I shook my head.

"So what will become of all of you?"

"We all have been salt-rakers so I expect that's what we'll keep doing after we're sold."

"What's salt-raking?"

The man in the cage gave me a strange look.

"You don't know much. Every year the ships go to Grand Quay and we set to work in the salt ponds. It's a horrible place. Each morning before the sun comes up we go to the salinas and we stand there all day, salt water up to our knees, raking the salt out. We get boiled corn for breakfast and blawly for lunch, and we stand there raking under the hot sun. When it gets dark we shovel up the salt we've raked all day into big heaps on the shore. Then we have more corn for dinner. Only relief we get is when it rains."

"Where does the salt go?"

"Master sells it to ships, but what I told you isn't the worst of it."

"What do you mean?"

"You stand in salt water all day you see what happens."

The man lifted up his leg and pulled his trousers back. The leg was covered in large red rings from his knee down to his ankle. His foot was one large patch of raw skin and his toes were all shortened with no nails. The top joint of each toe was gone. Mary, looking through another gap in the staked fence, gave a small gasp.

"Yessir, that's right and that's not the worst of it neither. These legs have healed; we haven't been in the salinas for quite a while now since you can't stay there in the winter. The salt eats away at everything, eats it right down to the bone. You can't ever get healed there, your legs get covered by boils and the skin falls off your feet so as you can't walk. Since you're standing out there all day in the heat of the sun, you get salt blisters on your back and the top of your head and they don't heal but stay open, leaking the whole summer."

"All of you do this work?"

"Yes. Lots of the slaves here are salt-rakers."

"What about the old man there? Is he a salt-raker too?"

I gestured towards an older man who was slumped against the far wall of the pen, his hand on his forehead.

"Yeah. Him too. Let me tell you what happened to him this past summer. He is older than most of the workers and he's been working the salt ponds for many years, but that doesn't count for anything with the master. He's not as fast as us and he finds it hard to wheel the barrow of salt through the sand, it being heavy and with his feet just about falling off with the sores and the salt water and the sand grinding into his skin. So the Buckra man stands watching this for a little while and then he goes and gets the long cow-skin and he starts whipping that poor old boy, just as hard as he can, across his back. Poor old Abel, he starts screaming but up he gets and starts pushing the barrow through the sand just as hard as he can. The next day it's the same thing and the next after that until his back is just one big raw ugly mess. Even that's not as bad as it really gets. Abel, come over here for a minute."

The old man, who I thought had been sleeping in the sun, grabbed hold of the fence and pulled himself to his feet. He didn't say anything but came over to where we stood.

"When we got back this year from Grand Quay, the master was very angry with Abel for not being able to work as hard as the rest of us. Every few days he whipped him with a briar stick so that his back would not heal. Look at this."

The man carefully lifted the back of Abel's shirt up. The cloth stuck to the old man's back and as it came loose the man grunted softly. Underneath the shirt was a most horrible sight. Abel's back was a mass of red, green, and gray flesh, all oozing blood and liquid. Each ragged island of flesh was edged by a clump of writhing maggots. His back looked like a map of the world I'd seen in a book a long time ago, with countries of different colors edged in white, except this map was alive and squirming in the hot sun. Mary, watching our conversation through the other hole in the fence, gasped again and went to sit by the side of the road, her head in her hands and her eyes looking at the dirt. I turned my head to watch her, then looked back at the men in the enclosure.

"Take them off. Are you humans or animals? How can you just leave them there on his back? Abel come here, I'll take them off myself if your friends won't help."

"No, sir, you can't do that. We did take them off at the beginning but then he got very sick and infected and had a bad fever and the worms came on faster than we could clean them off. After that, his back started to heal. The fact is they eat up the bad stuff. I swear he would be dead now without them. The master's gone and maybe he won't get whipped anymore. I think he'll heal up; those worms will eat up the bad skin and then we'll take them off."

I had never seen or heard anything like this before, but all I could do was stand still as the man nodded his head. Finally, I grabbed his arm.

"How can you stand all this?"

"What choice have we got? We run away, they catch us, it starts over again. There is nothing else. Maybe tomorrow we will be bought by a better master. Who knows? This is just the way the life is. Where are you from?"

"From the war in the States. We were on our way to Nova Scotia as free men but we got blown off course and landed here."

"Were you a slave before?"

"Yes. Then I was a runaway and fought in the war and now I'm a free man."

"Then you shouldn't ask how we stand it. You should know. Is that your wife?"

"Soon to be. Are you married?"

"Soon to be. That's her over there. Her name is Sarah."

"I'm Murphy. She's Mary."

"Ben's my name."

"Well, Ben, I think we'll be going. Is there anything I can do for you?"

"Can you buy me at the auction?"

"Sorry."

"Then it will be good-bye. Thanks for stopping. I enjoyed our conversation."

I called to Mary and we started walking back down the hill. We had lost our appetite for work or food and neither of us looked back at the pen.

We did not go back into town for many days. We were content to stay on the *Joseph* and somehow afraid to venture into Flatts Village, as if we thought we might be seized and forced to work in the salt ponds. Neither of us spoke of our encounter with Ben, but I knew that Mary thought about it as often as I did. As the repairs on the ship slowly began, it became clear to all of us that we would not be leaving Bermuda until the spring, and we became resigned to not arriving in Nova Scotia until much later than we had expected.

In March, an unexpected snow fell on Flatts Village; large flakes drifted down out of the sky and settled silently on the *Joseph*. The snow couldn't last, but it felt vaguely like New York, with the houses downy and silent. I was standing at the rail with Thomas, not talking but watching the snow fall on the tame water of the harbor. Each flake dissolved into an icy skeleton on the water before that too melted away. My friend's brow was knotted as he turned to me.

"Murphy, why isn't Blucke on this ship?"

"Well, you know he left earlier for Nova Scotia."

"I know that, but how is it he got to leave earlier and we're stuck here not even in Nova Scotia yet? Why isn't he the last one to leave, being our leader and all?"

"I don't know. Does it matter?"

"I'm not sure. It might matter if when we get there there's no land left or all the good land's been given to those who got there first."

"I hadn't thought of that."

"Here's what I think. I think Blucke always considers himself first and makes sure his interests are taken care of. I think we have to remember that about him. I also think we might be at a disadvantage getting to Nova Scotia so late. Maybe not, but it worries me. I wish we could get going."

"Soon, I think. The repairs are done and we're just waiting for better weather."

"Sooner the better."

Despite the spring snowfall, the days were getting warmer. We began to load barrels of salt and flats of tobacco leaves into the ship.

The loading of the *Joseph* took an amazing amount of time. A loaded barge had to be put off from the dock and the barrels rolled up a long plank into the hold of the ship. The ship took many barge loads. One day, as I was helping the crew with the heavy barrels, Captain Mitchell called me over to where he was standing near the rail.

"We'll be ready to go in two days."

"Finally."

"I thought you might say that. Are you going to the race tomorrow?"

"What race?"

"They race those small boats around the harbor every spring. They call them dinghies but they're actually bigger. This year's race is tomorrow."

"I didn't know about it."

"It's best to watch from the dock, I think. If you and your men want, I'll send the barge out tomorrow and it will take you to the dock."

"That would be fine."

The next day, the barge arrived at mid-morning and the Black Brigade got on board. Sally was worried about the drinking on shore during the race so she and the children stayed back on the *Joseph*. All the other passengers and the sailors made the short trip across the harbor to the shore, where a noisy crowd had already gathered. Two dinghies were bobbing in the water by the dock. Farther out in the harbor, a course had been laid out with floating flags. I was standing on the dock looking at the small boats when one of the members of the crew came up to me.

"Murphy."

"Ben. What are you doing here?"

"The new master put me on his dinghy."

"Do you know anything about it? Racing, I mean."

"No. One of the crew got sick so the new master bought me just to fill in. He said I didn't need to know about sailing as long as I did what I was told. Mostly what I'll be doing is bailing."

"What's bailing?"

"The boats get full of water so my job is to take this pail and bail it out as fast as I can so we don't sink. Less water means we go faster, I guess."

"Do you mean you might actually sink during the race?"

"Lots of boats sink in this race when they get full of water. My other job is to dive off the back if the captain tells me to. Good thing is, I don't need my sorry feet for bailing or diving."

"You mean jump right off the boat in the middle of the race?"

"Yes. There's six crew and if we want to go faster we jump off one by one during the race. Sometimes just the captain is left at the end but usually there's the captain and one other crew member."

"Six crew in this little boat."

"Yeah."

"Is the master the captain of the boat?"

Ben laughed.

"You're funny. The crew members are slaves and the master bets on the winner. There's a lot of money changing hands and lots of bragging after the race, especially from the man who owns the winning boat."

"So what do the crews get?"

"There's a big dinner tonight with turtle meat and lots of fish and lots of drink."

"Have you raced before?"

"No, but I watched before. I'll be all right. I can bail for sure. That's all I've got to do."

"And diving off maybe."

"Yeah."

"Well, good luck, Ben."

Mary and Thomas stood beside me as we watched the race. Ben's boat lagged behind the other for the first part of the race. I could see him bailing frantically, head down, as the dinghies turned towards the finish. Just as they made the turn, with the other boat well in the lead, a crew member dove off the back of the dinghy. The boat seemed to stop as the man jumped off, then took a big leap forward. Quickly, another member of the crew dove off and Ben's boat drew level with its competitor.

The two boats remained level as they drew closer to the finish line. The dinghy captain and Ben were the lone surviving crew members in one boat, while the captain alone was left in the other racer. The second boat had shed two crew members at a time as the distance to the finish got shorter and, finally, the bailer had jumped overboard. With less than thirty feet to the finish line and the boats even, Ben stood up at the stern of his dinghy and smoothly dove over the hull, pushing with his feet against the rail at the back of the boat. The little dinghy gave a small shake as he dove off and then jumped forward, pushing ahead of its competitor just in time for the flag at the finish. The crowd on shore gave a huge cheer as Ben's boat finished ahead of its rival, and I saw several people slapping the back of a florid-faced man in a large, white shirt. Ben swam swiftly to shore and pulled himself up on the dock. The other crew members who had jumped off the dinghy earlier in the race had been picked up by a rowboat in mid-harbor and were returning slowly to shore.

"Good race, Ben."

"Yeah. I'm about done in though."

"What now?"

"Now the party will start and there'll be dinner later."

"It looks to me like the whole town is here."

"It'll go on all night."

"Ben, come on over here. I want to talk to you for a minute."

Ben and I walked over to a corner of the quiet boatyard. Mary looked at me as we left but she and Thomas stayed by the dock as the other crew members came in. Already the rum was being passed around and men were gathering in groups along the waterfront, but there was no one near the boatyard.

"Ben, do you want to get out of here?"

"What do you mean?"

"We're leaving tomorrow for Nova Scotia. You could stow away on the ship."

"I can't leave here. They'll come after me."

"No, they won't. The *Joseph* is a British ship, commissioned by the redcoats. Nobody is going to come after us."

"But if the captain finds me?"

"Yeah. That's the risk all right but we'll hide you. We've got a full cargo and there will be lots of hiding spots."

Ben looked across the water at the *Joseph* lying heavy in the harbor.

"How would I get out there?"

"That's the beauty of it. Tonight you could leave after the dinner and the party. When everyone is drinking, no one will notice you gone and we'll row you out. There won't be anyone on the *Joseph* because they're all going to be on shore. No one will know you're gone for a day or so."

"What about Sarah?"

"She can come too. Abel too and the other fellow. There's enough room for all four of you, if you want."

"Let me think for a minute."

Ben walked into the woodshop and sat on a short bench. He picked up a piece of curled shaving and idly drew it through his fingers, back and forth, watching his hand with a vacant look.

"There is nothing for me here but work and pain. Sometimes when I'm raking the salt and the sun is beating hard on my head, I dream of being free. You know, I kind of go into a sleep, like I'm not really there. I mean, I'm up to my knees in salt, my legs are sore, but my mind is somewhere else. Murphy, I'll tell you what I dream but don't laugh at me."

"What do you dream?"

"I dream of a place where it's cold, where the sun warms my arms but the wind is cold and never hot. Where the water is cold on my legs, so cold that my feet get numb, and the wind blows so I have to wear a coat and a hat all the time. A place where I can plant and tend some pigs, maybe a sheep or a cow. In my dream nobody ever tells me what to do. There are no Buckra men with long terrible whips."

"That's our dream too. All the Black Pioneers are runaways. We're free men now but it wasn't always that way. We had to push

162

and push and push, until they got tired of pushing back."

"I've run twice before. They caught me both times. They gave me these ears. Next time it's the hanging tree for me."

"Ben, don't you see my cheek? They gave Thomas and me that brand when we ran the second time. That was after they flogged us so we nearly died. You have to push back until they're more afraid of you than you of them. If you want to live your dream, you're going to have to take that chance. I can't do it for you."

"Who's Thomas?"

"He's my friend. He's going to meet you at the *Joseph* when I row you there."

"I'm just not sure and I can't speak for Sarah and the others."

"All right. Here's the thing. Thomas and Mary and I will row out to the *Joseph* and we'll wait for a few hours. We'll wait until we hear the voices carrying strong and loud and drunk over the water. Then I'll row back and wait for you by the dock. If you want to come with us, meet me there. I'll wait for an hour or so."

"All right."

We walked together back to where the benches and tables were being set up for the upcoming banquet. I was relieved to see that the eating area was set well back from the waterfront where I would be waiting for Ben in a few hours. Mary and Thomas were sitting and talking on a bench. They both rose when we came up and I introduced Ben to Thomas. Mary and I began walking down to the barge and the rowboat. Thomas jogged to catch up to us. We climbed down into the boat and I picked up the oars and began slowly rowing back to the *Joseph*. We didn't talk but both Mary and Thomas looked at me sideways as we worked our way towards the ship. Finally, Thomas laughed and threw a piece of yellowed rope at me.

"Hell, Murphy, what is it you want us to do? You look like a man who swallowed a peach pit. Why don't you just spit it out?"

"It's about Ben."

"Well for God's sake. We know what it's about, we just want to know what it is you want us to do."

Mary looked up at me, her eyes sparkling.

"Murphy, do you think we just ran into you on the street? Thomas and I have been talking about how we were going to get Ben and Sarah off this hideous place, but it looks like you already have it figured out. So why don't you just share it with us?"

I told them of my simple plan and where they fit in. Thomas would be waiting on the *Joseph* at the ladder to help the runaways up on the deck and Mary would take them to the hold and hide them behind the barrels of salt or beneath the leaves of tobacco. Sally would get them food and water to keep them during the voyage to Nova Scotia.

We waited anxiously on the *Joseph* for the party onshore to get into full swing. There were no sailors or Black Pioneers left on the ship so I was not worried about being discovered. I was only worried about Ben. I was most anxious that he take the chance. I felt like it was my own life in the balance. I leaned on the rail, the night passing slowly and the noise from the party onshore getting more and more raucous. Finally, with many lights on the shore and the singing and yelling at its peak, I climbed down to the rowboat and pushed off.

When I got to the dock, I could see Ben, Sarah, and Abel standing together. I turned to Ben.

"You been waiting long?"

"Yeah. We didn't want to miss you. Then we were afraid you might not come."

"I said I'd come."

"You might have changed your mind when you thought about the risk. To you, I mean."

"I'm not scared for myself. Mostly I was afraid you might decide to stay in this hell-hole."

"No. I'm ready. Sarah is too."

"Where's the other fellow?"

"David? He's not here, he was bought by a privateer and they've gone wracking."

"Wracking?"

"Yeah, diving on wrecks to get supplies and whatever they've got on board. It's tough."

"Sounds hard."

"Lots of men drown. It's hard to hold your breath for so long and the wrecks are deep. Sometimes you've got to go inside them and it's very easy to get hung up and not be able to get back to the surface."

"You ever done this wracking?"

"I did once, a long time ago, when I was younger. I was stronger then but still it was very bad and always dangerous. I was lucky because my master sold me off quickly enough when he saw I didn't have the lungs for it, but I don't know if it's worse than salt raking. In the one, there's always the risk of drowning, but the other is like a slow death. I don't know. They're both bad in different ways."

"What about Abel?"

"Ask him."

Abel had been standing off to one side while Ben and I talked. The old man had a frightened look on his face.

"Abel, are you going to come with us?"

"Not sure."

"Well now's the time to be sure. You can stay here and get whipped for the rest of your life. Or you can take a chance to get away."

"I was born here. This place is all I know."

"Well it looks to me like you'll be looking to die here pretty soon if you stay on this island."

Ben turned to the old man.

"You can stay if you want. We're not going to make you go, but we have to leave."

"It's just that my friends are here, everyone I know. I don't know any other place. I can't imagine living anywhere else and I'm not young like you fellows. I'm an old man and it's late to make changes and take risks. It's the risks, don't you see? I'm not scared to die but it's the risk of leaving somewhere I know and going somewhere I don't know. I'd like to go. I really would like to go, but I can't. Can you see that? I just can't leave here where everybody knows me. I know things are bad but they could be worse somewhere else. It's not getting caught. I'd take that risk. It's the not knowing about the future. The devil you know is better. That's what I mean. I wish I was young but I'm just too old now. That's it I guess."

"All right, Abel."

We climbed into the boat and Abel pushed us off from the dock. Ben turned to the old man, his wide eyes glistening in the dark.

"Good-bye, old friend. Get someone to check on your back and try to stay out of trouble."

"You too."

We rowed into the night and finally the *Joseph* loomed up before us. Thomas was waiting at the top of the ladder and took Ben and Sarah by the hands as they climbed aboard. I tethered the rowboat to the side of the ship. By the time I climbed the ladder, both of the runaways were nowhere to be seen. Thomas gave me a hand up.

"Now we hope for the best in Nova Scotia."

"Yeah."

"Just the two of them?"

"One is already gone. The old man wouldn't come."

"Huh. That's too bad."

"Just too settled in. Even though it's bad for him here, it's still his home, I guess. Can't say I ever thought that way myself."

"You're not old, though."

"Thanks for helping out on all this. You didn't have to."

"Yeah, I did."

"I guess maybe you did at that."

The *Joseph* lay quietly in the harbor and we sat the long night on the deck, waiting for the new day that would take us closer to Nova Scotia.

Twenty

It was not until just before noon of the next day that we heard the barge bumping against the side of the *Joseph*. It was full of complaining sailors returning from Flatts Village. Some of the men had taken up with women in the village and were living in small shacks along the curve of the harbor. They did not want to leave the warmth and cozy beds of Bermuda for the spare life on board the ship. The sailors had posted lookouts to warn of the approach of the ship's officers, but Captain Mitchell was not easily fooled and scoured the area until every crew member was located, before they could run to the caves along the coast.

The captain was in an ill humor as he made his way up the ladder and gave a terse order to get under way as soon as the last sailor's foot hit the deck. The crew was in a desperate state and several of the sailors leaned against the lines, morose and hungover. Others lay stretched full out on the deck. The brigade soldiers kept carefully apart from this group, anxious to be leaving the shore of that benighted island.

Captain Mitchell watched carefully as the *Joseph* slowly made her way to open water. He came up to me as I stood at the stern of the ship looking at the shoreline which was falling behind. As we left the inlet, a cannon was fired from shore.

"Know what that is?"

"No."

"There's to be a hanging today. Pequot slave, Quashi, killed his master. The cannon's calling everyone."

"So it's not to mark our leaving, or to shoot at us?"

Captain Mitchell smiled and shook his head. He walked over to his mate and they stood talking as the brisk ocean air filled the sails of the *Joseph*. Even the most wretched of the sailors was now hard at work. It was a fine day and we were on our way to our new home in Nova Scotia once again.

In Bermuda, I had seen slavery in forms I had not previously known. There were poor white men on that island too, indentured to their masters and slaves in everything but name, and there were others, sharecroppers, beholden to their landlords and grubbing out a hopeless existence. On that luckless island, many slaves were Pequot or other tribes, captured and sent to work in the tobacco fields. Others, like Ben and Sarah, were bought or stolen from rebel owners. The common thread, through the salt workers to the bought slaves to the sharecroppers and the indentured poor, was the ownership of one man by another for economic advantage, the imposition of will by the powerful on the weak.

I enjoyed standing on the deck of the *Joseph* in the night, the ebony dome above pricked with stars and the wind steady on the sails. Leaning on the rail at the bow, I could watch the ship as it cleaved through the sea, the water curling over itself in silver foam, stark and clear against the surrounding dark.

Thinking about my friends, I saw that Thomas and Mary and Sally had real courage, the kind of aching steadiness that only true believers own. It is one thing to be brave in battle. It is greater still to be brave on the scaffold, alone against a hostile and jeering crowd. But to be steadfast and constant when the future is dark and uncertain and when you do not know for months and years at a time if your husband is dead or wounded or captured—that is real bravery.

The stowaways, going to an unknown land on an uncertain ship and relying absolutely on people barely met, impressed me with their trust and courage. I wondered about this in the dark as we sailed like a ghost ship into the night. So many had died. The runaways now were running not from their masters but from a whole nation. We hoped for freedom in Nova Scotia but could it be? I had never seen a place where all men had an equal chance.

The loyalists, those men we had fought beside in the war for the States, often owned slaves of their own. After the war they would return to their farms and businesses, run in their absence by their slaves. Some of these loyalists would be our neighbors in Nova Scotia, still with slaves, as natural to them as their ownership of horses and cattle.

* * *

We did not want to bring attention to where Ben and Sarah were hiding, so we did not go near them until the second day of the trip. Thomas then gathered up some bread and pork to take to the couple. They had hardly stirred from their hidden corner and did not talk as we gave them the food.

Our voyage to Nova Scotia lasted eight days. As we came close to land, Thomas was occupied with the problem of getting Ben and Sarah off the *Joseph* without either Captain Mitchell or the officials on shore seeing them. If they were spotted they would be sent back to Bermuda, likely to the hangman's noose, and we could be sent back to a miserable fate in the States. We contemplated several plans as we stood on deck and I often thought of bizarre schemes while I stood alone at the rail at night. My nighttime thoughts were fanciful and without merit in the hot blast of daylight.

One night I was at the stern of the ship, throwing stale bread into the water for the gulls, when Captain Mitchell came up to me.

"Send him off with the crew."

"What?"

"We'll be ashore tomorrow. You take your soldiers and their families off so they can get checked off the list by the customs man. Then I'll send the crew to shore for leave. It's done all the time."

"Yeah?"

"Put your man in with the crew. Nobody ever checks who's in the crew. The sailors change all the time—some run away and we get new ones at the ports we're at."

169

"My man?"

"The stowaway. Murphy, please don't insult me. Do you think I'm blind or stupid? Do you think I don't know every inch of the *Joseph*? There's someone hiding behind the barrels in the hold. I've not been back there so as to not have to deal with it in front of the sailors, but it has to be a slave from the island, I figure. Here's what you do. Tell him to wait until your soldiers are all checked off. Then I'll give leave to the crew. I can tell you they'll be gone in a rush and the shore officials will leave then, too. Tell your fellow to wait until they're all gone, then he can leave just ahead of me. If anyone on shore asks, I'll just say he's a sailor."

"Why would you do that?"

"I don't cotton to slavery. Never have."

"Huh."

"Well, I'll tell you, Murphy. I think we should act with good grace towards each other. What do you think of that? It sounds simple, doesn't it? That's what I was taught and that's how I try to live. It sounds easy but if you try to live it you'll find out soon enough you'll be a threat and a problem to a whole lot of people. There'll be all sorts of folks, most folks, really, who'd like nothing better than to string you up. That's the truth of it, I'm sorry to say."

"They may catch up to you later on this thing."

"Slavery is an abomination, plain and simple. We might as well be animals if we're going to allow it. Not me, I'll take my chances like I always have. I'm not perfect by a long, long shot and I've done many things I'm not proud of. I expect there will be a few more yet and some of them likely on the wrong side of the law but I've tried to act towards people with good will, if they'll let me. The damned pasty-faces haven't slowed me down yet and I don't stay on shore long enough for them to grab me there neither. There aren't too many police officers on the ocean. I'll tell you something else."

"What?"

"You be careful of yourself on shore. Everyone will just be dying to be the next mayor or president or some damn thing. When they start talking that way, when they start saying they're being asked to serve all of you by being the one who tells you what to do, you start running the other way. Nothing worse than somebody looking to tell you what to do and telling you they're doing it for your own good. If ever things get really bad, you look me up, I'll have a bunk for you."

"Thanks. There is one thing."

"What?"

"There's two of them stowed away. One's a woman."

Captain Mitchell pushed his cap off his forehead and looked over at me with a little smile on his face.

"Well I'll be. That is a surprise, but it's no matter, just do like I said. They can both come out. Let the man go first and the woman can go behind me. If anyone asks, I'll say she was someone I picked up in Bermuda to keep my bed warm."

We sailed into the harbor at Shelburne. Captain Mitchell set off with a sailor in the rowboat and we waited impatiently on the deck of the *Joseph*. We could see little of the town but there were several small fishing boats bobbing on the water near our anchor. After a couple of hours, the captain came back with the tender and climbed on board with a heavy step. He called Thomas and me over.

"There's no room for you here."

"What do you mean?"

"They say there's too many settlers already. They don't want any more. They say we have to go around to Annapolis Royal. I'm sorry, but that's what we're going to do."

Captain Mitchell turned to his mate and told him to make sail for Annapolis. I looked over at Thomas.

"This is not a good start."

"No, and I wonder where Blucke is. Could be he's already settled in while we're wandering around. I'll bet he's got his land already."

It was not a long voyage around the peninsula to the Bay of Fundy and then to the Annapolis Basin. Our excitement on arriving at Nova Scotia had been etched with anxiety at actually finding a place where we would be given the land we had been promised, but the harbor at Annapolis was perfect, with neat white houses lined along the shore and a large number of British guns facing the bay.

A British officer counted off the names of the Black Pioneers and their families as we left the *Joseph*. Thomas and I waited nervously on the dock as Captain Mitchell addressed the crew and gave them leave. We had told Ben and Sarah to wait until the crew were off and then come out of their hiding place and off the *Joseph*. The British officer turned away as the last of the passengers disembarked. He paid little attention to the crew members laughing and jostling as they spilled onto the dock. He did not, however, go back into the customs office, but stopped where Thomas and I leaned against a squat iron pillar. He looked directly in my eyes as he talked.

"Are you fellows waiting for something?"

"Yeah. We're waiting to say good-bye to the captain and thank him for the fine trip."

He nodded and turned to walk away. I could see Ben leaving the *Joseph* and walking stiff-legged along the edge of the dock. Sarah stood at the edge of the ship, stretching out her legs, with Captain Mitchell directly behind her. The customs official turned back to me as Ben walked slowly along the dock.

"Do you know where you're going?"

"Not really. To town, I guess."

"Nope, I think they're taking you to Digby. You're supposed to muster at the square. Here comes the captain now so you can say your good-byes."

The British officer turned to Captain Mitchell, who was just stepping off his ship, but his gaze quickly shifted to Sarah, who was walking unsteadily along the dock. Ben was nowhere to be seen, having stumbled around the corner of the customs office.

The officer looked hard at Sarah, then called to Captain Mitchell.

"Sir. Sir. Who is that?"

The captain, walking calmly away from his ship, turned slightly and slowed, but did not stop.

"Just a likely little thing I picked up."

"Is she yours?"

"Yeah, well I guess you could say she's part of the crew if you want. You might say she's for entertainment."

The British officer gave a short laugh.

"Wait a second. These men want to talk to you."

He shook his head once and walked back towards his office.

Thomas and I caught up to Captain Mitchell, who was now striding purposefully up to Sarah and off the dock. Mary and Sally had taken the children and Ben well up the road into town.

"See, Murphy. I told you there was nothing to it."

"You should be a pirate with that sort of nerve."

"So they say. Where are you off to now?"

"They say we're going to Digby to settle. We're meeting at the square."

The captain's eyes narrowed.

"One place after another. It seems like you fellows are bound to wander and wander."

Captain Mitchell smiled and reached into his pocket. He took out a small jingling bag and gave it to me.

"Here's something to help you on your way to prosperity if you ever do find a place to settle."

I stopped walking and opened the small string on the top of the bag. There were coins, mostly pennies but several shillings mixed in, the first money I could ever call my own. Thomas, standing at my side, did not say anything but looked at Captain Mitchell with a thoughtful look on his face. I was silent, thinking of the man who had already risked much for us and now gave more.

"I don't know what to say."

"Well then, don't say a word. It's not much but who knows, it might come in handy some time. You go on with Thomas and get to the square, but remember, you're free men now and you've been promised land by the British. Don't let them weasel out of it. If things get too bad, you get down to Shelburne and ask for me. They'll know where to find me."

Captain Mitchell shook our hands and took off in the direction of the grog shop. Thomas and I met up with our families and walked towards the meeting area.

The members of the Black Pioneers and their families milled aimlessly around the meeting area while several British officers talked together at the front of the crowd. Finally, a sergeant called for silence and we stood quietly as an officer told us that we were to go to Digby, which would be a fair hike over a rough road. Most of us would be able to go on wagons, as would the supplies and tents. We walked over to a wagon waiting by the road and put Mary, Sarah, and Sally with the children on the back. Ben climbed in with them and Thomas and I sat on the seat. A team of two small grays nodded in the morning heat, the flies swarming above their twitching necks. Being on that wagon brought me back in time to when Thomas and I had lain, hidden, in the back of a similar cart for day after day on our way to Wilmington. Now we were driving and our family and friends sat as bright as day in the back.

The trip to Digby was a slow affair, with the wagons of the brigade stretched out for several miles. The trail between Digby and Annapolis was well-worn but uneven, and generally followed the coastline. After we had been traveling for several hours, we made one detour inland to cross a large river and got to Digby just before dark. It was a shabby-looking place in the twilight, the only dwellings consisting of small huts and shacks gathered together around the wharf. The smoke from the cooking fires in these cabins hung around the town like a greasy shroud.

We set up a tent town just outside of Digby at a place the British called Brindley. We fed and watered the horses at a poor paddock and ate a military meal of pork and biscuits. Thomas came over to me as I sat on a log, mopping up the pork juice with a thick crust.

"Not much, is it?"

"Nope."

"Still, it is something, and I expect we can make it better. Will you and Mary start building tomorrow?"

"I figure we will once we know where we can."

"Yeah, I guess that will be the next thing."

In that, Thomas was wrong. The real next thing, as soon as my friend went back to Sally and his children, was to lie in my tent, Mary curled up next to me. It wasn't our home, just a way-station, but it was ours, together, and that was something good to hold on to.

Twenty-One

The town looked no better in the morning light.

Mary elbowed me in the ribs and pushed herself up so that she sat hunched over with the top of her head just touching the tent wall. She had opened up the front flap of the tent and the morning light streamed in.

"Murphy, will you get up and have a look?"

I scrambled out of the tent and looked back towards Digby. A fog had rolled in off the ocean during the night and mixed with the grime of the cooking fires. The gray mist floated a short distance above the ground so that the tops of the spruce trees were cut off and the sun was a vague glow. Digby itself was a collection of dark shadows in the fog, with buildings shifting in and out of the gloom. The whole place had a kind of underworld feel to it with topped trees, barely-seen buildings, and residents drifting just slightly beyond sight.

Mary crawled out of the tent and stood beside me.

"Tough to look at," I said.

"I don't know about that. It looks like home to me."

All around us on the grassy field were the tents of the Black Pioneers and their families. The British had put up three large tents of their own where the tall grass was overtaken by the spruce and aspen of the surrounding forest. Thomas, Sally, Clairy, and little John had a tent next to ours. Sally was cooking breakfast over a

175

small campfire. Ben and Sarah had their tent on our other side but were sitting on big rocks around Sally's cooking fire.

"Murphy and Mary, come on over and have a bite."

We went over and Sally dished out eggs, pork, and sharp-smelling coffee. Thomas was anxious to see the British agent to get our provisions squared away and determine where we could start to build. I had barely finished my cup when he jumped up and started towards the British headquarters. Ben, Mary, and Sarah stayed behind to help Sally tidy up the campsite.

The British commissary, Williams, was a stump of a man. He was not happy with our arrival, which took him away from his breakfast. We sat like supplicants across his table as he sopped up his plate of eggs with a soggy crust. He looked carefully at Thomas.

"What do you boys want?"

"We'd like to know about the provisions. We'd also like to find out where we can build and get some lumber and tools."

Williams wiped his chin with a dirty rag and belched.

"Provisions are coming just as fast as they can. Boards and shingles too. As to where to build, guess you're going to have to wait a while for that."

"What are we waiting for?"

"The surveying's not done. The surveyor hasn't finished drawing up the lots for the farms. In fact, he hasn't even finished drawing up the town lots. It could be we don't quite know where to put you fellows just yet. Not that we don't want to find a place for you, of course. We're just not sure where that place is."

In the corner of my eye, I could see Thomas glancing sideways at me but I didn't say anything and kept looking straight at the ground. My friend spoke up, an edge in his voice.

"When do you figure on having all that surveying done?"

"Well, I don't know. It's not up to me. It's up to Millidge, the surveyor. He'll have to check with the governor, of course, who will have the final say on things. But as to provisions, they should be here later today. We wouldn't want you people starving."

Williams gave a little laugh.

"You're Peters, aren't you?"

"Yep."

"I heard about you. Guess you'll be Steele, then. I've heard about both of you. You fellows will be the ones in charge of the provisions when they get here."

Thomas stood up.

"We've taken an awful long time and gone an awful long way to get here and we don't intend on waiting too much longer. We want this surveying done as fast as it can so we can finish building before the winter."

"Well now, we just want to make sure everything is checked out and fine. No need to get all upset about things."

"Is Blucke around here anywhere?"

"Colonel Blucke?"

Thomas put both of his hands flat on the table.

"Here's the question. It's actually pretty simple—is Colonel Blucke here? He's our commanding officer and I'd expect him to want to take things in hand here."

"He's in Shelburne, I think."

"Has he got his land?"

"I think he's got a house in town and a farm outside."

"Williams, you need to get this surveying done really soon and you need to get us supplies for the year. We have to get houses up, a town built, and farmland cleared. I don't quite know what the problem is, but we're not just going to sit here in our tents starving for the whole summer. All of this should have been done before we got here."

And with that, Thomas turned and walked away from the table. I stood up and left without a word, Williams looking after us with a surly smile on his face.

I wasn't sure whether the simple process of getting the town surveyed was going slowly because of design or neglect. I had seen before that it was generally hard to tell in these messes whether the fellow flat-out disliked you and was messing things up on purpose, or was just inept.

Lack of action can be blamed on either one and it can be convenient to be usually negligent and lazy so that a specific and

177

focused inactivity will be set aside as common practice by outside observers. Thomas had a different idea altogether. His thought was that Williams and Millidge were likely both in the pocket of some land profiteer in Nova Scotia.

Any lingering goodwill I had towards the British agent was ground up like so much dust when our provisions failed to arrive. Thomas and I went to see Williams every day that first week. Every day he told us our food would arrive the next morning. The British army doled out enough food to enable us to get through each day, but we felt like beggars with our hands out as the sun ate away each morning's heavy mist.

We had been promised to be supplied with provisions for three years, which would be long enough for us to plant our feet on the ground and be able to make our own way. It was obvious to all the veterans that, having fought for the British in the conflict in the States, we deserved compensation.

It is a plain fact that idleness and uncertainty breed discontent and impatience, so it was no surprise to Thomas or me that, as the days of inactivity stretched on, fights between tenting neighbors became more frequent. Some little character flaw, easily tolerated in times of industry, would now set long-time friends into a fierce argument. We had no real solution for the general lassitude in the camp.

Mary and I went for long walks. We would take off shortly after breakfast, sometimes with Clairy and John but more often by ourselves. Thomas wanted to stay in camp to keep peace among the men and prod Williams. Sally would not go without him and Ben and Sarah were too sore still to go any distance.

Sometimes we walked into the woods and other times back along the trail to Annapolis. Mostly we strolled along the big rocks around the shore. I came to know the shoreline in the area very well. One place in particular struck me. It was a small cove where the water, deep and black, rose to a single sheet of rock just offshore. Twenty feet out, the water was very deep and then, as if placed exactly by a giant's hand, a single sheet of red rock rose like a ramp straight from the bottom. At the shore, the rock shelf went right up to the puny and stunted spruce trees that guarded the fringe of the looming forest.

Mary and I often sat on the edge of the shelf and speculated on the depth of the ocean and on when we would finally get our land. We also wondered what would become of Ben and Sarah.

The two stowaways had blended easily into the camp. By never talking too loudly and staying in the background, Ben and Sarah had come to be accepted by all the families. The British, still trying to figure out what to do with all of us, never noticed that there was an extra family. After the initial roll call coming off the boat we were never mustered and Thomas warned me repeatedly not to think of the men as still under our command. The Black Pioneers had been disbanded in New York, but of course the soldiers were as loyal as ever to Thomas.

One day as we were sitting by the edge of the shelf watching the waves roll in close to our feet and eating our lunch of pork and biscuits and wild strawberries, Mary asked me when I planned on marrying her. I laughed and stroked her cheek.

"Bold as brass and twice as shiny."

That's what I said and she laughed back, coiled like a mermaid on the smooth rock.

"Fortune favors the bold, so they say. Besides which, if I waited for you to get on with it I'd be an old maid. As if I'm not one already, and that's your fault too."

"Now how would that be my doing? I would have married you back in New York, but I seem to recall you saying no, so I don't see how this is on me now."

"Oh, I see; I see now what it is you've been waiting for all these long days. How could I have been so blind? Please, please forgive me Murphy."

And she raised up on one knee in front of me.

"Murphy Steele, will you marry me?"

Before I could swallow, she got a little piece of driftwood out of her pocket and held it in her palm. The smoothed wood had a hole just the size of a finger right through the middle.

"Well, I don't know. I've had a lot of offers, especially lately. Seems there's more of a demand for a worn-out old veteran than you might think."

179

"Is that a fact? I think you need to do more thinking about women. It seems your education is lacking in that area. Else you'd know what they say about a woman scorned."

I looked over at my Mary and laughed harder than I had for a long time. She told me that she'd heard there was a traveling preacher who made rounds of the country, and the next time he was out we could get married. We didn't know if he was a Baptist or an Anglican or some other denomination and we didn't care. A whole lot of my God-fearing had dribbled out of me over the fighting years and the biggest part of it had left when God called on me to tell the generals to stop fighting. Nobody had listened then and I figured that if God couldn't make the killing stop then maybe there wasn't much to Him anyway.

Mary did have something she wanted me to do before the marriage. She'd heard that her mother was in Shelburne and she wanted me to fetch her. That was fine with me. I was itching to do something and, though Shelburne was a fair hike, it wasn't as if I was doing anything else. That was just what Thomas said when I told him about it later that day.

"Of course you have to get her. I'm kind of looking forward to seeing Jean too, it sure has been a while. I'd love to go with you and maybe have one of our old adventures, but Williams keeps saying our provisions are coming every day and I have to keep him heading in the right direction. He's like a damn jug-headed mule."

On no account would I let Mary come along. The walk to Shelburne was going to take days and I had no idea if we were really welcome in that place. It could be there'd be enemies there like everywhere else. I told Mary that Sally could use her help with the cooking and looking after the kids, particularly since she was pregnant again.

Hoisting my small sack over one shoulder, my Roman sword belted on my side, I left before the sun came up the next day. The path to Shelburne was clear, if thin in spots. It was July and the days were hot and dripping with abundance, the woods filled with fragrant smells and swollen leaves. The spruce stood all around, new growth bursting out, fresh and green as a wet frog against the darker green of the tree. As I walked, I could not help but feel that this was my home, my land. I was fresh, too, and ready to make it a place where Mary and I would be free to live and prosper. I felt better than I had ever felt before. Shelburne was three steady days ahead but that was just fine with me.

The first day, I did not see a soul. That night, after dinner and tea, I settled on the ground under a large aspen in a grove that smelled fresh and new. I wrapped myself in my old army blanket and was just nodding off to sleep when I heard a commotion on the trail coming from the direction of Shelburne. I left the blanket on the ground, bundled up as if someone was asleep in it, and crawled to a different tree trunk nearby with my sword in my hand. The cooking fire had burned down but was still slightly glowing and the leaves and branches nearby were jumping, swirling ghosts, one moment huge and orange and threatening, then small and shadowed and harmless.

A boy, perhaps fourteen or fifteen years old, burst off the trail and into my small clearing, breathing hard and looking back over his shoulder. I sat motionless in the shadows. The boy glanced at the fire and walked over to my bed. As he bent over to lift the corner of the blanket, I came up quietly behind him and grabbed him about the neck with my left arm, my right still holding the short knife.

"Who might you be, and what do you want?"

The boy had not struggled from the moment I wrapped my forearm around his neck. He stood still, his hands at his side. It was clear there was no fight in him. I dropped my left arm from the boy's head and spun him around, still holding the sword in my right hand. He stood quietly, looking at me, his mouth open and his eyes glancing wildly around the clearing.

"Don't even think of running. Have you got a tongue in your head, boy?"

"Yes, sir, I mean no harm."

If he hadn't been such a poor bag of bones, I expect my night would have been harder. As it was, I felt sorry for this child who was afraid and alone. I told him to build up the fire and when we had a decent blaze, I made tea and he ate biscuits. All that time we spoke little and I waited for him to finish his dinner. He was wiping the crumbs from his shirt and licking his fingers when I asked him to tell me how he came to be roaming through the dark forest like some beast of the night. He hadn't seemed to be much of a talker but once he got the bit in his mouth, there was just no stopping him. I sat quietly, sipping my tea and listening.

His name was Daniel. He had been a slave working in the tobacco fields on a huge farm in Virginia. When the war came, his father was sent to fight for the rebels in place of the master. Daniel never heard from his father again. One day, his master, a man who was cruel to his slaves and generous to his friends, had Daniel sent to his office in the big house. There he told the boy, barely thirteen, that he was to go to the camp of the Sons of Liberty and tell them that he was volunteering to fill the place of the master. When Daniel said that his father had been sent to do the same thing, the master told him his father was dead and gone and that his place was to be taken by the boy.

Daniel went off to the fighting on the side of the Virginians and had fought at the debacle of Great Bridge. That miserable fight, when Moses had been killed, seemed like a generation away but the boy's words brought it back. He had never fired a gun at that battle, the truth being he didn't know how and had no wish to do anyone harm. He stood at the back of the ranks and kept his head down. Daniel had been scared right down to the soles of his feet and was determined to run when the battle was over. The rebels had other ideas and kept a close guard on all the slaves. It was many days before he got a chance to go and during that time all the black surrogates were watched day and night.

His chance finally came when the Virginians marched into a village—more like a crossroads—where the loyalist residents had packed up and left. The windows on the houses were open and the doors swung in the wisp of a breeze. Even the dogs had left and the place was as quiet as the grave. The front window of the lone store in the forsaken place gazed on the soldiers like a great eye but it didn't take too long before someone smashed it with a brick and stormed inside.

Daniel and the rest of the slaves were taken just outside the town to a little wooded glen and left there with one guard. Inside the town, the sounds of looting and burning and shooting could be heard. The store had enough liquor to make the whole outfit good and drunk and the men worked hard to prove the point. The guard got tired of sitting outside the town and went to join the party, and that was the signal for the slaves to strike off by themselves in the opposite direction. Not all of them left. A large number stayed, feeling some kind of strange loyalty to the Virginians, but Daniel and a few others took off down the road as if the hounds of hell were at their heels.

The boy was young but he wasn't stupid and as he ran he figured on two things. First, he would go by himself so as to lessen the chance of being persuaded by someone else to do something he didn't want to do. Second, he would find himself some slaves working on a farm and sneak into their bunkhouse at night to determine the where and why of things and the direction he might go. He told the slaves running down the road with him that he planned on going it alone. One of them, an older man, tried to talk him out of it, but Daniel took the first path off the road that led into the woods and ran like a deer.

He ran and walked a considerable distance along the wagon track. When he came to a farm, he looked carefully to see the lay of the land, then walked calmly by as if he owned the world. No one stopped him and he walked for quite a time until he came to a large outfit with slaves in the fields. Daniel stepped quickly back into the shadows of the surrounding forest before anyone could see him and waited until night. When it was good and dark he crept to the bunkhouse and opened the unlocked door. He could hardly grope his way over the stoop but inside the long cabin there was a lone candle burning and he could vaguely see people sitting around a small table.

"Hey there, who is that?"

"Just me."

"And who might 'just me' be? If you're some kind of wandering ghost or some other more human vagrant, you ought to know there's five strong men here."

"Nope, I'm no ghost. Just a poor boy looking for a little dinner and some water."

The men around the table had moved around Daniel in a tight circle and one of them had his back to the closed door, so the boy knew he was well and truly committed. He didn't know what else to say and stood there gaping foolishly. One of the men came up close to him and turned his face from side to side.

"Why, he's just a child. I don't think he's much of a worry at all. What are you doing here?"

"I've left the army and I'm trying to figure out what to do now."

They got some hard bread and water for Daniel and sat him down at the table while he told his story. Finally, the man who had first looked him over told the boy that there was only one thing he could do, having run from both the rebels and his master.

"You have to join up with the British in this war. They've said they'll free all the slaves that will come and fight for them. I've thought of going with them myself."

Daniel knew nothing about the redcoats but he had little choice about which road to take, seeing as how all other paths were closed to him. So he finished his meal, thanked his hosts, and asked for directions to the British forces. They wouldn't talk more about it that night and told him to sleep and stay hidden in the bunkhouse the next day and they would show him the way the following night.

After the men returned to the house the next evening, they brought extra food and drink with them. The leader turned to him.

"We can leave just as soon as it's dark."

"What do you mean 'we'?" asked Daniel.

"Well here it is, son. I've been hankering to join those British myself, so I figure I'll be your guide and we'll both of us sign up to be free men."

So it was that Daniel got what he hadn't wanted in the first place, a traveling companion, but he also had food and a pack on his back and a scout who knew the land like the creases on his worn hands. His guide was a quiet man who went from dawn to dusk keeping his own counsel, which was just fine with Daniel.

They made the coast on the evening of the second day. Daniel and his friend didn't even break stride. They walked over to the dock in the gathering darkness and untied the closest rowboat. It was a simple, if long, row out to the blockading British warship standing out in the harbor. The ship blazed like the gateway to heaven and the runaways rowed on the thin line between the black sky and the black sea. Ignorant of their place in the world and unsure of their destination, they rowed as if cursed towards the only light in their world of night.

They were not the first runaways to make it to the ship. The captain sent Daniel's friend to be a pilot on another warship lying further in the harbor but he kept Daniel as his cabin boy. The ship itself, a humble vessel, saw little action during the war and was mainly used to blockade harbors, which was a tedious affair that generally involved simply lying at anchor. After the war, the ship went back to the merchant class and Daniel could have remained as one of the crew, but the boy had heard stories of Nova Scotia and wanted nothing more than to be let off at Halifax, there to make his fortune as a free man in a free land. However, the captain had business in Shelburne and so it was there that Daniel took his leave and sought work among the tradesmen of that town.

He was hired as a stable hand at a farm just outside town and was content for several months, living in the field barracks and earning a small wage for the first time in his life. One day he was sent by the farmer into town to pick up a package from the general store. As he was coming out, he was hailed by a man slouched on the bench in front of the store, a yellowed hat low over his face.

"What's your name, son? Why don't you come on over and sit by me here?"

Daniel's hard past had made him skeptical but he felt he had no choice but to go over and sit by the man, at least to find out what he had in mind. As he sat down, the man pushed back his hat and reached inside his coat pocket, coming up with a paper.

"Your name wouldn't be Daniel, by any chance?"

Daniel just sat there, as dumb as the wooden horse standing outside the store.

"See, the reason I ask is that this paper here in my hand says that there's a reward for bringing back a runaway by the name of Daniel.

That runaway is said to be in Shelburne but owned by a fellow a ways from here. This description seems to fit your size and age and shape and all. If that be you, you might save us both a lot of trouble by saying so here and now."

Daniel sat there on the bench with a roaring jumble of wild thoughts running through his mind. He wondered if his old master could really have tracked him to Nova Scotia or if this fellow was just after the nearest likely candidate. But then how did he know his name? And what of the British promise of freedom in a free land? Could this gray man—and Daniel now saw that the man was really gray, not just in his skin but in a feeling that clung around him like a damp stench—actually take him back to slavery?

All of these thoughts came in a flash to the boy still sitting on the bench. The first solid idea he had was to run. He jumped up from the bench, leaving his package behind, and ran through the store and out the back door. He didn't look behind him but kept going all the way into the woods until he hit the trail to Digby.

He'd kept running and walking through a day and a night and another day until he walked right into my evening camp.

Daniel stopped talking and looked at me. I looked him straight in the eye.

"That's one hell of a story. It could be this fellow has no call on you at all. It seems to me that this is a free land and the British won't let this bounty hunter just grab you. Of course there is the other side and that is that maybe they won't do a thing about it and in that case you'll be dragged back."

I stopped and looked at the boy.

"The other thing is that you might not be the one this fellow is looking for at all. It could all be a big mistake."

Daniel didn't say a word. He just threw small twigs in the fire with a vacant look on his face.

"Here's what I think. I'm not sure if there's real trouble here or not but I think you'd be a whole lot better off with my friend than you are here. I think you should strike on out for Digby. When you get there, you ask the way to Brindley and look up Thomas Peters. Everyone knows him. You tell him that Murphy sent you and, if anyone cares, you're my son. He'll look after you. I'll give you a bit of food to get there."

"Should I keep going now?"

"If you can stand walking the path at night you should. It's bright enough and the sooner you get to Thomas, the better off you'll be."

I gave him some more biscuits and a little pork and the boy struck off along the path to Digby.

I wondered if anyone was actually chasing him. It seemed to me that a man with a mind to catching him would have caught him by now but I was past taking chances myself so I let the fire die down and wrapped my blanket back up on the ground to make it look like I was asleep. Then I crawled back to lean against a tree deeper in the woods. The night was warm and still and sleep came quickly.

I awoke with a start, cramped, with my head scraping against the bark. The night had gotten darker and although I could hear the short chuckle of a horse, I could not see the animal. My fire was just a small bed of orange coals casting no light into the surrounding forest. I could almost make out the shape of someone walking around the fire. The man leaned over to lift up the bunched blanket as I walked out of the woods and grabbed him around the neck from behind, just as I had grabbed Daniel earlier in the evening. He had a short knife in his hand but he dropped it as I lifted him clear off his feet and bent him backwards, my left arm around his neck and my sword in my right hand.

Things were working out just as I had figured, but then everything changed. Just at the edge of my vision I suddenly saw a sharp movement. Next thing I knew was a crushing pain across the back of my head and then blackness.

Twenty-Two

Climbing out of the blackness was like climbing a muddy bank in the pouring rain. I woke a little and tried to focus, swirling and sliding in the fog, then slid back into the mist despite my best efforts. Finally, desperately, I grabbed any slice of the world I could fix on and held my eyes on the now blazing campfire.

I was sitting against a large tree, my arms bent back around the trunk and my hands tied together. Two men were crouched on small logs around the fire, eating squirrels that were skewered on sticks. Roasting on sticks leaning across the blaze were four more squirrels, their eye sockets staring from bald heads.

The white man glanced over at me, then looked away, his teeth tearing at the small bones of the blackened squirrel. He didn't look at me as he spoke.

"Here's how I see it. You've got the boy hidden around here somewhere. I guess you didn't count on me being there as well to give you a little tap on the head."

The man was pale, as if the blood had been sucked from his face. His hat was low on his forehead. Below the brim, his eyes, set together like a weasel's, were black and stupid. He was as common as pond scum and I had seen his blank face a thousand times before. It was the face of the foremen who whipped me and the slave hunters who had tracked me down. It was the look of the rebels who covered a man with burning tar. It was the face of men who waited to be told to fight and who needed to be told the cause because they did not know how to live without orders. I was sick of the lot of them and sick especially of being held, again, by such evil men. My fingers worked at the unseen knots behind the tree trunk.

The other man was gray, as if the twilight had wrapped around and claimed him. He could have been a runaway himself if he had been a little darker, but instead looked faded and dusky. He turned to his friend.

"Shut up. We'll get gold for him just as well as the boy. You just let me do the talking."

The white man grunted and grabbed another squirrel from the fire. He finished two more squirrels, rolled out a blanket, lay down, and within a few minutes was snoring.

The gray man sat against a stump and started smoking a short pipe. He leaned his head back, staring up at the small circle of stars that showed through the tops of the trees. The smoke curled around his head like a halo.

"Where do you mean to take me?" I asked.

"Likely as not to Florida."

"I'm not a runaway, I'm a free man. You've got no say here."

The gray man looked at me and blew smoke towards the stars.

"It's all the same to me. Free man or slave makes no difference to me at all. You'll still fetch a good price. I don't know or care about the rules in this country or any other. I'm here free and you're there tied to a tree. You're going to be a slave on some southern island and I'm bound to get a good price for you. Nothing else matters and there's nobody to say what's the law and what isn't. The plain fact is that nobody with any say cares what happens to you."

My shoulders were aching deep in the bone where my arms were bent back. The gray man sat watching me from across the fire. His blue rings of smoke rose straight up in the air.

"How is it that a man like you comes to be hooked up with a worm like that?"

"What do you mean, a man like me? You don't know anything about me."

"You're a runaway yourself, I think."

The gray man chuckled, a deep sound that slowly spilled from his mouth.

"You're about half right, I guess. My momma was a house slave, sure as hell, but my daddy was a great hunter with many horses and a chief to boot. Iroquois. So I reckon you could say I'm a half-breed of sorts."

When the man laughed, he tipped his head straight back and showed his long tongue. His whole body twitched and his feet shook down to the ends of his boots.

"If your mother was a slave, how can you be hunting them down now?"

"Well now, she didn't stay a slave because my daddy happened to see her one day and bought her off. Then he took her and made her his wife. The thing you have to think on is this—he bought her with gold. Have you got any gold to buy yourself or that boy off?"

I shook my head.

"That's what I figured. Now if you had the gold we could be talking about price and such. You'd be well on your way to going home, if you even have a home, but seeing as you don't have any gold, I guess you'll be sold to someone who does."

"So it's just about the gold to you then? There's nothing else in it?"

The gray man looked straight across the fire.

"There is nothing else. It's just as plain here as it is in any other case. If you want to know the right and wrong of a thing you need to just look at where the coins are and that'll be where the right is. Let's look at you. You have that brand on your face that says you're a runaway. You have no money. You say you're a free man; maybe so, but who cares? The only man that matters in all this is the one that's going to buy you. Well, I guess I matter too, 'cause I'm the one that's going to sell you. But then I'm just a means for the man with the money to spend some of that on something that's going to make him more money. That'd be you. See both me and the man with the money say you're a slave and that's that. There's no one going to say different. So what we've got here is a simple business transaction. Now you're saying you're a free man and not a slave to be sold but that's wrong and must be a lie because you don't have the coin to back it and we do."

"No, that's not the right of it. That's just you saying something and other idiots believing it to be true."

The man threw his head back and laughed so hard that his boots hit against the logs at the edge of the fire.

"That's the same thing. If I and the money man say it is so, then so it is. Maybe the government says no slaves are allowed, but there are plenty of slaves down in Shelburne and others too that might just as well be slaves. Those slaves belong to men of money and power and nobody in this crap-pot government says boo to them. I can tell you that nobody will say anything to me either when I drag you and that boy back across the border. Nobody's going to give you anything and you have to take what you want, plain and simple. The taking of it by itself makes it right. There's nobody going to say differently."

"It doesn't bother you to break the law?"

"Whose law might that be? By my lights there's no law against hunting runaways. Fact is, a good bounty hunter is respected by all men because we do what them that have the money don't want to do. In any event, it's plainly illegal for slaves to run and plainly legal for a good hunter to track them down and bring them back. Now the law elsewhere might be different. Laws change from place to place and from time to time. I wouldn't be putting too much faith in any law if I was you, tied to that tree and all. I surely wouldn't be trying to figure out right or wrong from a law."

I pulled hard at my wrists but the ropes just bit further into my skin. There was no loosening of the knots that I could feel. The gray man looked at me and puffed on his pipe. His partner was dead asleep—even the snoring had dwindled away.

"I have friends in this country and they'll come looking for me."

"See, now you're getting the hang of this situation. Your friends could come with their knives and guns and such and shoot me and rescue you. That would be the right thing for them to do and who could argue with them? They'd have the power then and then the right would be on their side, but I'm figuring they won't get here in time to rescue you and, until that time comes, I have the power and the right's on my side. See, right follows power like a whipped dog follows his master and until you get that little bit of power, you're always going to be in the wrong and begging for scraps from the righteous men on top."

"That's not how I see it. When I was a slave I had to do what the owner wanted, had to work where he said and go where he wanted. Now that I got my freedom I can do what I want and go wherever I feel the urge. Now you can talk of right and wrong and different laws for the powerful and such. All of that may be so but I'm a free man now and free to do what I want when I want. You can tie me to this tree but you can't change the simple truth that you're not hunting slaves, you're just grabbing anyone you come across. If you were chasing after runaways that would make you a snake, but seeing as how you're grabbing anyone who can make you money, slave or not, why you're just a plain criminal despite all your fancy talk. One day someone's going to tie your evil hide to a tree and it'll be by the neck."

The gray man leaned forward and spit into the fire.

"Those are fancy words I've heard before but I'll tell you something—your so-called freedom will only last as long as the big men want it and that's only as long as it suits their purpose. Now you have freedom because the redcoats needed you to do their fighting for them. All that time that rolled on before the war they didn't do a thing about the slaves. So they gave you freedom in exchange for you giving them your lives but now they're done fighting and I can tell you they don't care at all about you. If you starve or freeze or get killed by bears here, there's nobody that's going to raise a finger to help. Nobody is going to stop a slave hunter because it doesn't suit them to do that. They don't need you to fight and die for them now so there's nothing in it for them."

The slave hunter leaned forward and looked hard at me, his eyes shining with a strange intensity.

"I'll tell you this one story so you can sit there and stew on it. Then I'm turning in—we've got some hunting ahead of us tomorrow for that runaway boy and then we got some hard traveling ahead. Now, I told you my daddy was a big chief and so he was. You talk about freedom, why he was as free as the hawk. We used to walk from morning to dusk and not see another person. All of the land was the hunting grounds for our village and we had respect from everyone around. The whites respected us too and they came often to trade and sometimes just to yap. Soon, though, they started to build little farms and then little towns near us. Then they built more little farms right on our hunting ground."

The gray man poked at the fire with a stick.

"Still they came to talk and they told us not to worry, that those settlers were just a few crazy farmers and nobody else would get too close to us. My father listened to them and believed what they had to say. These were our friends, after all, and we'd known them a long time. So we let the few farms creep closer and closer and then, one fall when we were out hunting for winter provisions, we realized that there were so many farms on our old hunting ground that lots of the animals had left and there wasn't much left to hunt. So we went back to our village and my father called a council."

The gray man stopped talking, stood up, and went over to one of the packs. He rummaged through the top pocket and came back with a plug of tobacco, which he stuffed in the top of his pipe. He tamped the leaves down with his thumb and, taking a thin stick from the fire, lit the mixture with a few deep puffs. I said nothing, trying to relax my arms behind the tree.

"Some spoke of war at the council. Others wanted more talk and still others said we should leave and move west. My father talked about the right and wrong of the whole thing. He said it was wrong for the white man to move into our grounds and scare the deer away. But the whites were our friends too, he said, and when your friend makes a mistake you tell him that but you don't kill him and you don't run away from him. You stick by and help him get over the mistake. That's what my father said, and because he was a great man the others listened to him. We thought that the right thing to do was to stick by our white friends and help them see their mistake. The council decided to talk to the whites, so the next day my father and twenty men from the village went off to the settlement office. I went with them because my father wanted me to learn how to negotiate. My father began to talk with the settlement officer right after he got there. But it wasn't too long after that, on the very same day, that a troop of soldiers surrounded the settlement office. All of us village men, talking and laughing in the yard outside the office, were trapped inside the circle. When my father came outside to see what the ruckus was about, one of the soldiers shot him square though the chest. Before the rest of us had time to gather our wits together, there was a general firing. In the melee I jumped on a horse and made off back to the village. There was nothing left to be done at the settlement office."

The gray man stopped for a moment and stood up. He kicked a loose stick back into the fire and scuffed at the dirt with the toe of his boot.

"A couple of miles from the village I could see the smoke. There really wasn't anything left to see. There were many dead on the ground. Everything was on fire. I sat on the horse a long time and tried to figure out what to do. Finally I turned away, to the east. I rode a long time, traveling at night and hiding in the woods during the day. I wasn't sure if I was being chased. Finally I rode into a town and there, on the first post, I saw a reward poster for a runaway. Right then I knew what I could do to get by. It was something I was sure to be good at, and so it's been."

The man was quiet for a minute, his eyes closed. Then he sat up quickly.

"After a time it came to me that the whole thing ended up the way it had to end up, simply because the right of it was with the white men. There's no other way to figure it. My father was in the wrong with all his talk, and the settlers were in the right with their guns and horses. I came to see that it's the powerful who decide what's right. Not the laws, not the priests, and not the teacher. So if you want to know the right and wrong of a situation you need to simply look at where the strong arm is and you'll get a good idea of the rightness. If you're on the other side you had just better change and start going with the flow or you'll be swept away."

The hunter went over to his pack and took out a thick wool blanket. He laid himself flat on the ground without another word, his eyes fixed on the small hole in the trees outlining the night sky, and his breath slowing.

"Wherever it is you take me, you know I'll run away."

The gray man rolled over and looked me square in the eyes.

"I'm counting on it, but not until after you've been sold."

The night crawled on and I slept in patches, my head sinking down to my chest then bouncing back up as the pain in my cramped arms woke me. The bark of the tree scraped along the inside of my forearms.

I could see that by having everything taken away, a man could change and become something different, walking like an outcast in a shadowy world where normal laws and ways of men did not apply. I never had anything in the first place and only ever wanted to be free. I thought that if you have nothing and struggle to be free, the threat to that freedom, once gained, is more important than anything. The freedom is worth more than your own life.

These thoughts churned through my mind. Sleep eluded me as the stars wheeled above me. I could see no way clear. I wondered, too, about the boy. It would be hard to walk to Digby in the dark, not knowing if you were going the right way and worried about the hunters behind you. If Daniel made it he might bring Thomas back to help but I would likely be long gone by then and maybe out of reach of help. It seemed to me that I had to work out a plan myself but I was unable to sort out any sort of actions through the jumble of my thoughts.

When the darkness began to fade into morning, I was half-asleep, my chin resting on my chest, and I still had no idea of how to get away from the hunters.

Twenty-Three

The men began arguing before the sun had penetrated fully into our little glade. The gray man said that the two should split up, with him staying behind to watch over me and the other hunter going after Daniel. However, his companion with the narrow eyes was scared to travel along the road closer to Digby. He was afraid he would run into travelers and perhaps even stumble into friends of mine. They argued until the sun had finally dappled the leaves of the forest and then the gray man packed up his simple kit and mounted his horse. He trotted down the road back in the direction I had come from, but not before spitting on the ground in front of the white man and telling him he was the biggest coward he'd ever had the misfortune to encounter.

The bounty hunter hardly glanced at me. I asked him to loosen the ropes binding my hands behind the tree or at least tie them in front of me to relieve the cramping. He didn't bother to answer. Sitting next to the fire, he ate big red strips of jerky and drank from a blue bottle. Then he took to laughing to himself and whittling away at a long tree limb, cutting off the short branches.

"Know what this is?"

"What?"

"It's a slave stick. You ought to know that. It's about to become your companion for the next while."

The man took the stick and ran it horizontally across his shoulders so it stuck out on both sides of his back. He then put his hands and forearms on the top of the pole and they dangled loosely over the front.

"See, this is how you'll wear it. There's no way you can get away from me with this stick on your back and your hands hanging like an ape's. There's just no way for you to run at all."

He began laughing and capering around the campfire, the branch riding across his shoulders and his hands swinging loosely. Finally he stopped and bent over. A short chuckle began deep in his chest and ended with him coughing and sputtering, spitting green streaks on the ground.

"If it was up to me I'd just tie you really simple so maybe you'd try to run. Then we could track you down and maybe have a little fun. You know what we used to do with your running kind back where I came from? Why we'd fire them up. We'd tie them up to a tree, just like you right there, and we'd fire them. Oh my how they'd shriek; enough to waken the dead. It's not that easy to fire up a body, even a greasy slave, but a huge big roasting fire will do it."

The man laughed and spit and laughed some more. Then he stopped suddenly, as if a shadow had crossed his mind.

"It could be I should do that to you right now, just for fun. I could tell my buddy you tried to run. I'll just bet you'd burn like a torch."

The man came over to where I sat hunched over trying to take some of the pain away from my bent-back shoulders. He stood over me with his head cocked to one side like a crow's. Then he leaned forward and sniffed the top of my head and ran his hand down the side of my arm. He stood back up straight again, his face twisted in a strange smile, then suddenly bent forward and licked my cheek before going back to the fire.

"I would do it, too, but he'd like as not be mad since you'll fetch a pretty price down at market."

The man started muttering quietly to himself, then lapsed into silence, pulling steadily from the bottle and looking at me through the fire with his squinty eyes. Pretty soon he lay back on the ground and loud wet snores rolled across the campsite. My hands had been tied behind my back for so long that they were pretty much numb, but my shoulders, twisted and pulled behind, blazed as if knives were being pushed through them, and still I had no plan, no thought of how to get away from that tree. I could clearly see my sword stuck in the dirt near the man's pack, but it may as well have been back in Brindley. I thought of that old tent town and I thought of my Mary going about her daily chores or maybe walking out to the seashore. Here I was, roped and stuck in a dismal camp with the worst sort of man, a man who thought no more of setting me on fire than he did of spitting. I had been a fool to think this new land would have better men in it than the old.

I felt rage welling up in me and, like a chained bear, slowly stood up tall on my feet, my tied hands rising behind the trunk of the tree. I used my feet as leverage and pushed against the trunk, my hands rasping against the bark of the tree. Still, there was no slack to the rope at all. I was about to give up when a small voice came from behind me.

"Keep doing that and I'll never get these ropes off. Can you stand still for a minute?"

I stood stock still and felt hands ripping at my ropes. Soon the bindings parted and I brought my hands forward to hang loosely at my side. The hunter slept noisily on the far side of the fire. Before I could look behind the tree, Daniel came to my side and began rubbing my chaffed wrists. He talked in a low whisper.

"I think we should get out of here. Can you walk?"

"Yeah, but I can't move my arms."

I went to crouch in the short bushes behind the tree. Daniel looked at me and I put my finger to my lips for him to keep quiet. He nodded. The bounty hunter remained asleep beyond the fire and I could hear his breath coming in deep, even sighs. We sat for several minutes. The truth was that I was unsure of what we should do. If we went down the road back to Brindley we could run into the gray man. If we left for Shelburne, the man by the fire could catch us. We could not wander far in the thick woods. Also, foolish though it was, I wanted my sword back.

After several minutes the feeling returned to my arms. I clenched my fists until they were able to grip, then cautiously began to edge out of the woods towards my sword. Bent low at the waist, Daniel crept after me. As I gripped the handle of the sword to pull it from the ground, the bounty hunter gave a gasp and sat straight up. Before I could move, he brought a small hatchet out from under his blanket and threw it straight at my chest. The distance was close, just across the diminished fire, but whether from the drink or the sleep, the man's aim was off and the hatchet went whistling past my arm and thudded against a tree. Sword in hand, I looked across the fire at the hunter, who had grabbed a short knife from his belt and was standing square to me, a peculiar grin on his face.

The man was used to dealing with runaways who were unarmed and cowed by his bluster, but I was a soldier, not a slave, and I'd seen his kind before and knew just how to finish him. He gestured to me as I grabbed up my sword and took a firm grip. Before he finished his taunt and got set I jumped quickly through the fire and, not looking at the knife in his hand, closed in tight to him. My sword found the soft spot between his ribs and I lifted the man up right off his feet. He tried to stab my back with his short knife, his hand curling around my shoulder, but he could get no purchase with that difficult angle and the blade barely pierced my shirt.

I jerked hard and harder again and the man's knife dropped to the ground. He slid to the dirt. Slumped in his blood in the dirt and the filth, the man looked directly at me and struggled to speak. Before he managed a word his body gave a huge heave and his eyes stared away. I sat down heavily beside the body and looked across the fire at Daniel, who was leaning against my old tying tree. His eyes were like an owl's, peering this way and that, unsettled and scared.

"It's all right, boy. It's over. Come and sit by me here."

Daniel walked over and sat beside me.

"Here now, let me catch my breath."

Not saying a word, the boy just looked at me.

"It had to be, Daniel, that's the way of it. It just had to be and the world's better for it happening. Now we just have to think what we're going to do. Here's what I'm thinking. If we go to Brindley, we're liable to run into the gray man and he might be a harder stone to throw than this fellow. So I figure we might as well go on to Shelburne, if you can stand to go back there."

Daniel just nodded his head. I figured if we took the horse and rode slowly and carefully all day and all night along the trail, we could just about get to Shelburne the next day.

I wasn't sure if we could expect protection from the law in Shelburne or if the gray man was right and the British didn't care what happened to us, but I did think that more people around would give us a better chance against the hunter if he did follow us to Shelburne. Also, I knew that Colonel Blucke was there, along with other Pioneers. All of them would back us, I hoped. Of course, Jean was there too. I bent over and took the right arm of the dead man. Daniel took the hunter's left arm and we half-carried, half-dragged the body out of the campsite and into the woods. After we went a dozen steps I dropped the arm and turned to walk back to the fire. The boy stood still beside the body, making no move to go back to the fire.

"We need to bury him. We can't just leave him here for the animals and all."

"We can't, Daniel. We've got no shovel and we have no time to be digging a grave for him. I'm sorry. Best we can do is get him out of plain view so it delays his friend a little."

"It's not right to do this. Everyone deserves a decent burial. It is a bad thing for us to do, to leave him here for the wolves."

I looked at Daniel.

"This fellow was a devil and deserves nothing more than to have his bones scattered. The plain fact is that even if he was the Lord himself we have no time to be burying anyone. It can't be bad to look after ourselves so we don't get taken for slaves. I'm sorry if that's not good enough for you but that's the way it's going to have to be."

I turned and walked back to the fire. Daniel came out of the woods as I was tying the hatchet and small knife to the leather strings hanging off the saddle of the horse. I threw my bloody shirt far off into the woods and wrapped my old war jacket around my shoulders. It was warm under the morning sun. I strapped my Roman knife on my belt.

"Do you know anything about riding a horse?"

Daniel shook his head.

"Well I know just about nothing, too. Now if we were driving, that'd be a different story but since we've got no wagon I guess we'll have to learn as we go."

I put the saddle on the horse, fastening it the way I had seen it done, and lifted myself up. I reached down and swung the boy up behind me. The horse, placid but curious, stood still, his ears flicking back and forth. We set off up the road to Shelburne.

The trail to the town was seldom used and we didn't see anyone for the rest of the day. A couple of times we thought we heard hoofbeats behind us and I pulled the horse into the woods, but the noises turned out to be the trees rubbing together in the soft wind or maybe the chuckles of the crows that followed us. Daniel slept in the hot sun of the afternoon, his head resting against my back. I wanted to sleep too and did nod off a few times, only to be jerked back awake as the horse stumbled over a downed tree or spooked a little at a strange shadow. My shoulders still ached from being stretched back for so long, but the day was warm, the woods were quiet, and it was peaceful and calm. As the shadows grew long and the night noises began, we stopped in a small clearing to let the horse graze. There was a narrow stream at the edge of the woods and Daniel and I sat by its edge and ate pork from my pack. The hunters had left my goods untouched. Even my small coin sack, given to me by Captain Mitchell, was still in the pocket of my pants. Neither of us had the stomach to look in the personal pack of the hunter and I finally cut it off the saddle of the horse and left it on the bank of the stream, along with his food sack and its contents of stinking jerky.

"What do you want to do when we get to Shelburne? I'll be off to see Colonel Blucke and you can come too if you want."

"I could go and see if I can get my job back."

"Yeah, but what about the gray man? He'll likely come looking for you and then you're back in the same soup."

I'd been thinking about Daniel for most of the day. There was only one way out for the boy that I could see. He'd have to come back with me to Brindley after I'd visited with the Colonel and found Jean. Otherwise he'd always be at risk in Shelburne. I thought maybe once we got to town we'd just ride on to Colonel Blucke's house and play things out as they came.

The night's ride was as quiet as the day's. The trail was clear in the moonlight and there was no sound from behind us. The horse plodded on and both of us slept for long stretches, only to suddenly wake up when the animal stumbled. We did not talk.

It was early in the morning when we finally rode into Shelburne. Barely visible through the morning mist, a large British warship was standing in the harbor with its masts poking through the top of the fog. The city itself was alive with activity and we were scarcely given a glance as workers bustled about their tasks. It was a large town—a small city, really—and when we came out of the woods it spread out before us in straight lines, the houses and stores laid out on a careful grid.

We walked the horse slowly into the town and I asked the first person I came upon how to find Colonel Blucke, but that man just shook his head and walked away, his pace quickening. The woman behind him, a basket of laundry in her arms, said that we needed to go to Birchtown, on the northern edge of Shelburne. When I asked her how we would find the Colonel's house, she laughed and told me to look for the biggest place in the town.

We made our way through Shelburne and out to Birchtown, which was a short distance further on, and came upon a large frame house standing on a cleared corner, dwarfing the buildings next to it. While Shelburne was a busy place, Birchtown was quiet and the houses were mostly small and set close together, but the Colonel's house would have been a gracious home no matter where it was located.

A young woman answered our knock and led us into the front parlor, where we waited for the Colonel. He came into the room buttoning his waistcoat and looking like a magistrate. He had not changed in appearance from the time I saw him last in New York, but he didn't recognize me.

"Sir, what can I do for you?"

"Murphy Steele, colonel. I served with you in the war and this is my friend, Daniel."

The man looked hard at me, squinting under his heavy brows. Finally a flash of recognition streaked across his face.

"Yes, now I remember. Sorry, so many things have happened since then. My memory is not what it used to be. Now, Murphy, how are you? I heard that some of the Pioneers were blown to Bermuda and only just landed in Annapolis. I suppose that would be you and your friend, um, Peters. Yes, I suppose you two have only just landed."

"Yes, sir, we're at Brindley, just by Digby, and looking to get set up there with some land, but we're having some trouble getting the surveying done."

"Yes. Well here it is, Murphy. The land here is terribly bad, you know, there's a lot of rocks and all that blasted moss. Clearing the land is hard, hard work. Now I've heard that the Annapolis area is different. People say that the land is better there, much better for farming."

"Well, sir, I've never been a farmer and I don't know much about it but the land at Brindley will do for us, I think. The problem we're having is in the getting of it. We can't get the British to lay out the plots so as we can get to clearing and building. Maybe you could help us get them going is what I've been thinking on the way over here and now that I've seen your house, I'm thinking you might have some pull with them."

I had been wrong about Blucke's unchanging aspect. The man had become a bundle of nerves since I had last seen him in New York. First he sat, then quickly he stood and paced about the room, his hands clasped behind him. Then he sat again and scratched the top of his bald head, his eyes squinting and his foot tapping the floor. All of this he did while he talked with me, his eyes rarely leaving my face. Daniel sat in a far corner of the room, barely able to keep his eyes open, his chin resting on his chest.

"Yes, I can do that. I'll talk to the governor and maybe we can get things moving for you."

"The governor?"

"Yes. I've talked with him about several items previous to this. We need to get everyone settled and working. You know, Murphy, this is a great, great land. We have the chance here to make a country of our own and we've got the people to do it."

He stood again.

"Is there anything else I can do? Are you looking for work? I've got crews working on the roads around here. Let me give you some advice, Murphy. Build a fishing boat; the ocean is everyone's, the fish are boundless, and our fish are worth the same as the white's. Build a boat and you'll not go hungry and you'll not be on scanty wages."

"Well I was thinking more along the lines of lumbering. It's more what I know."

Colonel Blucke stopped his pacing and looked down at me, his hands in his pockets.

"Yes, that will do too, and with the same thought behind it as the fishing. After all, there's no shortage of trees in this place. I think there is a mill in Digby so if you start taking the logs out there will be a need for them. Yes, that's a good idea what with all the building to be done and the shipbuilding too. The woods or the sea, either one will do, I think. It's hard to eke a living out of the ground though and that's what most of them are doing; that's a mistake, I think."

"Colonel, I'm looking for an old friend of mine. It's said she's in Shelburne. Jean Brown is her name."

The colonel sat down, crossed his legs, and began tapping his knee with his left hand.

"Jean Brown. No, I don't know that name. She's not with the Pioneers, I think. In Shelburne you say? Wait a minute. Let me ask

Tess, she knows everyone in town."

He summoned the woman who had answered my knock on the door. Her face brightened when he asked about Jean's whereabouts.

"Why Colonel, I'm surprised you don't know her. She lives above the butcher's shop on Water Street, down by the docks. She's always at the frolics in town, as lively as a youngster, though who knows how old she is. She works at Jamieson's, the old doctor down there, two roads back of the water."

"There you go then, Murphy. You'll find her down on Water Street."

I went over to Daniel and nudged him a little. The boy woke with a start and grabbed his short jacket. As we were leaving the house, I turned to Colonel Blucke and related to him the story of the bounty hunters and how the gray man might come looking for us in Shelburne. The colonel's face grew hard and he stopped his nervous pacing.

"We'll show him short shrift if he shows up here. Don't you worry, Murphy, bounty hunters have to go through the courts to get runaways back to the States. They can't just show up and take free men away. We won't allow it, even if the British are lax."

"I don't think these two were planning on letting anyone know what they were doing."

"You say there were two, but there's just this one gray man hunting you now. What about the other one?"

I didn't say anything. He stared at me and Daniel, then glanced over my head at the horse tied up to a post at the road.

"Decent-looking horse you got there. Must have been you got him in Digby in trade for work, which is what I'd be saying if anyone asked me. Nice seeing you again, Murphy, I'll surely look you up if I get out your way."

We rode back into town slowly. The sun was high in the sky as we went down to the docks and on to Water Street. The yards were busy with men unloading several ships. Barrels and boxes were piled high and many wagons waited along the road with the horses nodding in the heat. The butcher shop was easy to find, both by the fresh smell coming from its open front door and by the cart with a large salted pork standing by its side door. On the other side was a small entranceway with stairs leading up to the rooms above the row of stores. I left the horse tied to a post and we went up the stairs.

It was close to noon and our hope was that Jean would come back to her room for a meal before returning to her work at Jamieson's. When we got to the top of the stairs, there were three separate doors and we were uncertain where to look, but luck was with us and as we stood talking on the landing, the first door opened and out came Jean, older and bigger than I remembered. It took a second for her face to register the two of us standing there and just another short minute for her to recognize me. She let out a gasp, then a whoop, and came over and hugged me tight about the waist.

"Murphy Steele, Murphy Steele, I never thought I'd see your face again. What are you doing here and what have you done with that girl of mine? Wait. Don't tell me. I've got to get back to work, tell me tonight. No. Wait. Tell me now. Is Mary all right? I heard that you two were together. You're not here with bad news, are you? I want to hear it all but not now. Just tell me if it's bad news."

I just shook my head and grinned and Jean, now standing back from me but still holding my shoulders in her hands, leaned forward and gave me a big kiss on my cheek.

"All right, I have to go but I'll be back tonight and we'll talk. You go in here and make yourself comfortable and I'll see you later."

With that, she was off down the stairs in a cloud of billowing skirts and flapping hands. Daniel and I went into her room and sat down on two big pillows. It was a simple room but homey. There was a wood table and chairs and several large cushions on the floor. In one corner of the room was a bed with a straw tick and woolen blankets. A small stove sat in the opposite corner.

The room was warm with the sun blazing through windows that looked out over the street and on to the docks. I got up and opened one window slightly and a mild gust of salty air blew into the room. It was calm and pleasant and I gazed for several minutes out the window as the dock workers scurried back and forth loading a small whaling boat. When I turned back, Daniel was sleeping soundly on one of the large pillows.

I went back downstairs and untied the horse. At the end of the street was a small livery with a round-faced, heavy man minding the stable. I took five pennies out of my bag and gave them to the man and left the horse in his care.

Then I returned to Jean's room. I kicked off my boots and lay on the cozy tick, the sun warm upon my face, and sleep found me in a moment.

Twenty-Four

Jean opened the door and woke me up. She went to the table and began unloading her canvas bags as I sat on the edge of the bed rubbing my eyes.

"We're going to have us a dinner tonight. It's too hot to cook here but I've got this roasted chicken ready to eat and some makings for a salad and an apple pie for dessert. You wake your friend and we'll sit right down."

Daniel was already stirring and the smell of the chicken, still warm in its brown paper wrapping, filled the room and drew him to the table. Jean gave me the rum bottle and I pulled the soft wooden stopper out of the end and poured the liquid into the cups on the table. As Jean began mixing the salad together, I told her about the war and about leaving New York and being blown off course to Bermuda and ending up in Brindley Town. She laughed when I told her about finding Mary and her eyes glistened when I spoke of my dark days of lying sick with fever and closer to death than to life. I told her that it was Mary who had saved me then, and Mary who had been my rock through all the long days since. Finally I told her of our marriage plans and her face broke into a wide grin. Jean wiped her hands on her apron and came over and wrapped her thick arms around me. Her bear hug nearly lifted me off the ground and I let out a gasp.

"You're still not too big for that and I doubt you ever will be. I couldn't be happier for the two of you. Of course I'll go back with you, I wouldn't miss it for the world. Imagine seeing my girl again after all these years."

Mary had never spoken to me about her childhood. She also rarely spoke of her brother, who was taken to the West Indies and never heard from again. News spread easily across the States but did not come so quickly from the West Indies. Those islands seemed to be a giant hole, and few who went there as slaves were ever heard from again. As we sat down to eat, Jean told us of her life since Thomas and I had run away from the Richardson farm. The war had destroyed the farm soon after we escaped. Richardson and the overseers had gone off to war. The slaves were left to fend for themselves as rampaging soldiers and villains roamed the countryside. Jean thought her best path was to head north and she gradually made her way to New York, stopping along the way to work in small towns. A good cook could always find work. When she finally got to New York she worked in a hospital kitchen, and through our hard New York winter, the hot summer, and that cruel autumn when Colonel Tye died, Jean had been in the same city as us, cooking at the hospital across town. Of course, our paths never crossed.

As it became clear to Jean that the war was ending, she began to worry about her future. She had never been released from slavery and had never been guaranteed freedom by the British. She had heard stories about rebels returning from the fighting and tracking down their dispersed slaves and she knew that Richardson, if alive, would do the same. One day as she sat at the huge kitchen work table in the hospital sipping on a mug of tea, a doctor came through the swinging doors. He sat opposite her without a word. The doctor's name was Jamieson and he could see the end of the war coming as plain as he could see Jean, wiping her hands on her apron as she began to slice the carrots.

The doctor was completely without politics. He was interested solely in making people well and improving his knowledge of the world. To say he was not politically inclined is not accurate. He was not disinterested but had seen that politicians were unprincipled and corrupt. Dr. Jamieson was very interested in history and knew quite well that with the end of the war would come all manner of cruelty, much of it directed against British sympathizers and runaways. He also knew that most of the abuse would be directed against those with no power, namely the ex-slaves.

He liked Jean.

Dr. Jamieson knew her to be hard working, genial, and good with children, and she made the best apple pie he'd ever tasted. He asked Jean if she would come with him and his wife and children to Halifax. Jean needed no convincing. She had a pretty clear idea herself of what the end of the war would mean for her. Dr. Jamieson was looking for a change and Nova Scotia looked like an interesting new home; as a well-respected doctor, he had some influence to get his own way.

The fact that Jean had never been granted her freedom, a real obstacle for many ex-slaves when Thomas and I boarded the transport ships with the rest of the Black Pioneers, was not a concern for the doctor. When we left New York, ex-slaves who were not Black Pioneers or members of the general army and who had no papers to establish their freedom had great difficulty boarding ships, but the doctor booked passage for his family and his staff, including Jean, who was listed as a cook and nanny, and no questions were asked.

Halifax did not suit Dr. Jamieson. He disliked pretense and the city, to his eye, was full of hypocrisies. Shelburne, raw and youthful, was perfect. Jean told us that the doctor's practice had thrived. He was honest and caring and he treated the wealthiest members of Shelburne and the poorest inhabitants of Birchtown. Jean loved her patron and his family and told Daniel and me that she had never been happier.

"I'll go back to Brindley with you for the wedding, but I can't stay. Dr. Jamieson needs me here, and this is my home. When will we leave? How will we get out there?"

That was a good question. On the trail to Shelburne it had never crossed my mind that Jean would not be able to walk back with us, but, now that I saw her, I realized that walking that tough path through long days and hard nights to Brindley was about near to impossible. Riding the horse was a possibility, but Jean was not used to riding, and then there was the gray man, who was still possibly on the trail and might be lurking around any corner. I was responsible for young Daniel but to be responsible for Jean as well on that dangerous path was unsettling. I looked over at my young friend but his head was on his folded hands on the table. He was fast asleep again.

"Jean, can we meet Dr. Jamieson? I'd like to thank him for looking out for you."

"Of course, I'll take you down with me tomorrow."

Jean had many questions about Mary and, of course, she wondered who Daniel was. The boy was not much of a talker. He was happy simply to have a warm place to sleep and a good meal to eat. Of course, I knew something about Daniel's history, as he'd told me of it around the campfire just a few days ago, but I didn't know anything of his early life and that was fine. I liked his uncomplicated courage and good humor. He was an excellent companion. I tried to answer Jean's questions about Daniel and Mary as well as I could, but the simple truth was that I didn't know a lot about either one before the time that they had come into my life. There were many things about my own past that no one but Thomas knew and neither he nor I talked about those troubled times. I suspected the same was true for both my love and my young friend. Jean, too, had known hard times and, perhaps because of that, she did not press her questions too much.

"It's been hard for all of us, Murphy. I know that as well as anyone."

She put her head on her hand for just a moment.

"Never mind, Murphy. Today is a happy day. I never thought I'd see Mary again. I heard she had been killed in the war. So today is a day for miracles and tomorrow will be a time for hope renewed. It's wonderful to see you again."

We sat in silence for a long while, the boy sleeping with his head resting on the hard table and Jean and I eating our way through the chicken. Finally Jean stood and said she was headed for bed. I nudged Daniel and the two of us made our way to the large floor cushions. I was nearly asleep before my head hit the pillow.

The sea air was clear and fresh in the morning and the bright sun was already streaming through the window when I finally shook the sleep out of my head. Jean was nowhere to be seen but Daniel was still sleeping soundly beside me. I sat at the table and had some cheese and bread and filled my cup with water from the pitcher. As I ate, Daniel stirred and finally sat up.

"Dan, will you have some breakfast and just wander around the town a little? Not too far, mind, and have a quick look about before you go anywhere. Jean's gone to work and I think I'd like to talk with that Dr. Jamieson. Be back for lunch."

Daniel nodded his head.

I was unsure where Dr. Jamieson's office was located but it turned out to be just around the corner and up the hill, barely fifty paces from Jean's flat. Jean herself was just inside the doctor's door, tending to a small girl who was crying and holding her hand. She smiled at me as I came in and asked me to sit on a small wooden chair. In just a few minutes, the door to the back room opened and a balding man with a bandage in his hand came out and went straight to the little girl. The doctor spoke softly. He poured alcohol from a bottle onto the bandage and then wrapped it around the little one's hand. She winced with the sting but stopped crying. The doctor gave her a piece of rock candy and sent her out the door.

He turned to Jean.

"She'll be fine, just a little cut is all she's got. I wish she'd stay away from that wood pile; she's always coming in with slivers or scrapes."

The doctor looked at me.

"You must be the Murphy I've been hearing about."

I wanted to talk with Dr. Jamieson so I asked him to step outside and, with a nod to Jean, we walked out the door and down the boardwalk towards the dock. Jean had told her employer about my adventures on the trail and her intentions to go back with me to Brindley Town for the wedding. He was also concerned about the three of us travelling along the same path that had held so much danger for Daniel and me, and had other worries as well, most of them centered around the mood in Shelburne.

"The town is a powder keg, Murphy. The black loyalists have been forced to work for almost nothing. A lot of them haven't been given land so they're basically begging for food most of the time. The white veterans and laborers are a bitter, sour lot. They're mad about losing the war, and they're mad about losing their homes, and they're mad about being stuck here. Some haven't been given land, either, so when they get to drinking they blame the blacks in town and want to kick them out."

The doctor shook his head.

"I just don't see how all of this is going to end well around here. There's no decent government and hardly a police force."

We walked down the dock to a small bench. Dr. Jamieson sat down and I leaned on the back of the bench, gazing out over the waves. I wondered if my old commander, Stephen Blucke, could help make peace in the community, but when I mentioned Blucke the doctor spat into the water and began to laugh.

"Murphy, you'll get no help from that quarter. He's in cahoots with the British agent, Skinner, and the two of them are taking both the blacks and the whites for everything they can get their greedy little hands on."

I'd always thought Blucke was self-absorbed and manipulative but I'd never featured him as turning on his own war veterans, but the doctor explained that my old leader had contracted with Stephen Skinner, a government agent and a leading Shelburne businessman, to supply black workers for the building of roads and bridges in the area. He said it was common knowledge that Skinner received thirty-five pence per day from the government for each worker, gave Blucke twenty-eight pence, and pocketed the other seven pence for doing nothing. And Blucke turned around and hired workers, most of whom were Black Pioneers, and paid them eight pence each. It was that extra twenty pence per worker that enabled Blucke to not only build the nicest house in Birchtown, but also be the only black member of the privileged Christ Church in Shelburne.

"For God's sake, Murphy, it's enough to make me sick. He went ahead and bought a pew at that church. That's about the only way they'd let him in. It costs twenty shillings to buy a pew and here he is hiring his old soldiers out at eight pence a day. You can't live on that. Nobody can. Even the worst of the white workers are making two shillings a day."

That pay gap was the start of the simmering anger in the town. Many Black Pioneers took the job, even if it meant fishing or laboring as well to augment their wages, because the eight pence a day was better than nothing. The white laborers in town were also mostly disbanded soldiers. They thought they were entitled to decent pay, some property for farming, and overall good treatment from the government that they had fought for in the war. They would not work for starvation wages and their resentment towards the black workers was strong.

That was not the end of it, either. Skinner was the government agent, a man Dr. Jamieson said was roundly disliked for his arrogance, but his word was beyond reproach in Shelburne, mainly because he controlled the courts and the flow of government funds for the town. Colonel Blucke was viewed as the leader of the Birchtown community because he was the former leader of the Black Pioneers. The two became not only business partners but also friends, and Skinner arranged that only through Blucke could workers be hired for roadwork, thereby benefitting both of them, impoverishing the black community, and creating bitterness in the white community.

"You have no idea how bad things are here for some of the people. The winters are hard and there's no doubt that some people are simply starving. Not just the Black Pioneers, Murphy, but the poor whites too. Those that aren't starving are scrambling for anything they can get, working all day and all night. You know, if the road workers could get the thirty-five pence that the government is paying Skinner, they could likely scrape through, but at eight a day and with a family, there is no chance."

The doctor shook his head and for a long while neither of us said a thing. We looked out over the rolling waves to the long horizon. There were several brigs in the harbor along with smaller fishing boats and the war-ship. A red sun was beating down, creating a haze over the cool water. It was serene and peaceful but I was thinking about the doctor's words and wondering when slavery would end and we would be treated as free men, not indentured to anyone and especially not killed or captured by slave hunters or slowly destroyed by our corrupt leaders.

"You know, Murphy, I don't know how it is with your group in Brindley but here most of the blacks and some of the loyalist whites have not been given any land to work. Most of the land is hard enough to work anyways with the rocks and the sparse soil and the winters and all, but even to be given just a town plot won't work. Blucke, I hear, has been given two hundred acres and, besides, he's got a fishing business going too. Some say he and Skinner are in charge of the surveying. I don't know the truth of that but I know for damn sure that a fellow can't raise a family on two or three acres, no matter what sort he is, and there's few that have land close enough to town to make a go of it."

But, I thought, Birchtown wasn't Brindley Town and Blucke couldn't make trouble for Thomas and our group that far away. Besides, I had a more pressing problem, namely how to get Jean and Daniel back to Brindley without running into the bounty hunter. Dr. Jamieson agreed that it would be too tiring for Jean and far too dangerous for any of us to take the road back, but there were ships that sailed between Digby and Shelburne on a regular basis and he was confident that we could find passage there if we could afford the fares. The doctor looked hard at me as he told me this but I assured him that I did have the money. My parting gift from Captain Mitchell was in a leather bag around my neck, underneath my shirt. We walked slowly back to his office. The street was now crowded with people as the business day wore on.

"Don't stay here too long, Murphy. Bad days are coming to this town. I can feel it."

Jean was minding another child when we got back to the doctor's office. I told her of our traveling plans and set off to find Daniel to arrange passage as quickly as possible.

The boy was sitting on the edge of the commercial dock, his feet dangling in the brackish water, watching the gulls swoop down for pieces of food that floated on the tide. He was startled when I came up behind him, still nervous after our ordeal in the woods. We bought buns and cheese from a waterfront vendor and went down to where two ships were being unloaded. A short, thin man was leaning against the rail around the landing, watching the unloading and smoking a large cigar. I caught his eye and asked him if he knew where we could arrange passage to Digby. He nodded his head towards the smaller of the two ships where the activity was less intense. Sitting on a large trunk next to the vessel was a man with a pencil making marks on a long list of names. He looked up as we walked towards him.

"What can I do for you fellows?"

Captain Josh Terrell was pleased to take two more passengers to Digby but that was all he had room for. Normally, he said, he was booked two weeks in advance, so if we wanted to wait for a few weeks then we could all go. He shrugged his shoulders and said that he really only had berths for two and we were lucky to get them for a passage in two days. I thought for a few minutes while Daniel went over to the ship and looked her over closely. If we waited for two more weeks it would put us behind in our wedding plans back at Brindley. And what would Daniel and I do for all that time in Shelburne? I was getting increasingly anxious about getting started on a cabin before winter came. I knew the cold weather was around the corner and I was determined to have a comfortable, safe home for Mary before the snow flew. Dr. Jamieson's warning about trouble ahead in Shelburne also echoed in my head. I turned to the captain, who was looking at me curiously.

"All right, two berths then. They'll be for the boy here and an older woman."

"Money up front. No credit, no barter, no trades."

"All right, will you transport a horse, too?"

The captain looked at me with a small smile on his face. He was a hard old bastard, clear enough, but there was something about him that I liked.

"Yes, we've got room below for a horse, at least as long as it doesn't mind sharing stables with a couple of cows and a dozen goats. A shilling for the horse and I'll throw in hay and water for the passage. No oats though."

We shook on the deal and he looked me straight in the eye. On a whim, I asked him if he knew Captain Mitchell and he smiled broadly.

"Everybody knows him, the rascal. He's a good man but many will tell you differently. He's south right now, I hear, but he'll be back here when everybody least expects it."

The captain laid his finger against the side of his nose and winked at me, but I had no idea what he meant by that gesture and simply smiled and nodded. Now that I had booked berths for Daniel and Jean, I felt a huge relief. I was prepared to walk back to Brindley by myself, if need be, keeping a close eye for the slave catcher. Captain Terrell looked at me closely.

"I know you wanted three fares. There are no other ships leaving here for Digby before we get back and, like I said, you're looking at two weeks of waiting. If you want to put the two on and take yourself there by other means, you've only got two choices. You can walk the trail through the woods, which I hear is infested with bandits, or you can hire one of those Mi'kmaq guides to paddle you there. There's always one or two waiting by the river just as it flows into town."

He pointed to the north end of Shelburne.

"It's only a half hour walk from here. Then you can settle down in one of those bark canoes and paddle your way to Digby. I hear tell it's only a three-day trip and, depending on the winds, you could even get there before us. That's if you can stand sitting in a little wee boat that floats way too low and is way too tippy."

I arranged to bring Jean, Daniel, and the horse to the dock early in the morning in two days, and the boy and I walked back up to the town. My mind was churning with the idea of taking a small boat to Digby. I'd never been in a canoe before and couldn't imagine how any vessel could be made of bark. It didn't sound likely. Still, it might be better than taking the forest road and wondering all the time if the hunter was catching up to me.

When Jean arrived home that night, I told her about arranging the passage to Digby and she was pleased we were leaving soon but worried about me traveling alone. By that time I had made up my mind to try my luck on the river and had put aside my fears.

The next day passed quickly. Jean packed her trunk after saying her good-byes to Dr. Jamieson. He pulled her aside and gave her a little money wrapped in a white handkerchief. He told her that if she decided to stay in Brindley after the wedding he would not hold it against her, but if she came back there would be a place for her. Jean was a little teary-eyed as she left the doctor's office but she was excited too at the prospect of seeing Mary again. We went to bed so as to get an early start on the traveling day but just after midnight we were awakened by a terrible roaring in the street down below. I ran over to the window and looked down at a mob of people, some holding torches and others with pitchforks, clubs, and sticks. A few had muskets which they fired in the air randomly. The roaring came from across the street, near the water, where a large collection of furniture and boards was burning. In the very middle of this blaze could clearly be seen a wagon, wheels and bed engulfed with orange flames. On the bed were bales of salt hay, each bale emitting thick clouds of oily, black smoke. It was a fascinating, horrible sight, as if hell itself had been imported to the middle of Shelburne. Before I could turn around, there was a fierce pounding at the door. Daniel was sitting straight up on his bed and moved quickly towards the door to answer the knocking, but I was quicker and stayed his hand. I put on the belt with my Roman sword that I had hung on the corner of a chair and opened the door. To my surprise, Dr. Jamieson was standing there, his hair pointing in all directions and his coat pulled on directly over flannel night pants.

"Quick, Murphy, let me in and lock the door behind me."

The doctor quickly explained the situation to us. He had come directly to our flat from his bed, sneaking around the corners of the houses on the hill and, at times, pretending to be part of the chaos that was present outside our window in order to avoid being damaged by it. His house, being in the comfortable white part of Shelburne, was safe enough, but his office, just around the block, had been broken into and the windows smashed. It was exactly as he had feared when we talked earlier. The mob was made up of laborers who were unable to find work at more than starvation wages. Some of these men were simply layabouts, not about to work in any event, but the real danger was in the core of the group, which was composed of former soldiers. These were dangerous, capable, and desperate men who had been tipped past the breaking point by a corrupt local government.

"These are not bad men, Murphy. They have families they cannot feed and there is no reasoning with a man once he is pushed to this point, especially when there are hundreds of them egging each other on."

The doctor had heard that the riot started after a small group of loyalists drinking at the waterfront tavern had begun discussing their plight. The men blamed the influx of black loyalists into the community for the loss of work. It was simple reasoning. Before the former Black Pioneers had arrived, the men had had jobs. Now those jobs were going to the new arrivals who were willing to work for lower wages. There was no work left for the whites. The combined influences of alcohol and a mob mentality had made the answer self-evident. Evict the blacks and the jobs would be left for the whites.

The appeal of this wisdom was irresistible to all who were seated in the tavern, and when the group took to the streets, every low-life and gutter rat that normally frequented the wharves also felt drawn to the expanding mob. The first store window was broken on a lark, but more followed quickly and with determination. It would be only a matter of time before floggings and hangings of blacks followed. I hadn't seen this exact scene before but I had witnessed and experienced enough of its cousins to have a very good idea of the ending to this sorry story. It was also very clear to the doctor.

"Murphy, you have to take Jean and Daniel away tonight. Not tomorrow; right now. Who knows where this will end? I think they'll search through the apartments and do terrible things before this night is over."

We obviously could not leave by the front door, but Jamieson did have a kernel of an idea to get out of the turmoil. The mob was mostly leaderless with the loudest and most lawless drunks having their way. He had heard some of the rioters talking about making their way to Birchtown now that several houses had been pulled down in Shelburne and a few unlucky black residents caught and beaten. The time that the mob actually went to Birchtown would be our best chance to make our way down to the waterfront and to Captain Terrell, who would hopefully let us on his ship. Otherwise we would have to hide out in the apartment and hope that the mob passed us by, a chance that I was loath to take. Dr. Jamieson felt that the rioting would likely continue for several more days.

I peered out the window and when it appeared that the crowd had melted into the surrounding lanes that led up to Birchtown, I turned to my comrades. Jean had her trunk full of her belongings, which we lugged down the stairs. She had not said a word since Dr. Jamieson came into the room. The street outside the flat was littered with glass from the broken window of the butcher's shop. Across the street, the old wagon was still burning while the hay smoldered with thick black smoke.

I shook Dr. Jamieson's hand and he left us quietly, going up the lane towards his house. The three of us made our way quickly to the water's edge, where I thought we would be less visible. All the time I kept a sharp lookout for any laggards from the mob. The crisis had brought my soldier's wits to the fore and my eyes darted in that familiar fighting way, looking at everything and staring at nothing, but there was nobody on the street and no sound from the surrounding flats.

When we got next to Captain Terrell's brig, I was surprised to see lanterns on at all stations and a small boat tied to the bow. The captain himself was leaning against the rail smoking a pipe with a stem that had to be two feet long.

"Well you took your time getting here. We're about to push off and the mate's been at me for an hour already to leave. The sooner we take leave of this hell-hole, the better."

The captain told us that all the passengers had been rounded up in town by the ship's crew for an early departure, with the exception of Jean and Daniel. The mate had begged him to leave without us when the mob passed right by the tied-up ship and the crew were frantic to get away, but Captain Terrell had had the thought firmly in his head that we would show up, so he waited. His ship, the *Heather*, was ready to leave Shelburne as soon as we were aboard. I grabbed the captain by the elbow and asked him to give me just ten minutes more so I could get the horse to him. Terrell said it would take fifteen for the crew to prepare the ship for departure and if I was not back by then, they were leaving, horse or not. I took off down the loading plank at a dead run. Jean and Daniel were already grappling the trunk into the bowels of the *Heather*.

Fortunately, the livery was just down the deserted street. I had no idea what to expect at the barn, which was right in the path of the mob, but everything appeared to be quiet and calm. The livery owner was not around and it was an easy matter of untying my horse and leading him out of his stable. I looked as carefully as I could for the saddle but it was nowhere to be seen and as the moments ticked by, I abandoned my search and led the horse out with a rope halter.

I could see the crew of the *Heather* getting ready to cast off the huge mooring ropes. Fortunately, Captain Terrell had left the wide plank down, even as his crew had picked up all but one of the ropes. The horse balked at going up the ramp and I was at a loss as to how to get him on. Behind me, I could hear the mob moving back towards the waterfront.

Terrell, however, had undoubtedly had this problem before; he quickly dropped a sack over the horse's eyes and led him around the wharf in a few circles to confuse him. Then up the ramp he went, with two sailors on either side of the beast, arms linked together and pushing on his back legs. As soon as the captain and horse hit the deck, he gave the order to push off. I scrambled to throw off the last mooring rope and a sailor picked up the ramp. Four men in the small tender at the bow of the *Heather* began rowing and she slowly got under way. There was no sign of Daniel or Jean but the captain yelled down at me as the ship gradually moved into the darkness of the bay.

"Don't worry, they'll see you in Digby. Go now to the river; don't wait, there'll be someone there who can help you. Watch out for those louts and keep your wits about you."

I waved back but there was little time for good-byes; the torches from the mob were clearly visible a few blocks up from the waterfront. It would not be good for me to be caught down in the shadows of the wharf. I ran quickly to the street where the doctor's office was and, darting from doorway to doorway, made my way to the outskirts of town. I had seen the river as it left the forest, not far from where the rough track from Digby came out of the woods, but I had not seen anybody there when Daniel and I crossed its shallow, slow-moving waters a few days ago. It was hard for me to imagine any boat making its way through the shallow water. Now I hoped that the captain was right and there would be a Mi'kmaq guide camped by its waters.

The river was still when I got there, the water smell hanging in the breeze and the air cool by the banks. There was no sign of anyone and it was very quiet as I crossed to the other side. The river left the pasture, immediately entering the thick woods, and I walked along the bank, happy to be back in the calm forest and away from the unsettling town. There was a low growling noise coming from Shelburne and there were several patches of orange fire visible, particularly in the direction of Birchtown. I had my money bag hanging around my neck and my other items in a sack over my shoulder. If there was no guide at the river, I would have to make my way back to the forest trail, traveling by night and hiding by day to avoid the slave hunter.

A short walk along the river led me into bush so thick and black that I had to stop. I sat against a large oak tree and thought about the day and how trouble seemed to follow me, but at least the boy and Jean were safe and on their way to Brindley. Mary would be thrilled to see her mother and surprised to see the boy. My last thought before I fell asleep was of Mary picking strawberries by the side of the deep rock shelf where it entered the ocean.

When I woke the sun was streaming through the long oak leaves and birds were dancing above the top of the water. A large man in leather leggings and a long leather robe was looking down at me silently with his arms crossed. As I shook my head and looked up at him, he slowly bent from the waist and stared directly into my eyes.

"Where do you want to go?"

"Digby. Brindley."

It was obvious that I had met my guide. I wondered just how much English this Mi'kmaq could speak, but that question was soon answered. His English had a strange twist to it but was as good as my own, though with an occasional unknown word thrown in.

"Well, Bear River then. You can walk to Digby from there, it's not far. Half a day's walk for a man. How much will you pay if I take you there?"

I had no idea how much it would cost to go to Bear River, nor how long it would take, but I'd sent a horse by a ship for a shilling.

"One shilling?"

"If you don't eat, it can be one shilling. If you eat with me it will be two shillings."

"All right two shillings, then. How long will it take?"

"That depends."

"On what?"

"On if we see a moose to kill. Then say five days to get there. If we don't see a moose then four days."

The guide pivoted on his foot and went into the woods. Back fifty paces or so from the edge of the river was a small camp with an open fire and a pot boiling on a small grate. Next to some bedding was a small vessel, the first canoe I'd ever seen. I wondered why he'd dragged the boat so far from the water's edge. The guide told me his name was Noele and said that I was welcome to the boiling tea. He walked over to the canoe. The guide picked it up with one hand, his arm linked under one of the wooden spars that ran across its width, and walked down to the river. When he returned and began packing his gear, I grabbed my traveling sack and took my tea down to the canoe that was resting, half-in and half-out of the river. It did not resemble any boat that I had ever seen. About sixteen feet long, it was held together with wooden beams that made a curve the length of the canoe with a single long span of wood along the bottom. Smaller laths were stretched horizontally across the main beams at about two-inch intervals. Above it all was birch bark, layered on top of the beams and held together with a sticky substance that felt like sap or tar. There was not a nail in the whole vessel that I could see. The canoe was held together with sinew tied so tightly that the cords, shellacked with the same tar, appeared to be one with the wood.

Noele came down to the river's edge and flung his two traveling sacks into the bottom of the canoe. He looked down the length of the river, then back at me.

"It's time to go."

There were no seats in the canoe but he gestured for me to get in and I clambered up the canoe to the front. The craft was surprisingly strong. Noele lifted the boat by its stern spar and pushed it easily into the river. He hopped into the rear and passed a wooden paddle up to me. I watched him paddle us out to the middle of the river and found I could easily get into the rhythm of the strokes. The current of the river was against us, but the flow was so slow that it was a simple matter to work the canoe upriver and I found it enjoyable to watch the forest gliding steadily past us.

It was a quiet voyage. Just before noon on the first day, Noele steered the canoe to the bank and we had a lunch of smoked meat and hard bread. There were raspberries growing on bushes next to the forest wall and, barely ripe, they made a nice finish to the meal.

We ate in silence until the end of the lunch. Then Noele turned to me and asked if I was British. I shook my head.

"Then what are you? You speak the same language."

And what was I, really? I shrugged my shoulders. I suppose I could have called the United States my home once, but I had no rights in that country and no future there either. So I could not be that. I had fought for the British but had no feeling for them and, from what I'd seen in Shelburne and my brief time in Brindley, I wasn't sure things were much better in this country. Nova Scotia was a colony, not a country, but could it be home to me? I meant really home where Mary and I could raise a family and make a living? It already looked like everything we gained could only be kept through simple hard work and plain stubbornness against the usual entrenched interests and prejudices, but then again there were always some people like Dr. Jamieson and Captain Terrell, who were honest and generous.

Noele looked at me and laughed.

"Well it's a good thing that you aren't British, even if you can't decide where you come from. I hate the British."

He drew his finger across his throat, his eyes glinting in the sunlight.

"We used to be friends with the French. When they left, the British brought death and hunger to us and hunted us like rats. Lapigot came with them, too."

I glanced back at my guide, my eyebrows raised. Noele grunted.

"Smallpox. The British brought smallpox to my people."

The canoe rode easily over the shallow river, even when the depth was less than a foot. I got used to the uncertain balance and learned to lean back on the cross-beam near the bow. We made good time and I could tell that my guide was pleased with our progress. We slept under the stars and forest canopy each night, enjoying the cool river air and the clear skies. Before noon on the fourth day, after paddling for several hours, we beached the canoe and walked for a small stretch. Finally we arrived at a small settlement. Noele pointed as we rounded the final corner into the settlement.

"This is Bear River. This is my home."

We were met by Luce, Noele's wife, who led us to their wigwam, a tall structure supported by fifteen or so saplings, six feet in height and spaced about two feet apart. The saplings were placed in the ground on one end then bent together and lashed at the top, leaving a small opening for smoke to escape. On top of the limbs were placed strips of bark and fir boughs to make the structure safe against wind and rain. There was an opening at the front of the wigwam but we had to enter on hands and knees given its restricted height. Inside the wigwam a pole was set across at a height of four feet with a pot hanging from it, suspended over a small fire. Once inside, I told my guide that I wanted to leave for Brindley as quickly as possible, but he insisted that I stay for the day, share dinner with the community, and leave in the morning.

"Listen to me, Murphy. It's best to walk there when you're full and feeling good, not tired from paddling the canoe for four days."

So I stayed, lying in the hot sun and listening while Noele sat beside me smoking a small pipe and greeting the other members of the Bear River community who came up and spoke with him. He told me how his people had been at Bear River for a long time and had been friendly with the first fishermen who had come from across the sea. As settlers arrived, the Mi'kmaq had been pushed into smaller and smaller areas. The French settlers treated them well, trading with them, and many French had married into Mi'kmaq families. Some people at Bear River had both French and Mi'kmaq ancestors and now had French names but, when the British defeated the French, life became very hard for both the Mi'kmaq and their friends. Their numbers had been declining for many years and smallpox plagues regularly ravaged the populace. That and starvation were frequent visitors to the Mi'kmaq, who depended on moose, deer, and beaver to provide furs and food to get through the long winters.

This year, however, had been a fine one for the Bear River community. The game had been plentiful and the Mi'kmaq had also been able to smoke many fish taken from the bay. The past year's porpoise harvest had been excellent. I had never heard of a fish called a porpoise. Noele explained that a porpoise was a big fish that swam in the bay and could be caught when it came to the surface to breathe. When I shook my head at the idea of a fish that could breathe, he laughed and said we would go on a porpoise hunt in his canoe sometime.

I told my guide of our escape from slavery, and the war, and the settlement in Brindley. I also told him about Mary and going to Shelburne to get Jean. His face darkened when I spoke of meeting Daniel and our fight in the forest against the slave hunter.

"I have heard of men like this. The British always bring trouble and bad men with them. It is like they are devils with curses on their heads and they poison everything they touch."

Noele said that the Mi'kmaq had never experienced smallpox and other diseases before the arrival of the British. Some people said they were given the disease on purpose by the settlers through blankets that were deliberately infected then sold to the Mi'kmaq. When I told him that this seemed unlikely, even for the British, he leaned back against the wigwam and puffed on his pipe. Then he looked down at me.

"Murphy, three times in my life the British have paid for the scalps of my people. Two times these were not just bounties on warriors but also on old men, women, and children. They were paid to men like your slave hunter for each scalp they brought to their government. It was as if we were wild dogs to be hunted down. We have lost many, many people to the pox, which did not exist here before the British came. In one sickness, almost half of this place was gone to dust. The British hate us because we were friends with the French. Do you know why they finally stopped giving money for our scalps? I will tell you. It was because those evil bounty hunters started bringing back the scalps of people who were not Mi'kmaq. They killed their own to get the money. They were running out of the heads of my people to scalp so they brought others. You say they would not give us sickness on purpose? Bah."

We sat together in silence for a long time. Finally I stood up.

"Noele, I'm sorry. You'd think—after seeing the mess of things that I have—that I'd have a clearer idea of just how cruel men can be. Still, I hope things will get better for both of us."

Noele got to his feet.

"It's all right, we will be good friends, you and I."

He showed me around the Bear River community and, afterwards, we had a dinner of venison, dried fish, and berries. That night, with a cool wind blowing and the sky threatening rain, we slept in the wigwam, warmed by the embers of the dying fire.

Twenty-Five

I was up with the sun the next morning. Luce gave me a sack filled with smoked meat, and Noele, serious and silent, embraced me as I left. The trail from Bear River to Digby was clear and well-used. I thought of the slave hunter and kept my guard up but, gradually, in the brilliant heat of the day, my worry faded.

It was not a long way to Brindley Town. I walked into Digby just past noon and Brindley a short while later. It seemed like I'd been gone for a very long time as I thought about my troubles along the trail. Several people called out as I made my way through the forest of army tents, until there, sitting in front of a small fire, was Mary with Daniel and Jean. It was a sight to warm my heart. Mary ran over and gave me a great hug, but it was Jean who spoke first.

"Well, Murphy, here you are and we've been here a day and a little more already. Did you have a good trip? Is everything all right?"

But I said nothing as I looked into Mary's eyes and saw her fear and anxiety shining back. She talked in a low voice so the others would not hear.

"Murphy, are you really all right? Jean told us about your trip down through the woods. Did you have trouble coming back?"

I held her tight to my chest and whispered in her ear.

"Listen, we'll go for a walk later and I'll tell you all about it. Everything is just fine; there is a lot to talk about, but not with everyone around. Let's talk with the others here a while, then I'll go see Thomas."

So we sat and chatted and I told them about Noele and our canoe trip. Daniel and Jean's voyage was uneventful once they cleared the Shelburne harbor. The weather had been clear the whole way and the ship made steady time to Digby. Captain Terrell had treated them well and they and the horse had been well fed. The horse was staked at the edge of the tent town, grazing on long grass. Mary had given him the name Moses in memory of my long-gone friend.

Daniel had not said a word since I got back but when Mary asked him to fetch more wood from the huge pile at the edge of the clearing, he went off willingly. She turned to me with a broad grin on her face.

"He's been a blessing, Murphy. He does everything he's asked and more and never questions or complains about anything. These are strange times we live in where you can add to your family just by taking a walk in the woods. It's good for him here, too, I think, though he says very little."

"The plain fact, Mary, is that he saved my life. He has nowhere else to go and I know he doesn't say much, but when he has to he speaks up."

The sun was high in the sky when I left our tent and went looking for Thomas. His tent was right next to ours but he was nowhere to be seen. Sally said he was checking the water tank near the British army barracks and, as I wandered in that direction, I could hear his voice, angry and loud. Thomas was standing next to the cart where the water tank sat, talking to a British soldier who looked barely interested as he fiddled with a fitting on the tank.

"What is it that you don't understand? We must have more water each day. Bringing the tank here once a day isn't enough, it runs out by afternoon and then there's nothing the rest of the day. Lend me a horse and I'll get it myself."

The soldier was unmoved, shrugging his shoulders and ignoring the outburst, but I could see that here was a problem that I could do something about.

"It just so happens I have a horse that's available and he would love to have some work to do."

Thomas turned around, his frown turning to a broad laugh in an instant. He grabbed me in a bear hug.

"Murphy, just the man I need, and your horse too, of course. I was just thinking I might have to borrow it before you even got back."

"You would have been welcome to it. Thomas why don't you have the people go to the well by themselves rather than haul it here on the cart?"

The well had been dug even before we'd arrived at Brindley. It was just a half mile or so west of the tent town towards Digby, but access to it had always been limited to the water cart with the huge tank on its bed.

"Murphy, if we let everyone in the camp go to the well by themselves, the ground around it will be a muddy bog in a day or two. In a week or so the sides will cave in. No, the tank cart is the best way, but we need to have fresh water on hand all the time. Come with me for a minute, I want to talk to Ben."

Ben and Sarah were sitting inside their tent. They greeted us, and Thomas asked Ben if he had any experience with horses.

"Yep, I worked with them one whole season, hauling flats of salt."

The old salt worker said that he could easily hitch Moses to the tank cart and haul some water back to the camp. I told him to take Daniel with him for help. As he was heading over to our tent, Thomas took my arm and asked me to walk with him. We made our way out of the tent town to the shore, where he stopped and sat on an old log. I thought he was going to ask me about my trip or how I came to meet up with Daniel but his worries were so serious that he talked for a long time without a pause.

He told me that the situation at Digby was dire. We had been promised a full ration of food for a year, then partial rations for another two years as we got settled into our new country. Most of the Black Pioneers were men who needed land to make a living but no land had been forthcoming from the British and the rations were dwindling as summer ran on. With no cabins being built, the food rations running out, and no help from the local officials, Thomas was almost frantic about the coming winter. Worse than that, some of the officials were holding back rations in Digby, doling them out to those they favored and insisting that the new arrivals work on the road from Digby to Annapolis before they received food. He had heard that there were more than 12,000 pounds of flour and another 9,000 pounds of salt pork stored in Digby under the direction of Reverend Edward Brundenell. That man used Richard Hall's cellar to store the supply barrels and Hall had made himself the judge of who was to receive the food.

Although the local British agent, Williams, had told Thomas and me that we were to be in charge of issuing rations, it was Hall and Brundenell who actually gave out the food. Hall was in charge of the local work crews that were building the road to Annapolis and so used the government rations as payment for work on the road. Food for road work was not what had been promised us when we left the British army, so Thomas had talked to both Brundenell and Hall, but neither had the wit or the will to listen.

Looking beyond the petty corruption of the food distribution system, the lack of land was the greater problem for us and it was the lack of surveyed plots that troubled Thomas the most. Without town plots for houses and farm plots for working, most of the Black Pioneers would never be independent and would have to rely on the favors of local residents to survive. Thomas had talked with the surveyor, Millidge, about getting at least the town surveyed, but the man said that his resources were too few and that he was focused on getting the white loyalist settlers established in Halifax and Shelburne. He hoped to get to Brindley Town in the fall or early winter.

Many of the brightest members of Brindley had already figured out the situation and had left for Halifax or were making plans to do so. Others had found work locally as house servants or farm laborers or had gone to Shelburne or Annapolis for work. Some had become indentured to families in Annapolis for extended periods of time. These unfortunates, usually pressed by the needs of their families, had sold their liberty for wages that were barely above starvation level. All through the long years of war and suffering we had been told by the British that we would be given land and the means to become independent once the war was over. Instead, we were back to scrambling for a living and some had even returned to slavery. The families left at Brindley were made up of people who relied on Thomas to find solutions to the food shortage and lack of land to farm. It was no wonder he was feeling anxious. The awful truth was that there was no local solution to either of these problems. Thomas explained to me that he had talked to all the local agents and could not cut through the corruption and self-interest. He asked me if I thought Colonel Blucke could help us from Shelburne and wondered if it was worthwhile for him to make the trek to that town.

"Thomas, the simple fact is that Blucke is no good either. They say he has two hundred acres of the best land around Birchtown, and the biggest house there, and a pew in the white church in Shelburne. He's got all that by working with the government agent in town to steal the money supposed to go to the road workers there. Most of the members of our old brigade, his soldiers, haven't got enough to eat and can't feed their families on what's left of the money that dribbles through to them. They've got no land to work, no land in town to live on. Thomas, they're begging on the streets, our old fellows, while he's living high on the hog in a house with servants and the like. I saw him and there's no help from that end, and there's worse news than that."

I told him about my fight with the slave hunters in the forest and the gray man who had headed towards Brindley more than a week ago. I wasn't worried about the bounty hunter coming to our town but any lone travelers would have to be careful. I was also uncertain about how the British officials would react to slave hunters. Would the British back them or support us? Thomas wasn't sure either, and had not previously considered the possibility of slave hunters coming to Nova Scotia. It was yet another worry.

"With no help coming from Blucke, there's no reason for me to go to Shelburne. Sounds like things are no better there anyway. It's too late in the year to plant. I think I should tell our people to try and get some work, even on the road if need be, to be able to get through the winter. Some will likely have to live in tents through the cold, but some can build shacks if they can get the materials together. What are you going to do?"

I'd actually been doing a lot of thinking about just that. I was lucky in two ways—first by having some money left in my leather bag that I could use to buy an ax, a saw, and other tools, and second, by having a horse. The way I figured it, Mary, Daniel, and I could build a simple cabin to get us through the winter. I was unsure whether Jean would go back to Shelburne, so it would have to be big enough for the four of us. I was thinking I'd build it back from the water near the rocky shelf where Mary and I often walked. It struck me that such a natural harbor might have some advantages. Near the water's edge, stunted trees grew, but farther back the land was thick with fir trees, straight and long and perfect for ship's masts. I did not see myself as a farmer and I didn't really care how thin the soil was, but I did know a thing or two about cutting trees and it seemed to me that there might be a living in that. I told Thomas about my plans and he grunted in agreement. I figured that logging here would be pretty much the same as logging in the south. First, I'd go and see the Digby sawmill owner and see if he'd take any logs I'd cut. Logging had no appeal to Thomas, who was a millwright by trade. He thought he would work on the road with the others until he could get a more suitable job and some land.

The most important thing was to keep pressing the British to have the farm plots surveyed so that the remaining Pioneers could make a start at farming and have a small town plot for somewhere to build a house. He had an idea of how to pressure the authorities beyond our local area. With so much local corruption, Thomas thought our best plan was to write a letter to Nova Scotia Governor

Parr to see if he would take an interest in our problems.

"Murphy, we'll sit down in a day or so to put a letter together. I've got some thoughts about what to write in it and you can put it down on paper for me."

But it was more than a week before we actually got together to write the note. Thomas thought it was important to make the petition seem official and respectful. He dictated and I wrote the letter. He had already written it many times in his head so he wasn't prepared to accept much in the way of suggestion. Frankly, I thought the whole exercise was a waste of time and had no chance of success, but Thomas was my friend so I kept my mouth shut and wrote down what he told me. Somehow his words, which were so moving and powerful when he spoke to crowds, sounded stiff and silly when I wrote them:

"This humble petition of the Black Pioneer begs your Honour would be so good as to look at the following description.

We first enlisted in the year 1776 and we promised when we were sworn in by Thomas Waddle by order of Henry Clinton to serve faithfully and loyally during the American Rebellion and, when it was over, we were to be at our own liberty and provide for ourselves after which time we came to this place. We have not received what we were promised, and we would be very much obliged to your Excellency if you would be so good as to grant what the articles allowed by Government to us, the same as the rest of the disbanded soldiers of his Majesty's army. When we first enlisted and were sworn we were promised that we shall have land and provisions the same as the rest of the disbanded soldiers, which we have not received. We would be ever bound to pray for your Excellency if you would be so good as to Order us what was allowed by Government to the rest of the New Colony."

It went on from there. To me it sounded awkward and begging, but my nature was not the same as Thomas' and he was always much better at the art of persuasion. Thomas gave the document to a British soldier to carry to Annapolis and on to Governor Parr. He didn't hear a word from Governor Parr about this letter.

The sun was glowing orange and low in the sky when I got back to my tent that day. Mary was sitting on a log outside, sipping slowly on a cup of tea. The others were nowhere to be seen. I took her hand and we walked to the rocky shore that I had already started to think of as our home. Mary wanted to know all about my trip to Shelburne and my run-in with the slave hunters. She'd heard it all before, of course, from her mother and Dan, but she wanted to hear it again from my lips. I skipped quickly over the fight around the campfire but Mary was not easily deceived and her eyes flickered, but she said nothing. I told her, too, of the kindness of the Shelburne skipper who had waited for us despite the peril to his ship and crew when the white soldiers had rampaged through the town. Of course I also told her about the simple generosity of the Mi'kmaq guide, Noele, who had become my friend through our days of paddling and nights under the starry skies.

It was not a difficult job to persuade Mary to leave the tent town for the thin woods around the salty shore. She loved the huge rocks at the edge of the water and had always been intrigued by the sharp drop to the depths just off shore. The rocky shore, crashing ocean, and thin soil had a bewitching form, simple and startling in its bleak beauty. She hated the crowding of Brindley Town. Even more, she disliked the uncertainty of not knowing our future, of always wondering where our food would come from, when we would get our land, and how we would survive the winter. The only certainty was the monotonous salt pork and biscuits. After all our wandering, she wanted permanence and security and the chance of a life together.

We packed up and moved the next day. While Mary and Jean set up the tent and our household in a small clearing not far from the ocean, Daniel and I walked the couple of miles to Digby to see the mill owner, John Belanger, who was a short, stocky man with the shoulders of a blacksmith and hands as rough as the bark of the logs his mill was cutting. Belanger was given to swearing and pawing in the dirt with his boot while he worked out the prices of logs and lumber. He calculated everything in his head and could easily do complicated sums. I found him fair and honest. He was no tougher with me than he was with any other logger who hauled logs to him and certainly not as hard on me as he was with his mill employees, who feared him. He was skeptical at first about my ability to regularly bring him logs, but when I told him I had a horse his eyes widened and he nodded thoughtfully.

"And an ax? Do you have tools and ropes and chains?"

I confessed I had none of the makings yet but did have enough money to buy them. Belanger agreed to take any logs that I would bring him, paying six shillings a ton for straight logs, weighed on the mill scale. It was not a large return but would be enough to keep my family over the winter and buy hay and oats for Moses.

I had decided to build a board and batten cabin. This type of construction was more common in barns than in houses but was sturdy and simple to make. Better still, I had been part of a team that had put up a machine shed of board and batten at the Richardson farm and I knew that this style had two big advantages—it was quick to build and precise measurements were not needed. It was also weatherproof. The mill owner agreed to trade me cut lumber for some of my hauled logs. He asked me if I planned on skidding the logs behind the horse and, when I nodded, he pointed at a rough, low-slung wagon that was pulled off by the side of the wall of the mill. Belanger told me I could have the use of it and the harness too if I would bring him at least forty logs a month. I thought for a moment and realized that I could bring at least three times as many logs with each wagon load as I could by simply skidding them along the road, and they would also arrive at the mill in better condition. Lending me the wagon also tied me to Belanger, thereby ensuring another constant supply of logs for his mill. We shook on the deal.

Belanger went to his pocket for a scrap of paper and wrote a short note to the merchant at the general store, telling him that I worked for the mill owner and should be given fair trade. When I went to the store I was very happy that I had Belanger's note. The store owner at first attempted to sell me an old ax that was not balanced and had a poor handle. I knew what I needed, however, and insisted on an oak handle, long and true, and a balanced head with a straight edge.

There was a good ax sitting by the window and after I pointed to it and gave the shop owner the note, he looked at me sharply and then presented only the best quality chains, ropes, and block and tackles. I added several hatchets for limbing, two long saws, and one short saw. The tools left me with just enough coin in my bag to buy marzipan in the shape of a rose for Mary. The shopkeeper agreed to keep the items until the next day when Dan and I returned with Moses to pick up the wagon. My head was swimming with thoughts about building our cabin and the upcoming logging. I would start cutting right away but the best logging, I thought, would be in the winter when the leaves would be off the trees and the ground would be hard for skidding the logs out of the woods.

That night, lying in the quiet of the tent, I had a terrible nightmare about the gray man. He had me up against the edge of a cliff, gradually pushing me over despite my best efforts to hold on, my fingers scrambling in the dirt. After I awoke I lay for a long time thinking of the Black Pioneers and where we were.

I did not feel the same duty to the remaining Brindley residents that Thomas did. Sometimes I thought that if I could find a way to carve out a life in the wilderness, then why couldn't the rest of them? But then, I had had the gift of the leather money bag to thank for most of that and the horse for the rest.

I had sympathy for the men but I did not feel the same responsibility for them that Thomas did. That was the difference between being a leader of men and being a man who only really cares about those close to him. It had always been that way with Thomas and me. He had always wanted to lead, and I only to take care of my own. Still I knew he relied on me more than any other and for that I did feel responsible. To listen to him and give him advice when he asked, to do the plain jobs, the blunt work that he could not accomplish, was my service. Thomas was my friend and I intended to be his support as long as he needed, so I would help the remaining Pioneers, too, as much as I could.

Twenty-Six

Some of the Brindley residents thought Daniel was a little slow. Even Jean took me by the elbow one day and asked me in a whisper if I thought the boy might be a little thick in the head.

I knew better.

It was true that Dan didn't speak much and it was true that he seldom spoke first. He usually waited to be asked but I knew where he'd come from and it was a dark place where slaves never spoke unless spoken to. Daniel had told his whole story easily enough to me that night in the woods and he would speak to me when needed. It was a relief to me to have a quiet, capable worker on the other end of the long saw. Many mornings we spent together in the quiet woods, neither of us speaking before lunch.

He was an able and willing worker. There was never a day when he rolled over in his bed saying it was too early, and never a time when he wanted to quit before dusk. Most often it was me that tired before him as he grew in strength and confidence. My experience, gained through past mistakes, made the work easier, and Dan learned all my lessons. The best one was the old one of keeping the ax sharp. Nothing makes the job finer than having a sharp ax, and using the file for half an hour saved two hours of hard work with a dull blade.

When I took off my shirt to work in the heat of the mid-day

239

sun, Dan never asked about the scars that crossed my back like the veins in a leaf. He did a man's job even though he was still not fully grown. He didn't know his age or his birthday so we resolved to make it Christmas, the same as mine, and I figured him for about fifteen. He was tall for his age, though thin, and had a kind of elastic strength. I was a bear compared to him. Together we could cut and move just about anything we needed.

Our horse, Moses, turned out to be the foundation of all our endeavors. Not only did he pull our wagon of limbed logs to the mill every third day or so, but he also skidded the logs out of the woods and brought the wagon load of boards back to our clearing so we could build our cabin. After Dan learned about building we took turns taking the horse to town with the wood on mill day, while the other worked on the little house and, in this fashion, had the cabin just about completed as the summer drew to a close.

Thomas came out to our house in the woods several times each week. He, along with most of the remaining Brindley residents, was working on the road to Annapolis but he had managed to secure a place in Digby for his family by maintaining the machines at Belanger's mill, along with helping at the flour mill and two of the wheelwrights' shops. By working extra hours, he had picked up enough money to rent a small shack on the outskirts of Digby so that his family would have shelter for the winter. He worried constantly about the Pioneers left in tents at Brindley. Thomas chafed at the inaction of the British authorities and the corruption of the local officials. Our provisions were still doled out in a haphazard fashion at the whim of the local agents, all of whom were interested in receiving payments themselves for the road improvement and were, therefore, motivated to hand out food to those who would work on the Annapolis trail. It was not what any of us had expected. One day, while Daniel was cutting in the woods, Thomas came into our clearing just as I was nailing the stoop onto the front wall of the cabin.

"I've got one thing to tell you and one thing to ask you," he said.

"And what might those two be?"

"Well the telling is that there's been a fellow at Belanger's looking for you. The asking is just when are you going to get married after all the fuss and palaver?"

My first thought was that the gray man had shown up in town to track me down, and I felt my stomach drop. Thomas saw my face and realized at once what I was thinking. He told me quickly that it wasn't the gray man at all but my friend Noele from Bear River, who was in town to sell some oil and asking how to get hold of me. The second thought I had was that Thomas was right—in the midst of moving and settling into the logging, my wedding with Mary had slipped from my mind. It was past time, though Mary had not said a word about it as she bustled around maintaining the household and helping with the building of the cabin and the logging, when needed.

Thomas told me that there was a preacher in town who would do the job for us if we didn't want too much ceremony. We hadn't been to a regular church since landing at Nova Scotia—the old churches in Digby did not take kindly to the wave of Black Pioneers. The only black loyalist I'd seen who had joined a white church was Blucke in Shelburne. We had seen a few traveling preachers who held services when they hit town but I hadn't been too worried about that for quite some time now, and I thought my churchgoing days might be mostly behind me. Still we'd need a churchman if we wanted to marry and I did want to make Mary an honest woman now that things had settled down some.

As for Mary, she had not much use for ceremony, so she was thrilled when I told her about the preacher in Brindley.

"I was starting to think maybe you'd changed your mind."

Of course there was no change of mind for me when it came to Mary. She was my one and only. We gathered up Jean and Dan, hitched up Moses to the logging cart, and headed out for the tent town. Thomas, Dan, and Jean sat in the back of the cart as we rumbled the short distance to Brindley. As we got closer to the settlement, we could hear a single voice raised from inside a large white tent and Jean, dangling her legs over the cart at the back, called out that she recognized it.

"It's David George for sure. There couldn't be anyone else with that set of pipes."

It was David George, a Baptist preacher from Shelburne who had been burned out of that town during the riot. His meeting hall had been burned to the ground even as he preached inside and he had barely made it out of the back door along with his small congregation. The mob of angry white settlers had seen him sneak out the back and had pursued him to the swamps on the east side of town. He had plunged into the murky water and the rioters did not follow. Pastor George remained worried about the angry mob the whole night through and sat shivering in the cool, misty swamp until the sun came up. His mission in ruin, and his purpose threatened, the Baptist preacher, known for his loud ministry in Shelburne, which had become the largest in that city for former slaves, wondered where he would go next. David George was well known throughout the area. Jean had mentioned him to me when I was in Shelburne as a fine man who provided support for our ex-soldiers at every turn. He had a calling to establish his New Light churches across Nova Scotia and even into New Brunswick. Jean had told me about his preaching and about baptisms in the river at Shelburne where he baptized dozens of people at a time, but I didn't really care about that. I'd be happy so long as he made Mary my wife.

We opened the tent flaps and stepped inside. Sweat beading down his brow, the preacher was just finishing an impassioned sermon. The tent was filled with people sitting on long wooden benches, many of them Black Pioneers with their families. Pastor George was a wonderful speaker and the congregation was attentive, with heads nodding as he jabbed his finger in the air and slammed his fist down on the pulpit. The sermon concerned his recent flight from Shelburne, comparing it to the ordeal of Jesus in the wilderness. I frankly thought it was a bit of a reach, but I noticed that Jean was captivated and the rest of our little party, standing quietly at the back of the tent, was listening carefully. It was not the first time that I had seen a good speaker captivate a crowd and I thought to myself that Thomas could have made a brilliant preacher if he'd had the inclination.

The congregation filed slowly out of the tent at the conclusion of the service and I hung back, waiting, as Pastor George said his good-byes. Then, as he bustled about at the front of the tent, I approached and asked him if he would perform a marriage. He straightened up and, looking at me closely under thick eyebrows, asked if I was baptized. I had been, as a boy many years ago, but not into the Baptists. I was uncertain if this would be enough for the minister, but as his eyes wandered from my face and took in the small group standing at the back of the tent, his face suddenly broke into a broad smile.

"Jean. Come here, girl. I never thought I'd see your face again."

My soon-to-be mother-in-law walked up the aisle between the benches and, to my surprise, gave the preacher a hug. He gasped and sputtered.

"You saved me for this? So you could crush me to death later on?"

He then told us that, on one of his mission trips along the coast of Nova Scotia, the small fishing vessel that he was on was carried far out to sea by an early winter gale. It took several days for the ship to beat its way back to Shelburne and, by that time, his feet had frozen and he was unable to stand up. The crew left before him and he stumbled off the vessel onto the dock and lay there, the snow beating down relentlessly, not able to walk or stand and growing steadily weaker.

The minister would have died on the dock that gloomy night but for the concern of a captain for his ship. Our friend, Captain Terrell, had docked his brig at Shelburne several days before and was enjoying himself at one of the waterfront bars, but the storm preyed on his mind and the gruff captain had wandered down to the dock to check on his ship, where he stumbled across the form of David George, covered with snow and unconscious with the cold. Terrell was a hard man, but he had his own code of behavior and that did not allow him to leave a frozen man dying on the icy planks of the wharf.

Terrell picked up the preacher and, carrying him over his

243

shoulder like a sack of potatoes, carried him up to Dr. Jamieson's clinic. The doctor had not yet gone home after the clinic had closed for the day. He was working on his accounts in his small office at the front of his practice when Terrell kicked at the front door. It took a day for David George to stop shivering and a week before he was able to stand on his frozen feet. It was Jean who helped him with his balance and massaged his feet to renew the blood circulation. Still, he would never again walk without a cane, and his feet hurt in the cold or after a day of preaching. A night in the cool swamps of Shelburne had also been hard on him. His health after his hardships was not good, but, without Jean's help, the minister would never have been able to continue his work and he had never forgotten her.

There was no longer any question about Pastor George performing the marriage ceremony. Mary and I were finally married after so many years and travails. It was a joining of two people who were only meant to be together. There could be no better partnership for either of us. It was the happiest day of my life.

We did not celebrate for long after the ceremony but we did walk into Digby and have a town meal, which Jean insisted on buying for us. Daniel had never eaten in an inn before. Sitting in a corner of the inn, near the fire, was John Belanger, the mill owner. He was eating a roast beef dinner with a large tankard of beer before him. Belanger, one of Digby's most successful businessmen, was solitary and took all his meals at the inn. Although he seldom sought the companionship of others, the residents of the town were often attracted to him to help solve their many political or economic problems. It was not uncommon for me to see him engaged in animated conversation when I delivered logs to the mill. Today, a thin man with spectacles was leaving his table as we took our place across the nearly empty room. The man glanced over at us as he left and Thomas elbowed me slightly in the ribs.

"That's the Reverend Brundenell, Murphy. He's the one who's in charge of the rations for the Pioneers. He and that Hall. They're both as crooked as a dog's hind leg."

Thomas had never heard back from Governor Parr about the

petition we had sent to him, but he had finally received a promise from the local British agent that town and farm lots would be surveyed for us next spring, and he pinned his hopes for the future on that. Many of the remaining Black Pioneers still lived in the tent town and worked on the Annapolis road or in other jobs in town. Ben and Sarah had left for Halifax a week before. Ben had not been able to stand long enough on his damaged legs to do the hard work on the road. However, he was very strong in his arms and shoulders and had signed on a fishing boat that had stopped at Digby but normally fished the rich waters off Halifax. It was true that some of the work on the boat involved standing, but much of it was hauling in heavy nets, work that punished the arms and especially the shoulders of the crew. The captain of the ship, impressed with Ben's massive shoulders and arms, agreed to let him sit for spells during the day, knowing that he would do the work of two men when it mattered most. Sarah would stay in Halifax to find work as a maid or kitchen help.

It was sad to see our friends leave but they were content with their work, so different from their labors in the salt ponds. They could both scarcely believe that they were no longer slaves. The excuses and corruptions that plagued Thomas and the rest of the Pioneers were nothing to Ben and Sarah, who were thankful that they were not standing all day up to their knees in salt water. We naturally expected the British to keep their war-time promises to us and were appalled and angered when they did not, but Ben and Sarah were simply grateful to be removed from slavery and horror.

Belanger glanced over and gestured for me to come to his table, so I excused myself and sat down opposite him. The mill owner took a pull from his tankard and nodded in the direction of the thin man who had just left his table.

"Murphy, do you know him? The Reverend Brundenell? He's about as close to God as me, I reckon. If I was you, I'd have as little as I could to do with him but I guess that isn't possible since he's got all that pork and such for you fellows. Well now he wants to trade me for planks to build a house. He wants to trade me your food for planks for his house, Murphy. What do you think of that?"

Belanger shook his shaggy head from side to side and gave a short laugh.

"But that's another story altogether. Murphy, there's been a fellow from Bear River looking for you. Noele, he's a good man; not as tough as his daddy maybe but still in all a good one. He wants you to go visit him. Here's what I've been thinking. You and that boy of yours are about the best loggers I've got. He's a real chip off the old block, that child; a man could tell he's yours without even knowing it."

I smiled because while it was surely true that Dan and I were much alike, it was also a plain fact that we were not related.

"Now if you go to Bear River to visit Noele, I'll give you my riding wagon to take and one of the mill horses. I'll load the wagon with cut lumber and when you get there, you can trade it for all the oil they've got. Mind you, all of it, or at least as much as you can possibly take. Then bring it on back to the mill and we'll see about selling it. What do you say?"

I thought about the miller's proposition for a minute or so. I didn't have a lot of schooling but I liked to think that my experiences had made up for any lack of formal training and I've always been pretty good about reading a situation. Here I could see a way for Belanger to help out all the remaining Pioneers at Brindley.

"Yep, I can see my way to do that, but I need you to do something for me. This Brundenell and his friends all look up to you. You've got the best mill around and you're a sharp businessman. The British agent listens to you, too. So I need you to lean a little on them all to release the food to the Pioneers, not in small amounts, like now, but all of it. Enough for them to live on and more to get them through the winter. Now you know as well as I do that it's our food, really, and these crooks have no right to it anyway. So it's the right thing to do. I'm not asking for any assurances, just your word that you'll have a talk with them. What do you say about that?"

Belanger was used to negotiating. There was nothing that happened at the mill that did not involve some give and take.

Smiling, he stood up and offered me his hand.

"Now you best get back to that bride of yours before someone comes along and steals her."

As I went back to our table I smiled a little to myself. How did the miller even know about our wedding? There wasn't much around the area that Belanger didn't know, is what I figured.

Mary and I never did stand on formality, so I left for Bear River the very next day. Seeing as how we'd been living together for quite some time, practical Mary was not at all concerned about my going so soon after our wedding. Dan gave a short nod when I told him I'd be gone for a while and carried on with limbing a large tree. I had no worries on that account. I walked to Belanger's mill and the owner loaded me up with one of his top horses in no time. The road to Bear River was well traveled and it was a smooth trip to the settlement. I had barely pulled back on the big horse to halt the wagon when Noele came up, a smile on his face.

"Just in time. I was beginning to wonder if you'd come."

He gestured with his hand and two of the young boys who had gathered around the wagon came around to unhitch the horse. Noele led me by the arm to his wigwam, where Luce was sitting by a pot of boiling water. She smiled as we came up and poured cups of tea. Noele looked at me, a glint in his eyes.

"I have a story for you and an adventure too, if you're willing to take it on."

Twenty-Seven

Actually, the adventure and the storytelling were linked together.

The people at Bear River waited in the late summer for the large fish called porpoises to appear in the little bay that led into the main waters of the big bay. Why the porpoises appeared, Noele did not know, but they had for his lifetime and those of his father and grandfather. Some said the strange fish were returning home, others that a favorite food was present in August. It may have been that the big fish followed the smaller mackerel into the bay.

The Bear River people had a way of hunting the big fish that was a mixture of necessity and sport. They would go far out into the water in their long birch-bark canoes, one man kneeling in the back of the craft and the other kneeling against a thwart in the front. The bow man had several spears, each about twelve feet long and tipped with twelve inches of iron, shaped to a point and with a blade as hard and sharp as one of my fine axes. The spears were as thick as a child's wrist and chosen to be free of cracks and flaws. Each hunter selected his own spears from the surrounding forest and was careful to dry the wood well, since his life could rest on them not breaking in a moment of stress.

Noele told me the story of the hunt as we sipped our tea by the fire. As he talked, he handed me a spear and I could feel the power and strength in its straight, polished shaft. The spears were placed along the length of the canoe and pointed out the bow like gleaming tusks. The canoe put out from shore along with dozens of others from the village and the two men in each craft paddled hard until they were in the midst of the porpoises, which swam a couple of miles out. The canoes spread out among the fish, both paddlers in each boat looking carefully for the rising porpoises. The fish broke the water like large billowing bubbles and arched their way along the surface. As soon as a porpoise was seen, both men paddled as hard and fast as possible toward it. Drawing near the fish, the bow man selected one of his spears and plunged it as hard as he could into the front part of the prey. The real battle then began, with the man in the bow holding on for dear life as the fish tried to wrench its way free of the spear. The man in the stern tried to anticipate the movements of the porpoise to reduce the strain on the spear and the man holding on to it. Finally, when the porpoise tired, it was lifted into the canoe.

I found Noele's tale of the porpoise hunt interesting and compelling but could not think why he was telling me. Surely the telling of this story was not why he had asked Belanger to let me know that he wanted to see me. I looked at him quizzically when he paused at the end of the description and he laughed and slapped his thigh.

"Okay," he said. "All right, I'll tell you why I need you here. Two months ago, the man who was my spear man died."

As he said this, Luce coughed across the fire and threw a small piece of wood that thudded lightly against Noele's shin.

"Yes. I will tell it all to you. The man who died was my uncle and he was the best spear man in our village. He had hunted with me for many years. We always brought back the biggest fish. Three months ago, the porpoise were seen in the bay. It was not usual at that time of year but we thought perhaps it was a favor to us, so we set off in our canoes. Some of the fishermen did not because they felt it was wrong to hunt at that time. Maybe half the village hunters went. It was very cold and windy. We had already landed two fish when a large one surfaced right beside our canoe. I did not have to paddle a stroke to get beside it and my uncle quickly speared the beast. It was then that the bad thing happened. Most porpoises I have seen stay near the top of the water when speared, but not this one. He dove straight down, so fast that the spear that was sticking out of his side flung straight up and struck my uncle across the side of his face. He grunted and toppled straight into the water, following the porpoise to the bottom of the sea. He was lost forever."

Noele stopped speaking and was quiet for a few moments.

"Since then, I have not hunted. At first I did not have the heart for it. Then I lacked the strength and courage. Finally, I simply could not find a spear man to go with me. The man in the bow has to be large and strong and he must be without fear and he should be a pleasing companion. There are men in this village who are strong but they are not big. There are men who have abundant courage. There are those who are trustworthy and are good to be with. Those few who are strong and friendly and without fear are not tall, and being tall is a big advantage since a tall man can lean down on the spear with all his weight. I am afraid that there are some here, too, who do not want to fish with me because of the death of my uncle."

Noele stopped and looked into the little fire. Luce stirred the tea-pot, a small grin on her face.

"Murphy, can you think of anyone who is big and strong and fearless and a good companion?"

I looked from one to the other.

The idea of paddling a light canoe a couple of miles into the cold waters of the bay, then spearing a large fish and battling it into the boat did not appeal to me, but Noele was my friend, he needed a hand, and it was a job I thought I could do.

We fished for five days along with others from the village. The porpoise was a strange fish, not like any others I have seen. Its body is gray, silver, and blue, and does not look like a fish body, and seems to be without scales. It has a long nose and active eyes.

The first day was simple—we caught three fish, each about four feet long, and it was not a hard task to spear them just behind their heads as they hunched over on the surface of the bay. Noele was a master at steering our canoe alongside a surfacing porpoise so that I could easily drive the spear hard into the fish and lift him into the canoe as he tired. I enjoyed the hunt and even liked the long paddle that took us far out into the bay. When we beached the canoe at the end of the day, the women and children of Bear River already had fires going to boil the oil out of the porpoises and smoke the meat.

On the second day, far out into the bay, we watched another canoe just one hundred yards or so from us. The boat had just turned against a rising porpoise and the spear man plunged his weapon hard into the body. At that instant, the fish flipped over on its side and the man with the spear, still holding on fast, was flung straight up in the air. His foot caught on the thwart of the canoe and the whole outfit—spear man, stern paddler, and canoe—flipped directly over, the canoe floating hull up on the surface of the bay. Noele yelled at the men to hold on to the upside-down canoe and we paddled furiously. The men were cold and shivering as we hauled them into our canoe. Noele reached over the hull of the craft and flipped it back upright by having three of us sitting low and grasping each side of our canoe to stabilize it. The soaked men were too cold to continue their hunt, and their paddles and spears had drifted away or sank, so we paddled them back to shore with their canoe tied firmly to the back of ours.

It was early afternoon by the time we got back to shore so there was not enough light left to paddle back out. We sat and watched the women work the fires and the smokehouse for a while. I was napping, my back against a tree, when Noele jumped up and said he wanted to show me something. We walked along a path to the river to Shelburne. As we rounded the final corner into the sleepy river that had been our road from that cursed town, I saw a long log-like shape on the ground. Noele pulled back a deer hide that was wrapped around the bundle and revealed a body within. Bluebottle flies were buzzing around the hide and swarming over the corpse.

"Hell," I said, "what is that?"

Noele leaned close to me.

"Look closer," he said. "Look closer at this man."

The last thing I wanted to do was look at the face of the unfortunate creature, flies buzzing around his head, but I faced it and was startled to see the drained and wrinkled but unmistakable face of the gray man. The man-hunter who had chased Daniel and haunted my thoughts had reached an end here, where the river curved towards the Bear River settlement.

I sat down on a stump.

Noele smiled.

"I take it that this is your gray man," he said.

I nodded.

"Now let me tell you a story. I have already told you that I could not hunt the fishes for the last few months. So I have been traveling the river, trading and sometimes paddling other travelers. A few weeks ago I paddled some skins and wooden staffs to Shelburne. The skins I traded for flour and salt. The poles were for hunting and I had the smith in Shelburne fix points to them with iron. He is the best at this. I landed my canoe at the carrying place here but it was dark and it had been a very long day. I carried the spears up and lay them upright against a tree. By this time I was tired to the point that I did not want to take the small walk to the village. I made a small fire and had a pot of tea, then I rolled into my blankets and slept easily. In the night, I woke up because I heard the nicker of a horse and there standing across the ashes of the fire was this man. He was pointing a gun at me.

"I found this strange since the path to Shelburne does not run past this point so travelers on horses would not usually be here. When I knocked the sleep out of my eyes, I saw at once who he was. It was your gray man. He spoke slowly.

"'I'm looking for a black runaway. Young boy, thin but strong looking. I've been riding this trail up and down for a while with no sign and I figure now he must be here or close by,' said the man. I looked at him across the fire. He was still pointing the gun at me.

"'I know who you are,' I said. 'You're not welcome here, this is our land and you need to leave now. I've seen no boy.'

"But the man's face was hard and his expression mean. He came up next to me and, raising the butt of the rifle, slammed it into the side of my head. The blow knocked me sideways to the ground and my vision blurred. I lay there, unable to move, not knocked out but dazed and confused and with a crushing pain.

"'I tell you, I've ridden up and down the trail to Shelburne and he's not there,' he said. 'That means he's just about got to be here or in Digby. I think either way you know where he went and I think you're going to tell me. Now we're going to your village and we'll see if your friends would rather watch you die than tell me where the boy is.'

"The bounty hunter tried to lift me up with one hand, still pointing the gun at my chest, but I was a dead weight so he let me fall back down for a few minutes. Gradually, my senses returned but still I lay there, unmoving, pretending to be insensible while I was making a plan in my mind. The spears were well within arm's reach but the man had his gun aimed directly at my chest.

"Finally, with a curse, he came over and grabbed my arm to lift me up. I stumbled as I rose, now wide awake but pretending to still be dazed and slow on my feet. As he reached forward to support me, the gun in his other arm dipped down. This is what I had hoped for and as soon as the gun barrel lowered, I grabbed the nearest porpoise spear. Without hesitating or taking the time to look, I rammed it with a backward swing as hard as I could into the man. It went a long way into his stomach. As he fell back with the force of the blow, he released his hold on my arm and fired his gun. The bullet grazed my shoulder."

Noele pulled back his shirt and showed me a large bandage that wound around his shoulder and under his arm. I looked at him with a question in my eyes.

"I'm fine, it just grazed me," he said. "The gray man flopped around on the ground with the spear sticking out of his stomach. Finally he stopped and lay still. I knelt on one knee to catch my breath and pressed my shirt against my shoulder to stop the bleeding. Then I went over and pulled the spear all the way through and out.

I left the man where he was lying and went into the village. Luce bandaged me and one of my friends came and wrapped the man's body in this hide. I told him to leave it until you could see."

My friend paused and there was silence in the little glade, the only noise the steady buzzing of bluebottles.

Finally he spoke again.

"I wanted you to see the body so you'd know you no longer have to worry about him hunting you or your friend Daniel. Now we will bury him. He was an evil man, traveling the hidden paths and threatening your people. He was a man with bad intent who had committed crimes in the past. I think he deserved to die. Still, I would not have killed him if he had not hit me and threatened to kill me."

Noele stopped speaking. He sat on a log that had washed up high on the sand, the end of which touched the stump I crouched on.

"The evilness of these times seems to be without end," he said. "The coming of the white man changed everything and now we have come again to men hunting other men for money. First came the French, and we were their friends and allies in war but, when they lost, the British knew us as enemies. They drove us from our homes, put bounties on our heads and killed our women and children when the men were out hunting. I have seen these things. Worse, they brought their missionaries, hard on the heels of their traders and those men took the heart out of us. They brought pox and fever and the animals left the land, so we starved. When your family is sick and dying and starving, you lose heart. It is much worse than any war because it takes and takes and takes. We lost many people to the British soldiers but we have lost many more to the traders with their flea-filled blankets and more still to the missionaries with their preaching and white man's medicine. We have lost our way in our own land and this country has become our tomb.

"Murphy, when I look at you I think that you already know these things in your heart. You are a tribe of slaves far from your home, taken away from your families and flogged by vicious men. Your people too have had the hearts carved out of their chests by these white men and you are left with no home here and no knowledge of your past. I have heard tales about your people and how they are owned by white men in the States. It sickens me."

I thought of my past floggings and a small shiver went down my spine.

"Noele, I have seen things in war that I would like to forget and now in peace there are men who will take and take. You asked me when we first met which country I called home and I could not answer. I still have no answer to that. My ancestors came from across the ocean but I did not know my parents. My friends and my wife, Mary, and her mother and the boy, are all that is dear to me. The rest does not matter. All that matters is my home, my own land, my family, and friends like you."

There was a long silence. Noele drew aimless curves and circles in the sand while I gazed down the river, my eyes always drawn back to the wrapped bundle. Finally my friend looked up from the sand and threw his short stick into the water.

"That way is the end of our tribe and the end of our hopes. Murphy, we are defined by who our ancestors were. My tribe has lived here for more generations than I can count and only now are we without our souls and unable to see our futures. Here is what I think. When the white man first came to our shores, yours across the ocean and mine here, we should have killed them all. The same the next time the big boats came. And the next. I think if we had done that, the white man would not have kept coming back. Your people would not be slaves in a foreign country and mine would not be without heart."

Neither of us looked at the other. The flies droned around the body. My parents had come from a place that was across the ocean but I felt no attachment to that land. The flogging and the branding, the death of Moses, and the cruelties of war, and pain of sickness and poverty only had meaning to me because they affected me directly. Nothing else mattered, surely not injustice in the past of my ancestors, but I did understand Noele's words because they were similar to Thomas'. I have always envied men who can truly feel the pain of others and can fight as fiercely for those they do not love as I would for those I love.

Noele stood and kicked a stone into the river. I got up off the stump and we began walking slowly back to Bear River. After a little ways I stopped and shook my head.

"What about his horse?"

"Hanging in the smokehouse. There's lots of meat there for the winter."

We walked on a little further.

"And his guns and such?"

"The guns were given to the young men. Everything else he had is at the bottom of the river."

By this time we were nearly back at the settlement.

"Thanks for killing the gray man. I'll have no more bad dreams about him stealing into my home."

But Noele was already thinking about the next day's porpoise hunt.

We fished for three more days and caught three fish one day and four the next. All of the fish were just under four feet long. I could tell that Noele was pleased with our steady catches but I also knew that he wanted to kill at least one large fish. The largest porpoise caught so far in this hunt was just over five feet.

On the final day of the hunt, we paddled far out into the bay, farther than before. By noon we had caught four good fish, and I thought we might turn for shore but my friend asked if I wanted to go after a big one. He said that the biggest porpoise may be found either at the front of a group or right at the rear. It was easiest to pick them out at the rear since we could follow the rest of the fish. It was not a recipe for a steady catch since the whole group could escape while waiting for a large one at the back, but we already had a good catch for the day and I was feeling lucky.

We paddled through the school, the porpoises clearly visible as they swam to either side of the canoe. All of them were right around the length of three or four feet. We went through the group and as we got to the back, the number of fish dwindled and large gaps appeared between them. When I turned towards him, Noele gestured with his paddle and we continued to move until there were no more fish visible. Finally, he whistled low and shallow. Noele had told me at the start of the hunt that the fish could hear sounds above the surface so we talked quietly when we got near the beasts. When I turned to look at him, he pointed with his paddle, about twenty feet to my left. I could see a large shadow just under the water, with a hint of a fin creasing the surface.

I put my paddle on the bottom of the canoe between two of the fish already caught and grabbed my favorite spear. It lay in my hand with a perfect smooth balance, the shaft sanded and polished until it shone with a dull light. I hefted it above my shoulder and moved into a kneeling position in the bow as Noele paddled to the shadow with long strokes that moved the canoe forward while barely disturbing the surface of the water. My heels were hooked under the edge of the cross-spar that I normally leaned against while paddling. As we came up to the porpoise it became clear just how big the fish was. The monster was more than half the length of our canoe and our vessel was sixteen feet long. I heard Noele whistle again softly under his breath and so I moved my right leg out from under the thwart and, levering myself to a crouched position, thrust the spear with all my weight just behind the head of the fish.

Immediately the beast attempted to dive, the spear sticking straight out by its gill, its eye rolling and staring at me as I leaned over the edge of the canoe just a foot or so away. I would have gone straight into the sea with the spear pole lodged under both of my arms, except that my one heel was still hooked around the spar. I quickly moved back to a full kneel, hooked my other foot around the spar, and, pushing down the spear on the side of the canoe, levered my whole body against the thick shaft.

A smaller man would have been propelled overboard by the weight of the monster, but my weight and strength were just equal to that of the thrashing fish. My shoulders and upper arms ached from the power of the fish as it pulled us through the water, but with our weights at each end bending the thick wood of the spear, my only concern was that the pole would break in the middle or the point snap off. I could hear Noele grunting at the stern as he tried to maintain balance against the fish's weight on the side and, at the same time, paddle backwards against the forward pull that was now moving us out of the bay and into the main channel.

We stayed this way for a long time, the fish pulling us farther from the shore, the light dimming as evening wore on, and neither of us saying anything. Finally, I felt the porpoise weaken and saw it roll slightly onto its side. Its head broke the surface, its large eye now wildly moving up and down. My weight was still firmly on the pole but I reached quickly with one hand to my belt, to the Roman sword that was always tucked there. I grabbed the short sword in my right hand, not in a fighting grasp but rather as a dagger, and plunged the knife with the full force of my right arm straight into the eye of the fish. The sword sank deep, almost to the hilt, and the water around became dark and red. It took me a few minutes to realize that the porpoise was no longer moving and it was not until Noele scuttled up from the stern of the canoe that I knew the fight was over.

There was much work to do and our danger was not yet past. We tried to lift the fish over the side and into the canoe but the beast was too heavy for that. The canoe, already loaded with the four smaller fish, tipped dangerously as we leaned over. Finally, we lashed the pole with the monster still impaled across the bow of the canoe and tied the tail and hindquarters to the thwart near the stern. With this in place and with the canoe heeled over sharply, we paddled toward the shore. Both of us paddled hard but the going was slow with the heavy drag of the monster. In the gathering gloom I could no longer see the shore and could only count on Noele's sense of direction. With the darkness came a fine mist and pockets of fog that gave the waters a mystical look. Neither of us said a word as we coursed slowly through the blackness. The excitement that I'd felt during the long haul to kill the beast had drained away and I now felt empty and exhausted, as if the chase had sucked the life out of both the fish and me. I could sense that Noele felt the same and the one time that I glanced at the rear of the boat I saw him staring at the bloody eye of the porpoise.

We paddled for hours and I never had the heart to ask Noele if he was sure of our direction. Through the night and the mist we persevered until, as the darkness melted into a gray morning, I could see that we were moving deep into our home bay. Silently we beached the canoe. I lay on the beach with Noele beside me on the damp sand and slept as the sun rose in the sky.

It was the gulls that first woke me as they wheeled and plunged over the fish carcasses. I sat up and waved them off. I could see the women and children coming from the village and, farther down the beach, the fire to render the fat from the fish into oil was already burning. Noele was working by the side of the canoe, cutting strips of flesh from the fish in the boat. When the women reached us, they each grabbed slabs of meat and hurried back to the fire. My friend cut the rope binding the huge porpoise from the canoe. Noele and I grabbed the spear still sticking out below the head of the beast and a group of village children lifted the tail as we carried the monster back to Bear River. The closer we got to the village, the bigger the crowd grew around the fish. Finally Noele glanced over at me and we dropped the load near the fire.

"My friend, it is the biggest fish of the year. Only a man as large as yourself could land such a beast. It was a wise decision to have you as my man in the bow, the man with the big spear."

It was a fish that had nearly dragged me, the canoe, and Noele so far out to sea that we could never return. Suddenly, all at once, I felt a wave of homesickness and knew that it was time to go back home to Mary and our cabin.

Twenty-Eight

Belanger was pleased with the load of oil that I drove to the sawmill on my way home, but the sawmill owner was a canny man and he wondered aloud if I had taken all the oil in the Bear River settlement in return for his lumber. Clearly he wanted to corner the market in oil in Digby, a clever strategy with the winter months looming. If he had the only supply of oil in Digby during the winter he would be able to name his price. I assured him that there was no more oil to be had in Bear River but I knew that this was not quite true. Noele was just as careful a man as Belanger and I knew that he had held back some barrels of oil for trade later on in the year. The sawmill owner would never know the difference; Noele could always say that the oil had come from fish killed after my visit. My friend planned on using the lumber to build a smokehouse on the beach. I left the wagon and horse at the mill and was hoisting my small pack on my back when Belanger came over to give me a ladle of cool water.

"About the other matter, Murphy. It's taken care of, I think. Your men should be getting their full rations now."

I had hoped that the sawmill owner would be able to help get the food released to the Pioneers, but I had had no expectation that it could be accomplished so quickly.

"Richard Hall is one of the biggest scoundrels in Nova Scotia. He also happens to owe me money that he is behind on. He was easily forced to release the food that was never his to begin with, and Brundenell is the usual sort of small man who can be persuaded by a cart full of lumber."

Belanger snorted and spat on the ground.

"Neither one can be trusted. They're just the sort that the British would hire. If you're smart you'll have as little to do with them now as possible. By the way, that boy of yours was here twice while you were gone. He had two good loads of fine logs. They were straight and solid and not a trace of rot. When you get settled in, come and see me and bring the boy, too."

The trail home was as familiar and solid as the full moon that was just rising as I walked into our yard. Mary was sitting on the stoop watching the first stars twinkling in the deep blue sky. She came running into my arms without a word. Daniel, too, was outside and he came over and hugged the two of us with his long arms, his eyes sparkling. Jean came to the doorway and stood there, smiling. The warm smell of baking bread wafted out of the open door.

Autumn and winter are close brothers in this part of the world and sometimes could scarcely be separated. We had snow one day and a clear sky the next. The snow would build up, then quickly melt as the warm weather returned and turned the trails into holes of water and muddy tracks. It became difficult to haul the wagon through either the snow or the mud.

Belanger's proposition for Daniel and me solved the growing problem of how to get our logs to the mill. The mill owner supplied us with a solid Canadian horse and a sled with long runners on it to haul the timber to town. We had become his best suppliers of the long, straight timber needed for masts and spars. It was a smart move by the mill owner to ensure a steady supply of excellent logs through the winter. For the two of us it was a means of not only moving the logs to town through the snow but, with the extra horse, a way to almost double our trade. Now one of us could stay logging during the day with our old horse, Moses, while the other drove to town with Willy, the strong new Canadian gelding. We took turns with the drive to town and found that we could take three loads into Digby every week.

Sometimes Daniel and I would take a morning off of our work and wander the forest, marking trees that we saw were particularly straight for future cutting. In the evenings we sat on our front steps sharpening our tools. Only occasionally would we talk and then almost always about the condition of the horses, the shape of the path into town, or the comings and goings at the mill. We found our living very comfortable. The winter was bitter but it was cozy inside our cabin, if close. Our horses had oats only as a special treat but they had plenty of good hay that we had bought and hauled from a local farmer.

For others, the winter was not so fine.

Soon after I returned from Bear River, Thomas came to the house. He and his family were managing in town and some of the other Pioneers had found jobs, but many were barely getting by, selling any possessions they owned, even down to their clothes and beds and furniture. The food was finally getting released, as Belanger had said, but the Pioneers were still not in control of how it was released. The British agents were responsible for building the road to Annapolis and continued to use the food as a lever, still requiring the ex-soldiers to work on the road in return for food. For the men with families, there was no choice. Many of the men who had come with us from Bermuda had left for Shelburne or Halifax. Others had actually returned to the States. Returning to the States meant returning to slavery, but for some of the Pioneers slavery was better than starving to death or freezing in the bitter winds of Nova Scotia.

The worst off were those who had hoped to have built their houses on town lots before the winter blast. The delay in the surveying of the plots meant that some Pioneers were living in tents which provided only slight protection against the fierce winter storms. Thomas told me that he had heard that many veterans in Shelburne were even worse off, living with their families in a crude form of shelter known as a pit house. My friend said that these families, caught out in the open as the winter approached and unable to secure lodging of any sort in Birchtown, had dug down as far as they could into the shallow ground or had located a fault or trench in the hard rock. They put small logs and branches on top of the trench in a criss-cross fashion to form a sort of peaked roof with vertical logs nailed on the front and back. In this way, a simple shelter was made that kept out some of the snow, but it was a shelter that a man could not stand up in and one where the angry winds blew through with barely a pause. Some of these pit houses had small stoves but many did not, and the cold had already claimed the lives of several infants.

My friend could hardly wait for the winter to end so that the British surveyor could lay out our town plots and the Pioneers who were left could begin their new lives. We had been promised that we would be first in line to receive surveyed plots when the ground thawed, and it was this promise that sustained the veterans who were left in Digby.

Without giving any details, I told Thomas that we would no longer have to worry about the slave-hunting gray man. He looked sharply at me for a moment but he'd known me long enough to know that it was pointless to ask questions. Instead, he remarked that the end of any slave hunter was a relief.

There were two aspects of that winter that sapped the strength from us all. The first was the length of the season. Just when we thought the hard weather was over, it returned, shoving aside the fair days and blustering through the woods with a roar. Then there was the depth of the cold. We were not used to such bitter blasts from the sea and the icy wind quickly stole away our natural warmth. We were a stubborn, hardy lot, though, or we would not have been in this cold country in the first place. So hang on we did, until finally the winter abated and blessed spring arrived. I had my doubts that any surveyor would appear, so I was surprised when Thomas tracked me down in the forest one sparkling spring day, with the light bouncing off the young, green leaves and the warmth of the sun full on my bare shoulders. He was as excited as a child and just as full of energy. The British agent, Williams, the same stubby bureaucrat who had first welcomed us to Nova Scotia, had come to Thomas and told him that the surveyor would begin his work in Brindley within the week.

"Murphy, we finally will have our own homes and then he can survey farms for us. It's really the start of our lives here. It's going to be all right."

A week later, in town with a load for the mill, I walked over to where the British surveyor, Millidge, had set up his equipment. Already there were several sticks pounded into the ground that marked town plots and some of my countrymen were hard at work erecting small cabins and sinking postholes into the rocky ground. Thomas was there supervising the building and keeping a close eye on the work of the surveyors. My friend and I had not spent much time together during the winter, as Dan and I worked in the woods and Thomas stayed in town with his milling and handyman jobs. Often the only times I spoke with him were if he came to the house or happened to be working at Belanger's mill when I arrived with a load of timber.

The Thomas Peters that I saw that bright spring day in 1785 was full of hope and energized by his vision of the future. The long road to Nova Scotia was forgotten and optimism in a new start was as clear as the small crocuses poking through the last remnants of snow. The words tumbled out of his mouth quickly.

"Murphy, this is it. We're really going to build a town here. Millidge is a good man, I think. He's working hard here and, when he's done, he's going to lay out the farm plots for us. We'll be able to plant this spring and have a crop for the fall. We're going to get a town laid out and have our own people living and working and making a life for themselves. It's everything we wanted and worked for, Murphy, and it's really going to happen."

In many ways the farm plots were more important than those in town. The plots were not large, about twenty acres, but they were big enough to provide for a family during the winter and, hopefully, enough to trade some of the crop. With a means of making a living, the Pioneers could make the tent town that had existed for nearly a year into a real town with houses and streets and stores. Brindley Town's close proximity to Digby meant that real trade could exist between the two. Brindley would initially serve to house the farmers as they cleared and worked their farmland but later there would be merchants and then teachers and doctors and bankers. Enterprises other than farming would spring up to serve the farmers and the town would grow.

I also quickly saw an opportunity for myself. Many of the Pioneers did not have the tools needed to clear their farm plots. Others did not know how to wield an ax or saw and none had the capacity to haul the logs any distance, certainly not to the mill. Most of the plots were thickly treed; only a few had open, grassy spaces that could be broken right away. Daniel and I wouldn't be able to clear all the land for its timber but we could surely do some of the plots, especially if the new owners helped. It looked to me like a chance to get our people squared away, while at the same time increasing our logging business.

I was running these thoughts through my head as I walked back to the mill. With Brindley being much closer to the mill than our cabin, Dan and I figured we could make a loaded trip every day. Belanger furrowed his brow when I told him of my plans, but the shipbuilding industry needed a continuous supply of straight timber and the new town and farm buildings that would be built also required milled wood. He agreed to take all the wood I could send him.

I also talked to Thomas about my idea. My friend had been troubled by the absence of axes and saws. He also knew that logging required skill. There was a lot of land to clear and many willing, if unskilled, hands. Thomas determined that it was best initially to clear just five acres out of every twenty-acre plot. That would be enough to grow a crop to support a family through the upcoming winter. Next spring, more land could be cleared. We had many workers and even with only a few axes, and poor ones at that, we could clear five acres fairly quickly and move on to the next farm plot. The farmer with the cleared land would be able to till and plant as soon as we were done. There would be no stump pulling that first year either, the seeding would have to be done around the stumps. We both knew how time consuming it was to pull stumps, even with two strong horses, and we decided that the most important thing that first year was to get a crop in the ground.

As soon as Millidge got the first farm plot surveyed, we got to work. The British agent supplied us with a dozen axes and half that number of saws, and we also had my own tools to work with. Thomas sent the strongest Pioneers to work with me on the clearing while he worked with the rest on building small houses on the town lots. It worked out pretty much as we had planned. Daniel kept one horse delivering loads to the mill while I kept the other back for hauling timber out of the plots. I showed my friends how to work their axes properly and the logs piled up quickly. After Dan's first week of trips to the mill, Belanger gave us another wagon. This was a huge improvement for us. It meant that I could load a wagon while Dan was gone, and he could hitch the horse to that wagon the next day without having to wait.

We tried to adhere to the five-acre rule. If a farm plot had three acres of open land on it when we got there, we only cleared another two. If it had no open spots, we cleared five full acres. Thomas and I determined together the actual area of five acres and no one ever argued with us. The land was given out by drawing lots and, as spring turned into summer, it became clear that we would have clearings made in each farm plot in time for at least a small crop for everyone.

We agreed to split the proceeds of the timber sales half and half between myself and the new owners of the land. Even with this split, the sheer steady volume of timber provided more funds than I had been earning from the woodlot around our cabin.

We set up two tents as we worked on each farm plot, one for Dan and one for Mary and myself. Jean had chosen to stay in our cabin in the woods but Mary had been determined to move with me as we went from lot to lot. She made meals for all of us on an open fire she kept going all day. Dan often chose to sleep in the open on those warm spring nights, and Mary and I would also often leave our tent for the back of the wagon where we could talk. One night, as Mary and I lay close together on the floor of the wagon, she told me in a matter-of-fact way that she was pregnant. I was tongue-tied and simply held her close while we watched the stars wheel overhead.

Twenty-Nine

Barely had the farm plots been surveyed and half of them partially cleared and seeded, when word came from Millidge that we could not have them. Millidge said that the governor told him the land he had surveyed for our farms had already been pledged to a church group with the unlikely name of the Society for the Propagation of the Gospel. We had never heard of such a group and suspected a conspiracy by the government in collusion with a local official. The whole place seemed so corrupt that it was not surprising to get this latest blow. Yet it was difficult not to feel bitter, especially after all our hard work and combined efforts to make the farm plots workable. All our work on the farm plots was in vain and our hopes for the future were scattered like the seeds planted on the thin soil.

We could not think what was worse, the actual loss of our future farms or the betrayal of the British again after we had reluctantly started to trust their words. We had a problem, too, with the land that had been surveyed in Brindley Town. What good were the town plots, many of which already had small cabins or houses on them, without the farmland to support the Pioneers?

Some, disillusioned and angry, left for Shelburne or Halifax when word spread that we had been cheated. It was hard for anyone to retain faith in our new land after so many disappointments and setbacks.

I felt the betrayal acutely because of my work clearing the farm plots—work now done for the benefit of the church group—but my disappointment was nothing to the bitterness of Thomas Peters. My friend looked like the worries of our past years had finally caught up to him. He had aged overnight after Millidge told us the bad news.

Thomas could not accept what had happened. All spring, as the town lots and then the farm lots were finally surveyed, he had been full of confidence and optimism. Everyone had been enthusiastic in our ideas for the future. Now our plans were all deflated and chaotic. For Thomas, the loss of our farmland seemed almost like a loss of his sense of himself. Mary and I took Thomas and Sally and their growing family back to our house in the woods so that he could at least remove himself from the general confusion for a few days. There was nothing more he could accomplish in town at this point, and he needed time to work things out in his own mind. We set up two army tents in the yard with the children in one tent and Thomas and Sally in the other. The weather was fine and we cooked our meals over an open fire in the yard, just like in our campaigning days.

Thomas and I stayed up very late for two nights in a row, smoking and talking about the state of things. Dan also joined us a few times, quietly puffing on a long-stemmed pipe but saying little. Thomas wanted to know if I would come with him if he left for a different part of the country or even back to the States or overseas. When he asked me this, I saw Daniel, sitting on a log across the fire, start and look keenly at me through the smoke and rising ash, but he shouldn't have worried. There was no question of moving back to the country I had run from and it disturbed me to hear my old friend considering it. It was a sign of the extreme frustration that Thomas was feeling. I made a comment to Thomas about having to talk with Mary about any move but I knew it was not in my heart to return to the States.

The betrayal of the British agents was only the first of several setbacks that year.

We had not been logging our home woods for several weeks, as all our efforts went towards the surveyed farm lots. The horses were tired from the weeks of heavy work without rest and I decided to give them time to recover in the fresh green grass of the meadows scattered among the forest. Without old Moses and the stout mill horse, Willy, all our efforts in the woods would be for nothing.

After a few days, Thomas and Sally went back to Brindley and a few days after that, Daniel and I roused the horses from their lazy days on pasture and put them to work. Dan and I continued to take turns in the woods and on the wagon, a practice that gave each of us a rest, or, at least, a change to keep us alert and content. That first day, both of us worked a short distance from the house, Dan ahead with Willy, cutting and skidding trees that we had previously marked for harvest, and me with Moses with the easier job of moving the skidded logs on to the bed of the wagon. Waiting in the small clearing that we used to load the wagon, I could hear the bite of the ax as Dan felled his first tree and quickly rough-trimmed it, then the rustle and groan of the tack as Willy strained to pull the log through the undergrowth back to the small clearing where I stood quietly with Moses.

Willy, the Canadian horse, seemed like he was made for the woods and the trade. Shorter than Moses, but stronger through the chest and hardy in all manner of weather, he had a stubborn but pleasing personality that got us both through many a mishap where a lesser horse would have stumbled. Whatever training he might have needed had already been done at the sawmill. I preferred to keep him busy logging at home while Moses strained his way to town with a load of timber on the wagon.

The most Moses could pull to town was five small logs or two or three larger ones. Loading the harvested logs involved placing three thin but sturdy logs on the side of the wagon to be used as a loading ramp. Moses was then led to the other side of the wagon. Two chains were stretched from the horse's tack across the wagon bed to the recently-felled log. With sharp commands and luck on my side, Moses would pull the log up the poles and onto the bed of the wagon. It generally did not work perfectly. Often the log would not be pulled cleanly and would come off the end, or perhaps Moses would not stop in time and the log would clear the bed and land on the other side, or would stick on the frame of the wagon. More work back and forth would be involved. Loading a wagon with logs for town was a job that looked like it should take two hours and often ended up taking a full day.

That morning was brilliant. The sun shone and the air was hot and heavy. Willy strained into the little clearing and Daniel halted him and unhooked a log. As I finished trimming it, I took a close look at the log. It was a strange shape, almost flat on one side so that it would not roll properly, but would roll then stick on the flat side, and it was fat at one end, almost as thick around as a butt log from a large tree, but then tapered sharply to a thin peak. I shook my head and Dan, catching my look, smiled as he made his way back into the woods. We both knew the log would be hard to load.

The first part of the loading went well. Moses and I had the log halfway up the pole ramp, the trunk thumping every time it landed flat on the poles, but we could not get it beyond a large knot on one of the poles. When I urged Moses to pull hard, the pole bent and seemed ready to break. I left Moses on the pulling side of the wagon and went back to the log on the other side, thinking to lever the log over the knot to enable the horse to pull it onto the bed of the wagon. As I neared the back of the wagon, the brush at the edge of the woods rustled and a large garter snake slithered quickly through the tall grass. In an instant, it was past me. The snake was about three feet long and thicker than my thumb. With a white stripe along its side and its head held high above its curving body, it was easily seen. I was startled and reached to the stuck log to steady myself. As I put my hand on the log, the snake reached the other side of the wagon and slithered directly between Moses' legs. Moses reared back on his haunches, then hopped sideways against the weight of the log. The chain tightened on the log, trapping my little finger and ring finger between the wood and the chain. The knot on the stubborn pole gave way against the rapid movements of the horse, sending the near side of the log tilting down towards my boot. My fingers were crushed and I was trapped against the log, which was now supported on just two poles and was very close to landing on my foot. Moses, lathered and trembling, was continuing to crow-hop on the other side of the wagon, moving the log back and forth with every lurch. My hand was a throbbing agony.

My first job had to be to calm the horse. The pain from my two crushed fingers was constant and fierce but I knew that if the log fell, it would break my leg. Gradually I quieted Moses down with gentle words through gritted teeth, all the while hoping that the two poles would hold the log, which was balanced precariously above my leg. Finally, I could see Moses return to his normal self, his head hanging in front of his chest and his tongue lolling out of his mouth as he took more even breaths.

I did not know how to get free of the log. If I ordered Moses to move forward, the chain would likely tighten further and trap even more of my hand, but if I told him to back up, the chain would slacken quickly and the unrestrained log might then careen off the poles and onto my leg. The horse had the full weight of the log and was holding it still, which, it seemed to me, was the best available situation. My fingers were torn and blue beneath the chain and the blood continued to flow freely onto the grass. I called for Dan but it seemed like a very long time before he and Willy clattered into the clearing. He quickly took in the situation, grabbed a spare pole, and levered it against the thickness of the log near my trapped hand. The log weighed more than any man could lift but by levering one end of the pole against the ground and the shaft against the stuck log, there was a chance that Dan could move one end just enough for me to get my mangled fingers loose. As he strained on the log, I pulled on my trapped left hand with my good right hand and it finally sprang free. My little finger, which had been trapped beneath the chain all the way up to my hand, remained behind, still caught between the chain and the log. My ring finger was free but mangled, and the blood, which had stopped as we worked to free my hand, flowed again.

I felt dizzy and it was through filmy eyes that I saw Daniel back Moses up so that the log fell back on the ground, then quickly unhitch the log harness and hook up the wagon. He gently helped me into the back of the wagon and took me to the house. As we came into the clearing, both Mary and Jean came out of the cabin, surprised by our early return. Seeing the blood, Jean quickly stuck my hand in cold water and tied a small rag tightly around my wrist. After a few minutes she took my hand out, unloosed the tourniquet, and laid it on her apron. The coldness had stopped the pain as well as the flow of blood, but now that my hand was back in the warmth of the sun, the pain returned.

"I'm not a doctor, Murphy, you know that, but I'm about as close as you're going to get to one around here and I've seen a few mangled fingers from my time in Doc Jamieson's. Here's what he'd say to you. He'd say that you're lucky with that little finger, seeing as how it's gone. Yeah, you've lost it but we can sew the skin up over that hole and you'll be none the worse for it. Now the other finger, that's the problem. It's broke sure enough but that's just the half of it. The fact is it's crushed and cut all along the length and pulled half out of its socket. I know old Doc Jamieson would say that we should take it off like the little one and just sew it up. That way you'd likely get no infection whereas if we try to save it, you could end up with infection and lose your whole hand. Maybe even your arm."

I asked Jean to let me think for a moment so I could clear my head. Mary, her face drawn, came over and sat next to me on the wagon. I asked her what she thought I should do.

"Jean's got lots of knowledge in the healing area, Murphy. She's about as good as a doctor, I think, and you know from the war what an infection in a wound can be like. You might lose your hand or more. Two fingers gone is nothing, and on your left hand to boot. You'll hardly miss them, but a hand, that's another matter, and who knows where an infection can end up. You think on poor old Colonel Tye. I think you should do what she says."

Dan was standing behind Mary as she spoke and as I looked up at him, he gave a short nod and turned for an ax and a hammer. He took my crippled hand and laid it flat on the bed of the wagon. Dan looked in my eyes and gave another short nod, his face pinched. I turned my face away from the wagon. Through the pain, I could feel the sharp blade of the axe against the loose skin at the base of my finger. Out of the corner of my eye, I saw Daniel take up the hammer. A short rap on the back of the ax was enough to sever the damaged finger. Quickly, Jean grabbed my hand again and thrust it into the cold bucket of water. The flow of blood spread like a cloud through the water but gradually slowed. Finally, Jean took my hand from the bucket and, using a simple sewing needle and thread, sewed both knuckles shut. Strangely, the loss of my second finger did not cause me any additional pain and the cold water had relieved much of the throbbing. Mary wrapped me in a thick wool blanket and I lay back on the wagon bed and slept.

My hand gaped where my fingers had been, but the sewn knuckles did not become infected and a man could get by just fine with two fingers gone, especially on his left hand. There were many in Brindley and Digby with worse injuries.

Jean insisted that I not do hard work for a week. So I watched Dan load the wagon with logs that he had cut, then drive the wagon to town. My partner blamed himself, attributing the accident to the strange shape of the log he had hauled out of the forest that day, but I laughed at his long face and gradually pulled him out of his guilt.

Two weeks after my accident I was leaning against the gate at the entrance to the mill, watching a load of logs being unloaded from my wagon. Thomas had been working on the giant sluice of the mill, which funneled the water against a large wheel and powered the inside saw blades. Wiping his hands with a rag, he came over to me, his eyes widening as he saw my crippled hand. I told him of the accident and he sat shaking his head for a spell. Then he started to laugh.

"Well I wish I knew what was so damn funny."

"Sorry, Murphy, it's just that we made it through the war and the slave hunters and the trip here and all without losing any parts, and then you go and cut off your fingers after you're all settled down. It just struck me as funny or something. I expect you'll do just fine with what you've got left."

My friend had some disturbing news. He told me that the Society for the Propagation of the Gospel, the group that had claimed our farmland, was based in Shelburne. The British surveyor, Millidge, had told him that the governor had ordered him to give the surveyed farmland to that mysterious church group. When the surveyor had balked at the order, the governor had informed him that the Society was supported by influential and wealthy patrons in Shelburne, one of whom was our old commander, Stephen Blucke.

Since assuming the command of the Pioneers from the stalwart

Colonel Tye, Stephen Blucke had always struck me as careful to look after his own interests first. He was one of the first to be evacuated, and he was the owner of the largest tract of farmland and the biggest house in Birchtown. I wondered what it was about our land that had attracted Blucke and his friends. Perhaps the motivation was simply to thwart our efforts to build an independent community and thereby deprive Blucke of cheap labor. There was no doubt that many Pioneers living in desperate situations in Birchtown would come to Brindley if we could establish a self-supporting town.

I was still thinking of Blucke and his British friends when Thomas delivered another blow. He planned to move across the bay to New Brunswick when his summer work at Belanger's mill was complete. Thomas had had enough of broken promises in Nova Scotia and hoped to find a home and stability in a different land.

"Some of the men will likely come with me and some will stay behind. I won't ask you to come, Murphy. I know you're well settled here, more than just about anyone else, I think, but don't forget that you don't have the title to your land, either, and could be moved. So you'll have to keep your wits about you and look after our people."

Mary and I had built a snug life in the woods and my business was steady and sure. I would not leave. Thomas and I had been through so much together, it was hard for me to think of him moving away, but I saw his point. There was nothing for him here and little hope for the future.

Thomas' departure seemed barely real to me but as the rest of the summer wore on and I saw his plans start to come together, it grew more and more substantial. Finally, as the brown leaves curled on the trees and floated on the harbor breeze, my friend and several of the Pioneers and their families boarded a ship bound for the New Brunswick shore. I wondered if this would be the last I would see of Thomas Peters.

Thirty

With Thomas across the bay and the Pioneers scattered between New Brunswick, Shelburne, Halifax, and Digby, I wondered how we would ever have the community and united purpose necessary to push for the changes that were needed to let us prosper. The betrayal of all the promises made to us stung, but it was the practical need for titled land that was most crucial. Without title to land, we could be moved at the whim of any corrupt official or politician.

I knew that I was in a precarious position because I also did not have the title to the land where we had built our cabin. Dan and I had a good business, we had good terms with Belanger and his mill, and we owned our tools, our blades, and one of the horses. It was unlikely that any farmer would want our rocky outcrop and we could always move and build again, if necessary. Still, it made me uneasy to know that any person of influence could shift us for any selfish excuse.

The loss of Thomas to our community was huge. He had sustained us through many hard times with his enthusiasm, his trust in a better future, and his practical guidance in advancing day-by-day. Without him we drifted along, each Pioneer looking after his own family and no one looking out for our overall good. We had no leader in our unformed town and each was left to fend for himself.

For me, it was more than that. Thomas and I had been through so much together that it was hard to get used to having him far away. Even when we had not been living next to each other, as had been the case for a while now, I'd still felt that he was as close as town. Now my friend was over the bay and I could not help but think that our lives had moved apart.

My life with Mary, though, was as perfect as I could imagine. Never had I dreamed that I would have the love of a fine woman, a trade that would provide for a family, and a partner like Daniel, who was so much more than my comrade in the woods. When I was a slave, I had never dared hope for anything more than freedom. I had no clear idea of what lay beyond that freedom. The idea of having a life with the satisfactions and demands of a family, and work that was for our gain, had been beyond any thoughts that flew through my mind as I labored on my old master's farm. I had slipped into the role of family man and provider easily. Now there was nothing else for me and I could not imagine any other life. So it was that the struggles of others were interesting to watch but did not really affect me. I had a vague wish to help the Pioneers but it was not solid and could be quickly left behind. Still, that fall I began to hear stories from around Nova Scotia that troubled me.

I heard from Belanger that a man had been whipped in Shelburne for stealing a potato. A former Pioneer, this unlucky man had pulled the potato, top and all, from a garden in town that belonged to the local magistrate. The official's wife happened to be sitting near the window of the house and, witnessing the theft, had called loudly from the window. Two men passing on the street had apprehended the potato-stealer and tied him to a post. Without the benefit of trial, the magistrate had ordered the man taken to a wagon, tied to the back, and whipped as the vehicle made its way along the main street, dragging the thief behind it.

I wondered at how luckless a man had to be, to be whipped for the theft of a vegetable, and how desperate he must have been to lift the plant from the ground. Oddly, Daniel had a different view altogether when I related this unhappy tale to him. Why, he wondered, had the man thought to steal a potato? Daniel said that the food to steal when in hunger should be able to be devoured on the spot, both to satisfy the thief's appetite and destroy the evidence. He recommended carrots, or tomatoes, or apples from the garden, or a pie or loaf cooling on the window sill.

When I thought on this, my mind wandered back to my conversation with the gray man in the woods. Like him, I found the law to be crafted to favor the rich and powerful and used as a club to crush the poor and weak. When I thought of the man who was flogged for stealing the potato, I could not think of myself in his place.

If it came to stealing to provide for my family, I had no qualms about this any more than the magistrate had misgivings about flogging a man for stealing less than the rabbits took each summer. I could see no difference between my thoughts and those of the government bureaucrats, corrupt and cruel. Violence passed into law for the benefit of those who passed the law and supported by the strength of the police is not just, but only expedient.

So I have always acted, closer in spirit to the gray man than to any man I have ever seen with ruffles around his throat. As to being caught, I have thoughts on that also. There is almost no risk of being caught if a man can keep his head without relating the incident to others. Most men are not capable of this small achievement, but those who are can be successful in any endeavor. I had often thought of myself as a deep well where deeds have been tossed down, never to be seen again. If a man can keep his own counsel it is unlikely that any violent deed done in the dark of night may reach the light of day.

All these ideas whirled through my mind as I considered the plight of the man being whipped through Shelburne, but mostly I thought of what I would do to that magistrate if it was me who had been flogged.

Yet the people accepted it.

Even when hungry and whipped and despised, the people stayed quiet and subdued. I often wondered how this could be, since these were the same men who had risked so much to leave their masters behind and who lacked nothing in courage. The same men who had quickly slit a throat in the war now stayed silent and meek as they worked for menial pay and their families starved. I thought perhaps they were tired of it all, tired of the running and fighting and endless glances over their shoulders. There was nowhere left to go. This was to be our last stand. Many men had died with the thought of where we now lived on their minds. So it was that we who had achieved this goal seemed reluctant to do anything to endanger our standing. We submitted to all manner of indignities. Perhaps, too, we placed faith in our children who, at least, would grow up with the appearance of freedom and equality. Our lives might be lived in this land with that dream of the future. Theirs, as adults, might be lived in the reality of it.

I thought that our single hope for a united purpose lay with Thomas, who had the capacity to unite the people and drive change in our lives, but my friend was seldom seen on our side of the water and we heard only scattered tales from travelers of his frustrations with obtaining land in New Brunswick. It seemed that his troubles had traveled with him. There were rumors, too, of slave hunters and human smugglers. I heard of men and women and sometimes whole families stolen in the night and put aboard ships bound for the States. These ships operated under commission to slave owners in Virginia or South Carolina who claimed ownership of former slaves. The law forbade this practice, but the law was seldom seen in the poorer communities of this land.

* * *

The fall bled into winter with the fierce snowstorms and days of icy rain that always marked that transition. Just before Christmas, with the winter well entrenched, Mary gave birth to twin boys as alike as the stars twinkling in the cold stillness.

I had fears about the birth all through the autumn nights. My sleep, always uncertain and troubled, was now impeded by dark dreams of death—both Mary's and the unborn infant's—but the event was actually very calm, guided by Jean's steady hand. We named the boys Tye and Sam after my friends from the past. They were strong, active boys, and that winter our small cabin echoed with their cries. After a few weeks of this, Dan came to me as I sat by the stove one night.

"Murphy, I think it's time I had my own house."

"Well I can hardly blame you for that with all the racket in this place. As soon as the frost is out of the ground we'll start right in on it."

And with the snow finally melting in the ditches and the geese winging overhead, we began work on his small hut. In two weeks we had the cabin completed and Dan moved in. It was nice to have more room in our house and it was good for him to have some privacy.

I ran into Noele on one of my trips to the sawmill in early May and he told me that the winter had been a fine one at Bear River. Since the British raids and bounty hunting had stopped a decade past, the biggest concerns that his people now faced during the winter were a prolonged cold spell or, worse, a time of disease. The past winter had been harsh but free of the dreaded pox, and the coming of spring meant easier travel and abundant food. He agreed to bring Luce for a visit during the summer and, in return, I eagerly promised to help with the porpoise hunt in early autumn.

Thomas surprised me in late July as I was cutting a tall maple that stood in a clearing not far from the cabin. I did not hear him and was startled when, jumping back from the cut to watch the tree fall, I almost landed in his arms. My friend laughed but I could see lines of wear and fatigue on his face. Thomas was getting older and the strain was showing. Difficult enough as it was to earn a living to support a family, he also had the burden of trying to create a sustainable life for the whole community.

"Here's the thing, Murphy. Across the bay they'll give us town plots but the plots are small and full of stones. A man cannot make a living from them. When we ask for farm plots, they show us land that is so distant we can't walk to it. They don't want to talk with us. It's the same there as it is here, maybe worse. All the things we were promised have not happened. The local agents are worthless, so I'm going to try with the New Brunswick governor."

Thomas was visiting to get my help in drafting the petition for the governor, a task I was more than happy to do, despite my misgivings about its effectiveness.

That evening, sitting around a small fire in our clearing, he recounted many of the same troubling rumors that I had already heard. He said there had been many stories of kidnappings of former slaves to be returned to their old masters in the States. There was also talk of bounty hunters roaming the countryside and capturing unsuspecting, careless wanderers who were chained and taken on ships to the West Indies. There were other cases of loyalists in Shelburne who had kept their slaves when they took up residence in Nova Scotia. The law seemed uncertain and the government was generally supportive of the power brokers who owned many of the slaves and wanted the old system to continue. I wondered aloud about Shelburne, with Colonel Blucke and Birchtown so close by.

"Murphy, Blucke is not our friend. He does not care what happens to the Pioneers. Remember it is he and that rascal Skinner who skim off most of the government funding for the road work that is meant to go to the Black Pioneers who are actually doing the labor. It was Blucke's church society that stole our farmland in Digby. He cares only for himself and for gaining power and money."

Thomas stayed with us for two weeks. Many nights we sat by the fire, talking and playing with little Tye and Sam, who were as alike as peas on the outside but had very different personalities. Tye was generally loud and complaining, but Sam was quiet and calm. Jean, smiling on the other side of the fire, said they were much like us in personalities. Both Thomas and I claimed quiet Sam as similar to ourselves. Mary, who was tending to a small cut on Dan's hand, laughed aloud and said she did not agree. We were both, she said, like Tye, loud and boisterous and, Jean added, interested only in eating and sleeping.

Thirty-One

The fall of 1786 was a brilliant one. The forest became a jumble of red and gold and brown pieces. Individual trees stood like torches in the woods but, from a hill, the forest was a child's paint-box of smeared colors running into each other and out into the gray rock ledges. Soon after the first frost, Noele and Luce walked into our yard. Noele was pulling a small wagonload of smoked fish, as brown and tough as rawhide but tasty and fine. The porpoise hunt had been early that year and I had missed it, but Noele was unconcerned about my absence. The hunt had been a huge success with a large amount of meat smoked. My friends were impressed with our little cabin in the woods and more so with the twins, who took to both Noele and Luce.

"I think it will be a good winter for us this year, Murphy. We have lots of food put by and the people are strong and healthy. There hasn't been sickness for a while."

It was a fact that the mildest winters seemed to correspond to the times when much food had been put by the previous summer. It was when the winters were long and cold, and the hunting for the deer in their winter yards tough and fruitless, that the food was most needed. It always seemed that the summers before those hard winters were difficult hunting times, with the catches few and far between. The

Mi'kmaq felt that a summer of poor hunting and fishing was a bad omen leading toward a winter of sickness and despair. It was hard to hunt during a cold winter, with the snow deep and difficult to slog through and the deer thin and hard to find. A man could not live solely on squirrels and rabbits and if the porpoise hunt failed, a bleak winter was ahead.

Weakness through lack of food and prolonged cold spells could bring on outbreaks of smallpox and other diseases. Heading into the winter with good supplies and in strong physical condition was a reasonable indicator that the dreaded diseases would not appear. I had seen during the war that smallpox claimed many soldiers who were already weak and easy victims.

Many of the British soldiers and a few of the Black Pioneers had been given a medical treatment known as 'variolation' when we joined the British army. Before the battle at Kemp's Landing, both Moses and I had been lined up with the rest of the runaways. A vein on the inside of my arm was opened and a smear of white matter from a small jar was wiped on my cut. We were not told the reasoning behind this procedure at the time, but Colonel Tye later told us that the treatment had been done to prevent smallpox. It had been hard to believe that this could work, especially since he also said that the matter in the jar had been collected from the open sores of smallpox victims. He said that the small sickness we experienced after the procedure would prevent the larger horror of smallpox in the future. It was true that both Moses and I had been slightly ill a few days after the scratching. My old friend had not lived long enough to determine if the variolation would prevent smallpox, but I had been exposed to the disease several times, along with swamp fever. Although I had been very ill with the fever, smallpox had not touched me.

Most of the Black Pioneers had not been given the treatment and almost all of the runaways who had not joined the regular army, but who had hung around the camps doing odd jobs and trying to simply stay alive, were also overlooked. Many of these men died. Some died from smallpox and others from starvation or exposure to the damp weather. Some of the Pioneers and their families continued to get sick in Nova Scotia, where doctors were few and far between and variolation was not generally practiced. The disease cut wide swaths through several communities in our new land.

I had also seen the British commanders use smallpox as a weapon during the war by turning infected runaways back into the rebel towns to spread the disease among the occupants of these places. The plan had been effective against the citizens but had not worked against the soldiers who had also been treated. If what Noele had told me about the British in Nova Scotia purposefully giving blankets from smallpox victims to the Mi'kmaq in years past was true, then the idea of using disease as a military tactic had not had its origins in the war.

But there was plenty of food for everyone that fall, enough for Noele to share the fruits of the annual hunt with us, and even enough for the Black Pioneers who were left in town. Supplies from the government's stores were finally being released, albeit slowly, and the winter did not prove to be very cold. Many of the Pioneers still lived in pit homes. Gradually some had built shacks in town or taken over abandoned buildings. Only about thirty of the original Pioneers were left in Brindley. The rest had either died, left for other parts of Nova Scotia, or gone with Thomas to New Brunswick. A few of the most desperate had gone back to the States to face certain slavery. Of those who remained, several were indentured to merchants and farmers in the area. There was supposed to be a small payment attached to this and a term limit of ten years, but often the payment was not made, the term was extended indefinitely, and the indentured servant lived with the owner and was expected to work all day and every day. When the winter winds began to blow was when the old Pioneers were persuaded by the lure of a warm house and food and when indentures took place. And it was not just the old soldiers who were enticed. Most of the indentured servants were women, unable to support themselves or their children in any other way, and with no place left to go but the hearth of a rich merchant or officer who sought domestic help.

We rarely saw Thomas but heard that he was having his old fights with the government in New Brunswick. The good land had already been given to the white settlers, many of whom had not even fought in the war. Only two of the men who had left with my friend had been given farm plots there. The rest got by as they had in Nova Scotia with odd jobs and temporary work.

The twins were growing like weeds and often went with Daniel on his scouting trips into the woods. Our lives were quiet but content. Belanger's mill had grown and he took all the lumber we could bring him. He was as close to a friend as we had in the Digby community and he was fair with us, both in pricing and in other dealings. For my part, I provided him with the straightest trunks we could find to be made into masts and spars for the boat-building business, which was booming. My hand pained me when the weather turned cold but I could still do my fair share of the physical work. Jean would frequently heat a poultice for me to apply to my fingers when they were frozen into a claw by the work, the cold, and the damp. She had a good grasp of basic medical procedures learned from Dr. Jamieson and word of her skill in healing, and especially in administering treatments for wounds and accidents, had spread through the Brindley community.

It was common for my mother-in-law to be called to tend to the afflicted in both Digby and Brindley. Often an injured man would arrive on our doorstep. Jean was passionate about attention to the sick and neglected her own well-being in favor of her patients. The only other medical person in either Digby or Brindley was a traveling surgeon who performed operations in a careless manner and was universally feared by all residents. At least Jean did not kill anyone, which could not be said about the hapless surgeon.

While the hunting in the summer of 1786 had been good and steady, the opposite was true in the summer of 1787. It was a miserable summer in many ways, wet and cold, and with freezing zephyrs from the sea blowing frequently along the coast. It was hard logging. The ground never seemed to dry and the mud pulled against the horses and gummed up the wheels of the wagon. The logs would not slide well on the gumbo and dug into the ground. Also it always seemed more difficult to cut a wet tree than a dry one.

The hunting was terrible. Some said that the cold, wet spring meant that the deer had lost many fawns and had therefore strayed further afield than usual. Others thought that we had over-hunted the deer in the past, resulting in lesser numbers now. The cold spring meant that the leaves and grass did not green up at the usual time, which may have forced the deer further into the forest than was commonly the case. Everything was delayed, it seemed. Even the ducks and geese did not fly their long formations until well into May.

I thought about Noele many times that summer and asked Belanger if he had seen my friend, but the mill owner had nothing to add to what I already knew. He had not seen any of the Mi'kmaq in town and did not know how the porpoise hunt had gone. As for deer hunting, he did not need to tell me how poor that was. Just after the first snow covered the ground, I loaded up the wagon with as much food as we could spare. It had not been a prosperous year for us, either, with the poor logging, and we had little surplus, but I knew that anything we could take to Bear River would be welcome.

As I drove past the mill in town, Belanger came over to the wagon.

"Murphy, it's timely seeing you here. I've had a message from Bear River. They've got a sickness and want you to bring Jean out there. I was just about to come and tell you."

"I was just going there anyways. I'll go and get her."

"Well, you may want to think this whole thing through before you go. The messenger that came here was a young fellow. It's smallpox, Murphy. That's what they have out there. The boy made a sign with his hand to me, a slash across his chest meaning many are sick. Now I know you want to go and that's fine but if you go and bring the sickness back here, we could have an epidemic here, too. Jean's a fine healer and better than any doctor I've ever seen, but she's no spring chicken. Can she handle an epidemic with the Mi'kmaq and possibly also at Digby and Brindley?"

I leaned back in the wagon's seat. Belanger was right; bringing smallpox to our communities would be catastrophic, but I couldn't sit back and do nothing while Noele's village sickened and died.

"Murphy, you went through the war, did you ever get the pox?"

"No, I had a treatment that they said made me immune. I guess they were right because I never got it."

Belanger shuffled his feet.

"I asked you because they say that if you had the disease once, you can't get it again. You could go out there and help them and not get sick yourself. I haven't heard of this treatment you had, are you sure it worked?"

"Well, I always wondered about it too, but I did spend a lot of time with fellows who had the pox and I never got sick. Half the army was very sick, many were dying and it never got to me at all. So, yeah, I guess it did work."

The mill owner looked hard at me and I knew what he was thinking. I could go out there with supplies and food for the tribe and not get sick.

"I'll just go back and let Mary know that I'll be gone a little longer than expected and maybe Jean can tell me a few things to do to help the sick ones."

"Leave the wagon, Murphy, and I'll get some bandages and more food and blankets together. Just take the horse and we can hitch the wagon up when you come back through."

Mary was calm when I told her the plan but Jean was determined that she must go to Bear River herself.

"Now Murphy, you know that you know nothing about treating the sick, and don't sit there and ask me to tell you how to do something that you have got no ability to do at all. It's just plain dumb. You can barely take care of yourself, let alone someone else. Why, you couldn't even take care of yourself when you had two good hands and now that you've only got one, well..."

The worst of it all was that she was right. I never was very good at tending to people. Even in the war I always felt kind of helpless when men got sick. It always seemed random to me, whether or not the ill got well—whatever anyone did seemed to have little actual influence on the outcome. But Jean had not received the variolation and that meant she could get sick herself. I was not prepared to risk that, even if she was.

As usual, she had an answer to that.

"Here's what we'll do. We'll both go to Bear River but I'll stay just beyond the village where there aren't any people and I'll set up a kind of hospital. You can bring the sick out there on the wagon and I'll treat them there so I don't have to go into the village itself."

It wasn't a perfect plan and Jean could easily still get sick herself, but it seemed like the best idea around and I reluctantly agreed. There was no point in going out to Bear River at all if we weren't going to treat those who were infected with the pox, and the only way to treat people is to get close enough to see the problem. But, when I asked her what the treatment was for smallpox, her face darkened and she was hesitant and vague in the way that doctors often are.

"Well, we'll have to see what we are up against. I only saw a couple of smallpox cases in Shelburne and we never did much except give the person plenty of water, wash the sores, and keep them cool and away from everyone else."

"Yeah, but did they get better with that treatment?"

"Some did, some didn't. There was nothing else we could do. Dr. Jamieson said there were no cures but rest, cool coverings, and prayer."

I had believed in prayer once but the war had beaten that belief out of me.

Belanger had collected a wagon load of food and supplies along with a couple of large tents. We hitched up and the day was bright, crisp, and cool as we left Digby. We saw no one on the path to the village, but that was not unusual in that thinly-settled country. However, this time it gave me a creepy feeling.

When we made the final turn and saw the village laid out before us, I felt the skin on the back of my neck tighten and my stomach churn. Bear River was completely quiet. Usually when I came into town, children would be running and chasing, men would be fixing

Kevin Bannister

the fishing nets and talking in small groups, and women would be preparing food on fires, but that day there was no playing, no working, no food smells, not even any fires burning. There were no sounds of people at all. All we could hear was the wind whistling through the spruce around the settlement. Closer in, we heard the flapping of bark and branches against pegs and posts and the snuffling of several feral dogs who were working under the pile of nets near the shore, looking for mice or voles. I told Jean to stay on the wagon. I jumped off well short of the settlement, and walked slowly towards Noele's wigwam. Large black birds were circling high up in the sky.

As I drew near Noele's wigwam, I realized that I had been mistaken about the silence, which had seemed to shroud the village. In fact, there were small noises coming from many of the wigwams. I pulled back the flap from my friend's dwelling and was met by an absolute wave of stench, a smell like I had never experienced before, even on the war-time sick boat. It was concentrated because of the close walls of the dwelling. Lying on a bare mat on the floor was Luce, curled in a bundle, her knees drawn up under her chin. Kneeling beside her was Noele, but a Noele with a face that I barely recognized, so marked and crusted was it. He looked up as I entered the wigwam and a small smile creased the lumpy skin beneath his nose.

"Murphy. I knew you would come."

Noele began coughing and the rag that he was using to wipe Luce's face fell from his grasp and settled on the floor.

"Come outside and we will talk."

My friend heaved himself upright with a groan and we sat outside on the logs that ringed the cold fire pit. There was a stack of wood beside the pit and, as Noele talked, I lit a small fire.

"Of course it is the pox again, but worse than that—we have little food for the winter and it will be a hard one, I fear. Every family here is sick. Many children, too. I am over the worst of it, I think, and will be left with this scarred face, but Luce is not. We were not able to fish because of the sickness and that makes things worse."

"I brought food and bandages. Also, Jean is here. We can tend to the sick and feed the well. Do you have men who are strong enough to help us?"

Noele said that since the smallpox began, all the families had kept to themselves. Several families, afraid of contact with others, had moved off by themselves to the edge of Bear River, but there was no stopping the spread of the sickness. On Noele's last walk around the settlement, he found that every wigwam sheltered at least one sick person and most had two or more. Several sheltered entire families that were ill. Noele said that he would try to round up half a dozen healthy men. We would meet back at his wigwam.

I walked back to the wagon where Jean was waiting and explained the situation to her. Her face hardened.

"We need to set up hospital tents by the town. I can give the men bandages and get them to start fires to boil water to clean the sores. Also, we should bring the food to Noele's wigwam so he can look after it, and some of the men can start taking fresh water to all the families. I suppose the first thing I should do is walk the village to see how many we can still help. You and Noele can organize unloading the goods from the wagon so we can pile the bodies on it. We can't have sick people lying next to the dead."

I was amazed. This was like no Jean I'd ever seen before. She'd already thought of what to do while I was still thinking about Noele's broken face.

"For God's sake, Murphy, are you just going to stand there looking stunned? I've seen quite a few things, you know, and I've learned a lesson or two along the way. We're going to do this my way because that's the only way to make this better. The first thing you're going to do is drive this wagon up to Noele's wigwam so we can get started."

So that's just what I did.

Thirty-Two

It turned out that there were eighteen people in the village who were willing to help because they had either not become sick or, like Noele, had survived the pox. A few of the other residents were reluctant to leave their wigwams and their own sick relatives. Others, recovering, were too weak or debilitated to help. Most of the residents were in the iron grip of the illness themselves. The smallpox was such a terrifying and mysterious affliction that there were a few people sitting by themselves by the edge of the clearing, afraid to move, afraid even to tend to their sick families or feed themselves.

We left the majority of the men at the wagon to set up the tents, collect fresh water and firewood, and unload the food and supplies. Two men who had survived the sickness came with us as we walked slowly around the village. We stopped at each wigwam to determine the status of every family in Bear River.

Noele opened each tent flap with hesitation. His fears were well-founded—every wigwam had at least one sick person. Most had several victims, and in a few, all of the residents were ill. Many of the homes had a corpse lying in the bed next to the sick. Saddest of all were the quiet wigwams where the entire family was dead.

Noele stopped and talked with the family members at each

wigwam as the two men who accompanied us carefully wrapped the corpses in bedding and placed them on the ground outside the wigwams. I kept a count in my head of the sick, the dead, and the healthy. Jean had stopped at the first wigwam we visited to tend to the sick inside and had called to one of the men working by the wagon to bring her water, bandages, and firewood. As we worked our way around the settlement, Noele sent several women back to work with Jean. They did not want to leave their sick relatives but they realized that the healthy members of the settlement had to care for all, not just their family members. There were so few healthy and so many sick that a healthy person would have to look after several victims that were outside his family circle.

The simple and brutal fact was that little could be done to help victims of smallpox and that was as much the case in Bear River as it was anywhere else. Some people got the pox and lived through it, some did not. One person might be in close contact with smallpox sufferers and never even get the disease. I had seen this during the war when some former slaves who had helped treat many pox victims did not get sick. Another person might be in only slight contact with the sick yet get ill and die. The young and strong were no more likely to survive than the old and weak. It was an all-encompassing disease, sparing no one in particular, and spreading suffering among all classes, but there was one exception to that rule. Smallpox seemed to be the worst among those living in crowded conditions. I did not know if this was because the disease spread more readily through close contact or if the general health of those living close together was worse.

As we made the rounds, we met several old women who were already tending to the sick. My friend told me that these seniors were people who had been ill with smallpox the last time the disease had swept through Bear River and seemed to have developed a resistance to it. No one who had lived through that epidemic of twenty years past had become sick.

Rarely were the sick able to even summon the strength to move the dead bodies out of their beds and the buzzing of the green bottleneck flies and small no-see-ums that gathered in clouds over the bodies was sickening. We dreaded lifting the tent flaps to peer inside. The sweet smallpox stench poured out to greet us everywhere. At first we tried to make the victims, who were often stuck to their bedding by the oozing of their pustules, more comfortable by turning them to a drier side of the coverings, but many times that resulted in an entire section of skin remaining stuck to the sheet and sloughing off as we turned them. So desperate were the sick that even this act, painful as it had to be, was usually met with little more than groans.

Noele was looking more drawn with every wigwam that we peered into and, finally, with just a few more to look at, he sat on a log with his head in his hands and his eyes on the dirt.

"Murphy, I need to sit. You finish up and meet me back here when you're done."

My friend had told me that he had been one of the first people at the village to become sick. How the disease had arrived in Bear River was a mystery that would never be solved, but Noele had been lucky. He had been covered with raised pustules which, when they finally faded after a couple of weeks, had left scars which he would bear to the end of his days, and he had been feverish for much of that time. Gradually, however, he improved and started feeling healthy at just about the same time that Luce and much of the rest of the village became sick. We had arrived soon after.

I sent the two men back to get the wagon and they began the awful task of loading the dead bodies and stacking them down on the beach. As Jean came out of a wigwam, I beckoned to her, and we met with Noele who was still sitting quietly. All of us were still for a moment. The only sounds were the wind moaning through the trees and the soft whisper of dull voices from the village.

Jean spoke first.

"There are a few things we can do. I can organize the women who are healthy to make soup and a little food every morning. Then we can go through the wigwams and clean everyone. The men can dispose of the dead. Murphy, can you go back to town in the wagon and get some blankets so we can burn these dirty ones?"

I wondered at the reception I would receive in Digby but clean blankets were needed and I could pick up more food at the same time. Noele had told me during our walk that food supplies were running low, although with many of the ill not eating, that was not the most pressing need. He looked up as I began to walk towards the returning wagon.

"I can organize the men to remove the dead. First thing, I think, is to gather firewood to burn the bodies down at the water. Then we can help with taking care of the sick. Hurry back, Murphy, I feel the cold is going to come on us soon."

I needed no words to spur me. The wagon had been emptied by the men. The bandages we had brought would be needed right away. The pressing need now was for blankets and sheets and more bandages and rags. There were no balms that we could apply to help relieve the pain and suffering but at least we could try to keep the patients clean and warm.

I pulled into Digby with a good deal of anxiety. Everyone feared an outbreak of smallpox in town and, although I was seemingly protected against the disease, most in the town were not. I was unsure if I could bring the pox into the town on my clothes or even on the horse or wagon. I yelled for Belanger as I came to the mill and the owner appeared, looking worried. I told him to stay away from the wagon and my friend stopped about ten feet away.

"Is it bad, Murphy?"

"Bad enough. I haven't got the pox but I don't know if the horse or my clothes can carry it, so you just stay away. I need to go back there. Can you get blankets and sheets and bandages together?"

"I'll see what we can do. What about food?"

"Nobody's eating much. Those that are still alive."

Belanger's face paled.

"How many are dead?"

"So far maybe thirty or so. I'm afraid there's many more to come."

Belanger shook his head.

"I've seen the pox work its way through a town before. All right,

Murphy, I'll get things together but you'd best just stay put on that wagon seat. I'll send someone out with something to eat for you and water for the horse and when you're gone, I'll go out and let Mary know you and Jean are going to be tied up for a while. Should I scout around in town and see if we can find some people willing to go out there and help you?"

But there were enough people already in Bear River who had lived through the sickness to help with the pox victims and I was reluctant to expose more people to the disease, especially since there was little anyone could really do to help. I was happy to take up my friend's offer for him to speak with Mary. I dozed on my seat in the autumn sun until one of the mill workers arrived with a small loaf of bread, a chicken leg, and a jar of water. The man, terrified of getting near me, the wagon, or the horse, threw the food and water to me. Then he came back with a tub of water for the horse which he carefully placed ten yards ahead before scampering back to the mill. I drove the wagon up to the tub and let the horse have a long drink of the water.

No more than an hour later, Belanger came back with an armful of blankets that he put on the back of the wagon.

"More will be along in a few minutes. We'll have enough to fill the wagon, I guess, and some rags for bandages and such. I can round up some more supplies for the next time you're back. I reckon you'll need more heavy blankets and maybe a few coats next time. The winter's going to be coming on sooner rather than later."

A few men straggled after Belanger, their arms full of rag bags and, further down the road, a small wagon loaded with blankets drew closer, but none of these men would come near me. I smiled at Belanger.

"How is it you're not afraid and these others are petrified of me?"

The mill owner's face, still dusty from the mill, split as he chuckled.

"Oh, I guess I just figure either I'll get it or I won't. These things are a bit beyond my understanding. I'm not about to walk around being afraid."

He let out a loud laugh and walked over to the closest man, took his bag, and put it on my wagon. In no time he had the wagon full. I told him I'd be back in a few days and he said he'd have a load of supplies waiting by the front of the mill. As I pulled away, he yelled that he'd ride down and see Mary that evening and I thought how lucky I was to have at least one good friend in the Digby community. But, then, Belanger was French and the French had been friends with the Mi'kmaq for many years.

Little had changed at Bear River. It was still quiet, so quiet that I could clearly hear an owl hooting and hunting in the gathering gloom and the soft rustle of night creatures in the underbrush at the edge of the settlement. A huge fire was burning on the beach, flames shooting high into the night. At regular intervals, one man would grab the shoulders and another the feet of one of the corpses which had been brought down to the sand and toss it far into the flames. The men, their faces florid and shining with the heat of the blaze and the effort of the toss, would sit on a log for a few minutes between each toss. It was a testament to their resilient natures that they were not despondent but rather quiet and absorbed in their task, careful to keep the fire hot and the wood piled high, calling to others to bring more wood as the supply was diminished.

No family members were present at the cremation. The few strong people in Bear River were busy tending to the needs of the sick. Prayers for the dead would come later.

Jean and her small band of helpers tended to the needs of the sick as well as they could, but the nightly cremations were as constant as the crows and ravens lining the edge of the settlement. These scavenging blackbirds got on my nerves after a while, so on one of my trips to town I got a barrel-shortened fowling piece from Belanger. This I learned to use to great effect, which surprised me and would certainly have surprised my old friend Moses, who used to say that he only felt safe fighting right beside me or to my rear, given my inability to hit anything I aimed at. The fact was that there was not much more for me to do than plink at the diminishing flocks of carrion birds, help with some of the physical work, gather wood and water, and go to town every few days with the wagon for blankets, coats, and other supplies,. Belanger had proven his worth during these Digby trips, both by being forceful in his efforts to push the townsfolk to supplying many, many blankets and coats and good food in abundance, and by keeping Mary informed of our progress.

Jean was tireless in her efforts to tend to the needs of the sick and, after two weeks, had begun to look drawn. I worried about her health but there was no talking to her about leaving. Noele and I would often share our meals and he worried almost as much about Jean as he did about Luce. Thankfully, his wife did recover after an illness that lasted ten days and seemed, at times, to be leading her to death. Both Noele and Luce were left with terrible scars, but they would live.

The number of daily deaths did not diminish until we had been at Bear River for two and a half weeks. At first I wondered if there were simply fewer people left in the settlement, but gradually it became clear that the number of smallpox cases had peaked and was on the decrease. Fewer corpses appeared down at the beach and Jean told me that there were fewer new cases appearing. We knew this was the disease simply running its course, rather than a result of our attention, but it was still a huge relief. Bear River had lost a considerable number of its residents. One day Jean came to me, wiping her brow with a dirty rag, and said that we should think about returning home in the next couple of days. She had lost weight but, beyond that, she looked tired and flushed and told me she was going to lie down. When she awoke, she called for me. Her forehead was damp with beads of sweat and her eyes told me what we both knew.

The pox advanced in the usual way. What started as a simple fever became an inferno raging beneath Jean's skin. After a week and a half, her face suddenly lost its hot look and, one day, she sat up in bed. I had seen enough of the progress of the disease by this time to know that this could be just a lull in the storm with the main tempest yet to come. Despite knowing this, I could not help but have a fool's optimism that she had beaten the disease. This hope was dashed in just a couple of days as the tell-tale rash appeared, first on Jean's forehead and then on her face, arms, neck, and finally on the rest of her body.

We tried to keep her body clean with gentle baths, but the pox always seemed to run ahead and the cleaning process itself was very painful to Jean, who was slipping in and out of consciousness. Still, I held on to the hope of a recovery for Jean since we had observed that, while the skin was the most obvious horror of smallpox, it was damage to unseen organs that resulted in death and this did not necessarily correspond to appearances.

The pox became a solid covering on Jean's face just two days after it first appeared, but we knew that if she could battle on for just a day more, the worst would be over and the disease would disappear as quickly as it had appeared. However, that night as I was sitting by her bedside, she gave a sharp cry and her breathing, which had been very rapid, suddenly ceased.

There was nothing any of us could do.

Jean was one of the last victims of the smallpox in Bear River. The settlement itself would live on with its small group of survivors and rebuild. Food would not be a problem now that most of the residents were dead. The cremation fires were slowly fading as I turned my back on the settlement and drove the wagon back to my home in the woods, where my family waited.

Thirty-Three

I did not pause in Digby on my way back but instead went straight home. Before I got there, I stopped at a clearing in the woods, stripped off all my clothes, and heaped them and my bedding in a pile which I set on fire. I put the wagon away from the house and tied the horse to a tree with grass around its roots. Finally, I went to the rock shelf that Mary and I had visited so often in the past and dove into the water.

The ocean water was very cold in autumn and I let out a whoop as I surfaced, loud enough to bring Mary and the boys running to the water's edge. She smiled when she saw me clambering out of the water but her face held a question as she looked back to the woods.

"Where's the wagon, Murphy? And Jean?"

I shook my head. I could think of few words to speak but I knew I had to say something.

"She's gone, Mary, and most of Bear River too. She's gone with the sickness and I'm as sorry as can be. I wished I'd talked her out of going but it's too late now and that's a fact. She's gone doing what she wanted to do. She was sure she had to help and she helped more than I can tell you. She got us all organized so that some were able to live and she cared for those that were sick. Mary, it's what she wanted. She had a tough life but she died doing what she wanted and none of us can ask much more than that."

Mary had always been of a mind to take the knocks with a level outlook, but this was something she had not foreseen. She hid her face in her hands and sat on a rock, her shoulders shaking with her sobs. I told her about the smallpox ravaging the settlement and I told her how it had finally claimed Jean. I told her about burning my clothes and warned her to not go near the wagon or the horse. I didn't know if they could carry the pox but I could not take the chance with Mary and the boys.

Mary's grief settled in her like an anchor that she carried with her day-to-day. I knew that Jean was always with her. Memories of Jean also stayed with me. Often I would think of her and frequently my thoughts would dwell on the long-ago time at the plantation when she tended to the raw welts on our backs from the overseer's whip.

I had seen many deaths over the years but now there was an undefined darkness in my soul which I felt as an ongoing uneasiness. For, if Bear River, in its innocence, could be crushed, then why not Digby; why not Nova Scotia; why not the world? How could I protect my loved ones from things unknown, unseen, and devastating? It was a darkness which devoured the light that had stayed at the core of my life through Great Bridge, through Kemp's Landing, through my fever and the torments of Bermuda, and the frustrations of our new land. I had always kept my good spirit, but now I felt it fading away.

I went back to work the very next day, as much to dispel the gloom as to actually be productive. Daniel had worked hard in my absence and the logs had accumulated in a pile in the yard. I began to get back into the rhythm of the logging and tried to fit into the hard schedule that Daniel had established.

It was exactly two weeks after I returned from Bear River that Daniel got sick. I knew the signs well. At first he was weak, dizzy, and tired and kept to his bed after sunrise. Two days later came the first of the rash, spreading along his neck and face. I tended to him and kept him away from the others but a cold weight had settled in my heart. I wondered how this had happened after the precautions I had taken. It could only be that I was somehow carrying the disease myself. I had taken great pains to burn my clothes and anything else that could have carried smallpox but I could do nothing about my own body if it was working to destroy that which was most important to me.

There was no sparing my family.

Daniel did recover but within short order and within hours of each other, Tye and Sam grew feverish and, soon after that, Mary ran outside our cabin to vomit in the woods. The disease followed the same deadly track I had witnessed in Bear River. There was nothing I could do to help any of them, even with Daniel now well enough to assist. They had to either get better or succumb solely through their own devices and that too seemed entirely capricious, or worse, pre-determined but unknowable.

Sam died just three days after first getting ill, his little body wracked in spasms coming from deep inside him that convulsed his limbs and left a trail of beaded sweat on his brow and above his lip. By this time, Mary was unable to care for the boys, unable even to talk. I do not know if she was even aware of me. Her eyes, though wide open, stared only at the ceiling and did not move to look when I drew near to care for her. Perhaps she did know I was there but did not want to look at me because she recognized that I was the bringer of death and destruction to our family.

Mary died while I was outside filling the water jars. Her eyes stared still at the ceiling and her fists were clenched. I cried for Daniel and he came on the run and took little Tye back to his cabin in his arms. The darkness that had tainted me since Jean's death now came to steal my heart.

I did not know what to do. I vaguely remember Daniel taking care of things over the next few days, burying the dead, saying a few words, and tending to Tye. Often he would bring me water, sometimes food, but I drank little and ate less. I had forgotten how to be hungry and thirsty. I could not recall my life or what we had planned for the future. I had no life beyond my thoughts of Mary and the boys. These memories, too, became the fiber of the dark web which entangled me. At times I was mute, my mind exhausted and blank, unable to think or even comprehend my surroundings.

Sleep, when it came, was a relief, but this oblivion was short-lived. I rarely slept more than two hours at a time. Upon awakening, memories of Mary and Sam flooded back and I was left without sense. This is how I was during the cool days of autumn and so I remained as the cold days of winter crept in. I had no sense of the weather and would not have recognized the cold except that Daniel brought me extra blankets and began lighting the small stove in the cabin. He often brought Tye when he made my meals but I had no mind for the boy. He reminded me too closely of what I had lost.

I did not work anymore. Daniel, with Tye bouncing on the seat beside him, had taken the wagon into town several times and exchanged the logs for food and goods which would sustain us through the winter. He continued to work in the woods when he could and spent much of his time tending to Tye and me. My winter of despair dragged on.

One night, I awoke in my cold cabin. It was as still as the grave, the air crystalline and misty. I walked barefoot to the door and out onto the landing. Above, the stars were remote, piercing the ebony sky. A sliver of a moon dangled halfway up from the horizon, providing just a trickle of light. Everything was far away and uncaring. I made my way through the darkened woods along the path I knew so well, to our rock ledge by the ocean.

I gathered a bundle of firewood along the way and walked along the frozen ground to the edge of the water. Here I lit a fire and sat, cross-legged, next to the blaze. I was tormented by not being able to figure out how I had brought the smallpox back from Bear River, despite the precautions I had taken, but there was no doubt that if I had not gone there, Jean, Mary, and Sam would all be alive. I thought I had provided a measure of relief to the poor souls at Bear River which they would not have had if I had not come, and certainly Jean had been a godsend to the sick people there. The cost was paid not by me but by my family. It was a cost that had not been known when the burden was taken on.

I took a glowing stick from the fire and deliberately put the red-hot end on the skin at the back of my arm. There was a flare as the hair burned off, and then a twist of putrid smoke as the skin burned and charred. I held the stick there briefly, then threw it back on the fire. The pain was the first real thing I had known since the deaths of Mary and Sam. I didn't know why I was alive, I didn't know why they were dead, and I surely did not know and did not want to think about what my choice would have been had all the futures been revealed to me that day of my journey when I sat on the wagon outside of Belanger's. But I did know the pain of the burn.

I lay on the flat rock and slept as the stars wheeled and turned above me like vultures in their sinister circles.

My sleep would have led into eternal rest after that cold night but for a number of unlikely coincidences. The next day, I still lay sleeping on the granite with the waves crashing at my feet. Daniel had taken little Tye into town with a small load of logs. He had not told anyone about the pox at our place because he was naturally secretive, and also because he was afraid of the reaction of the townsfolk if they found out that smallpox was right on the edge of their settlement. The workers at the mill quickly unloaded and marked the logs for future grading and Daniel prepared to drive away. However, as he turned the wagon onto the path, Tye, hungry and tired, began to cry. The cries of the youngster attracted the attention of Belanger, who came out of his office to determine the cause of the commotion. Seeing Tye with Daniel, the mill owner asked after me. Daniel, caught off-guard by the wails of the child and Belanger rushing out, told him our story. Belanger was stunned. This was the first he had heard of the calamity and he promised Daniel that he would be out to check on me later that day. Daniel continued on to our home and Tye, soothed by the steady rocking of the wagon, soon stopped his crying and went to sleep.

Later in the morning, as Belanger was hitching up the wagon to make the trip to our cabin, he spied Noele further down the road to town. My friend had come to town to sell some oil and had stayed for a while. He found it hard to return to the Bear River village with so many of his friends and family gone and the settlement itself reduced to a fraction of its former size. It was the quiet, the lack of laughter, and the absence of happy voices at Bear River that he said troubled him. Mainly, though, he blamed himself for the pox destroying his village, thinking that his frequent trips to the outside world had resulted in him bringing the disease back.

Belanger knew all this but he also knew that Noele was my friend, so he called to him and helped him clamber up on the wagon seat. The mill owner did not know what to expect when he pulled the wagon into our clearing but when I was not in our cabin, he feared the worst, and the two men began calling my name. Not knowing that I was not in bed, Daniel had taken little Tye with him on a scouting trip into the woods, but when he heard the voices, he came back into the clearing as well.

Daniel pointed out the well-worn path to the shore and it took little time for the men to locate me lying next to the dead fire. I was covered with a thick layer of frost and could not be wakened so they carried me back to the wagon, covered me with blankets, and quickly drove me back to town, leaving Daniel with the child. Belanger took me to his house, where I stayed in a coma for the next two weeks. I could hear people speak sometimes and on other occasions re-visited events that had taken place in the past as if I was still there, but most of that time I lay in a deep sleep.

Luce had come from the settlement to help nurse me back to health and, slowly, I did recover. Eventually I was able to hobble around the room, although my toes were sore. Oddly, my fingers were unaffected, perhaps because my hands had curled close to the heat of my chest as I lay on the granite shelf. Belanger and Noele had made plans during my convalescence. Although the mill owner was content to have me as his guest, he was eventually persuaded by the arguments of Noele and Luce that I would be more at ease and more easily treated at the Bear River settlement. Daniel had visited me several times and had been judged quite capable of managing the logging operations and looking after Tye for at least a few months. The truth was that I had been little help to him or Tye since the deaths of Mary and Sam.

It was a sunny winter day when we left Belanger's house and headed for Bear River. I owed the mill owner and Noele and Luce my life, but I did not care about living and often thought that they had done me a bad turn by rescuing me from the cold. I remained in the same dark cloud that had enveloped me since I had destroyed my family, a feeling of guilt and shame that overwhelmed me.

Noele put me in a wigwam close to his own with a good supply of blankets and firewood. Every morning, and throughout the day, Luce would come with smoked meat, soup, and bread, of which there was ample supply. The settlement remained very quiet.

I spent the rest of the winter and the following spring by myself. Luce came to bring me food and Noele came to provide wood and small talk, but both quickly realized that I was not capable of carrying on a conversation or even listening to another person. In fact, I loathed myself and was not able to think beyond the small confines of the wigwam. Noele and Luce were subdued and sad but they had a long history of loss and suffering and had learned to cope with death and adversity. Bear River had suffered several disasters, both man-made and natural, in its past. Despite the suffering I had experienced in my life and the loss of Moses at Kemp Bridge, it was clear that I was being taught another lesson in grief. I grieved for my lost family and I felt sorry for myself and guilty for what I had delivered.

Noele, of course, knew all this. He knew too that grief cannot be understood by anyone who has not suffered tremendous loss and could not be told by one person to another. Because of this, he largely left me alone to my own nightmares and trusted in my ability to learn my own grief lesson my own way. Every now and then he would come to my wigwam to ask if I wanted to take part in a hunt he was going on, or perhaps to go fishing in the woods, or collecting berries. When I shook my head, he would leave without a word.

I was not a quick learner. Through the spring of 1788 and into the summer, I thought of no one but myself and indulging my sadness. Gradually my capacity for guilt and despair was filled, then over-flowed. I became tired of my own inactivity, then tired of my self-indulgence. One day when Noele asked if I wanted to go with him to pick raspberries, which grew like weeds around the village, I nodded. He did not express surprise but merely handed me a bucket, and we walked in silence to the woods.

However, the grief never really left me. It sat, heavy, in the pit of my stomach. Each morning, I woke with thoughts of my wife and son first in my mind. My lesson was to learn to live with these memories which would not diminish with time or experience. I did not learn how to do this through a cathartic event but rather through the force of life still coursing through me. I would never feel completely whole again.

The most important lesson in grief was that life was meant to be endured, not enjoyed, and so it would be with me until the end of my days.

Thirty-Four

I spent the summer and fall of 1788 at Bear River taking part in the porpoise chase, now reduced to just a few canoes in the bay, and helping in the fall deer and moose hunt. I had never been a great talker and now I was an even more quiet companion, but not morose. Often I went into town to chat with Belanger and sometimes to meet with Daniel and little Tye, who was growing into an active boy and was curious about everything. When I saw him, I remembered, and when I remembered, a chill seized my heart and I felt like roaring at the wind. But still I lived and so I did not roar, I did not moan, I did not despair.

I endured.

My heart had frozen solid and nothing would thaw it again but I would carry on, almost as if it were a duty to be alive. I felt like I owed it to someone.

In the early winter of 1788, Daniel asked if I would come back to live at the cabin in the woods. At first I was anxious about moving back but eventually I realized I was needed there and that it was my home. Daniel had grown into an excellent young man but it was clear to me that he needed help, both with the logging and with the raising of Tye. It was apparent that I should be with my son and return to being busy in the old way.

The logging had never been better. Although we had to go further afield to find the straight trees that were favored for the making of masts and spars, the premium these logs commanded was high and so we did very well. My crippled hand ached sometimes in the cold as I hooked a chain on a log and onto the harness of the heaving horse, his breath white in the still air, but I welcomed the pain and muttered quietly to encourage him through the drifts and deadfalls. Daniel and I always looked forward to the trip to Belanger's with our wagon of logs. We often celebrated our work with a dinner in town, which was a chance to catch up on the latest news and show off Tye.

We heard little news about Thomas. He had not returned to Nova Scotia since his last visit to our cabin but, one day, a former Black Pioneer named Smith who was trying to scratch out a living as a teamster came up to me as we unloaded at the mill and told me that he had heard from a friend of his who had left with Thomas for New Brunswick. The friend had told him that Thomas and the people who had left Nova Scotia to join him in New Brunswick had had no luck in securing farmland within a short distance from town and the petitions had fallen on deaf ears, not just refused but generally ignored. The men were making do on small jobs with scant pay and even Thomas had gone from job to job, his dreams diminished.

That winter was mild but it was not until the spring of 1789 that we saw Thomas again. He walked into our clearing with his hat in his hands, a thinner man with more gray about his temples and worry lines etched around his eyes. Of course he was very sad about the news of the sickness and our loss, but he was still the same old Thomas, frustrated with his current place and eager to work towards a better future. His enthusiasm had been dimmed but not extinguished by his frustration in New Brunswick and the refusal of the many petitions he had drafted with the help of a literate settler. The few that had been answered by the governor had not given satisfaction but that, to my mind, had to be expected in a province where many of the loyalist immigrants had come from the plantations of Virginia.

Thomas had a new plan. I could only listen as he outlined his idea after dinner. Daniel said little, but I could see he was listening intently.

"I have to go to London to present our case. There is nothing more to be done here. No one will listen and nothing will change. If we wish to become real citizens with the ability to support ourselves and make a life for our children, we must have land, and the governments here will not grant it."

"Thomas, the governments here represent the interests of the government overseas. What makes you think you will get a better reception there?"

"Because I have heard that the government in London is in favor of better treatment for us. Because the local governments are full of corruption and theft, and because most of us have nothing left to lose, nowhere else to go. Think, Murphy, this is our last chance to make a home here. Without a change we will always be in chains. The key to freedom is in the ownership of land and that can only come from government decree. If not from here then from the ruler in London."

Thomas would not be dissuaded from the trip to London which would be, at the very least, long and arduous, and at its worst, dangerous. Fortune hunters patrolled the coast off of Nova Scotia and often halted vessels heading for Britain to check for former slaves on board. These people were now free and residents of another country, but often they were seized and returned to the States where they could be sold at auction or returned for a reward to their former owners. These profiteers often ignored the paperwork that most of the black loyalists carried which acknowledged their status as free men. The captains of the British vessels were not above co-operating with the brigands for a small fee and, in any event, had no real interest in protecting their passengers from seizure once the passage fee had been paid.

Thomas, of all people, well knew the risks of a trip to London. He was also aware that only by demonstrating that he represented the interests of most of the black settlers in Nova Scotia and New Brunswick would he be able to deliver a credible message to the leaders in London. I thought that there was almost no chance of meaningful change. The only changes that I had seen in my life that actually benefited a large group of people had come at the round end of a long gun. Or, more specifically, many guns. However, Thomas was right in his intent. The Black Pioneers had never received the land they had been promised and were still treated as second-class citizens by the government they had fought for. It was also true that there was no local path to justice which had not already been tried by Thomas. It was easy to be cynical while sitting idle on the outside looking in, and so I resolved to help my friend, at least in the drafting of a petition which he could circulate and use as a demonstration of support when he arrived in London. Before I could tell Thomas I would help him draft the petition, Daniel, sitting quietly away from the fire, spoke.

"I would like to come with you. I can't read and I can't write but I can work all day and half the night, and you might need someone there to run errands and keep the day-to-day stuff going while you're talking with the high and mighty."

As he was talking, Daniel looked squarely at me and, as he finished, both of my friends stared at me. My first response was guilt. It should have been me that volunteered to go with Thomas on his mission, but I did not want to go. Since the death of my family, I had little enthusiasm for anything and certainly not a long overseas voyage. I also knew I was not of sound mind. My guilt and depression waited like a conquering army inside my head, watching only for a sign of weakness to gain the advantage. What little responsibility I had ever felt for my fellow Pioneers had dwindled.

"If you want to go, Dan, I think that would be fine. I can look after the logging and little Tye and I think you could be a great help to Thomas, if he would like it. For my part, I can help draft a petition that can demonstrate that you have the support of the people when you go to London."

Thomas nodded and looked at Dan.

"That will be fine and I gratefully accept your help."

He cast his glance at me.

"Both of your help, I should say. It will be good to have a companion on the expedition if only to share ideas. I thought you might like to come along, Murphy, but I did not know then about Mary and the sickness."

His voice trailed off and he looked away. In my self-absorption, I had forgotten that Thomas had had a close bond with Jean and Mary, and in fact had known them both as long as me. He had also lost a child to fever, so he was not a stranger to grief. He looked back at me. The passing of the years had not spared Thomas. His face was lined with worry and his eyes were not as sharp as they had been. His mouth, which had always looked ready to laugh at a joke or tell a story, was now turned down at the ends. And were we really further ahead? Living in perpetual poverty was another form of slavery and many of the Pioneers still teetered on the edge of starvation.

"Here's what we need. We need to draft a petition outlining our need for decent land and recognition of our status as veterans and free men. Then we need to figure out a way to raise our passage over there, or work it off, or something."

"And you need to have yourself named in the petition as the representative of the black settlers here," I said.

"Yes. Of course. Can Dan leave here with me tomorrow so we can start signing people up for the petition?"

It was tempting to agree, to crawl back into my shell and stay in the woods and leave the politicking and traveling to my two friends, but I was the only one of the three who could read and write and the only one who could witness the marks of those who would sign the petition. So, I agreed to travel with Thomas around Nova Scotia and across the bay to New Brunswick to obtain as many signatures as possible. Dan would stay behind to look after Tye and take care of the logging. He would accompany Thomas on the trip to Britain.

We spent the rest of the summer and fall traveling throughout Nova Scotia and New Brunswick, explaining our plan to the black loyalists and obtaining their signatures in support. It was a long job, knocking on each door and explaining the reason for the overseas trip over and over. I was able to continue with an outward appearance of strength and calmness. It helped that the plan was always greeted with enthusiasm. Some of our friends were skeptical of the eventual results and a few would not sign for fear of repercussions from their bosses, but most signed and expressed support for Thomas. Many gave us as much money as they could afford to pay for the trip and it soon became apparent that passage fees would not be a problem. Only a few of the Black Pioneers could sign their names—most got by with a mark—but I named and witnessed them all, and by the time the frost settled hard in the ground, we had 202 names on the petition. That represented a whole lot of walking and talking, and we felt it would be enough to present to the government in London and be taken seriously. The petition not only named Thomas as our representative in London but also asked the government to help with obtaining land and rights in Nova Scotia and New Brunswick or, failing that, settling the Black Pioneers in another place. It had become clear to us in our travels that most of the Pioneers were living in poverty and were desperate to change their circumstances.

Thomas stayed in New Brunswick as the winter came on and I returned to my home. Everything had gone well at our logging camp and we had another good winter taking many logs to Belanger. Prices had remained high.

Tye was now older than a toddler but not quite yet a lad. We knew that he missed his mother but, being young, he had strong capacity for bouncing back after being beaten down and Dan was an excellent substitute parent. He often took Tye to the woods, showing him the secrets of the trees, the tracks made by the wildlife, and the stories of the seasons. I was not so good, though I tried in my own clumsy way to meet my son's needs. I found it difficult to separate Tye from Sam and Mary and when I watched my boy play, my mind would often wander down melancholy lanes that were endless and tortured.

As the winter wore on, I came to realize that my lessons in grief were not yet concluded. I was like a pariah dog, unpredictable and capable of only living on the outskirts of settlements, scattering and skulking and snapping at the approach of kindness and cruelty alike, afraid to stay long enough to determine the difference. I ate little and felt no hunger or cold. I did still go into the woods to help but now felt like a stranger in my own forest. My hands, so used to the feel of the ax, were now cold and stiff and unfamiliar.

Daniel began avoiding me as much as he could and I rarely spoke to him when he came back from cutting trees. Often I would sit in the corner, muttering small words and staring at the floor. Eventually, as the spring light curled over the treetops, he became uneasy about leaving Tye with me and always took him with him to the woods.

In all of this, Daniel was right.

I remained strange and less than a man.

One spring evening, Daniel came to me and told me he was leaving in the morning to find Thomas. He told me he would take Tye with him and leave him with Noele in Bear River. So faded was I that I had no thought on the matter and said nothing, just waved my friend away and made small, meaningless sounds that had no more gravity than the whisperings of mice moving through the long grass.

Half way along the path to Digby, Dan and Tye met my old friend, Captain Mitchell of the *Joseph*, striding along towards our home. The captain told him to go directly to the dock at Digby, thereby to meet the tender for the waiting *Joseph*. Tye was to go, too. As for Captain Mitchell, he continued to the cabin, where I was lying on my bed.

"Murphy, what is going on here?"

When I made no reply, Captain Mitchell dragged me—feet first with my head bumping on the floor—to a chair. There he plopped my feet on the seat and stood looking down at my face, which was staring up at the ceiling from the floor.

"What a sorry god-damn sight you are. I sure as hell never figured on you being a suicide but I guess I might have been wrong about that. I'll tell you what, I've heard about all your troubles so you don't need to be crying about them to me again. I've got a few things to say, then I'm going to go and you can do as you like."

His face was red and his lips tight.

"Here it is, Murphy, you've got three choices. You can lie

here like a sniveling child and just kind of fade away. You can kill yourself, if you figure you can't live with yourself anymore. Or you can put your sadness somewhere in your mind, so you take it out now and again and look it over, and then live your life like the rest of us. Now the first way is the worst way since it shows you don't even have the guts to kill yourself. The second way is at least choosing to do something. But then you could choose the third way and live."

He kicked my feet off the chair and sat looking down at me.

"Murphy, do you think you're the only person who's lost someone, the only guilty one, the only one who has the sort of sorrow that gnaws at your guts? You are so occupied with what you've done wrong and with your own guilt that you can't see beyond your nose. All of us are guilty of something, haven't you learned that by now? There are no innocents, Murphy, and you are not the judge of who is guilty and who is not. That pox may have been brought back by you from the settlement but it may not have been, too, and even if it was, how were you to know? These are things that you will never get the answer for, try as you might to pry it out of the Almighty. And you can riddle yourself to death over this if you want."

"Here's the thing. I'm going to take Thomas and Daniel and Tye to London, and then I'm going to bring them back here when they're ready. Don't try to explain everything to me, I know it all; I've talked with Thomas about it for hours on end. You should be going with him; you know that and I know that, but since you aren't capable of getting out of bed, let alone helping him or even looking after your boy, then I guess you'll just have to stay here until we get back. Then I'll have a little talk with you, I think, and if you're not up to it, you'll never hear from me again. If you don't think you can handle even that then I think you'd best go and drown yourself and put us all out of your misery."

He paused and passed his hand over his hair.

"You need to stop thinking so much and start doing. If I was you, I'd be working in those woods from sun-up to sun-down and sharpening my tools at night. Then I'd be planting my garden on a spare day and weeding on another day. Why not a pig and some chickens, maybe a cow? You see what I mean, Murphy? You got to keep busy to keep the demons from roaming around your skull. We all do. The devil is not in the doing, it's in the thinking, and here's something else to do besides building up your homestead here. Instead of lying around feeling sorry for yourself, how about taking an interest in some of your old comrades and those out there that are having a tough time getting by. A lot tougher than you, I'd say. The people look up to you, Murphy. Thomas is doing the best he can but he needs help. He's got his role to play but you've got one too. For God's sake, you can do something. Christ, it makes me puke to see you waste yourself like this."

With that, and without a good-bye, Captain Mitchell turned on his heel and left the cabin. By the time I pulled myself off the floor, all I could see was his back as he walked briskly back to town.

I hadn't said a word.

Thirty-Five

I was sure Captain Mitchell did not know what was going through my head, and as I lay on my bed feeling sorry for myself, my fevered brain even worked up a sense of outrage that the captain would dare come to the cabin in order to tell me things he knew little about.

However, over time, it's hard to feel outraged when you're lying in your bed by yourself. There seemed no point in ranting to the walls and eventually I got sick of myself lying like a slug on the bed. Finally, I got so fed up that I began to put in a regular day of work. That meant getting up early, harnessing one of the horses, and dragging logs out of the woods or cutting the branches from fallen timbers. Sometimes I'd take some blankets and food with me and I'd lie out on the cutting, watching the stars peeking through the tops of the trees until sleep closed my eyes.

I had little time to think and I was so tired that sleep came easily. The demons in my head were still waiting for me, but they could not break through as long as I kept them in a box in my mind that was separate from day-to-day work. Logging looks simple, but it's not. You have to pay attention. I'd already been caught unawares once—my crippled hand was the proof—but now I was careful, methodical, and controlled. Once again the ax became a part of me and the trees were interesting anew. I slowly began to remember the subtle joy of working in the forest and the sublime pleasure of being the only human in a wild place. In the past I had taken pride in my skill with the tree-cutting tools, and that sense of being in the right place and of fulfilling my correct role in life slowly returned. I began to feel good again.

I did not feel lonely.

Belanger visited the cabin occasionally and I saw him in town regularly when I went to drop off logs. I saw Noele and Luce a couple of times. The Bear River settlement was slowly returning to a sustainable size but had not yet regained its previous strength. Mostly I kept to myself, busy now with my work and too tired at the end of the day to think about things that could not be changed.

I heard from Belanger that the *Joseph* had sailed on a fine day and, given a good passage, Thomas, Dan, and Tye would be in Britain in late September or early October. The voyage might be perilous but I had great faith in Captain Mitchell's abilities and so did not worry about bad weather or marauding bounty seekers. Sometimes I wondered how my friends would make out in London and if they would get any satisfaction in resolving our problems. It was hard for me to see how the trip could end in success, since the local governors who had given us so little satisfaction were representatives of the home government in London. But, if anyone could explain our situation, it was Thomas, so I hoped for good results.

I sometimes contemplated the captain's words about leadership but could think of no way that I could provide help to my peers. Stories about various injustices filtered through to me, mostly from Belanger, but I could see nothing that I could do to help address these cruelties. The winter wore on and was thankfully mild, though snowy.

Early in 1791, Belanger told me that a ship that had arrived in Halifax, after a fast trip from Britain, sent word that the *Joseph* had completed its voyage in October of the previous year. It wasn't until early summer that the ship returned to Halifax, along with my friends.

The trees were already in leaf and the air full of the dull buzz of insects when the trio strode into my yard. I could tell by their aspects that they had news to relate and I could tell, also, that the news was good. I made a fire in the rock circle and boiled tea while they told me their story.

The *Joseph* had made a quick trip to Britain, encountering fair winds and no vessels from the United States. Once there, Thomas quickly met with the small community of black loyalists who lived in London. Several former Black Pioneers worked on the docks and recognized my friend as he came off the *Joseph*. This was a good thing, since the three had limited funds. They found loyalist families who were happy to put them up during their stay in London.

After hearing about our plight, the loyalists put Thomas in touch with our old general, Sir Henry Clinton, who remembered him from the war and even asked after me, likely because of the strange vision I had related to his assistant in New York. The general did not hesitate to provide Thomas with a recommendation to several leading politicians in London whom, it was thought, would be able to help my friend. These were politicians who were eager to hear about the situation in the colonies and quickly reassured my friend that the injustices would be addressed. As Thomas continued to speak about his experience in London, I began to realize that the motives behind their support were not entirely selfless.

"Murphy, they provide three choices. Every man will have to decide which to take. First, they promise to have an investigation into our difficulties getting the title to land, and to address the problems that are discovered. Second, for those not interested in waiting for this inquiry to be completed, they offer military service in the West Indies with a full military pension. And third, for everyone who wishes to move to the Province of Freedom, they offer transport and support.

I blinked through the smoke of the fire.

"Did you say the Province of Freedom?"

"Yes, Sierra Leone, on the coast of Africa. They call it the Province of Freedom. They want to move settlers onto the land there. It's warm and it's on the ocean, so there's easy trade and good farming, and there is the Sierra Leone Company in Britain set up to support anyone wanting to go there to get established."

"Thomas, are you saying we should move across the ocean to a new country and start over?"

"For those who want to, yes. It's not exactly starting over, Murphy. We've never gained even a toehold here so it's not like we're giving anything up. They'll give us land there and the tools to work it. It won't be cold half the year. We will be going home, Murphy."

"Well it's not home for me. It's not home for Daniel."

"You know what I mean, Murphy. Your parents and Dan's didn't choose to come across the ocean. They were sold into it and so was I, and our heritage is across the sea in that land. It really will be going home."

There was a long pause.

"Thomas, what's in it for them?"

"For them?"

"For the Sierra Leone Company."

"They want this land settled for trade. It's true there is a business aspect to this but they also see this as a way to fight slavery. The men running it are against slavery. They want this settlement to attract slaves from around the world but, yes, they want to make money too, I guess."

"Will we get land there?"

"Yes, so they say, and I trust them. Anyway, it's up to each man to decide if he wants to stay here and wait for the inquiry to finish and then maybe get land, or to go to a place where he won't freeze in the winter and establish our own settlement."

He went on to explain that there had been a settlement in Sierra Leone before but it had been abandoned and burned after repeated attacks from the various tribes that lived in the area. That did not sound promising or welcoming, but Thomas assured me that the new settlement would be considerably larger and would be protected by British forces. He could barely contain his excitement as he explained that the Province of Freedom would attract settlers from Nova Scotia and New Brunswick, and also from Britain and the West

Indies. It would be a refuge for the dispossessed and downtrodden and power would be given to the settlers. They would be able to rule themselves with their own laws and their own leaders. Thomas had met with the men behind the effort to create the Province of Freedom and was convinced of their good intentions. It was clear that this was the option favored by my friend. The years of waiting for a response from the local governments had ground Thomas down to the point where he did not want to wait for an inquiry to take place.

The choices were clear enough and it was hard to see what would hold many back from setting sail across the ocean to yet another homeland. Most of the Black Pioneers had not established a real life for themselves and their families in Nova Scotia or New Brunswick. Many had trouble adapting to the harsh climate and others found they had no real skills to market. Most knew how to farm but needed better growing conditions and their own land. This, it was said, they would find in Sierra Leone. I had no doubt that many would take the offer to leave.

The fire burned low and Thomas, weary and travel-worn, took to his bed. Tye had long been asleep, but Daniel and I still sat around the embers, poking at them with sticks to keep the fire alive. I looked at my young partner across the fire ring.

"Will you go?"

"I think I will, Murphy. Thomas thinks it will be a new beginning for us."

"We have a pretty good life here."

"Yes, for the two of us, but I want a family someday and we have no title to this land. They could kick us off whenever they want. The winter is long and cold. Yes, I'll go. What about you?"

"I don't know, Dan. There's not much holding me here now. I guess they likely have trees of some sort in Sierra Leone, so my tools will be just as good there and, if not, I could likely find something else to do. I feel like I owe it to Thomas to go. We've been friends for a long time. It was always his dream, I think, to create his own country for his own people and I think I should help him with that. It's pretty hard to picture living here by myself with the both of you gone. So yes, I'll make a new start too."

In truth, leaving Nova Scotia had never previously entered my mind, but there was little reason not to leave and a few good ones to make the voyage. Daniel explained that an English politician would be arriving in a few months to arrange the transportation of those wishing to re-settle and also to begin the inquiry into the distribution of land. The Sierra Leone Company would pay for everything. The Company would restrict transportation to those persons registered in the government's books, which would result in many potential emigrants but would also leave some non-registered settlers remaining in Nova Scotia and New Brunswick. I could see that there was a fine line to be walked here, since the Company wanted to have a viable base for settlement in Sierra Leone while also leaving a core group behind. It was of little concern to me since all of the names of the Pioneers were on the list created when we left New York.

The next few months were a whirl of activity. Thomas and I traveled from town to town to explain the options to the Pioneers and other registered folks. The response was overwhelming and the crowds grew steadily. Although we had obtained signatures from just over two hundred people on the petition which Thomas had taken to London, it seemed to me that there would be many more than that who would sign up to leave Nova Scotia for the Province of Freedom, and I could not fault them for this. Many of the people we saw were in very desperate situations, some with few clothes and many with no permanent homes and an uncertain food supply. Although I had always thought that prosperity resided in the ownership of land, it was becoming clearer to me with every step that the immediate solution for the ever-present poverty was for laborers to receive decent wages. These wages were, in fact, available to the many workers on the roads, but the lion's share of the government payment was still skimmed off the top by middlemen such as Stephen Skinner and Stephen Blucke.

Word of the English proposal had spread throughout the province and the settlers were eager to meet us as soon as we arrived in a town. At a large outdoor gathering in Shelburne, we ran into our old shipmates, Sarah and Ben. Sarah was working still as a maid, but her employer had moved to Shelburne from Halifax. She had a long indenture to the man and Ben had quit being a sailor because his poor legs gave him constant trouble. Ben came up to Thomas as he sat on a bench and I soon joined them. A crowd had already started to gather around but we had a few minutes before Thomas would begin his speech. Ben told us a tale from Shelburne, the likes of which I thought we had left far behind.

A woman, a former slave of a rebel officer, had fled from that man's estate and taken refuge with the British forces in the war. She stayed with the army, doing laundry and kitchen duties as it traveled. The woman, Mary Postell, was one of the many refugees from slavery who sought freedom by joining the British and had been guaranteed that freedom by government leaders. She was, in point of fact, little different than any of the other Pioneers in Nova Scotia. However, Mary Postell was different in one way from the war veterans. She was married to a man who had not joined the Pioneers but had served the British military by doing some of the hundreds of support jobs behind the scenes, like digging braceworks, cooking, roadwork, and repairs. At the end of the war he persuaded Mary to leave and take work with a British loyalist who fled to Florida, named Jesse Gray. Florida was just a stop along the way for Gray, who eventually made his way to Nova Scotia, taking Mary Postell and her two children, Flora and Nell, along with him.

Mary may have continued to live with the estate owner for the rest of her life except for something that happened shortly after the household settled in Shelburne. Mary, who mainly worked in the kitchen, happened to overhear Gray talking during dinner about selling her. Mary had been sure that her flight to the British lines during the war meant that she was now a free person, able to make her own decisions, and not about to be bought and sold by any man. She believed that she was working in the Gray household freely and of her own will and was not owned by anyone, so she took her two children off the estate and moved away from Gray and into a small cabin on the north end of Shelburne. Gray attempted to stop her from moving, but Mary was a stubborn, proud woman and she was not ready to return to a life of slavery—so the three, Mary, Flora, and Nell, moved into a small flat above a shop in town. She sought work as a maid in Shelburne and obtained a job with a barrister, looking after his ailing wife and attending to the duties of the house.

Some people are born in a cursed phase of the moon and have no luck in their lives in any endeavor. For such people, any good fortune is seen for just what it is—a prelude to a more intense and protracted period of misery and injustice. Mary Postell was such a person. On her way to work one warm day in spring, Mary was grabbed by three thugs who lay in wait for her in a dark alley a few steps from her door. These vicious men packed Mary into an enclosed buggy and took her directly to the town of Argyle, where Gray waited. The loyalist had grown tired of her ways and sold her to a family friend, James Mingham, for 113 bushels of potatoes. Gray had also sold her children, but not to Mingham. Flora and Nell went to separate homes in other parts of Nova Scotia.

Mary's spirit was broken by the loss of her children. She stayed with Mingham for three years and would have stayed there until the end of her days except for two events. First, she heard that Flora was living in Shelburne, and second, a passing carpenter who worked for a short time on Mingham's barn told her that she would have some relief in the courts if she brought a case to seek her freedom. So, in the night, she slipped away from the Mingham farm and made her way to Shelburne, where she arrived at the courtroom proclaiming her freedom and asking for her children. The court appointed a lawyer to support her cause and in due time the case was heard.

Mary Postell's lawyer uncovered a witness to support her claim of freedom, a man by the name of Scipio Wearing, who was also a friend of Ben and Sarah's. Scipio Wearing had known Mary during the war, and even before when she was a slave in Charleston. Both Thomas and I had known Wearing when he was a Black Pioneer, but his friendship with Mary Postell went even further back than that. He had left with one of the first vessels out of New York and had settled in Shelburne while we were still languishing in Bermuda.

He was a reliable soldier, which is about as good as anyone can say about any man.

Wearing testified that he had known Mary for many years and that she had joined the British lines and come to Nova Scotia as a free person. Further, he told the court that she had served the British well during the war and was entitled to all the protection and rights that all the settlers had.

Wearing lacked nothing in courage. Others had been asked to testify but had declined, afraid of repercussions from the powerful local men of whom Jesse Gray was a leading member. It was all too predictable that his testimony would be in vain. The judge ruled that Gray had not taken Mary to Shelburne by force, but that she came of her own free will. The courtroom was filled with Gray's supporters, who erupted into cheers and laughter as the verdict was read. Mary made her way out of the room but, as she started down the stairs, was grabbed by two men and whisked into another carriage.

At this point in the story Ben paused and, picking up a rock, tossed it at a squirrel that was chattering at us from a high branch.

"She was taken by Gray directly back to the States by way of a smuggler's ship. I have heard she was given to his brother and is a slave again in Carolina. But, Murphy, that is not the worst of it, though it is bad enough by itself.

"Scipio Wearing's house was fired while he was testifying. It was burned to the ground along with all his belongings. Inside the house was Sammy, his youngest child, who burned to death in the inferno. It is said that the child's screaming during the blaze was ignored by the men who gathered outside. No one has been charged with setting the fire because no one will come forward to testify."

Thomas groaned at this and leaned back against the bench, his eyes looking up at the squirrel, but Ben was not finished.

"All of this is bad, Thomas, but I have heard talk that is worse still. I do not know if I should even believe such talk, but here it is. Gray and his cohorts are leading men in Shelburne but the master of them all is Stephen Skinner, the grandest businessman and land developer in town and well connected to the government too. As you also likely know, Skinner and Blucke are as thick as thieves. I have heard that the burning of Scipio's house could not have been done without Skinner knowing about it beforehand. If Skinner knew, then so did his good friend, Blucke."

Ben paused and looked at me. I had known for a long while that Blucke placed his ambition and greed well ahead of any loyalty to the Black Pioneers. If indentures and enslavement were eliminated so that the Black Pioneers had more real rights, he might lose his control over the allotment of government funds. This was something that had clearly occurred to our former leader during the Mary Postell trial.

Thomas looked at me with a warning in his eyes.

"It may be just a rumor, Murphy. I see that look in your eyes and it's a look I haven't seen in a good while, but there may be nothing at all to this. Before you go blaming Blucke, we best make sure it's true. We're almost ready to get out of this so let's not do anything too wild now."

I wanted to believe that our old leader did not have a part in the burning, but I found it hard to think that he did not have prior knowledge of it. I wondered how Blucke would react if he realized that a big part of his cheap labor force would likely leave for the Province of Freedom. I thought it would be best if I stuck close to Thomas through the rest of his trip through Nova Scotia and kept a sharp eye out for trouble.

Thirty-Six

It was clear to me that Ben and Sarah would leave Nova Scotia for the Province of Freedom. There was little to hold them back from the trip and Ben found the cold weather hard on his legs. He had told me in Bermuda that he dreamed of living in a cold country, but the harsh winters of Nova Scotia had proven to be too much for his ravaged legs to bear. Thomas assumed that I would come with him, of course, and now there was little to hold me back. Dan was also keen to make the trip.

As we traveled around Nova Scotia, we saw more and more Pioneers who were disappointed and who were eager to make a fresh start in a more welcoming environment. The black settlers who were determined to stick were few and far between. By the time the Englishman, Clarkson, arrived in late summer, there were many hundreds who had said they were eager to leave and there would be more to come.

I met Clarkson only once, briefly, when Thomas went to talk with him about our progress and arrange for the ships which would transport us to the new world. He was very busy and bureaucratic but it was clear that he had the interests of the Black Pioneers at heart and was keen to address our grievances. The inquiry into our land-title problems would proceed but Clarkson was quickly confronted with the short-term logistics of transporting more and more people over a long distance. He had come to Nova Scotia to expedite the immigration solely on the strength of Thomas's word and the backing of the petition which had been signed by just over two hundred people. Now he found himself in a situation where hundreds of people, perhaps even a thousand, wanted to make the trip, and it was no surprise that the details were overwhelming. Thomas told me that Clarkson had originally planned for one vessel to make the trip to Sierra Leone but was now thinking that three might not be enough. Each ship had to be well stocked with food for the journey and supplies for the settlement at Sierra Leone.

Clarkson also had concerns about the colony that would be left behind in Nova Scotia. Obviously much of the interest in the African settlement had come from loyalists who were having a hard time making a living here. These people made up much of the labor force in the province. Their departure would make it more difficult to find workers and would result in higher wages for those who stayed behind. This was beneficial for those who would stay but not so for those who employed them.

The Shelburne business partnership of Blucke and Skinner had created this situation themselves by gouging our friends for so long, but it was clear that they, and other vested interests in the province, would not stand idly by as their cheap source of labor departed for warmer climes. First there came small petitions to Clarkson with concerns about the loss of workers. Then, subtle political pressure was applied to the visiting Englishman and, finally, overt shows of intimidation were made to individuals who were eager to leave.

All of this was in vain.

Clarkson would not be bullied by provincial businessmen and quickly saw their real intentions, which were often cloaked in soft words and disingenuous mannerisms. He pursued his task with a single-minded determination. However, he was firm about one condition—each applicant for emigration had to be registered as a landed loyalist in Nova Scotia or New Brunswick. For most of the loyalists, this did not present a problem. All had been registered when they left New York but I could see from the frown on Thomas's face when he told me of Clarkson's condition that things were not quite that simple.

"Murphy, don't you see? It's fine for you and me but what about Dan and Ben and Sarah? They are not registered anywhere. They won't be allowed to go unless we can figure out a way to get past these rules."

We did not tell the trio of the problem but it persisted as we wended our way across the province. We heard tales of people who had been turned away by Clarkson and his officials, either because they had no evidence they were loyalists or because they were indentured and could not provide a letter of release from their employer. There had been a case where a particular employer had been offered a sum of money by Clarkson in order to facilitate the release of his servant but had turned down the deal. The English official had then reluctantly told the unfortunate servant that he had to remain in the employer's control and could not emigrate. This was always on our minds but there seemed to be no way out, short of smuggling the three on board ship, and to do that, this time we would not have the help of Captain Mitchell. He had disappeared in a mysterious fashion and we had not seen the man for several months.

We had not run into Blucke on our travels either, but we had snippets of news about him. First we heard that his wife had left him and returned to the States, and that he was now living with his daughter. Then we heard that his daughter had had a child. Finally we heard rumors of stolen funds and embezzlement. None of this really surprised me but I kept waiting for another shoe to drop and that shoe finally did fall, in—of all places—our home town.

Digby was the final stop that Thomas made in Nova Scotia before heading across the bay to New Brunswick to round up the emigrants in that province. Word of his appearance had spread and a small crowd had gathered. Daniel and Tye had also come to watch. As Thomas climbed onto the back of the wagon to address our friends, there was a small commotion at the back of the crowd. A

327

small group of tough-looking men strode to the front of the wagon and stood in a line. I saw these men out of the corner of my eye as I was engaged in conversation with Dan and Tye, whom I had not seen for months.

Before I could fully comprehend what was happening, one of the men seized Thomas and, raising a short club, struck him on the back of his head. My friend slumped to the ground near one of the wheels. As I turned to his aid, the ruffian jumped on the wagon bed and addressed the crowd himself.

"This is what you get if you want to leave. This and a lot more. So instead of fancy words and promises, you think on that."

As I went to Thomas, the man jumped down from the wagon and disappeared into the crowd along with his friends. Thomas was kneeling on all fours, a small thread of blood trickling down his neck and onto the ground. I helped him sit, leaning him against one of the wheels of the wagon. As I stood up, Belanger, who had been standing by the edge of the crowd, came up with a wet rag that he gave to my friend. Belanger took me by the elbow and led me off to the side.

"Murphy, you have to watch out for him here. If they kill him, the whole plan may die and they know that. Tell him to go to New Brunswick and leave this place to Clarkson and his officials. I fear for his safety if he stays."

Belanger talked daily with travelers, suppliers, and customers, and had a network of subordinates around the area. If anyone knew who was responsible for the attack, it was him.

"So who did it? I don't think these knotheads thought this up all by themselves."

"Murphy, think on it for a moment. You know who is behind this. There are only a couple of men who have both the resources and the brains to do it. If you think on it, you'll come up with the answer. Just get Thomas across the bay before there is more harm done."

In any event, Digby was scheduled to be one of the last stops for Thomas in Nova Scotia. He was groggy but mostly unhurt from the attack, but he did see the ongoing threat from his enemies in the province. As the group registering to leave the colony for Sierra Leone got bigger, so rose the anger from those who would lose by the removal of cheap workers. Clarkson, being an emissary of the British government, was not in personal danger, but Thomas did not have that protection. The effort to mobilize emigrants was a huge success and had a momentum of its own, so his presence in Nova Scotia was no longer needed. He crossed the bay the following day and we resolved to meet back at the Halifax harbor early in the new year. Thomas had arranged for Sarah and Ben to meet us there also, although we had not yet figured out a way to get our friends onto the ships. Dan and Tye would come with me to Halifax.

It was a cold trip to Halifax harbor just after Christmas but we arrived in good condition. We had a short stay in a waterfront tenement and soon met up with Sarah and Ben, who were in a high state of anxiety, both about getting a place on the ships and, also, because Sarah had taken leave of her indentured service in Shelburne without a word, an act which could get her seized and put in jail.

There was no sign of Thomas. The third day we were in Halifax, we were idling by the waterfront, watching the ships loading, when we spied the *Joseph* well out in the harbor. I then cast about looking for Captain Mitchell, who I knew would be close by, and found him in a noisy bar by the low point along the harbor road.

The captain was in a much better frame of mind than the last time I had seen him, or perhaps I was more balanced. Captain Mitchell had told me he wanted to speak with me about something before he sailed to England. Now he drew me to a corner and spoke quickly with me.

"Murphy, are you looking after that son of yours?"

"Well he's with me, so, yes, I guess."

He looked at me sharply.

"Now don't lie to me. I want him to be my cabin boy. He's old enough now and I know from our trip overseas that he's a capable lad. What do you say? I promise you, he'll be treated as if he was my own son. He'll see many shores and I'll teach him his numbers and to read and write. He'll put in some work, no doubt, but he'll get his fair pay too. It's true that I walk a fine line with the law but I can't see you doing much with him in Sierra Leone."

I thought about the proposal, but only for a minute. I knew Captain Mitchell would take care of Tye, and I knew the lad would be better with him than with me. I had lost the heart for being a father when I lost the rest of my family. It was sad to say but I no longer felt committed to my son. I agreed to send Tye with the captain and stood up to leave, but then I had a second thought. I explained the situation regarding our three friends to the captain and asked him if there was anything he could do to help them. Mitchell hesitated for a moment, then asked if the three were capable and strong workers.

I told him that while Dan would work with the best of men, the same could not be said for Ben and Sarah, who could not recover from their long period of terrible work in Bermuda and were, in any event, not young anymore.

"Murphy, I know Daniel and I'll get him work on one of the ships as a hand so that he can get to the Province of Freedom. I know the captain of the *Eleanor* and can likely get him on there, but the other two, I don't know. Can you sneak them on with you?"

I knew there was actually little chance of this. The registration would have my name on the list but not my two friends' and the English had proven sticky about whom they would allow on the voyage. I thanked Captain Mitchell and agreed to meet him the next morning by the tender for the *Joseph* with Daniel and Tye. When I returned to my friends at the apartment and told them the plan, I could see that Dan was excited about his chance onboard the *Eleanor*, though he was reluctant to leave Tye. I had become convinced that my son's best opportunity rested with Captain Mitchell and was content with the decision. The next morning we met the captain at the quay and he sent Dan off with a sailor in the little rowboat to join the *Eleanor*. He had talked with the captain of the *Eleanor* during the night and arranged for Daniel to join the crew. We agreed to meet in the Province of Freedom and wished each other God-speed across the ocean.

Finally it was time to say good-bye to Tye, too. It was unlikely that I would see him again unless Captain Mitchell made his way to Sierra Leone. That was hard. Still, I knew it was the best course for the boy to take and so it was with conflicting emotions that I wished him well. For Tye, who was well on his way to becoming a good lad, it was just another adventure. He had come to know Captain Mitchell during the trip to England and was therefore not reluctant to go with him. I bade good tidings to the captain and turned away as the two made their way down the dock.

Thomas arrived with close to a hundred loyalists from New Brunswick before the close of the day. The sailing date had been set for two days hence, which gave us just that much time to figure out a way for Ben and Sarah to join the voyage. They were, by this time, in a state of desperation as they became convinced that they would not be able to join the emigration and would be left behind in Nova Scotia to face the harsh winter without funds and with no prospects. Thomas and I cast about wildly with fanciful ideas about how to get them on board, but we could find no way to sneak them past the registrar positioned at the head of the loading ramp on each ship to check off all the passengers against a list.

Thomas and I had been told to sail on the *Lucretia* along with Clarkson. On the morning of January 15, 1792, we went down to the docks to board her along with Ben and Sarah. They were in a worried state but held a forlorn hope of making the voyage. With us on the docks were the loyalists who had accompanied Thomas from New Brunswick and who were still nervous about committing to the endeavor. Thomas knew that their strength of conviction was shallow, so he led them quickly onto the ship. I watched closely as Thomas, his wife Sally, and their children were checked off against the same list used when we left New York. Their children, of course, were not on the list, but that was of no concern to the English, who were looking out for mature emigrants who were not loyalists.

As I watched the procedure, my thoughts went back to that difficult time when we all left New York. Mary had boarded using my last name even though we weren't married at the time. We thought this would make things simple and we were right. Suddenly, I had a flash of insight as to what I must do. Quickly, I turned to Ben and Sarah. Ben was sitting against a large sack of oats with his head in his hands and Sarah was quietly weeping beside him.

"Quickly now, Ben, stand up. Sarah you must dry your tears and put on a lively face. Here it is. Go up the ramp and tell the official that your names are Murphy Steele and his wife, Mary. They will have them both in the book. Don't let on who you really are."

Ben looked up at me, a flash of hope in his eyes, but then cast his gaze down again.

"We couldn't do that, Murphy. It is generous beyond measure but it will leave you here, stranded, with no way of getting to the Province of Freedom."

But as he spoke and nodded his head, my conviction grew that it was absolutely the correct thing to do. It felt right, better than anything I had done for a long time. It made no real difference to me where I lived. The spark in my life had gone out when my wife and son died from a disease that I had carried to them. Here was something akin to redemption, something that I could do that was the best thing to do and would help someone else.

"Quiet, Ben, it makes no difference to me where I live. Take Sarah and go and have a good life. When you get onboard, talk to Thomas and tell him he is my brother and always will be. Tell him I will always remember our times and what an adventure it has been. Tell him to lead our people in the Province of Freedom and make a grand settlement that is for the benefit of all and the disadvantage of none.

"Tell him I will write it all, all of our troubles and triumphs, the battles, the love, the losses, the freedom, and even the old times when we were whipped and chained. All of it I remember and none of it must ever be forgotten. I'll write it down so those who come after will see what men are made of, and, especially, I will write it for those who are still in chains."

I grabbed Ben's satchel and walked him and Sarah to the ramp. At the top, they paused briefly to talk with the official, then walked up the deck to where Thomas was standing against the rail. He turned sharply and, looking down at me, took his hat off and held it in both hands. He said nothing but gazed steadily down at me as I looked up at him. Ben and Sarah were the last people to board the *Lucretia* and she was underway in ten minutes. Thomas had not spoken during that time, though the space between us was small, but as the ship began to be pulled from her berth, he took his hat in one hand and began waving slowly with grand sweeps of his arm.

I took off my battered old logging cap and waved back.

About the Author

Kevin Bannister is the father of five children and lives on a ranch along a river in the beautiful foothills of central Alberta.

He has been a newspaper editor, sportswriter, reporter, investment house vice president, truck driver, farmer and steelworker amongst other jobs. Currently he ranches and is working on a sequel to *The Long Way Home*.

OTHER TITLES FROM FIRESHIP PRESS

THE PROPHET OF COBB HOLLOW

There is a world that runs parallel to our own;
a world in which legends are created...

When a New York novelist finds the dusty journal of a lost American legend, he can scarcely believe what he is reading. The story tells of a man having been rescued and raised by a Cherokee shaman named Three Crows, of riding with known gunslingers and a young Teddy Roosevelt, as a Confederate spy working for Mosby's Rangers during The Civil War, and the horrific conditions he experienced in the deadly trenches of World War I.

He tells the story of one man and his decades-long retribution to avenge his beloved. Whether seen as a realistic glimpse into our forgotten past—or as the mythic retelling of narratives spun around the mystery that spawned his legend— he is the only man to have walked through the portals of our national history. He is the oldest living human on earth and now his oral collections are told as it was lived. His name is Reuben Shadrack Judah, and he is: *The Prophet of Cobb Hollow.*

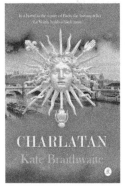

CHARLATAN

How do you keep the love of the King of France?

1676. In a hovel in the centre of Paris, the fortune-teller La Voisin holds a black mass, summoning the devil to help an unnamed client keep the love of the King of France, Louis XIV.

Three years later, Athénaïs, Madame de Montespan, the King's glamorous mistress, is nearly forty. She has borne Louis seven children but now seethes with rage as he falls for eighteen-year-old, Angélique de Fontanges.

At the same time, police chief La Reynie and his young assistant Bezons have uncovered a network of fortune-tellers and poisoners operating in the city. Athénaïs does not know it, but she is about to named as a favoured client of the infamous La Voisin.

For the Finest in Nautical and Historical Fiction and Non-Fiction
www.FireshipPress.com

Interesting • Informative • Authoritative

All Fireship Press books are available
through FireshipPress.com, Amazon.com and
other leading bookstores and wholesalers worldwide.

CPSIA information can be obtained
at www.ICGtesting.com
Printed in the USA
LVHW020806130819
627419LV00006B/39/P